THE GIBBERING

Vicki swatted at something. "I thought there was a wasp in here."

Phillip glanced quickly about the car's spacious interior, saw nothing. Something played a queer little tune on the chords of his mind, a cold little tune that chilled him.

"I remember . . . strange things sometimes," she said. "I remember being blind, and I remember dying."

Phillip Stone's jaw dropped, dropped more yet as his wife half-heartedly swatted at a wasp which clearly wasn't there. "They buzz so loud," she said. "In my head, they buzz . . ."

Stone wanted to pull over into the slow lane, find a layby, stop. His hands were clammy cold; he felt ill, wanted to be sick. So as Vicki commenced shaking her head and swatting furiously, he cursed, put his foot down hard, began to pull ahead of the lorries in the slow lane, and—

She stopped swatting, reached over and yanked the wheel, jerking it way over to the left. Her face was totally vacant; saliva trickled from the corner of her mouth; her strength was that . . . of a madwoman!

BRIAN LUMLEY

PSYCHAMOK

TOR
HORROR

A TOM DOHERTY ASSOCIATES BOOK
NEW YORK

For Les.
May his cup ever
flood over.

PSYCHAMOK

Cover art by Jim Thiesan

A Tor Book
Published by Tom Doherty Associates, Inc.
175 Fifth Avenue
New York, N.Y. 10010

Tor ® is a registered trademark of Tom Doherty Associates, Inc.

ISBN: 0-812-52032-7

First Tor edition: February 1993

Printed in the United States of America

0 9 8 7 6 5 4 3 2 1

Résumé One:
Psychomech

F OR EACH FORCE THERE EXISTS A COUNTERFORCE, AND
 every action has its reaction. For darkness
there is light, for day night. Time is measured in
space and space in time, and neither may exist
without the other. These are Laws of Nature which
apply to all matter, to every living creature in
every biosphere, and to every psychic emana-
tion—every *thought*—in the great Psychosphere
which encompasses all the worlds of space and
time wherever life exists.

And the Principle Law is this: There Shall Be A
Balance. For laughter there shall be sorrow, and
for life death. That is to say: for every birth or
emergence there shall be a life or existence, running its course and coming to an end. With time
tipping the scales, even mountains die and turn
into sand . . .

. . . Except that in 1952 a man was born on the
planet Earth who would break that Prime Law. His

name was Richard Allan Garrison, and his destiny was immortality.

Garrison's childhood was never easy, rarely happy. Life's knocks were hard; he was shaped on an anvil of pain. Finally the loss of his mother, the only one who ever cared or mattered, finished the job. Dipped naked in his sorrow, he emerged case-hardened. Cynical, a little—a rebel, some-what—and bitter, yes. But not completely.

Garrison's flesh was weak as all flesh, but his will was unbendable. He had taught himself a trick: he could take disappointments, hurts and frustrations, and absorb them, drown them in the deep dark wells at the back of his mind. A trick, a defense mechanism. One which would serve him well.

But there were other tricks in Garrison's mind of which he was unaware . . . until September 1972, in Northern Ireland. By then he was a Cor-poral in the Royal Military Police, a "target," as he and every other soldier out there thought of themselves. Boots and a uniform, a flak-jacket and a Sterling sub-machine-gun, and eyes in the back of your head if you fancy a pint in the mess tonight.

September 1972, and a dream—or nightmare—that persisted in bothering Garrison. A warning, an omen, a glimpse into a strange future, the dream had concerned a man-God, a dog and a Machine . . . and Garrison himself. And it had ended with a bomb. While its repetition worried him he could hardly hope to recognize it for what it was; in Northern Ireland many men dreamed of bombs. But Garrison's bomb was real . . .

Thomas Schroeder was in Belfast, too, on busi-ness. Millionaire industrialist, ex-Nazi, arms manufacturer, international financier, he was there with his aide, Willy Koenig, and with his family. Schroeder's young wife, their baby son and the child's nanny, had rooms in a hotel in an assumed "safe area" of the city. From there, upon conclusion of his business, they were to fly to Australia; a holiday in the sun. That holiday never happened.

Garrison was on duty when the bomb warning came, was there at the Europa when Schroeder and Koenig returned from certain "business" talks with the IRA (whose proposals they had viciously rejected) to find the building cordoned off and in process of evacuation. In an effort to get Schroeder's wife, child and nanny out of the hotel, Garrison had killed two young terrorists—after which he had been caught in the bomb blast. He was blinded, Schroeder crippled, the nanny killed outright. But Schroeder's wife and child were saved unharmed.

At the last, however, when the blast came, Garrison had expected it. He had *known* it was coming and also that it would blind him—as it had in his dream. He later remembered Schroeder's face from that dream, too—the face of the man-God . . .

In early 1973 Garrison accepted Schroeder's invitation out to his estate in the Harz Mountains. There he became aware of the man's consuming interest in ESP and the "fringe" sciences, theories and beliefs—especially reincarnation and immortality.

Like any vastly rich man as he grows old, the German loathed and feared death's inevitability. His intention had been gradually to transfer his own mind and personality into his child. A man is after all "reborn" in his son; but Schroeder had been intent upon a far more substantial rebirth. Now, however, it could not be. The boy was as yet a baby, his mind unformed, and Schroeder was dying as a result of the bomb. If he had had ten more years . . . but he had not even one.

On the other hand, he did have Richard Garrison . . .

Under Schroeder's tuition Garrison began to discover and practice the hidden talents of his mind, finally coming to believe that indeed a man might achieve immortality! They made between them a pact, which was this:

If Schroeder could return from beyond the grave—if there was any way in which his psyche could subsume or *Gestalt* itself within Garrison's— then that Garrison would accept him, become host to another's mind. In return . . .

Schroeder numbered among his friends the world's greatest seer, Adam Schenk. Schenk plumbed the future for Garrison and it was seen he would become rich and powerful beyond all dreams of human avarice. But money and power were not everything, there would be much, much more. The future was never lucid, ever misty; but there would be . . . a machine, *the* Machine of Garrison's dream. And through the Machine his sight would be restored to him.

His pact with Schroeder was sealed . . .

During his stay in the Harz Garrison met Vicki Maler. She, too, was blind and already beginning to burn bright with a rare cancer. But they loved each other, however briefly and intensely, before he lost her. Since she knew she was dying—unwilling to burden Garrison—Vicki simply went away.

Within six months Thomas Schroeder was dead, and not long after that Vicki Maler too. Schroeder was cremated; Vicki's ravaged body was cryogenically "suspended" at Schloss Zonigen in the Swiss Alps. This latter had been Garrison's wish and he had his reasons—even if he did not fully understand them.

Meanwhile, much of Schroeder's wealth had passed down to Garrison. Along with it came Willy Koenig, to look after the blind man as he had once looked after his beloved Colonel Schroeder; for Koenig believed that something of Schroeder had already found its way into Garrison. And there was also a dog: Suzy, a black Doberman bitch.

Years passed and Garrison married. Perhaps he loved Terri initially, it is doubtful that she loved him; there had been a man before Garrison and eventually she would turn to him again, though not for some years yet. He was the psychiatrist Gareth Wyatt, into whose hands had fallen a certain machine. A machine called Psychomech, a mechanical psychiatrist.

Wyatt was desperately in need of funds. His practice, once flourishing, was almost defunct; to make matters worse, there was a problem of a far more serious nature. Wyatt was a murderer. His victim had been the war criminal Otto Krippner who deserved death (even if he did *not* die for his crimes), and the weapon Wyatt had used was Psychomech.

Perhaps ironically, Psychomech had been built by Krippner, a man whose origins, background and ideals were as far removed from Thomas Schroeder's as the dark side of the moon. Krippner had been a psychiatrist in a so-called "remedial medicine unit" of the SS. Certain of his practices there had guaranteed his name's later appearance on the world's most-wanted lists of war criminals. Some years after the war, with the help of an organization known as Exodus, he had made his escape from Germany to England.

Wyatt, of sympathetic persuasions, had been recruited by Exodus in Germany while a student of psychiatry. When Krippner's escape was planned, Wyatt was contacted and instructed to "employ" the man and assist with his absorption into his new identity and environment. There was no way he could refuse (Exodus would take such a refusal very badly) but things would not be so bad. Krippner had been, still was, a brilliant psychiatrist in his own right. There was a great deal Wyatt might learn from him . . .

And so, after his many years of fear, flight and evasion, Krippner settled in to work—ostensibly as a gardener in the grounds of Wyatt's large but largely untended country home in Sussex—and at first he had seemed more than grateful. He displayed his gratitude, again ostensibly, by slowly constructing Psychomech in an empty upstairs room of Wyatt's house.

Psychomech was to be the culmination of many years of research and experiment, and through the machine Wyatt's fortunes would be restored to their previous standing. The German did *not* tell Wyatt that Psychomech was an unfinished Nazi project to create supermen—and that he, Otto Krippner, intended to be the very first of such!

By the time Psychomech was completed in 1976, Amira Hannes and her network of Israeli bloodhounds had already tracked down many of Krippner's contemporaries; it was only a matter of time before they got him, too. Exodus got in touch with Krippner, advised him to move on. Wyatt was also contacted, told to waste little time seeing Krippner on his way and covering the Nazi's tracks.

He did no such thing but used Psychomech to murder Krippner, weighed his body down and slipped it into a deep, dark, tree-shaded pool in the grounds of his home. This way Krippner could never be tracked down; Wyatt's connection with Exodus would never be discovered—

—All of which occurred three years before Wyatt's second affair with Terri Garrison.

In 1980 Terri arranged a meeting between her lover and her husband, and Garrison's ESP at once pinpointed Wyatt as a crucial factor in his future. In short, he "knew" that Wyatt was the key to the Machine, "knew" also that the psychiatrist actually had possession of Psychomech.

Wyatt was still desperately in need of money. He claimed that while Psychomech was incomplete and in need of much more work yet, nevertheless its potential was enormous. It would repay any investment many times over. If Garrison were willing to fund the project, he would surely reap a large share of the eventual profits. Garrison did better than that: he employed an expert in microelectronics to strip Psychomech down and replace bulky, obsolete and dangerous parts with new and compact high performance components.

When in 1981 the new Psychomech was ready to be tested, Garrison demanded that he himself be the guinea pig. This suited the illicit lovers very well. Their original plan had been this: that when Psychomech became a success, Terri would desert Garrison for Wyatt. They would manage a living on Psychomech's commercial earnings. But now . . . Wyatt had used Psychomech once to commit a murder. Why not twice? Terri's inheritance would be vast.

As for the Machine itself, Psychomech was *supposed* to function like this:

The patient would be caused to dream, to experience nightmares born of his own worst fears. This would be achieved by the stimulation of his brain's fear-centers. Psychomech would blow up his neuroses and psychoses out of all proportion, simultaneously supplying him with the physical (more properly mental) strength to overcome these fears. The conflicts within the patient's mind would be utterly real to him; having subconsciously "defeated" his personal, inner demons, he would discover upon awakening that the conscious manifestations of his neuroses were similarly vanquished.

And indeed the Machine might well effect just such cures—but that was merely a spin-off from its primary function, which was this:

That the subject's mind be utterly cleansed of *all* fear, and that his ego and potential ESP abilities— latent in all men—be expanded almost infinitely. So that he would emerge a fearless mental giant, a near-superman!

The mad dream of an insane Fuehrer? Perhaps . . .

Garrison went on to Psychomech on a Sunday morning in June 1981. Certain precautions had been taken to ensure that the "experiment" would not be interrupted; surprisingly, Garrison himself had been responsible for the arrangements. Willy Koenig had been sent on holiday to Hamburg; Suzy the Doberman pinscher— Garrison's "familiar"—was safely lodged in the kennels at Midhurst. Be that as it may, both Koenig and Suzy knew the exact moment that Garrison went on to the Machine, and they would later hear and answer his mental SOS when Wyatt tried to kill him.

Wyatt's method was simple—or should have been. He would magnify fear-stimulation to the full and cut the Machine's relief systems to their minimum. Garrison would be driven mad and the Machine would not be able to help him; its fail-safe would not function; eventually, in paroxysms of absolute terror, he would expire. The log of the experiment would be falsified, the controls re-set. It would all be seen as a terrible accident; Wyatt would sigh, shrug and point out that Garrison had known the dangers, had known that Psychomech was, after all, only a prototype . . .

But Garrison did not go insane and he did not die. While his wife and her lover sated themselves, he reached out from his mechanically-induced nightmares and took control of Psychomech *with his mind*, turning certain of the Machine's energies to his own advantage. The battle was joined, unendurable mental horror against almost limitless psychic strength! Something had to give, and because Psychomech was a machine that something must be the flesh-and-blood Garrison himself.

Unless—

The pact! That pact he had made with Thomas Schroeder, dead these eight years. Schroeder was there now in Garrison's bloated nightmares just as he had been in that much earlier dream in strife-torn Belfast, and his plea now was that same plea he had made then: that Garrison *let him in*! Even Psychomech could not destroy both of them.

Garrison capitulated, freely admitted Schroeder into his mind, subsumed the long-dead German's disembodied psyche within his own id, his own being.

After that . . .

Hitler's advisers had envisaged a machine to turn ordinary men into supermen. But what would happen if the subject was a man whose powers of ESP were already honed to an extraordinary edge? What if, instead of one mind returning from such a voyage, a multimind should emerge—a psychic sentience expanded to almost cosmic proportions? Superman—?

Or God?

Not God, no—not even a god—but a man with near-godlike powers. This was the Garrison/Schroeder which Psychomech had created. And this was the Garrison/Schroeder who freed himself from the Machine to find the lovers desperately, fearfully coupling in their bed—find them out in all their treachery.

Then . . . miracles and madness!

By the will of Garrison/Schroeder, Vicki Maler was *brought* from Schloss Zonigen to England and returned to life. *But it was Schroeder's will alone which transferred the living cancer that killed her into Gareth Wyatt and Terri Garrison!* And it was Garrison, humane as he had always been, who ended it by destroying both of them in an instant.

Outside Wyatt's house when all was done, Garrison/Schroeder and Vicki found Koenig waiting. Suzy was there, too, but she was dead; Wyatt had blown her apart with a shotgun. No longer blind—golden-eyed and awesome—Garrison/Schroeder had looked at Suzy, commanding her that she be whole again and live. And Suzy lived.

And Koenig, too—the ever-faithful Koenig—he also was rewarded. He and Garrison/Schroeder embraced, and when it was done Koenig's clothes fell empty to the earth.

Then, as the house of Wyatt and all it contained melted down behind them and became slag, Garrison/Schroeder/Koenig, Vicki and Suzy moved on toward their futures . . .

Résumé Two: Psychosphere

G ARRISON'S DREAM WAS NOW REALITY, ALL OF ITS
elements fulfilled. But still there were problems. The world was not ready for a superman,
certainly not one whose mind—whose multimind—
was flawed and faulted as is any human mind. (Or
any three minds.) Nor would the world be willing to
accept a resurrected woman whose body had lain
frozen in death for eight long years!

Perhaps more to the point, men had laws. Prime
amongst these and accepted worldwide was this
one: Thou Shalt Not Kill. Terri Garrison and Gareth
Wyatt, however, were indisputably dead. And what
of Willy Koenig? No court of law on the entire planet,
presented with the facts, would ever accept that
Koenig was *not* dead. In short, with all Garrison's
expanded ESP powers, there was still no way he
could reveal himself to the world.

Not that he considered this of any great importance in itself (in all truth Garrison did not desire

to be the new Messiah), but its implications most definitely were. For if he could not reveal himself, then he must keep himself hidden. Certainly he must hide his eyes, which were not the eyes of any ordinary human being; and Vicki must likewise hide hers. This was not difficult: the two remained, as it were, "blind," or at least part-blind, wearing deep-sided, dark-lensed spectacles whenever they were to be seen in public.

A vaster problem far was Garrison's multimind, the fact that he had a *Gestalt* psyche. The Schroeder facet was less than satisfied with the "immortality" he had achieved for himself: while Garrison lived, he "lived," yes, but not freely and by no means fully. True, the Schroeder/Koenig facets did occasionally surface and take ascendancy in their own rights, but usually Garrison himself was master. It was hardly the "sharing" Thomas Schroeder had envisioned, but it had to be a great improvement on death! Schroeder had been *there*, and he had not liked it.

In Koenig's case matters were far simpler. He had only desired to serve Schroeder and Garrison, and now as a *Gestalt* facet he was closer to both men than he had ever dreamed of being. The conflict between the two, of which he was of course aware, could never blossom into open warfare; there was no way in which they could spite or harm one another; anything one of them might maliciously engineer in his ascendancy could certainly be canceled by the other in his, which would only ensure mutual chaos. In short their relationship was balanced, as all *Gestalt*s are; and all three facets knew that in the event of some accident, should Garrison die, then that *all* of them were dead. Yes, and Vicki and Suzy too . . .

But between times:

When Schroeder was ascendant he lived as Schroeder; likewise Koenig. Both sub-facets had their foibles, their idiosyncrasies. Schroeder kept a woman in London; Koenig, as had always been his way, paid for his women wherever he found them. Vicki Maler was inviolate: she belonged to Garrison himself.

And yet in Vicki, too, a problem. While she knew it was not Garrison who went off on occasion to seek his pleasures in other beds, it *was* Garrison's body. And this created stress in her.

Finally, the greatest problem and by far the most disconcerting was this: ever since Psycho-mech had given Garrison's *Gestalt* mind its powers, those powers had been leaking into the Psychosphere. Each time he or his sub-facets used those powers, the battery of his mind grew that fraction weaker. For almost two years Garrison had suspected it, worried about it, before he finally became convinced that it was so.

By that time his financial empire was enormous. If he was not already the richest man the world had ever known, he soon would be. And yet, paradoxically—and chiefly because he must maintain a low profile—this was a fact of which the world was largely unaware. Certain people did know, however, and there was one person in particular who knew very nearly all there was to know about Garrison.

That person's name was Charon Gubwa . . .

Gubwa was a freak, the cumulative result of mutating genes piled one upon the next and passed down by successive generations.

An obese hermaphrodite albino (in fact of pure

African Negro descent, with typically negroid features, however leprous), Gubwa was also enor-
mously ESP-endowed. Frighteningly so. He had
known of Garrison's "coming" from the instant
Psychomech created the Garrison/Schroeder *Gestalt*, for he had "felt" the other's presence rend-
ing the Psychosphere as a great meteor rends the
atmosphere. And Gubwa had feared Garrison.

Gubwa knew that while his own mind was a mere
glowing dustmote in the Psychosphere, Garrison's
was a rising star. Of all men, Garrison was the one
who might one day stand in Gubwa's way, prevent
him from achieving his awful ambition. For the
albino, too, desired immortality—desired to make
himself the immortal and omnipotent Emperor of
Earth!

And his ambitions were greater (or more dire)
than even that. Gubwa was both man and woman,
a freak in the eyes of mankind's great majority.
But in the future he envisioned—after the world
had been devastated and when the remnants of
the human race began to climb back out of the
nuclear pit—hermaphrodism would be the norm,
bisexuality would cease to be. And only Garrison,
unknowing, unsuspecting, standing in his way.

And so Gubwa set wheels turning to crush Garrison. An attempt was made on his life, and more
would follow. And Garrison's powers deserting
him now, running out like water from a leaking
bucket. And of all three facets of his multimind,
his the ascendant one, and him the most vulner-
able.

Gubwa's weapon against Garrison was two-
pronged: he manipulated certain elements of
both the Mafia and a largely underground and
somewhat suspect branch of the Secret Service.
And with Garrison apparently on the run, finally

Gubwa kidnapped Vicki Maler and took her to his subterranean headquarters deep beneath London.

Gubwa's "Castle" originally had been designed as a nuclear shelter and command post toward the end of World War II, but was now largely forgotten. Gubwa had equipped it to his own needs, staffed and ran it in a paramilitary fashion.

There in the Castle, captive along with Vicki Maler, Gubwa also held Phillip Stone, an agent of M16. Stone, a dangerous man in his own right, had been the unwilling tool the albino had used in Vicki's kidnap; but he would later cause Gubwa to regret his enforced involvement.

Using telepathy to probe Vicki's mind, Gubwa found out about Psychomech, discovered the facts of Garrison's "creation." Since Garrison's death now seemed inevitable, Gubwa looked forward to the next phase of his plan for world domination. He would build a bigger, better Psychomech—and this time he would be the Machine's subject. His powers of ESP were spawned of radiation and mutation, and were greater far than Garrison's had been before Psychomech. Garrison had emerged an incredible, awesome power—Gubwa would emerge a God! An actual God: omniscient, omnipotent and utterly evil! Building Psychomech would take a little time, but time was on Gubwa's side.

Meanwhile . . . Garrison fled north for Scotland. He had dreamed again, a precognitive dream no less important than his Belfast dream of 1972. In this new dream he had courted the Goddess Immortality, and She had shown him the panoply of infinity, the glorious pathways of the universe. Also, there had been the glimmer of dawning awareness, the recognition of an imminent transition. Garrison knew that he was ready to take the next step, a step which *must* be taken. The gateway to his destiny lay in a wild valley where a new hydroelectric scheme was due to come into operation, but he must get there before his pursuers took him or his powers failed him entirely.

He was within an ace of his objective when the Mafia caught up with him. In the ensuing confrontation, Suzy was again fatally injured and Garrison driven to expend most of what was left of his ESP power. Of his pursuers . . . they were no more.

But Garrison was now merely a man once more, his powers very nearly spent, and still a way to go. He absorbed the essence of the dying Suzy into himself, adding her as a new facet to his *Gestalt* psyche, and with a dog's instinct set out on foot to cover the last leg of his journey . . .

With the fall of night he found the valley, taking shelter in a deserted house which stood in the shadow of a great hydroelectric dam of still, slumbering waters. And there, even as the last dregs of his power leaked from him, Garrison accidentally stumbled upon his salvation. By then he was very nearly blind again and the old house was dark. Fumbling with an electric lamp, attempting to insert naked wires into a socket, he received a shock—and a shocking, marvelous revelation!

For an instant, even as his body had been shaken, vibrating with the current surging through it, Garrison had felt strong again. His eyes had brightened and his multimind had been illuminated. Then, deliberately, he had plugged himself into the electrical source, jamming himself into a corner where he throbbed and burned and absorbed power as a sponge soaks up water.

Electrocuted, he felt only strength. Fingers, hands and forearms crisped and blackened, he knew no pain. Twice-blind, he saw again, saw more than mere eyes could ever show him. For at last he knew how to recharge his sorely depleted mental batteries, and charge them as never before!

With his mind he opened the great dam's gates, drawing off millions of volts from the energy so released. And when that was not enough he sought more power still, stretching out his mind and leeching from the atomic power station at Dounreay—until Scotland's very grid was dampened and lights burned low all across the land. Strange aurorae filled the skies, and the valley where the dam now thundered became luminous with eerie radiations and weirdly flickering energies.

And at last in one great blast of raw power, a Titan bolt of energy from the sky—finally Garrison underwent his transition. Every last physical vestige of Richard Allan Garrison was removed forever from the world of men, but the *mental* Garrison had ascended to a higher plane.

In his dream the Goddess Immortality had shown Garrison her abode—her House in the Stars, which was nothing less than the Infinite Universe itself—and now Garrison would go there, would venture to the limits of the very Psychosphere. Nor would he venture alone, for Schroeder and Koenig, yes, and Suzy too, would be with him.

But first there were things to do.

And Garrison reached out into the Psychosphere and made adjustments. He touched things and changed them. And as if the world were a vast book where Garrison's era was a single chapter written in pencil, he *rewrote* certain passages and *erased* others completely; all of which took a single microsecond of time before he wrote *finis* on that chapter. And in the world of men things were changed at a stroke and would never be the same again.

In the world of men . . .

. . . In Charon Gubwa's Castle, Phillip Stone and Vicki had made a bid for freedom. Recaptured by the albino madman, they had been inches from death when Garrison's transition took place—his and the world's! Gubwa was one of the changes Garrison made.

In his pre-supposed moment of triumph the leprous hermaphrodite felt defeat, felt another mind within his own. A mind awesome in its power and pitiless in its resolve. Garrison had seen the stars themselves and would now show them to Gubwa. But Gubwa's body was of flesh and his mind still mortal. Plunged like an upward-hurtling meteor into the vault of the sky, the ESP-master died horribly, his menace removed forever.

And also removed, dug out at their roots, many of the world's worst evils; and it was as if they had never been.

Another change was this:

That Vicki Maler was merely a woman now, whose husband, Phillip Stone, was rich and successful. And they were happy and had never known any other way. What memories there were were good ones, however vague or misty, but what mattered was not yesterday but today and tomorrow.

Especially tomorrow, for Vicki was pregnant . . .

* * *

Thus it was that Garrison and his companions left behind them a world very nearly perfect, a world largely purged and purified. They left a good world, a sane world. In short, they left a world where the Balance had been disrupted almost irreparably.

But the Balance is the Law. And just as there is Good so is there Evil, and for Great Good there is Great Evil.

And slowly but surely the Psychosphere moved to restore the Balance . . .

Part

I

Chapter One

*T*HERE HAD BEEN TWENTY YEARS OF A TRANQUILITY beyond all of Man's former expectations, such as never before existed in all his long and bloody history. Hot wars had simmered down into cold wars, into uneasy, puzzled periods of dialogue and treaty, finally metamorphosing into blossoming friendships. Border disputes and territorial arguments had fizzled out, been replaced by mutual trust, sharing and understanding. The Great Nations had made a prolonged, concerted effort to help the Not So Great, with the result that they were finally seen to be great and were no longer feared for their might; and the Lesser Lands in their turn had adopted those so long neglected or ignored technologies by use and means of which they were at last able to help themselves.

Economic crises had receded; creeping ideological territorialism had crept to a halt; the population explosion had not novaed but had in fact *sputtered and gone out like a damp squib. The old agricultural science of the land and the new science of sea-farming, together with an expanded and sympathetic awareness of Nature beyond the wildest dreams of the early conservationists, had for the first time provided food aplenty for the world's billions.*

It was an age of peace and plenty.

Twenty years, and 1984 left in the wake of the world's well-being (and Big Brother nowhere in sight), and the old arts and cultures revitalized and the new sciences surging ahead, reaching for a fair tomorrow. The turn of the Century only four years past, and life never so good on the green clean planet Earth . . .

And then the plague—or at least recognition that it had come amongst us. A plague not of vermin, not born of the new sciences or the atom, not of radiation or of wild chemicals or poisons—not physical in any way. A plague of madness!

The doctors had no explanation, no cure for it. To them and to those who suffered it, it was known only as The Gibbering . . .

The hospital was set in fifteen acres of landscaped gardens, its three floors spaciously appointed, its many-windowed, fresh-air appearance belying the conditions existing within. Not the physical conditions, for they could not be better— not in the circumstances. But the twelve-foot tall tight-meshed wire security fence surrounding the entire estate spoke all too ineloquently of its function. Tucked away in belts of shrouding pines and oaks, still that fence could not be hidden completely—neither it nor the fact that it was not there to keep people out.

Typical of dozens of similar retreats the hospital was new, had been standing for less than five years, was wholly state supported—and was filled with inmates. With poor mad people who had heard and heeded The Gibbering. The hospital had a name, Calm Lawns, but the lawns were the only calm things about it.

It was a sunny Saturday, early June of 2004 when the Stones made their eleventh monthly trip seventy miles north from their Sussex home to Calm Lawns in Oxfordshire, for it was just a month short of a year ago that their son, Richard Stone, had been committed. The thing had first come to him on a hot Friday night last July.

A tall, well-built youth of previously sound physical and mental strength, he had suddenly got up from his bed to prowl the house and complain of a sound in his ears: a faint murmur like the beating of waves heard in a sounding shell. A susurration of whispers growing ever louder, a tumult of tiny voices in chaotic conflict. In short, he heard The Gibbering.

The symptoms were unmistakable, their development inevitable. Before the eyes of his stricken parents Richard Stone's deterioration had accelerated with demonaic speed. Friday night the first shaking of his head, as if to dislodge some leech of the brain, to still the murmuring in his ears; Saturday his reeling and rushing about, and the sickness, the bile, the maelstrom of mad winds or waters howling in his skull; and Sunday . . . Sunday his *imitation* of those imagined sounds, the gabbled cries of souls in torment. The Gibbering.

Snatched aloft by unseen harpies, by Monday Richard had been a candidate for the straitjacket.

Heartbroken, they had visited him every third day through that first month; following which their visits had been restricted. It was known that too much proximity tended to induce the symptoms in certain people, and Phillip Stone was secretly glad when their trips to the asylum were curtailed by medical restrictions. Vicki had been almost "out of her mind" since Richard's committal; her husband did not want to see that condition become permanent.

He had even tried to persuade her that the monthly visit was too much—protesting that it could only damage her already ravaged nerves, or at best increase her unhappiness—but all such arguments had gone unheard. She loved her son, as did Phillip Stone himself, and she could see no harm in him express or implied, neither deliberate nor incidental. Heartbroken she was; faithless she could never be. She would always be faithful: to her son's sanity, to his memory as he had been. He was not the same now, no, but he could recover. She ignored the fact that no one—no single victim—had yet fully recovered from The Gibbering. Richard was different. He *would* recover. He was her son.

And there had been a girl. Vicki could not forgive her. Lynn had been the love of Richard's life. He had lived for her, and she had seemed to live for him. But the plague had taken him and she had visited him only twice before her father stepped in and forbade it. She had her own life to lead. She must forget Richard Stone and leave him to his padded cell and his gibbering . . .

Phillip Stone's large expensive car purred up to the gates of Calm Lawns and stopped at the security barrier. The guards were gray-uniformed, carried rifles that fired tranquilizer darts, wore helmets that filtered out all sounds except face-to-face conversation. In addition to filters the helmets contained radios tuned in to the hospital's security computer; through them the guards could "talk" to the computer, and to each other. The other function of the helmets—some would have it the main function, quite aside from communication—was isolation. No one, not even the doctors, liked to listen to The Gibbering for too long. For which reason Security and Staff alike worked in staggered six-hour shifts, and no one lived permanently within the Calm Lawns perimeter except the inmates themselves.

The Stones had visitors' passes but even so their prints were checked at the security barrier. Then, with their passes stamped, the barrier went up and they were allowed in. And while they drove through patrolled gardens—along gravel roads between lawns and fountains and low, rocky outcrops of moss-covered stone, where shrubs and rose bushes luxuriated and vines crept on arching trellises—Security alerted the hospital of their coming. At the car park they were met by a helmeted receptionist, a girl who smiled and checked that the doors of their car were locked, then gave them headphones that covered their ears and issued soft, calming background music; following which they were led into the hospital complex itself.

Richard's cell was on the second floor. His parents were taken up by elevator and led along a rubber-floored perimeter corridor where dust-motes danced in beams of sunlight through huge, reinforced glass windows. There were many, many cells; their inhabitants did not need a great deal of room. And while the soothing music was fed to the Stones through their headphones, they plodded on behind their guide until they reached

Richard's cell—his "room," as Vicki termed it, but it was a cell like all the others.

Its door had a number, 253, and there the guide paused, smiling again as she tapped out the three digits on her electronic wrist-key. The door hissed open, admitting them to a tiny antechamber no bigger than a cubicle. Inside were three chairs, one of which the girl in the helmet took out into the corridor, leaving the Stones on their own. Just before the doors hissed shut on them, she said, "I know you've seen him in a straitjacket before. It's for his own good," and she nodded sympathetically.

"Are you ready?" Phillip Stone asked, his voice a little shaky. His wife half-heard him, half-read his lips, nodded and took off her headphones. "Vicki," he pleaded, "why don't you leave them on?"

"I want to speak to him," she answered, "if I can. And when—if—he speaks to me, I want to hear what he says."

Her husband nodded, took off his own 'phones and hugged her. "Have it your own way, but—"

She wasn't listening. As soon as he released her she turned to the inner doors, stared for a moment at a slip-card in its metal frame, read the words she had come to dread through many previous visits:

"Richard Stone—No Positive Improvement."

Then, hands trembling, she reached toward the doors, reached for the handles which would slide those doors back on well-oiled rollers. An inch from grasping them she froze. The flesh of her cheek quivered. She glanced at her husband. "Phillip?"

"I hear it," he said, his color gray. "It's louder this time. Not only Richard. It's all of them. You

can hear it coming through the walls, the floor.
They're gibbering, all of them!"

"I . . . I *feel* it more than hear it," she said.

"Feel it, hear it," he shrugged defeatedly. "That's
why they give you headphones."

"Ma! Ma!" came a bubbling, rising, tormented
scream from behind the doors. *"Oh! Mamaaaaaaaa!"*

Hissing her horror from between colorless,
twitching lips, Vicki grasped the handles and
rolled back the doors. On the other side a wall
of lightly tinted plate glass separated the
Stones from their son, who lay on the thickly-
padded floor coiled in a near-fetal position. He
was in a jacket, as they had been warned he
would be, with a white froth drying on his lips;
but his face was turned toward them and his
eyes were open. Open wide and wild. The eyes
of a terrified animal, a rabid dog, their gaze
wasn't quite concentrated, their focus not entirely correct. There was a vacancy, a nameless
distance in them.

The antechamber and padded cell were audio-
linked. "Richard!" Vickie reached out her arms
uselessly toward him. "Oh, Richard!"

"Ma?" he repeated, a query in his voice, a half-
prayer. "Ma?"

"Yes," she sobbed, "it's me, son—it's only me."

"Do you understand, son?" Phillip Stone asked.
"We've come to see you."

"Understand? See me?" Richard's eyes were
suddenly awake, alert. He rolled, sat up, hitched
himself across the floor by inches, came up close
to the glass—but was careful not to touch it. On
his side the plate's surface was electrified. In the
early days he had used it deliberately, when
things got too tough, to shock himself uncon-

scious. Since then he had learned better. Learned the lessons of any poor dumb trapped animal.

"It's us, son—Ma and Da," his mother told him, her voice close to breaking. "How are you, Richard? How are . . . things?"

"Things?" he grinned, licking his lips with a furred tongue. "Things are fucking bad, Ma," he said matter-of-factly, rolling his eyes.

"Son, son," his father gently admonished. "Don't talk to your mother like that, please."

". . . Fucking, cunting, arse-picking, shit-stinking bad," Richard ignored him. "Why don't you get me out of here? Why did you put me *in* here? Do you know what it's like in here? Do you realize that I can hear them every second of every minute of every hour of every day and night? *Did you know that, Ma?*"

"Richard!" his father snapped. Then, less harshly, "Son, old chap, try to control—"

"Son?" Richard's eyes had shrunk down to yellow pinpoints burning into his father's through the tinted plate. Perhaps it was only a trick of the colored glass, but Phillip Stone could have sworn those pupils pulsed like a pair of amoebas, brimming like blobs of molten gold. "Did you say son?" Richard shook his head, his eyes fixed in their stare. "Ah, somebody's son, yes! But not *your* son, 'old chap!'"

Vicki could no longer hold back her tears. "Richard, oh my poor, poor boy! Oh my poor love, my lovely boy!"

Her husband threw an arm about her shoulders. "Vicki, don't. He understands nothing. We shouldn't have come. It's too much for you. He doesn't know what he's saying. He's . . . just gibbering!"

"*Ma!*" Richard screamed again. "*Maaaaa!* I do

understand, I *do!* Don't listen to him. He's not my father. You don't remember, do you? No, but I do. Ma, *you named me after my father!*"

His words seemed to conjure something within her. For the merest moment mad, impossible memories seemed to burn upon the surface of her mind's eyes—only to be brushed aside. The Gibbering was, after all, infectious. "Oh, son, son!" she collapsed against the plate glass, going on her knees, her face only inches from his and wet with tears. "You don't know what—"

"But I do I do I do!" he insisted. "Oh, I do! I'm the only one who *does* know!" He rolled his eyes again, the yellow pupils going up, up until the white showed. And slowly, slowly his lips drew back from his teeth in a horrific lunatic grin, and the saliva trickled and bubbled thickly from his gaping jaws. In mere moments his face had become a total nightmare.

"No want in all the world," he said, the words breaking glutinously through phlegmy foam like oily bubbles rising in mud. "No wars, no misery, no fear—except the misery of *this*, the fear of *this!* No prayers where there's nothing to pray for. Religion dead, faith dying. What use faith when the future's assured? No famine, no flood, no pestilence—except *this* pestilence! Nature herself bows to Man's science . . . but does she really? Peace and plenty? The land of milk and honey? A perfect battleground! With all the lesser evils out of the way, the field is clear for the greatest Evil of all. And it's coming, it's coming! The Gibbering is only the advance guard, and we are the fathers of the New Faith!"

The white balls of his eyes rolled down, seemed almost to click into place, like the reels of some

sentient slot machine. Their yellow pupils blazed
. . . and then a further deterioration.

The Stones had seen this twice before, this
abrupt and still more hideous alteration in their
son, which must invariably terminate any visit in
which it occurred. It was a transformation from
sub-human to complete alien. Without warning
his cheeks, all the flesh of his face seemed sucked
in, shriveled, wrinkling like a paper bag with its
air extracted. The yellow fires behind his eyes
flickered low. His head *wobbled* upon his neck,
jerking and twitching without coordination. His
color became chalk-white—a pale amber as seen
through the tinted glass—then rapidly darkened
to a purplish blotching. The rise and fall of his
chest beneath the straitjacket slowing, stilling.
Breathing coming to a halt. And the purple
spreading. His wrinkled, monkey-face darkening,
tongue protruding. And finally the blood trick-
ling, then spurting from gaping nostrils as his
mother screamed: "Oh, Richard—no, no, no!
Noooooo!"

In another moment consciousness fled him and
Richard toppled face forward against the glass
partition. The charged plate galvanized his muscles, flinging him back from its field. He tossed
for a moment, then lay still upon the deep-padded
floor, his face turned to one side and shiny with
blood.

Vicki had instinctively jerked back from the
tinted pane, lay half-fainting on the floor, her
hands propping her up. Phillip went down on his
knees beside her, wrapped his arms about her,
rocked her to and fro for a moment as she
sobbed. Then the door behind them hissed open
and their receptionist-guide was touching his
shoulder. "I'm afraid—" she gently began.

"It's all right," Phillip Stone cut her short, staring almost unseeingly up at her. "We'll be leaving now."

"Mr. Stone," she smiled concernedly, reached up a hand and tapped her clean pink nails upon the plastic casing of her headphones, "you really should wear them, you know."

"Yes, of course," he automatically answered, helping Vicki to her feet. Then his eyes focused. He stood stock still, his arm about his wife, holding her up. His air was that of a man who listens intently for something.

The girl looked at him questioningly. "Mr. Stone?"

"No need for the headphones now," he told her. "Can't you feel it? It's quiet as a tomb in here. They've all stopped, for the moment at least. They've stopped gibbering . . ."

Chapter Two

HALFWAY BACK TO THEIR SUSSEX HOME THE STONES stopped for a break at a roadside restaurant, a bright place dishing up snacks and salads on a serve-yourself basis. Vicki was not hungry but Phillip had a ham salad with eggs mayonnaise. He ate mechanically while she sipped coffee and smoked a cigarette. Conversation was absent; both were lost in their own thoughts.

But as he paid the bill and they made to leave she caught his elbow and said: "That . . . that gibbering. It's so horrible! Once it gets in your head you can't seem to shake it. It's like some feverish pop tune or jingle: you hate it but it gets fixed in your memory. Like a couple of silly words heard late at night, that keep repeating all through the dark hours and refuse to let you sleep. You know, I can still hear it."

He frowned and looked at her curiously for a moment, but she only gave him a wan smile and shook her head as if in denial of herself, then tugged his arm and drew him toward the exit.

The car was hot inside from the sun, and Phillip cursed under his breath as he started the engine. "I should have wound down the windows—at least left a gap. It's a bloody furnace in here!"

"That would have let in the wasps," she answered. "There are lots of them this year. Flies, too."

"Yes," he nodded, "—and thieves!" Pulling on to the road he frowned again. "Can't say I've noticed many wasps."

"Oh?" she stared out of her window, breathing deeply as the air conditioning did its work. "Oh, yes—lots of them."

He turned the car onto a southbound motorway where traffic was heavy, settling into the center lane of a three-lane system. Rumbling articulated lorries rolled on the slow outside lane, while long, squat, sharp and shiny cars flashed by on the fast inner. The Stones' car, while expensive and well kept, was a staider, older model, and Phillip Stone himself was respectful of speed where his wife's safety was concerned.

"Heavy," he commented. "All these cars heading for the sea. Like mechanical lemmings. A splash in the briny, heigh-ho!" But his levity was forced.

"Off for the weekend," she answered. "We were the same, last year. You and me, and Lynn, and—"

"Yes," he cut her off, "yes I know. I remember. We do have the memories, you know."

"Memories," she sighed.

"Remember when weekends were just Saturday and Sunday?" he asked, his tone deliberately light. "And we all used to wish they'd abolish Mondays? Well, finally they did. A four-day working week for most of us now, and only three for many."

"I remember . . . strange things sometimes," she said. "Things that didn't happen. Dreams, I suppose." She swatted at something. "I *thought* there was one in here! A fly—or a small wasp—I'm not sure."

Phillip glanced quickly about the car's spacious interior, saw nothing. He peered sharply at Vicki out of the corner of his eye. "Things that didn't happen?" he repeated her. "What things? What do you mean?" Something played a queer little tune on the chords of his mind, a cold little tune that chilled him.

She turned her head and looked at him, willing him to look back at her. "I remember being blind," she said. "And I remember dying." Her voice was cold and emotionless as ice, crystal clear. "And sometimes . . . sometimes I seem to remember a man called Richard. Richard Garrison. *My* Richard's father."

Phillip Stone's jaw dropped, dropped more yet as his wife halfheartedly swatted at a wasp which clearly wasn't there. "They buzz so loud," she said. "In my head, they buzz . . ."

Stone wanted to pull over into the slow lane, find a layby, stop. His hands were clammy cold; he felt ill, wanted to be sick. But the lorries were rumbling by on his left, their huge wheels coming up tall as the windows; and when he lifted his foot from the accelerator the line of traffic behind him flashed and tooted, apparently angry with his indecision. So that as Vicki commenced shaking her head and swatting furiously, he cursed, put his foot down hard, began to pull ahead of the lorries in the slow lane, and—

—She stopped swatting, reached over and

yanked at the wheel, jerking it way over to the left. Her face was totally vacant; saliva trickled from the corner of her mouth; her strength was that . . . of a madwoman!

The big car swerved over into the slow lane at the worst possible time, just as Stone hit the brakes. An articulated truck clipped his rear end, sending the car spinning across the hard-standing and through the thin metal sheeting of an advertising hoarding. Empty space beyond the hoarding, a railway embankment beneath. The car curved down through thin air, its nose crashing at an angle into the embankment's declining slope.

Phillip Stone had time only to hit the catch of his seat belt and lift the catch of his door, then all was pain and chaos. He was hurled free, bounced and felt ribs go, slid and felt his face torn, came up against something hard and felt his right leg snap below the knee. But all in a sort of vacuum of disbelief, in which the crashing of metal and roaring of an enraged engine came from a million miles away, in which even the pain was unreal, belonging to someone else.

He opened his eyes, saw the car bound across shiny ribbons of track below the arches of the bridge, saw it roll over onto its back and slide to a rocking halt halfway across the far track—

—And saw the train hurtle out from under the bridge, its blunt bullet nose tearing the car in two halves, smashing them aside, and rushing on down the track in a demon howling of brakes and showers of hot, bright sparks from the biting wheels.

Then he was crawling among the cinders and oil-blackened gravel, dragging himself across tracks and hand over hand along the ties, unaware of the pain of his body against the greater agony of his mind. The train had come to a halt further down the tracks; people were erupting from its doors, screaming and shouting, running toward him. He didn't see them, saw only the battered front half of his car, with the passenger's door forced open and the top half of his wife hanging head-down from her safety belt. Only her top half, scarlet with her blood.

The rest of her was somewhere else . . .

"How are you today, Richard?" Calm Lawns' governor and senior psychiatrist, Dr. Günther Gorvitch, sat on the safe side of the tinted glass partition.

"Fine," Richard Stone answered. *Fine, you bald-headed old bastard, you strained-through-a-blanket son of a scummy boil-sucker!* "I'm just fine—and I'm as sane as you are." He smiled, forcing The Gibbering from his brain, squeezing it out by use of an unending stream of mental obscenities.

Gorvitch was small, stocky, bulb-nosed and bespectacled. His eyes were a piercing blue behind thick lenses. He was dressed in a rumpled suit under his plain white hospital smock, seemed uncomfortable where he sat crossing, uncrossing and recrossing his legs. "Well, you've certainly got us thinking," he finally admitted.

"You mean you're about ready to let me out?" Richard raised a half-sarcastic eyebrow. *Turd-sucking, slime-dwelling, rat-shagging—*

"Oh, I wouldn't go as far as that," Gorvitch laughed, "not just yet. But I'd certainly like to think it possible—eventually. And if it is . . ."

"I'll be the first who's made it, right?" *Right?— you blob-nosed, analytic, syphilitic anus!*

"Right. If it was that which brought you in here in the first place. It might have been some lesser, er, aberration? The symptoms said it was The Gibbering, of course, but that might—just *might*—have been coincidental. On the other hand, it's our experience that mental disorders do metamorphose into The Gibbering. But—" the half-smile dropped from his face in a moment, "—whichever, you might yet prove to be an invaluable asset to this hospital."

"Just to this hospital?" *Fuck-face*.

Gorvitch nodded, smiled again, wryly, corrected himself: "To the world, of course."

"The first patient ever to beat The Gibbering," Richard grinned. "Hey!—I'll be something of a celebrity!"

"You'll be a lot of a celebrity," Gorvitch agreed. "If you've really beaten it. If you had it in the first place—and if we can discover *how* you beat it!" For the first time he allowed himself to look at his young patient from a purely physical viewpoint.

Richard Stone was a fine specimen, typical of his generation. He had been born in the years of plenty, had grown up in an era when the world prospered as never before. There were no starvelings anymore, certainly not in those lands which one constituted the first- and second-world countries. Even the tottery third-world economies were now solidly-based, whose children prospered in welfare states remote from the living-memory deprivations of their parents.

Richard was good-looking, rangy-limbed, broad in the shoulder and narrow in the hip. His dark hair was short in the modern vogue, crew-cut and trimmed evenly as a well kept lawn. That was the single demand (apart from the inevitable one) he had made since his arrival here: that his hair be trimmed once every ten days. His head itched, he said, if his hair got more than an inch long. As for jewelry: he adhered to the now outmoded affectation of wearing a single gold ring in the lobe of his right ear.

In short, there was little to distinguish him from any one of a million youths of his generation. Or maybe there was one thing, Gorvitch tentatively corrected himself: his eyes. They were perhaps the strangest eyes the psychiatrist had ever seen. Their color was hard to define. One might call them very light brown, but they were rather more yellow than that. A kind of bronze or gold color, but changeable as a moonstone. Sometimes they even seemed dark; but right now, through the tinted glass of the partition, they were a sort of gold-flecked green. Feral, almost . . .

They were alive, those eyes, brimming with a unique intelligence of their own, burning on Gorvitch and—

And he blinked, shook his head, found his patient speaking to him again, in the middle of a sentence:

". . . you distinguish between The Gibbering and just any old madness? I mean, *is* there any real distinction?"

Gorvitch coughed, pulled at an earlobe, covered his mind's wandering as best he might. "To go into that might take some little time," he said, carefully deflecting his gaze from that of the inmate. Had his mind wandered, he asked himself, or had it been something else? Hypnotism? That hardly seemed likely—unless it had been self-hypnotism. Maybe he was just tired.

"I have all the time in the world," *the world, all the time in the fucking wide world!*

The psychiatrist shrugged. "Very well. About five and a half years ago—we can't really put a finger on it more accurately than that—the world became aware of a peculiar, a frightening and

universal trend among its lunatics. Both its certified lunatics and people on the lunatic fringe,
as it were. It was The Gibbering, of course . . ."
Gorvitch shook his head, looked impatient or angry with himself.

"No, that won't do," he said. "That's not the
way to tell it, a very poor start indeed. Let me try
it differently."

"By all means," it was Richard's turn to shrug.
"Maybe I shouldn't have asked," *you farting old
fossil,* "but I mean, well, what's so difficult about
understanding The Gibbering? Ask a physician to
distinguish between cancer and the common
cold, or an astronomer between Mars and Venus,
or a geologist between granite and limestone, and
they'll—"

"But, that's just it!" Gorvitch cut in, his voice
suddenly animated.

*Or a priest to distinguish between good and
evil . . . !*

"In the examples you pose the distinction is
quite clear, indeed obvious," said Gorvitch. "And
similarly, there used to be clearcut definitions
and terms of reference for most of the mental ill-
nesses. But—" he slowed down and became calm
again, "but that all changed with The Gibbering."
His eyes had narrowed, were studying Richard's
face, watching and analyzing its every slightest
movement.

"Do you mind if I pace while we talk?" *You stinking shrink!* Richard began to plod to and fro across
the padded floor of his tiny cell, his hands clasped
behind his back. "I mean, it's a bloody good job I
don't have claustrophobia too, isn't it?"

Gorvitch laughed, relaxed. If he didn't know
better he'd swear his patient was normal. Even
knowing better, still Richard Stone was much im-

proved over when he first came in here. Very definitely. And after fifteen months of gibbering this sudden improvement might, just might, make him quite unique—eyes, mind, psyche and all! It already made him far more of a "celebrity" than Stone himself might ever suspect (or so Gorvitch mistakenly believed).

"But you were saying . . . ?" Richard prompted him. *You bald-pated, stunted little prick!*

As he paced—four paces to, four fro, back and forth, back and forth—Richard kept his hands clamped tightly together, hoping that the whiteness of his knuckles would not show through the tinted wall between. Clamped, yes, for if those hands escaped each other and crept round to his front, they might just leap at Gorvitch, might drag Richard Stone after them, crash him into the partition's electric field. Not that that would be a bad thing in itself; shocked unconscious he would doubtless dream his strange dreams, those dreams which he knew were more than merely nightmare visions conjured of a warped subconsciousness. But on the other hand it would lose him a great deal of ground with Gorvitch, and that was something he did not want. Not at all. Having gained the psychiatrist's confidence, he must now do all he could to maintain and improve their relationship. And with all of these thoughts rushing through his mind it was hard to concentrate, difficult to focus on what the good Dr. Gorvitch was even now telling him:

". . . madness? That all such disturbances would metamorphose into The Gibbering? Of course not! And yet that was what must ultimately happen. And after two years of gibbering, death—usually from cardiac arrest or a brain hemorrhage during a seizure. Now? We no longer bother to diagnose schizophrenia, melancholia, megalomania, paranoia, etcetera as such but simply as the First Phase of a disorder for which there is no known treatment. Not yet. All of them, without exception and however simply they start out, *must* deteriorate into The Gibbering! Small wonder we've made so little progress! What would be the state of things if doctors of the physical condition were faced with an epidemic where the common cold, mumps, anaemia, flu and ingrown toenails were all symptomatic of an imminent and completely incurable strain of leprosy?"

"Epidemic?" Richard repeated him. "You mean plague? Really?" He stopped pacing. Their eyes locked again through the tinted plate glass. For a moment the silent two-man tableau held . . . then Gorvitch nodded.

"Since it's highly unlikely you'll be going anywhere, I suppose I can tell you. Plague, yes. It's on the increase. The curve is—" he shrugged expansively, "—exponential. We don't know where, or if, it will end."

"And I might have the answer?" *I do have it, I do! It's locked somewhere inside me. Only let me out of here, let me track it down. I, Richard Stone, AM the answer—you poor dumb blind stupid bastard!*

Again the psychiatrist's nod. "You might have it, yes." *Oh, God!—let it be so!*

"Then how can it serve you to keep me locked up in here?" *Answer me that, witchdoctor!*

Gorvitch pursed his lips, began to concede, "There might well be something in what—" and paused abruptly, frowned, adopted an attitude of careful, concerned listening.

"Yes," said Richard after a moment, "I hear them too."

It was as if the hospital trembled, however minutely. Point zero, zero, zero, one on the Richter Scale. A sort of humming in the walls and floors. A slumbering hive suddenly whirring to life.

"A moment ago, silence," Gorvitch muttered, shaking his head. "Now—this! What turns them on, Richard, do you know?"

The inmate shook his head. "No," he answered, truthfully. *But I know that whatever it is, it turns me on, too. Leave me now, please leave me. Oh, God, go!—before I give myself away* . . .

"We'll talk again," said Gorvitch, tapping the cell's code into his wrist-key. "Tomorrow." Then the outer door hissed open and he stepped through into the corridor. "Tomorrow," he promised again as the door closed on him.

Alone—barely in time alone—now Richard Stone could relax, give himself over to The Gibbering. Except that he knew he must not do that. Features mobile as a rubber mask, he kneeled before the plate. Commencing a low, frenzied, uninterrupted and incredible stream of meaningless and meaningful obscenities, he turned his shining face to one side and held up his hands palms-forward on a level with his head.

Then he fell forward, chest, face and hands all coming into brief and simultaneous contact with the field.

Thank God! he thought, even through the great vibrating *rrrrip!* of physical agony which tossed him like a doll back from the plate. *Thank God for the padding!*

Thank God, too, for the merciful all-engulfing blackness . . .

Chapter Three

"**M**R. STONE?" THE HAND ON HIS SLUMPED shoulder was gentle but persistent. "Sir? *Sir?*"

Finally the anxious voice of Phillip Stone's housekeeper got through to him. He became aware of his surroundings almost as upon awakening, and yet he had not been asleep. He had not been *here*, no, but neither had he been asleep. He could not remember—not actually remember—sleeping at all since the accident, though he supposed he must have slept. Certainly he looked as if he had had no sleep for . . . days. At least, that had been his opinion when last he looked in a mirror. And from the worried look on his housekeeper's face things had not improved much since then, whenever "then" had been.

"A gentleman to see you, sir," she said when finally his eyes focused upon her. "A doctor, sir—a surgeon. He says it's to do with . . . with Mrs. Stone.''

In his time, Stone had suited his name well. Now, for all that the years were catching up with him, he was a crag of a man still. But the rock of his being was old and cracked, and weathering had started to soften its core.

He looked from his housekeeper to the empty glass in his hand, to the empty bottle on the table before him. Then he looked at his study, also empty. Full of his things, yes, but empty. Like his life.

His life. A year and a half ago it had been full. Where the hell had everything gone to?

''Sir?''

''Yes, yes,'' he finally answered, surprised to discover that his voice retained some of its former strength. ''What does he want? Papers to be signed? Tell him to leave them.''

''No papers, Mr. Stone,'' said a new voice, deep, powerful and polished. A speaker's voice, that of an orator or lecturer; not quite right for a surgeon, whose strength should be in his hands. ''It's simply that I have to talk to you, that's all.''

Stone eased himself upright in his deep leather armchair, put down his glass, looked beyond the dumpy figure of his housekeeper to the face of a tall, gaunt man who had followed her into the room. Mrs. Wells also looked at him, pursed her lips and said:

''I *did* ask the gentleman to wait, sir, but—''

''It's all right, Mary,'' Stone told her. He pushed himself to his feet. ''Since Mr.—er, Dr.—?''

''Likeman,'' the stranger obliged. ''Miles Likeman.''

Stone nodded. ''Since Dr. Likeman has already found his way in, I'll talk to him.''

When she had left the room, taking Likeman's overcoat with her, Stone offered his visitor a seat, opened a new bottle of Scotch and poured drinks. "You want to talk about my wife," he ventured at last, nodding. "You know of course that she died some four months ago, in a traffic accident?"

"Oh, yes, I do," came the answer. "I would have come to see you sooner, but it seemed only decent to—"

"I understand," Stone cut him short. "Thank you."

"As it is, today, since I happened to be down this way—I mean, I know it's off the cuff, that I really should have made an appointment or some such, but . . ."

While Dr. Likeman talked, Stone checked him over, growing steadily more conscious of his nervous agitation. A doctor? A surgeon? Not at all the sort who should suffer from his nerves. And yet he had a doctor's hands, and certainly he spoke with something of authority, however reluctantly. Maybe a few years more than fifty, about the same age as Stone himself. But why was he here? Whatever his mission was he didn't relish it, that was a sure thing. No, his reticence showed all too clearly in his worried hazel eyes.

Stone waited for him to continue anyway, and only when the pause threatened to stretch itself out indefinitely prompted: "I'm not much of a one for protocol, Dr. Likeman. As for appointments: I rarely make them and hate having them made for me. In fact, I often wonder how come I've got on so well in the world. In business, I mean. But come to think of it, I believe I do know your name. I've seen it quite recently, I think, on some documents." He frowned. "Yes, I remember now.

Weren't you the one who did some sort of post-mortem on Vicki? A medical autopsy?''

Likeman saw the change in Stone: his eyes had narrowed, peered at him more keenly now, and his huge frame had seemed to tense, tightening like a steel spring. His speech too, had sharpened, the words coming out hard-edged.

''You were unconscious for four days, Mr. Stone,'' Likeman said. ''And for another week you were doped-up against your injuries. I was in the middle of a course at the time of the accident, teaching student doctors. I did once have a Harley Street practice, yes, but now I prefer to instruct others. Part of my curriculum covered accidental death. Your wife carried a donor's card and is—was—total-body registered. The course was held at Oxford, in an emergency hospital for obvious reasons. The hospital computer confirmed Mrs. Stone's registration—yours, too, incidentally—and further told me that your only other living relative was your son. The law does not require permission, as you probably know, but I like to get it whenever possible. Getting your son's permission, however, was . . .''

''. . . Out of the question, yes,'' Stone nodded. Then he slumped back down into his armchair. ''It's all right, Dr. Likeman,'' he said after a moment. ''I'm not questioning anyone's ethics. It's just that some of these arrangements we make in cold blood . . . well, I'm sure you know what I mean.''

Likeman relaxed a little. ''Of course I do,'' he said. ''You must not let yourself believe that my familiarity with death has made me contemptuous of it—or callous. Quite the opposite: I'm one of the proverbial exceptions that prove the rule.''

Stone nodded again. ''Then let's get to it,'' he

said. "What do you want from me? For all your obvious sincerity, you didn't come here simply to commiserate."

Likeman sighed, blinked once or twice and got his thoughts in order, then leaned forward and took up his drink. "There are some questions I might ask you," he said. "A very odd thing has happened, perhaps several odd things, and your answers may be very important to me. Frankly, since my examination of your wife's body, I have been at something of a loss. Medical science is not exact, Mr. Stone, but it does have certain rules. And there are limits beyond which these may not bend. In your wife's case, the rules were not merely bent but broken—I might even say shattered!"

Stone recognized genuine concern when he saw it, but he wanted no man's pity. He sat up straighter, an angry retort rising and dying unspoken on his hard lips. Instead, very quietly, he said, "Why the hell don't you get on with it? Don't worry about hurting me, Likeman. Worry about getting tossed out of here on your neck—unless you start making sense pretty soon!"

"Very well," the other maintained an even tone, "I have to know about your wife. I have to know a lot about her."

"That's a start," Stone scowled, "but you already told me that. Now tell me *why* you need to know about her?"

"Because she was . . . different. She was very different, Mr. Stone." He leaned forward, his firm, strong hands trembling, however slightly, where he lay them on the table between them. "First, how old was she?" His eyes fixed and held those of the other man.

Stone frowned, shrugged huge shoulders, said,

"You know, I never asked her? But I'd hazard—"
again his shrug, "—oh, forty-five or six. Say, ten
or eleven years my junior."

"And you were born in . . . ?"

"1948," said Stone. "What are you getting at?"

"So you'd say your wife was maybe forty-five
years old?"

"I already *did* say so!"

Dr. Likeman sat back, pursed his lips for a moment, said: "She was born in 1947. She was a year
older than you."

Stone snorted. "Rubbish!" he said. "That would
make her thirty-seven when I married her, twenty
years ago. Thirty-seven? She was like a young girl.
I used to look at her and feel like an old man! You
must have made some sort of—"

"No, no mistake, Mr. Stone. A copy of her birth
certificate is in the new Central Registry in Köln."

"Birth certificate?" Stone's brow darkened.
"Köln? Who gave you the right to—"

"I had to! I had to corroborate the data from
the hospital computer. It was linked to Medcen in
London, but Medcen might have incorrect information. It was the computer first told me she was
born in '47; the source was her passport."

"Passport? That makes about as much sense to
me as 'ration book'!" Stone snorted again. "Pass-
ports went out nine, ten years ago. It's a free
world now, Dr. Likeman! No borders anymore.
Didn't anybody tell you?"

"But she had a passport in 1992," said Likeman, unruffled, "when she made herself a donor.
So . . . like you, I just couldn't believe she was
fifty-seven years old. Hers wasn't the corpse—
you'll forgive me—of an old woman. Not when I
first saw it, anyway . . ."

Silence fell in the room. Stone gulped at his

drink; but he was interested now. "What are you saying?" he asked. "What are you getting at? She didn't look old when you *first* saw her? What's that supposed to mean?"

His visitor held up a hand. "I'll get to that in a minute. Please be patient. You see, I have to have answers for all my questions before I can formulate any sort of explanation."

Stone gritted his teeth. "So get on with it," he said.

"About her blindness—" Likeman began.

"Her *what*?" Stone was incredulous.

The doctor looked at him in surprise. "Her blindness, Mr. Stone. How long had she been blind?"

Vicki, blind? Icy feet tiptoed on Phillip Stone's spine. He heard again Vicki's voice, echoing in the back of his mind:

"I remember being blind . . ."

"But she wasn't blind!" he said, and saw Likeman's eyebrows go up. Suddenly the doctor was looking at him as if he were a madman; and just as suddenly, Stone felt unsure of himself. "She . . . she wasn't," he said again. "She wasn't blind, and I'm not crazy. But I'm not so sure about you!"

"Mr. Stone, I—"

"Is that it? Are you some sort of madman?" Stone whispered, slowly uncoiling from his chair, stepping carefully round the table, looming huge. "You know what it sounds like to me, Dr. Likeman, or whoever you are? It sounds to me like you're gibbering!"

As Stone's hands reached down to grip the lapels on his jacket, Likeman shrank into his chair and closed his eyes. He was prepared to believe without demonstration that Stone was as strong as he looked. As for his mental state: the doctor wasn't sure he was fit to make comment on that anymore. And he could well understand Stone's doubts about him!

As Stone breathed Scotch into his face, Likeman said, "Please, Mr. Stone, do nothing rash." The authority Stone had at first noted was absent now. Likeman's voice shook.

Stone drew him upright, drew him close, held him limp as a damp rag, hanging from his hands. At last, carefully, the doctor opened his eyes. "I don't think either one of us is mad, Mr. Stone. There has to be some other explanation. Maybe a mistake. But the corpse I examined was certainly that of a woman who had been blind for a great many years."

Stone lowered him to the chair, reluctantly released him. "Are you saying it might not have been Vicki after all?"

"I'm not sure what I'm saying," Likeman sat still, waiting for Stone to uncoil. Finally he did, began to pace the floor.

"What do you remember of the accident?" Likeman quietly asked.

"I last saw my wife," Stone muttered, "—saw half of my wife—hanging out of what was left of our car. One of her eyes had been knocked out and was hanging on her cheek . . ."

Likeman nodded. "The body of the woman I examined had been severed at the waist. One eye was loose, the right one. I know a lot about eyes, Mr. Stone. They were my speciality when I was first starting out. Eyes and their diseases. This woman had been blind. Quite definitely. The optical nerves were completely eaten away. By disease."

Stone stopped pacing, shuddered violently, involuntarily, then flopped heavily into his chair and topped up their drinks. "Go on," he said.

"It was a very rare and insidious cancer. Whether the woman was your wife or not, she had it. Her accidental death had been sudden, violent, and was probably a mercy. We still don't have all the answers to cancer, and in this woman . . . well, it had gone too far. The eyes had been the first to succumb; that's the way it is with this form of the disease. That was my opinion at first sight, before the actual post-mortem. That is to say, before my class had assembled, shortly after the body had been brought in. It was also my opinion, at that time, that she was about forty-five years of age."

Stone waited for him to continue, finally prompting: "So you checked her . . . her *availability*, on the hospital's computer."

"Yes, and her age, etcetera, as I've told you. Then I made a few preparatory incisions and generally . . . you know, got her ready. I left her under a thin rubber sheet, secured the operating theater and went to welcome my class and give them a brief introductory talk. That took maybe half an hour, and—" Seeing Stone's face—how he had screwed his eyes tightly shut—Likeman waited.

Finally Stone took a deep breath, opened his eyes and said, "I'm sorry. Go on."

"I'm sorry too, Mr. Stone. Sorry right now that I'm a pathologist. Sorry to have to put you through this. Especially sorry that all of this happened to me. Anyway, the rest of it isn't pleasant."

"The *rest* of it?" Stone gave a sardonic snort. "I suppose I'd do well to remember that you make a living cutting people up! But . . . okay, we've had our fun, now let's have the serious part."

Likeman stared hard at him. "I understand the way you must feel, Mr. Stone, but try to imagine how I have felt for the last four months. You *will* understand by the time I've finished, believe me."

"Get on with it while I'm still willing to listen," Stone grated. "I've just about had enough. Ask the rest of your questions, or tell the rest of your tale, but get on with it."

"No more questions," the doctor shook his head. "I'll simply give you the facts. Then, if *you* have any ideas . . ."

"The facts, then," said Stone. "But quickly, please."

Likeman's face was shiny now with sweat. He nervously brushed back his hair, took up his drink, said, "Very well. I told my students that in the corpse we were to examine they'd find evidence of a rare cancer; I told them the accident had saved the woman a lot of suffering; and then I took them to the operating theater and removed the rubber sheet from your wife's—from the woman's—body."

Stone's heart was pounding in his chest. Suddenly he wanted to stop Likeman—but at the same time he had to know. It had to do with the things Vicki had told him in her last moments. Those mad things she said as she lapsed into The Gibbering.

"Under that rubber sheet—" Likeman paused to lick suddenly dry lips, "—how can I explain it? I had left a female corpse in that room just half an hour ago; the dead body of what had once been a very attractive woman; but now . . . ? Well, there was no autopsy, Mr. Stone. Not as such, certainly not as a lesson. Christ!—half of my class simply passed out, fainted away! I should have known—the smell . . .!"

"*Likeman!*" Stone croaked, his flesh crawling. "What the hell—?"

Likeman took out a handkerchief and held it to his mouth. His hands were shaking very badly now. "It was the same woman, I swear it. Same small scars, same injuries—everything. But . . ."

"But?"

"But *this* woman had been dead for . . . for quite some time. Do you understand? There had been a complete collapse of the tissues, the fluids. A katabolism. And it was still in progress. She . . . she *seethed*, Mr. Stone."

Stone could see that Likeman was neither mad nor lying. "Oh, Jesus!" he whispered.

"I got the students out of there," Likeman finally went on. "A little later I forced myself to go back in. By then it was all over. The corpse was quiescent—which is what you'd expect of a mummy! Bone and skin . . . and little else. I knew she had died only recently, but pathologically— this was a woman who had been dead for more than a quarter of a century!"

An hour, two hours later, still Stone sat there in his study, quite alone now. In his hand a pair of diamond earrings Dr. Likeman had given him— just as he had given them to his wife ten years ago—and in his mind Vicki's voice, crystal clear, repeating some of the last words she ever spoke to him:

"I remember being blind," she said again in his reeling head, "*and I remember dying . . .*"

Chapter Four

J. C. CRAIG DREAMED.

He dreamed a strange dream whose roots
went back to a man or creature long since passed
from all human knowledge, all minds and memories.
Except Craig's own.

The creature himself (he had been a huge hybrid Negro, a warped, ESP-endowed albino) featured only rarely in Craig's dreams, and then only
as a dark and enigmatic polyp on the periphery
of Craig's subconscious mind. He featured no
more than this because Craig had never known
him, and also because the Psychosphere had
struck his name and being from the face of the
Universe. Only his mental voice remained. Only
the thoughts and commands he had projected
into Craig's mind more than twenty years ago.

For deep in the vaults of James Christopher
Craig's awareness, hidden in the darkest reaches
of his subconscious mind, Charon Gubwa's tele-

pathically implanted seeds had taken root and grown. And with the passing of years they had fruited into post-hypnotic fungi, taking grotesque and malignant forms.

The fungi were his dreams; the malignancy was the way he had interpreted and acted upon them; the result was—

—Psychomech!

Psychomech the Oracle, through which Craig would one day talk to God in the waking world even as he now talked to him in dreams. And Craig *always* talked to God in his dreams, for that had been the essence of Charon Gubwa's instructions: that whenever Craig slept he would hear his voice, hear and obey! And over the years that voice had become the Voice of God himself, and His Word was the Law!

Craig's conversation with God was always the same, it had changed very little over the twenty-odd years since first he dreamed his strange dream. Craig *himself* had changed, certainly, but the conversation had grown almost meaningless through repetition until it was little more than a ritual liturgy. It always started the same way, and always in the same place. Craig was in that place now.

He looked about him in his dream and saw the usual, awesome things—awesome despite their familiarity.

As always, he was in a vast workshop whose walls must lie beyond the farthest horizon and whose ceiling was miles high and lit with great rows of glaring neons, curving away in dazzling procession over the edge of the world. Or perhaps the workshop was housed in a great dome, but a dome enormous beyond Craig's measure.

The floor of the place was of rubber-tiled concrete, where great lathes and grinders and cutting and stamping machines lay bedded, silent, waiting for the hand of some master machinist. Miles of cable, of electrical wiring, of tubing both metal and plastic, lay coiled on their drums; while overhead, bogy-mounted cranes and hoists crouched like monstrous mantis, or spiders poised upon webs of steel track. The bright gleam of metal was everywhere, everywhere the smell of plastic and oil and pent electricity; but nowhere a whisper of sound, nowhere the smallest motion, nowhere the slightest sign of life. Except in Craig himself.

Or perhaps there was life here—life of the Highest Order—but so hidden or strange or different from Craig's own that his knowledge of it was more instinct than intelligence. He *sensed* it was here but could never quite pin it down. Like being in a soaring cathedral—or on wild, wind-blown cliffs, overlooking a mighty, tormented ocean— or gazing up into the everlasting vault of heaven: one *senses* a Presence but is never allowed the smallest glimpse. Or very rarely.

God? Craig assumed that it must be God. He *more* than assumed, for Charon Gubwa's fungi had long since spread through all of his being. They no longer sprouted in his subconscious alone but had rooted in his very psyche, his id, his personality. And that made them part of his waking world, too.

But for the moment he dreamed, and in his dream he heard the Words of God:

Craig, are you listening?

"Oh, yes, Lord, I hear you."

You will hear and obey.

"You know I will, Lord. I am your obedient servant."

That is good! Only hear and obey me, James Christopher Craig, and I will make you a priest of my temple, and you shall know no other Lord but me.

"Lord, I embrace thy faith!"

Ah?—but it was not always so.

"No, for I was blind, Lord, and did not know you—and in my ignorance I sinned. Thus you have instructed me, Lord."

And what was the nature of your sin?

"I would have made a false god, Lord. He had man's face and form, but desired to be more than man."

He was evil, this man who would be a god!

"Yes, Lord, and through you I have come to know my sin—to know it and to repent and to humble myself."

. . . What was his name, this evil one?

"Garrison, Lord—or so you have told me."

And what work did you do for this . . . Garrison?

"I went in unto his temple, Lord—went in like an idolater—and there builded him an oracle."

A false oracle for a false god!

"Yes, O Great One!"

And did the oracle have a name?

"It was called Psychomech, Lord."

And you knew this Psychomech in all its parts and functions?

"Its parts were many. I am but a man. I—"

But did you not build the oracle?

"The machine *was*, Lord. I made it more powerful, more efficient. Garrison instructed, and I obeyed."

Garrison made you his fool, James Christopher Craig!

"Yes, Lord."

But I shall strike him down—not for your folly, but for his blasphemy!

"It shall be as my Lord desires."

And when he is no more and his works are made as nothing, then shall you be forgiven.

"Thank you! Oh, thank you, Lord!"

A weak, false god, this Garrison, and his oracle Psychomech flawed. For me you shall build a new, purer, more powerful Oracle; and I shall reward you; and you shall be a priest in my temple, James Christopher Craig.

"But . . . the oracle Psychomech was complex, Lord, and—"

Have you forgotten your skills? Are you not worthy of the Great Work I place in your hands?

"Worthy? Only let it be so, Lord! But how may I remember all that was—"

You WILL remember! Though it take a month, a year, ten years—you WILL remember!

"I . . . I will remember, Lord."

You will look back and see all as it was, as it still is in the eyes of your memory. No smallest detail shall escape you. Yea, and you shall build me a Psychomech! And soon I shall make myself known to you, James Christopher Craig; and you shall be first among my flock and shall be saved.

God's voice was fading now, echoing away in diminishing waves that were lost amidst horizon-silhouetted banks of machinery. Craig felt very small in the vast workshop, dwarfed by piles of inert components and wires and tubes and printed circuits and microchip matrices.

"Lord, don't leave me!" he cried in sudden terror.

Build me my Oracle, James Christopher Craig. Build me my Machine . . . The voice was a drifting whisper now.

"When shall I know you?" Craig wailed his desperation.

Soon, soon . . .

"When?" Craig was impatient, frustrated.

Build me my Psychomech . . .

And suddenly Craig remembered. "But I have built it! Psychomech *is*, Lord!" He waited with bated breath, but—

—Nothing! God had departed, as He always did at this stage. And mighty machine shadows pressing in on Craig, and the immense workshop silent and eerie as a tomb of robot kings . . .

Craig shrank down, down, down into himself.

And awakened.

High above the main gate and security control room of the huge PSISAC complex, two night watchkeepers looked down over the sprawling steel and concrete body of their ward, smoked cigarettes and talked in low voices as they kept vigil. Tonight's duty was largely static, for these two at least; in fact they merely tended PSISAC's security systems. Their official place of duty was down below, in the control room, but a smoke and a breath of fresh air had not seemed remiss.

They were two of ten such caretakers working in and from control points throughout the ninety-acre expanse of laboratories, processing plants, workshops, assembly areas, offices, reception and recreation areas, and loading bays which comprised PSISAC. The complex was a giant, but at the moment a slumbering giant. Neons around its perimeter glared its name like a challenge to the night, in tall letters of glowing light, far out in the Oxfordshire countryside:

PHILLIP STONE INDUSTRIES
(SATELLITES & COMPUTERS)

From the tower, the watchmen could mark the plodding progress of their fellow security operatives through PSISAC's streets and alleys, the narrow beams of their torches occasionally cutting into and probing the darker, deeper canyons. Ten men might seem a mere handful for an area so huge and mazy, but in fact they were more than sufficient. All were armed with dart-firing sleep pistols; huge alsatians were their companions and plodded beside the patrolmen where they quartered PSISAC's labyrinth; their forces were supplemented by a backup of security technology which could detect, pinpoint and track even the random excursions of night-venturing mice. More than sufficient, yes—but James Christopher Craig, PSISAC's Managing Director, was a very security conscious fellow.

"Work here, run the place, yes—but actually *live* here? Inside the complex?" One of the men in the tower, Geoff Bellamy, shook his head. "That's what I call over the top! Dedication run rampant!"

Bellamy was talking about Craig. Even as he stated his opinion lights came alive in the Dome, a structure standing roughly central in the rectangle of PSISAC's sprawling body. Lacking the accustomed naked industrial glare, subdued almost, the lights nevertheless showed that Craig was up and about, doing whatever it was that Managing Directors did at 3:00 in the morning of chilly October days. For Craig lived in the Dome; it was his home.

He might simply be making himself a sandwich or a coffee; he could be pacing the floor of his study, pondering the problems of some new project; possibly he was at his drawing board, intent upon some modification in the design of the communication or energy-broadcasting satellites which were his speciality. Or . . . he might be fast asleep, entirely innocent. His daughter Lynn could be the real culprit.

"See?" Bellamy inclined his head toward the Dome's lights. "The man's a workaholic!"

Bellamy's companion and instructor, Frank Harding, smiled at the other's comment. "He always has been," he said. "Can't say it's done him much harm, though. I wish I carried a half-percent of his weight around here—not to mention his wallet!"

"*Huh!*" Bellamy retorted. "Money and power aren't everything."

"No," Harding winked, "but they're a good start! Anyway, I don't see much wrong with Jimmy Craig. He's one of the old school—believes that if there's work to be done, the best way is to up and do it. Dedication? Over the top? Possibly—but some people work to forget, you know. It sometimes serves to take the sting out of life."

"But isn't that just what I'm getting at?" Bellamy was adamant. "I mean, with all he has going for him you'd think he'd take it easy. Christ, there'd be no sting in *my* life, I can tell you! But from what I've heard about him, it seems he tries to pack eight days into every week!"

"No," Harding shook his head, "seven days into six. He never does a stroke on Sundays. He's of a dying breed, Old Craig—a God-fearing man."

Bellamy was young and new to Phillip Stone Industries, which was why he was under instruction. Harding was an older man who had been at PSISAC since the days when it was called Miller Micros and consisted of a half-dozen Nissen huts in a three-acre plot. He had known Jimmy Craig—albeit from a distance—through all of those years and respected the man, and not alone for his energy and ideals.

"Not any old common-or-garden boffin, our Mr. Craig," he now informed Bellamy. "Long before he was a director, he was one of the country's top micro-engineers. Still is, they reckon. Has his name on more high-tech products than just about anyone else alive!"

If the younger man was impressed it hardly showed. "Holier than thou, I've heard," he grunted. "And there are lads on the factory floor who find his lifestyle more than a bit odd—I mean, him living in the complex and all, and only his daughter in the Dome there with him. Know what I mean . . . ?"

Harding nodded. "Oh, yes, I know," he answered gruffly. He spat his disgust over the tower's parapet. "Dirty-minded bastards!" Then he turned up the collar of his overcoat, stubbed out his cigarette and caught hold of Bellamy's arm, pushing his face close in the cold starlight.

"Listen, young Geoff," he said, "and I'll tell you a couple of things about James Christopher Craig. Not a lot because I don't know a lot—though I know a sight more than you!—but it might explain one or two things and ease your inquisitive mind a bit. Might even keep you out of a bit of trouble, too."

He released the other's arm, turned and leaned his elbows on the high parapet, cupping his chin in his hands. He gazed out over the silent complex. "Craig's wife died eleven years ago when their kid was only nine or ten years old. She was a lovely woman but pretty frail and her kidneys were up the creek. They tried dialysis but she couldn't face up to it, and her complaint was rapidly deteriorating. So . . . she had a transplant.

Her system rejected it and everything went wrong. Today—? No problem—but ten years ago . . ." he shrugged. "All in all, the thing was over in a couple of months. But it left Jimmy Craig on his knees, he'd loved that woman so much . . .

"But . . . he got himself together, got down to the job of bringing up his daughter. See, he had only two things left: his work and his daughter— and maybe his faith too. Anyway, the way I see it, PSISAC and the kid were all-important to him and he didn't want to cheat on either one of his responsibilities. So he took a short cut, killed both birds with one stone."

Bellamy nodded. "They came to live in the Dome," he said.

"Not just like that, no," Harding shook his head. "First he had to *build* the Dome! See, he'd always had his own private workshop right there in the center of the complex, where the Dome is now; so he got Phillip Stone's okay, built the Dome over his workshop and made his home there. And when all's said and done that's all the Dome is, a home."

"But *what* a home!" the other grunted, unable to keep the envy out of his voice.

Harding nodded. "I was a laborer on the construction team," he informed. "Oh, yes, it's quite a place. All built to Craig's own designs and powered by PSISAC, of course. Tropical gardens, solarium and swimming pool on the top floor—living rooms, library, kitchen, study and bedrooms in the middle— garage and workshop on the ground. And PSISAC's boardrooms and Craig's own offices round the perimeter. A hell of a place, yes, and all out-of-bounds to anyone not specifically invited. Not that anyone could ever break in; he'd have to get through PSISAC first, and that's what we're here for! One of the reasons, anyway." Harding nodded again. "Likes his privacy, our Mr. Craig."

"But what about the girl?" Bellamy was quick to ask. "What sort of a life is it for her, locked up in there with her old man?"

Harding laughed at that, but his amused expression soon changed to a scowl. "You don't want to pay too much attention to those shop-floor wankers," he said. "She has more freedom than most young women. Oh, I've heard some of the lads calling her a rich bitch; but that's all jealousy, Geoff, you take it from me. Sour grapes. Dogs with their tongues lolling, whining at a squirrel up a tree! 'Locked in there with her old man,' you say? You must be joking! She has her own car and a worthwhile job in Oxford—teaches backward kids. As for boyfriends: there was one I knew of, regular like, but—"

"Yes?"

Harding sighed. "It was Phillip Stone's lad, Richard. I suppose you'd say they were keeping it in the family, but they used to see a lot of each other. He was a regular visitor here. Then, maybe fifteen months ago in the summer, young Stone took ill. The Gibbering, I've heard it said—but least said about that the better. Since then, when she's not working, Lynn Craig usually spends her time at home. Can't say I blame her."

"I've only seen her once or twice," Bellamy admitted, "but I must say I'm impressed." He grinned and licked his lips. "Nice body! Altogether nice—and all going to waste, you say?"

Harding turned to him sharply. "Listen, Bellamy—your job will be going to waste if you keep letting your mouth run off like that! Anyway, we'd best get on back down to the gate and the control center. Before the night's out I want to show you how to isolate an intruder on the detector screens. Also the procedure for resetting the primary alarms."

"What?" the other's jaw fell open. He clambered after his instructor down the spiraling metal stairway. "But that'll take the best part of a week!"

"It'll take a single night—" it was Harding's turn to grin, however smugly, "—if you work hard at it. And it'll help clear all that smut out of your mind!"

As Frank Harding got down to the business of instructing his unhappy apprentice in the basics of PSISAC's security systems, the main subject of their conversation was just leaving the Dome's elevator to make his way through the spacious garage to the massive steel doors which guarded his private workshop and laboratory.

At the doors Craig inserted his ID key in the receptor slot and let the lab identify him. There was no time wasted, for his was the only key. Someone else might be using it, however, and so a beam scanned his face. He was recognized, the information passed to the door's hydraulics. As the steel wall cracked open and the doors moved apart on rubber rollers, interior lights flickered into life. They burned steadily as Craig stepped through into his . . . "laboratory."

There had been a time when this place was indeed Craig's lab and workshop, but as the work had progressed so he had required more room. Toward the end he had been obliged to build around himself, enclosing himself within the bulk of his creation. At first the lab had housed Psychomech—now it *was* Psychomech! And this had been Craig's main reason for building the Dome: so as to ensure Psychomech's security and secrecy. A reason neither Frank Harding nor any other man could ever be expected to guess or suspect.

As the doors closed silently behind him, Craig followed a narrow aisle into the center of the room, the heart of the Machine. Overhead and on both sides ducts and conduits and cables—bright metal pipes, twisted ropes of colored plastic tubing, endless miles of electrical wiring—were convoluted as the wrinkled surface of some great brain, behind which were banked the micromotor systems, servo-mechanisms and failsafes which supplied, monitored and regulated the Machine's energy flow. The floor beneath Craig's feet was of tough rubber, muffling his footfalls. With his dressing gown wrapped about him and his hands clasped before him, he might well be a solemn acolyte or priest as he reached a central dais and climbed its three steps to a throne-like chair.

There he paused to gaze raptly into the heart of what he had built.

At the top of the throne's backrest a hinged oval helmet or deep skullcap was tilted back, its interior lined with rubber-bedded sensors and electrodes. Curving overhead from the back of the throne, like some strange mechanical scorpion's stinger, a jointed metal arm bore a U-shaped clamp of steel-backed leather whose jaws were studded with a row of gleaming needles and tiny feed nozzles. Retracted now, still these "teeth" were strangely menacing. Even knowing that without these hypos there would be no Psychomech, still Craig hated them—and one of them in particular.

There were more needles in the wrist and ankle clamps, but they were more a nuisance than a threat. In fact it was only the needle which put him to sleep that really bothered Craig, the one he actually *felt*. A man would think he'd get used to it, but Craig never had. He supposed it was the idea that once one set the Machine in motion, one was at its mercy. In that respect the initial needle, the sleeper, was like the first tentative stroke of a vampire bat's anesthetic wing. But that, of course, was simple blasphemy. One must never confuse Evil as an analogy for Good.

All of the hypodermics and feeds were intravenous, and all were guided by their own microscanners. With their tiny "eyes," the needles couldn't possibly fail to hit their targets; no doctor or nurse in the entire history of the world had ever pierced a vein more accurately. The only thing they couldn't do was use the same holes every time. The epidermis, corium and cuticle seemed ever different, changing like the face of a desert and obscuring old points of entry. Access was therefore random, a matter of proximity. All Craig ever felt was a tiny prick, but still he hated it. Perhaps it was the small interval between setting the Machine in motion and feeling the prick: simply the *knowledge* that the prick was coming, and no way to avoid or stop it.

He sighed. Being one of God's chosen had its drawbacks . . .

. . . But it had its advantages, too.

Quite apart from the throne's mechanical and somehow menacing appurtenances, it was a remarkably comfortable chair indeed. During the Machine's various stages of construction, Craig had often fallen asleep in that chair. Padded in soft leather and built to conform and angle itself to the body's contours, it was heated from within and maintained a perfect body temperature. A man could hardly be more comfortable sitting in his mother's lap, or curled in her womb. One hour in that chair had seemed worth seven or eight in a bed. But that had been when it was simply a chair . . .

Yes, Craig was justifiably proud of Psychomech's throne. Of the entire Machine, it was the one component which bore the mark of his vanity. Surely God would allow him that much? After all, it was God's vanity, too, wasn't it? Why else would He let Craig be christened that way? In Craig's faith, there was no room for accidents or coincidences. All occurred according to the Great Design.

In the middle of the throne's padded backrest, the initials "J. C." were heavily embossed in two-inch letters of gold. "J. C."—meaning "James Craig" . . . If Craig didn't know better. But he did.

His name meant nothing, the initials were simply a sign!

Suddenly Craig felt uplifted, freed of the feelings of despondency and inadequacy which had driven him down here. There would be no requirement for Psychomech tonight. To use the Machine without need would be to admit dependency, addiction. It would be no better than self-gratification, mental masturbation. Craig didn't need that.

He turned on his heel, walked back down the aisle, caused the great doors to open and stepped out through them. Stepped out of Psychomech. Behind him the lights went out.

"J. C."—"James Craig." He grinned as the Dome's elevator bore him upward. A sign, yes!

As for the "Christopher": he never used his middle name himself. In any case, the last five letters were quite superfluous . . .

Chapter Five

RICHARD STONE AND DR. GÜNTER GORVITCH WALKED and talked together in the landscaped gardens of Calm Lawns. It was almost the end of October, some two weeks since their landmark conversation in Stone's cell. At least, Gorvitch considered it a landmark, for since then the improvement in his very special patient had been remarkable indeed. The visible improvement, anyway.

The sky was overcast and the afternoon a little chilly, too cold for the tough but rather lightweight coveralls which the inmates wore indoors. Thus Stone wore clothing he had not seen since his admittance: cord trousers, a casual jacket over an open-necked woolen shirt, and sturdy, thick-soled shoes. "Rough gear," he would have thought less than eighteen months ago; but now these common clothes felt wonderful against his skin, as did the air against his face, the wide expanse of deceptively open space before him, even the springy grass beneath his feet.

There were, however, other items of Stone's "dress" which were less appreciated and far less optional. It was not out of habit that Gorvitch walked with his hands behind his back but courtesy: he simply copied his patient, who had no choice. Stone's wrists were manacled, the long, single link between the cuffs being of tough rubber with very little of flexibility. His ankles were similarly fitted, but in their case the rubber link was longer and much less rigid. Suspended from a point between Stone's legs, it allowed him to take a full and comfortable stride. He could walk but could not run.

But for all the precautions, still the outing was a triumph for Stone no less than for Gorvitch. The latter saw it as an incredible advance for Stone in his personal battle with The Gibbering, an advance which might yet be shared by the rest of the world's madmen, in a colossal battle the world might yet win. Stone himself saw it as an opportunity he could not afford to waste, the chance to sway Gorvitch to even greater extravagances and favors.

For Richard Stone had things to do—a way to go, a quest to pursue—and they could not be accomplished here. Since he knew he would never be let out of Calm Lawns, he must break out. And that must be soon. A change was in progress and he knew it; despite all his wiles, his supposed "steps forward," his stratagem of self-imposed and -enforced "normalcy" could not sustain him and hide the truth for very much longer. He had evidence that suggested either he was weakening or The Gibbering was growing stronger, most likely the latter. Stronger *at its source*, which he did not believe lay in the minds of the poor lunatics who suffered it. And right or wrong, time was running out for him.

He had first become aware of the change one night just a week ago, when The Gibbering had come up out of nowhere to roar through the hospital's wards like a runaway fire. Security guards had been as numerous as doctors and nurses, racing through the cells, delivering knockout shots and cursing into their helmets, their booted feet shaking the floors of the endless and sterile corridors.

Stone, too, had heard The Gibbering, had felt its lure in his mind, had known he could not fight it. Before guard, doctor or nurse could find him also gibbering—which must of course give him away, reveal his susceptibility and thus conclude the game—he had thrown himself against his cell's electrical field. As a general anesthetic, however painful, it had worked yet again—but barely. His mind had been less willing to shut down this time, his muscles reluctant to convulse. Indeed his body had seemed almost to welcome the charge, had soaked it up as a sponge laps water . . . but in the end he had succumbed. And the dream he had dreamed then had been more strange and horrible than all those many dreams gone before.

Now while they walked, he brought up the matter of those earlier dreams.

"Oh?" said Gorvitch, at once interested. "You must tell me about them. A psychiatrist reads all sorts of things into dreams—often erroneously! But sometimes we do make pretty shrewd guesses."

"Oneiromancy," Stone answered. "Dream-reading—witch-doctoring—magic! Perhaps if I died you'd read my entrails, too? What does the Bible say about suffering witches to live amongst us? And should I let one into my dreams?"

Gorvitch laughed, entirely without malice. "You're an odd one," he said, "and no doubt about it. But . . . have it your own way. Only remember that if no one had ever practiced divination or necromancy or alchemy we probably wouldn't have a science, eh?"

Stone nodded, but added: "And by the same token we might not have any gibberers, right?"

Gorvitch frowned. "You're deep, Richard, I'll grant you that. Let me tell you something: even knowing that you're not entirely in control of yourself, still I suspect—I have this feeling—that you know more than you're saying." He stopped pacing, took Stone's arm and turned him until they stood facing each other. "By helping me, you know, you might just be helping an awful lot of people. Do you know that?"

I know that in that little tower over there in the trees, where the evergreens hide the security fence, there's a guard with a dart-rifle aimed right at me! I know the chances are he's looking down his telescopic sights at me right now!

Stone shrugged. "Fair's fair," he said. *You take me walkies, I'll run after your silly sticks.*

"These dreams of yours?" Gorvitch smiled into Stone's cloudy-yellow eyes, wondered what was going on behind them.

Stone stared back for a moment, nodded. They started out pacing again, side by side. "My dreams have always been very vivid," he began, "but these were clearer and much more real. They started shortly after I . . . came in here. And they've stayed in my mind when others are long since forgotten. They run in a series; I believe I've dreamed each one of them several times, not always in order. During my . . . attacks, they took on special meaning for me. I know that much, even though I can't remember what the meaning was."

"Go on," said Gorvitch.

Stone felt a sinister creeping in the core of his mind, heard the wicked whispers of a host unseen. *Be quiet! Be quiet! Not now—please not now!* he pleaded, driving them back. He blinked rapidly several times, gripped his hands behind his back, squeezed and squeezed them. Squeezed the turmoil of tiny voices out of his head. The Gibbering subsided.

"Well?" Gorvitch pressed.

Stone took a deep breath. "The first dream concerned my mother and father. Except . . . the man in the dream was *not* Phillip Stone. His first name was Richard, like mine, and his second was Garrison."

"Does the name have any relevance? Do you know of any man called—" Gorvitch started.

"No, no!" Stone was impatient. "I don't believe I ever heard the name before. A garrison is a large camp for soldiers, that's as much as I know. And yet he was my father . . ." He frowned.

"In our dreams," said Gorvitch, "we often put unfamiliar faces on familiar people or places or things. And sometimes we give them unfamiliar names. It's not so strange."

"It was strange for me!" Stone answered. "Anyway, he—this man, my father—was different. He was like a god. He glowed golden. His eyes were rods of gold like beams of sunlight. He had . . . a *power!*"

Stone's voice had taken on an intensity. Suddenly he felt the psychiatrist's gaze upon him. He looked at the other, tried to relax a little, licked his lips. "Vivid," he said, and managed to grin. "Like I told you."

"And interesting," said Gorvitch, waiting.

"Well, my mother was special, too. And she really *was* my mother—that is to say, she was Vicki Stone. She, too, was golden—but only when she stood beside him. Her eyes, too, were molten gold; but there was none of his terrific power in her. And I knew that she loved him and that she feared him . . .

"As for the world they lived in: it was a land of plenty. The promised land! It had great rivers, broad plains and mighty mountains. It was green and good and full of life. Its waters teemed with fish, its forests with game, its fields with all of Man's beasts. There was little of want, of misery, of pain. Oppression was dead or dying, war unthinkable."

"It was this world," said Gorvitch, smiling.

"There was no gibbering!"

The psychiatrist's smile faded.

"But there was . . . a Machine," Stone blurted. "An incredible Machine, with a capital 'M'—like the 'G' in God!"

"What sort of machine?" Gorvitch asked. "Can you describe it?"

Stone shook his head in confusion. "It was . . . an engine, a beast, a vehicle, a weapon! And it belonged to Richard Garrison. It wasn't like any other machine. It was *the* Machine. Not a car or a motorcycle, yet he rode it. In no way aerodynamic, and yet he soared with it over all the world's lands. Inanimate, it yet had sentience of a sort—and it *obeyed* him. Describe it?" he chewed his lip. "It was—" he shrugged, defeatedly, "—a Machine."

"PSISAC, perhaps?"

Stone's flesh crept. "Say that again!"

"PSISAC?" Gorvitch felt his own spine tingle at the sudden change come over the other's face.

Then the spell was broken. "No," Stone relaxed, shook his head. "It did have a name, I'm sure, and that name did have the ring of PSISAC—but that wasn't it."

Gorvitch was mildly disappointed. "The source of your real father's power," he pointed out, "is PSISAC. It's what made your world for you and filled it with good things. And I'm told that PSISAC is quite a place—big as a garrison? It would all have been yours one day. Did you perhaps fear the idea of all that power, that responsibility? Or perhaps—"

"Wrong track!" Stone bluntly cut him off.

"Oh?" Gorvitch raised his eyebrows. "Now you're the expert, are you?"

It was a trap, but Stone fell into it anyway. "Whose fucking dream was it?" he snapped.

Gorvitch nodded knowingly. "It's very important to you, isn't it? Very well, go on. I'm sorry I needled you."

Stone fought down his anger, his impatience. "Well, that was the first dream," he said after a moment. "Nothing much happened, it didn't frighten me."

"But the next one did?"

"Not much, only the setting. We were in a graveyard, and—"

"We?"

Stone sighed. "My mother, Richard Garrison, and me."

"You were physically there? You were with them?"

"I sort of . . . looked on, from outside, but I felt

I was with them. Anyway, we stood by a grave. There was a headstone. It had a name inscribed but I couldn't read it. The funny thing was, there was no sadness. Someone, something, was dead . . . but nobody cried. That's all there was to it."

"Nothing more? And yet it stayed in your mind. You remembered it. Are you sure that's all there was to it?"

Stone frowned, concentrated. "The sun was warm," he said, "the world seemed to be okay. All the graves were well-tended and the place looked very tidy. But—" he shrugged. "No, that's it."

"But there were more dreams." Gorvitch made it a statement.

Stone nodded silently. The whisperers in his head were on the move again, sneaking up on him. An awful lot of them. They were trying to draw his attention with their as yet distant, meaningless jabbering. If he let himself listen to them it was all over, his cover blown. Rational thought would be impossible. He would be reduced to gibbering.

"The third dream," he quickly went on, "was sort of sad. We were in the graveyard again, but the day was overcast—like today. While we stood there a mist rolled up. My father—Richard Garrison, anyway—kissed my mother, left us standing there, turned and walked off into the mist. He turned and waved, once. Then he was gone. His golden glow was swallowed up. I knew he was gone for good. My mother knew, too, but she wasn't sad. And she wasn't frightened anymore. She looked sort of dazed, but not sad or frightened. Then she turned up the collar of her coat, turned from the grave and walked to the gates of the graveyard. The gates were of wrought iron with spikes. The perimeter was of spiked iron railings mounted on a low brick wall. The mist rolled like a sullen, shallow ocean, knee-deep and opaque. At the gates, someone was waiting for her . . ."

"Yes?"

"It was my . . . father? It was Phillip Stone."

"I see," said Gorvitch. "And you were there?"

"I seemed to be, but . . . he didn't see me. They walked away together."

"Hmm! I shall give all this a lot of very careful thought," the psychiatrist mused, "—when I have the time. Meanwhile—"

"Meanwhile, there's the last dream," Stone hurriedly interrupted. "The last of that sequence, anyway. The dream that frightened me."

Gorvitch nodded. "Go on," he said.

Their walking had taken them close to the security fence. Stone was very much aware of that tall, tight-mesh wire screen standing between himself and the freedom of the world outside. He was aware, too, of the guard in the tower, the dull glint of metal in the shadows beneath the tower's hood. He felt trapped, a rabbit caught in a cruel snare. If he couldn't suppress it, a rabbit's squeal might rise unbidden in his throat, shrill and impotent.

"I feel . . . caged," he said. "These shackles . . ."

If Gorvitch was surprised at Stone's frankness, it hardly showed. "Sometimes," he said, "The Gibbering takes on very violent forms. And as we both know, it can come very quickly. There have been terrible crimes, murders. They get worse every day. Soon, perhaps, when there is trust and—"

"Soon!" Stone cut in, scowling. "Perhaps! Trust! You're a psychiatrist—doesn't it strike you as reasonable that when you shackle a man's body you might also shackle his mind? I can't think straight trussed up like this!" In his temper he lashed out with his foot at nothing. The link between his feet was stretched to its full. He stumbled, came close to falling against the wire mesh of the fence.

"*Careful!*" Gorvitch harshly warned, catching his shoulder and steadying him.

Stone glanced at him questioningly, stared for a moment at the fence, then turned his eyes back to the psychiatrist and glared accusingly. "So much for trust!" he spat the words out. "You've had them put a current through it. The fence is electrified!"

He was right, and Gorvitch silently cursed himself for a fool. He should have ensured that their walking kept them away from the fence, which under normal circumstances would only be switched on in the event of an attempted breakout, a fire, or some other potential disaster which might cause or make necessary a hasty, mass evacuation. On this occasion he had had it done purely as a matter of prudence, almost an afterthought. Prudent on the one hand, but imprudent on the other. It had probably lost him a lot of ground.

Now, seeing his patient's anger, he calmly advised: "Richard, I really think it's time we were getting back. This won't do at all. I really can't have you getting yourself all worked up, you know. Come on, we'll—"

"Wait!" Stone implored, his voice almost a moan of disappointment. *Wait you bastard, you bastard, you bastard! Look at me, look at me! Oh, listen to me! Heed me!*

Gorvitch sighed, turned and looked at him.

Stone's pleading was silent; his eyes did it for him. Those strange, molten eyes.

"Well?" said Gorvitch.

"I . . . I'm sorry," Stone gulped out the word. "It's just that I feel like an animal in here—in there!" he nodded toward the hospital building. "A little longer? Please? I was telling you about my dreams."

Gorvitch considered it. Nothing but a ruse to gain Stone a little more time out in the open, of course. The man had good as admitted that. But what harm in it? In any case, Gorvitch could not deny those eyes. They tugged at him. "Very well," he heard himself saying. "But just a little longer."

"The fourth dream was the one that frightened me—at its end, anyway," Stone began. "I was alone this time, walking. I walked through the world, but it was a different world now. It was night—it always seemed to be night in that changed world. The fields were withered, the forests black and frightening. If there were people, they were hiding. When there were birds, they were carrion-eaters. The oceans were oily, sluggish, poisoned . . ." He paused, partly to draw breath, for he had been speaking very rapidly, and partly to scan the abyss of his mind for signs of invasion. The enemy army was there and he knew it, but for the moment its hordes lay low.

Vigilant, Stone told himself. *Be vigilant!*

"You were frightened at what had become of your world?" Gorvitch questioned.

Stone shook his head. "Puzzled, saddened, yes—but not really frightened. Not yet. Then I came to the graveyard."

"Ah!" Gorvitch was keenly interested. He moved closer.

Stone shuddered. Just over the inner horizons of his mind the legions of chaos were massed as never before. Any time now they would come rushing to the attack, he knew. Out of the corner of his eyes he looked longingly beyond the tightly criss-crossed lattice of the fence . . .

"Yes?" said Gorvitch.

Stone looked at him, blinked his eyes. They were playing tricks with him: everything he saw seemed etched in monochrome. Gray sky, black tower, trees, wires of the fence—the psychiatrist's face milky, and the gaps between the trees showing a milky countryside beyond—the grass a lake of milk at his feet. A negative photograph. It was his eyes, yes . . . and it was his mind. All in his mind. The lull before the psychic storm.

Speak! he shouted inside. *He's waiting for you to say something!*

"I . . . I went in through the leaning, rusty, spiked iron gates and clambered over the tumbled tombstones to the one grave I knew. All the other graves were rank with weeds, overgrown, their headstones shattered. Only the one grave was in half-decent order. Its plot was a neat rectangle of moist, dark earth. It stood out in the darkness, seemed to gather the starlight to it. Its headstone was gleaming white."

Listening, Gorvitch studied his patient's eyes. Like Stone's description of his dream-father's eyes, they seemed fashioned of gold now. Golden amoebas that pulsed in his face. Fascinating eyes. Hypnotic, almost . . .

The two men continued their slow walk, parallel with and close to the fence. The tower was much closer now, half-camouflaged by the boughs of a great pine growing on the other side. The free side. Stone glanced once more at the watchtower, the fence, the tree whose branches came close to the tower's high, hooded platform. His mind photographed the scene, memorized it. It was an option, a way, an escape route. But it had a guardian.

He shook his head, tried to clear his mind. His thinking was growing misty—*and under cover of the mist, across the battleground of his sanity, an army silently advanced. Its weapon was its voice, but for now its breath was bated, even its breathing stilled in these final seconds.*

"About the grave?" Gorvitch heard himself say. He stared into Stone's eyes, felt himself sucked at as by a whirlpool.

Stone felt something unfolding inside himself. A power! Words were on his lips before he could fathom their meaning: "Show me the key," he breathed the words in astonishment. "The key to these shackles."

"The grave," said Gorvitch, reaching into a pocket of his jacket.

"Yes, the grave. I stood beside it, stared down at its dark soil. It began to rain, huge black raindrops that turned the soil to mud, the dark earth of the grave to quagmire. I stood there, soaked to the skin, waiting."

"Waiting?" Gorvitch held up the key.

"For the undead!" Stone half-turned toward the tower, placing himself between Gorvitch and the unseen guard. He forced his hands to one side across the small of his back, offered up the manacles to Gorvitch. All the time, looking back over his shoulder, he held the psychiatrist's eyes with his own.

Gorvitch stood as if frozen.

Do it! Do it! DO IT!

Still the psychiatrist stood, immobile.

And it was then, at that precise moment, that the barbarian mind-horde chose to attack! Their weapon was unleashed! It came crashing into Stone's mind like a battering-ram: the full, unbridled, mindless multitude Voice of The Gibbering! His defenses buckled. His mind began to cave in.

"What?" said Gorvitch. *"What?"* He saw the key in his trembling hand, wondered how it had got there.

"Doctor! Dr. Gorvitch!" the guard called down from where he leaned over the platform's timber parapet. "They're calling for you! It's come again, The Gibbering! I just got it from Security, through my helmet. The hospital's . . . *leaping!* Every single one of them is—"

"Gibbering!" Stone screamed.

Gorvitch stumbled back from him, the key still clutched in his hand.

Stone's face melted into a mad mask. His eyes were volcanic blowholes in pulsating lava. He swayed to and fro through fantastic angles, somehow remaining upright.

The guard in his tower aimed his rifle at Stone, trying to fix him in the sights.

Stop The Gibbering! Stop it, or at least deflect it! But how? How?

Stone stumbled, swayed toward the fence. He half-fell, half-threw himself against it—too late, he knew, for he was exposed now, his deception discovered. But at least this way there would be peace, a quick release from the torturing hordes who even now tore his mind out by its roots.

The fence seemed to grab at him, hugged him in electric arms. For a single instant as he vibrated, Stone's mind became crystal clear. All of his objectives stood out in stark silhouette against a background of exploding fire:

Key and manacles. Tower and tree and guard. Flight!

Then he was thrown back, hurled down.

In the tower the guard's finger tightened on the trigger of his rifle—which promptly burst into flames! Before he could think to drop it, he felt himself dragged across the parapet. Impossibly, he fell with more than the normal speed of a falling body. He crashed down across the wire fence, his torso almost severed before the mesh tore loose from its fixtures and wrapped round him in a crackling tangle of sparks. He hit the ground that way: blood and sparks and gouting flame from his rifle and uniform. The fence was down.

Gorvitch was witness to all of this, understood none of it. He saw Stone's form writhing and kicking spastically where it had been thrown. "What?" he uselessly mouthed. And yet again. *"What?"*

The key was wrenched from his hand, whisked away by invisible fingers. It flew unerringly to Stone's manacles, first the wrists, then the feet. A moment later, the manacles fell away.

Gorvitch saw Stone stand up. No—he saw him *stood* up!—as if some giant's hand had stilled his writhing, smoothed him flat, lifted him upright through ninety degrees. The psychiatrist reached out his trembling hands toward Stone. "No, no," he babbled. "Don't go! You *have* the answer . . ."

The guard's blazing rifle and uniform had set fire to several tufts of grass. Flames were already licking at one of the tower's legs. Smoke coiled skyward. Stone walked—no, drifted—through the smoke, across the fallen fence.

"No, no!" Gorvitch broke into a stumbling run.

Stone's body was limp. His arms and hands dangled, his feet hung downward, skimming the burning grass with inches to spare. His body seemed unconscious or dead, but something held his head erect—and his eyes were hideously alive! Almost mechanically, his head turned; his eyes shot warning golden beams at Gorvitch, who at once stumbled to a halt.

Stone drifted out through the gap and was soon lost in smoke and trees and distance.

Gorvitch went down on his knees, his head bowed. "The answer!" he wailed.

Great blowflies, coming from nowhere, buzzed around his bowed head and tried to find a way in. Almost unconsciously, as a reflex action, he swatted at them to ward them off. They weren't there but he swatted anyway . . .

Chapter Six

THE DAY HAD BEEN A BUSY ONE AT PSISAC.

Fridays usually were busy, when management and staff alike all hustled to get things tidied away and business settled in preparation for the long three-day weekend. But today had been special. The routine gossip and petty feuds of the offices and shop-floors—almost integral to the nervous system of any large industrial body or workforce—had been completely overshadowed by events of far greater magnitude, which might well have spelled disaster and utter chaos.

There had been two occurrences which at first had seemed linked, or at least to have their roots in the same dark earth, but as it later turned out this was not the case. At least, that was the verdict later passed down from head office.

The first of these had taken place in the late morning, just before lunch, and had involved storekeeper-foreman Andrew McClaren. This was the lesser of the two incidents: McClaren, a taciturn, middle-aged Scot who had been with the firm for years, had apparently suffered some sort of breakdown and been rushed off to the works Medical and First Aid Center.

Later in the afternoon, however, he had put in a brief appearance, pale and obviously shaken by his experience but otherwise little the worse for wear. One of PSISAC's younger executives, a firm favorite with J. C. Craig, had then driven him home in a company car. Rumors that he had suffered a mild initial attack of The Gibbering were firmly suppressed. He had been pushing himself a little too hard, that was all; his high blood pressure was playing him up again.

While McClaren ostensibly was being dealt with at First Aid, the second occurrence had taken place, and it had been of a far more serious nature.

Gordon Belcher, a burly young mechanic's laborer from Works Maintenance, had downed tools, shouldered the heavy body and bit of a large pneumatic drill in for repairs, and proceeded with it to PSISAC's power plant. Ignoring "Authorized Personnel Only" signs, he had caved-in the security door at the foot of the huge circular tower which housed PSISAC's Number One converter, climbed the spiralling perimeter staircase to the monitoring area and approached the safety rail overlooking the core and flux-field generator.

There an angry white-smocked senior technician had bluntly questioned Belcher's business in the place, only to be ignored and shoved roughly out of the way. When the astounded technician had tackled him again, grabbing his arm, Belcher had carefully put down his drill and bit, bunched up the other's lapels in one hand and drawn him very close. Only then, gazing up into Belcher's vacant, bloodshot eyes, had Senior Tech John Ganley taken note of the laborer's mental condition: the fact that he was "not himself." The man's face had been a quaking mass of flesh; beneath the grime and a beading of sweat, insistent tics had tugged the corners of his mouth into grotesque, meaningless smiles and grimaces.

With his free hand Belcher had pointed to his own head, informing, "It's not in here," in the patient, confidential tone of a grandfather instructing a very small child. "Not in here at all!" Then he had tightened his hold on Ganley, whispering: "I thought it was in my head, but it's not—it's *there!*" And with his face going through a fresh bout of hideous twitching, he had jerked his thumb toward the security rail. "It's down there—*down below!*"

"Down below" was the massive, inches thick, synthetic crystal inspection portal, beneath which PSISAC's main microwave converter turned satellite-beamed energy into countless megawatts of electricity. The sheer *power* of the flux about the central core of the converter was staggering. It was neither nuclear nor plasma energy but the next best thing—better, in that the level of radiation was low and never so scornful of human life—and it powered all of PSISAC and half of Oxfordshire besides. And for reasons known only to himself or not at all, Gordon Belcher had set himself against it.

In a man of Belcher's size, a man of his enormous strength and limited sensibilities, a bad attack of The Gibbering could lead to just one thing—mindless violence!

Senior Tech John Ganley saw this now, saw the

very plague itself writhing on Belcher's idiot face. He had time to yell for help—just one wild shriek—before the madman hit him and sent him skidding across the ceramic floor tiles to come up against the curving steel wall. The single blow had broken his jaw and knocked him unconscious; but his cry for help had brought three other technicians running from the monitoring and control room.

Too late, they saw what Belcher was about. "It's down there!" he had yelled hoarsely, pointing into the well beyond the safety rail. "It's there—and it has to *die!*"

To give them credit, the three techs had tried to stop him. One of them later explained that it had been like trying to stop a raging bull with a red flag! Belcher had picked up and used the ninety-pound drill as a flail, chopping down all three of them—two with shattered ribs—before launching the thing bit-first over the safety rail and down on top of the inspection portal.

After that it had been time to get out. Those who could crawl did so, dragging those who could not after them away from the rail. Radiation would be minimal outside the electromagnetic field, but heat was something else. And down below ninety pounds of metal had crashed through the portal and were being stripped down to nothing, atom by atom, while the core and flux went as mad as Belcher himself.

As for the maniac: he stood at the rail, clapped his hands to his head and reeled like a drunk, screaming as he staggered to and fro. And even as his eyes fried and the skin cracked open on his face and hands, still he kept on screaming, "It's down there—down there—*down there!*"

Whatever "it" was, Belcher feared it no longer

and would never fear it or anything again, for in
the next moment he had vaulted the rail and followed the drill into eternity.

From the door of the control room Chief Tech
Ian Dawson had caught the last of the action. He
threw himself back into the padded seat of his
swivel chair before the master monitors and took
a fearful look at the screens. One look was
enough.

Gordon Belcher was no more. Cooked as he
plummeted thirty feet through a roaring fountain
of heat from the shattered portal—bursting into
a sheet of flame in the next split-second and atomized before he could hit bottom—the flux had
scarcely noticed him. He had been a tiny foreign
body which was now flicked away forever . . . but
the pneumatic drill was something else entirely.

In a space which was normally forty percent
vacuum, the massive iron of the drill measured
up to an enormous imbalance: its disintegration,
however furious, was warping the flux away from
its standard symmetrical configuration. A few
seconds more and the mighty electromagnetic
shield would rupture, the crystal-lined steel walls
would buckle and melt like butter, the entire
tower and converter would collapse into a seething raw pool of energy. In converter terms, the
equivalent of a nuclear meltdown! Microwave radiation would lash outwards at the speed of light;
people in the immediate vicinity of the converter
complex would cook and others more distant
would be burned hideously; PSISAC itself would
be in jeopardy.

And quite apart from death and destruction at
PSISAC, there would be horror and havoc across
half the county. PSISAC's power lines were independent of the national grid; they fed industry,

offices, farms and homes. They powered surgical instruments in operating theaters . . . farm machinery . . . elevators, escalators and walkways, lighting and communications in the towns and cities . . . computers . . . railway signals, and traffic control systems . . . life support systems in hospitals.

There had never been this sort of crisis before at PSISAC, but Chief Tech Dawson was a man of split-second decision and unerring instinct. And he was knowledgeable as his rank demanded in all aspects of mechanical failure, practical and theoretical. If he could shut down the big converter quickly enough he might just save it, but there would still be county-wide chaos until the lesser converters could be cut in to restore power.

Or . . . Dawson could take a chance.

He could *boost* flux density to maximum and pray for rapid, total disintegration of the melting, atom-shedding drill. And that was exactly what he had done, and it had worked.

Minutes later, when flux was back to normal configuration and the injured were out of the way, heat- and radiation-suited techs had lowered crystal sheeting down the well to seal the break in the portal, following which it was a relatively simple matter of a slow, routine shut-down and transfer of load. A disaster had been averted, however narrowly.

But on a wider scale . . .

. . . It was not a coincidence that at the time of the incident—that is to say, at the precise moment when Belcher's insanity reached its peak, about 2:00 P.M.—Richard Stone had thrown himself against the electrified fence at Calm Lawns, but no one would ever have reason to connect the two occurrences.

It *would* later be noted that Belcher's had not been an isolated case—that the activity of lunatics in asylums all over the world had been at fever pitch when he died, and that new cases had been reported by the score over the rest of the afternoon—but again no one would find this of any special significance. The problem was after all worldwide. The Gibbering's toll was mounting, and men looked for answers in the wrong directions . . .

PSISAC, like a good many of the new industrial giants, looked after its employees. With the coming of the new sciences and the implementation of the four- (in some countries three-) day working week, the last of the mighty trade unions of the mid-20th Century had gone into liquidation and men had come to realize that they would nevermore have a "right" to work. There would no longer be a *need* to work, but those who were so fortunate would partake of benefits away and beyond anything their fathers had ever known. A majority of people had no hope of ever having a "regular job," and so saw little sense in training for one. First-class minds—even first-class labor—were therefore hard to find and worth hanging on to.

Two miles from PSISAC's mammoth complex, in a wooded, landscaped area on the banks of the Cherwell, a "model" village housed those of PSISAC's workers who desired company accommodation. This was where Andrew McClaren had made his home, and here he had lived for the last seven years, since first the place was built. His small, detached bachelor chalet overlooking the river was powered by cheap PSISAC electricity; every appliance, every item of leisure equipment within its walls bore the "PSI" trademark of Phillip Stone Industries. It was not that McClaren was especially loyal, simply that he was a true Scot of the old school. All of his stuff had been purchased on the company's discount system; in the event of breakdowns, repair or replacement was free.

It was almost 5:00 P.M., some three hours since the Belcher incident and two since McClaren had been sent home by J. C. Craig. In those two hours, or at any rate since Edward Bragg had at last left him on his own, McClaren had continuously paced the floor of his living room and considered over and over again the shattering revelations of the day.

For him the first of these had been his attack, the fact that he had fallen victim to The Gibbering. It had started shortly after 9:00 in the morning, a ringing as of tiny silver bells in his ears which would not stop. At first he had thought the bells were real, had actually sought to discover their whereabouts and still their constant tinkling; but by mid-morning the sheer volume of noise in his head had grown so as to shut out all else. It had become a great gonging that no one else could hear, which came to a crescendo and ceased . . . abruptly . . . shortly after 11:00 A.M.

The silence which followed had been almost deafening, but in no way a relief; with it had come a depression of spirit boding of worse things waiting.

Within the space of the next half hour, McClaren had heard the first insidious snigger—a distant tittering as of secret and evil glee, which came from nowhere to invade his innermost mind—and in just another ten minutes The Gibbering had been upon him in force.

Fleeing his stores accounting office, McClaren

had almost collided with a gang of apprentices on their way to lunch. One of them, a lad whose own father had suffered just such an attack less than a month ago and was now hopelessly mad in an asylum, recognized the symptoms and got in touch with his superior; he in turn contacted the medics at First Aid and they tracked Mc-Claren down.

After a short search, they found him crouched in a corner of the computer components warehouse, whimpering like a chastised puppy and covering his ears with hands that fluttered like trapped butterflies.

The medics had their routines. A certain standing order, the one that said any PSISAC employee suspected of the mind plague must be taken immediately to the office of the Managing Director, seemed to cover McClaren's case.

Craig had been told they were coming. When they arrived he gave the Scot a mild sedative and took him off their hands, ordering them back to their duties at Medical and First Aid. But first he made it understood that they were *not* to engage in casual gossip in respect of McClaren; in his case there was to be no speculation, no mention of The Gibbering. Then he had taken his dazed and twitching ward with him into the privacy of the Dome.

Most of this McClaren remembered like a bad dream, but the rest of it was warped as a psychedelic nightmare!

He had been vaguely aware that Craig took him into the Dome's ground-floor garage area, through huge steel doors and into a central chamber—and he dimly remembered how that chamber had seemed like a tunnel cut through the guts of some fantastic machine, where Craig had seated him upon a throne-like chair—but after that there was . . . nothing!

Oh, there had been *something*, but such a monstrous something that his mind point-blank refused to let him remember. Then, some time later, Craig had led him out of the room of the machine and slowly he had become aware that the horror had passed. The Gibbering was gone from his mind.

As he gradually recovered and knew that in fact he *was* still sane and had somehow been saved, McClaren had known intense relief and gratitude. Whatever it was Craig had done to or for him, it had saved his mind. His psyche was intact . . . for the moment, at least.

McClaren remembered the rest of it vividly, however surrealistically.

Craig had taken him back through the Dome's garage area and via a security door into one of the perimeter boardrooms. There, seated about a long conference table and coming to their feet for a respectful moment as Craig entered, a group of eleven PSISAC employees were convened and waiting. McClaren, still a little unsteady on his feet but believing himself fully in control of his faculties, had been offered a seat and Craig had moved to his own place at the head of the table. There he had paused to converse privately for a few moments with Edward Bragg, the young executive who would later drive McClaren home, before turning and resting his hands upon the polished top of the table.

He had remained standing, ignoring an empty chair and waiting until Bragg was seated, before commencing his address and "explaining" the purpose of the gathering. From the start, his words had burned themselves indelibly into McClaren's mind.

"Andrew McClaren, yours is a singular honor, for you have been chosen by a Higher Power to close the circle. You are the twelfth! As it was in Galilee, so is it here. As God is my witness, I have my disciples."

At that, McClaren might have spoken—if only to inquire as to Craig's meaning—but Craig had seen his confusion and quickly continued: "Be patient, Andy. Look about you. See your friends, these others of PSISAC who embrace the faith. And has not Psychomech saved them, too, and eased their troubled minds?"

As bidden, McClaren looked about the table.

There was a bald-headed technician from Computer Division, who had the seat to the right of a leggy, blowsy blonde from the Pay Office. Seated side by side were twin brothers from the 3-D TV assembly line. A broad-shouldered, blunt-featured man from Security sat close to them, and next to him a blocky supervisor from Repairs and Maintenance. McClaren recognized a flat-chested, shrew-faced spinster from one of the canteens, and a thin, bespectacled micro-electrician from Components. Of the rest one was Edward Bragg, who seemed to be something of Craig's confidant, and the other two were unknown to him.

All of these people sat silently staring at Craig, many of them in attitudes almost of adoration. A sort of fervor was in their eyes; they leaned *toward* Craig, hanging on his every word. And on the table before each one of them lay an identical headset, looking to all intents and purposes just like the individual hi-fi headphones of portable radios. McClaren noted that while the eyes of the eleven were fixed firmly upon Craig, the hands of most of them toyed almost unconsciously with these innocuous-seeming headsets.

"Let me tell you what this is all about, Andy," Craig finally continued, leaning forward, his knuckles and thumbs supporting him where they pressed down on the table. "Let me instruct you, as I have instructed these others. Unfortunately time is limited, for I am informed there are matters I must attend to—the matter of a serious accident, for one—and so I cannot at this time do much more than merely welcome you. I will therefore keep it short. But heed my words well, for one day they will form the first chapter of the new Holy Book!

"In the beginning, I was like other men. I had my prides and passions, my angers and petty jealousies, and to that extent I was a sinner. I considered myself and not my God. But God had placed in my head and my hands a great talent, and He had chosen me one day to become the instrument of His mercy—just as He has now chosen you to be my disciple."

Craig paused for a moment and smiled, cocking his head enquiringly on one side. "Does that sound like so much pseudo-religious claptrap, Andy? The hocus-pocus of some weird and esoteric sect? I suppose it must—" his smile fell away, was replaced by a penetrating stare, "—but it is not! If you will only listen to me with an open mind, you too shall soon come to know the truth.

"These are bad times, my friends," (he now addressed the entire table) "when Evil roams abroad in the world behind his twin masks of peace and plenty. The world is slothful and revels in its sloth, where people have forgotten the old skills and laws and moral codes in favor of the new sciences, idolatry and self-gratification. God Himself has been forsaken! He *gave* us this Garden of Eden, this land of milk and honey—and how badly have we used it, and how quickly have we forgotten Him!

"Four days only we labor—and many of us not at all—but do we keep a single day of the remaining three for Him? No! We eat of the fat of the land, all of us, in all the lands of His world, but do we make sacrifice unto Him? Do we offer Him Who Provides the merest tithe as witness of His bounty? No! His name is forgotten, His temples are empty. Men have turned their faces away and the churches are boarded up.

"Instead we are grown idolatrous: we worship the merest toys of our slothful existences—bright automobiles, sumptuous homes, our sparkling swimming pools—and worse, the human stars of our 3-Ds, who are become as gods in our eyes. And that is the worst blasphemy of all, for just as God made us in His image, so have we made them gods in His! None of us is wholly innocent—not one—and this has angered Him . . .

"Yes, for the Lord God is a jealous God and almighty—and His wrath is great!" Again Craig paused, looked from face to face about the table, finally returned his gaze to McClaren.

"I was not first chosen. Before me, God found Himself another prophet from among His angels and sent him down to do His will. This angel was given the face and form of a man, and a man's name. That name was Garrison—Richard Garrison—which is a cursed name! But . . . where is this fallen angel Garrison now? Search as you will, you will find no record of him. For he turned upon the Lord and set himself up in defiance of His laws; and he caused an oracle to be built which was his instrument of power, his weapon. I was the one Garrison chose to make his oracle work, and in my ignorance I was guilty of great sin. Mercifully, the Lord my God has taken away all memory of it, I remember only what He desires me to remember. Perhaps greater knowledge of my sin would kill me . . .

"However . . . When God saw what Garrison had done or caused to be done He waxed wrathful, and Garrison was struck from the face of the Earth, and his oracle with him. And nowhere is his name written, and nowhere are his works evident. He is no more.

"But, as I have said, in His mercy God forgave me; and He came to me in a dream and spoke to me!" Now Craig's eyes were full of glory. His hands trembled on the table and his voice fell to a sigh, a whisper. "*He* . . . spoke to me!" The room seemed to hold its breath.

Craig stood up straight, clasped his hands before him, closed his eyes. When he opened them again some of the glory was gone from them, and his voice was back to normal as he continued:

"Twenty years ago, my friends, God spoke to me for the first time—as He has done on countless occasions since. And the essence of His message was this: that I would be His prophet on Earth, and that I would make a Great Work!

"Oh, it was not without precedent, this manifestation of His presence, this visitation, this Command. Had He not instructed Noah in the building of the ark? And for what purpose? I will tell you: so that when he laid down the great waters upon the face of the world and drowned it, some would be spared. And just as Noah was commanded to build his ark, so was I guided in the construction of Psychomech.

"Psychomech the True Oracle ... through which one day, when He chooses, I shall speak to my God as freely as I speak to you—and not alone in my dreams. But until then I shall use the Machine to preserve you, the Elect, just as Noah used his ark to preserve them he found worthy. Has not God Himself given me signs, and have I not seen the writing on the wall? Did He not send each one of you to me? Yes, He did, else you were struck down! And has not Psychomech made you well and driven out the demons from your minds?

"But you would see signs, you would be convinced. So be it. Look at you, all of you—*lepers*! Victims of the Great Mind Plague itself—taken by The Gibbering. But do you shriek in asylums? Are you confined in straitjackets and padded cells? No! You, Dorothy Ellis, when did you first suffer an attack?"

He pointed to the blonde woman from the Pay Office, who now stood up. "Three years and two months ago, Mr. Craig," she answered.

"And since then?"

"Many times," her answer seemed ritualistic, as if this was nothing new to her.

"Yes," Craig nodded, "many times. For you were the first. And are there ill effects?"

"None. Through the will of God, Psychomech preserves!"

"And all of you are the same," Craig swept the table with his burning eyes. "When the brains of others collapse and shrivel, you go on, incorruptible. When they gibber and die, you thrive and await the coming and the pleasure of the Lord. What more would you have of signs and portents? And yet perhaps you still have doubts ...

"Very well, a sign:

"Stigmata!—the marks of my faith, the proof

of my devotion! For have I not—have *we* not—suffered and been crucified upon the cross of Psychomech? And are we not risen up, as it were, from the dead and enabled to walk among sane men?" Craig strode around the table, used his palms to hold back the graying locks of hair at his temples, displaying on both sides of his head a red stipple rash as of countless tiny teeth. Beneath his gray jacket he wore a thin black polo-necked pullover, whose neck he now yanked down to show marks in his own neck worthy of a drug addict's arm. And rolling back his cuffs, he revealed more marks of Psychomech's hypodermics on the insides of his wrists.

"And are these not signs?"

McClaren's eyes went wide. His own neck felt sore, his ankles, too. He glanced at his wrists. Fresh punctures were white as bee stings! He stared . . . and started violently as Craig's hand fell upon his shoulder.

"Andy, you are one of us now. The Lord has set a plague upon the Earth and the nations of the Earth shall die—but you will be saved. We shall all be saved, all of us here . . .

"And when the world reels and totters and screams in its madness, we shall wait. And when at last the holocaust is at an end—for The Gibbering *is* a great holocaust, destroying all unbelievers and idolaters, a fire *of the mind*, as was prophesied—then shall we go out and take the Word of the Lord with us unto the chosen few. Oh, some shall be spared, whom He finds worthy, and we shall seek them out in all corners of the world. And there shall be tribes upon the face of the Earth, and we shall be the priests in His temples, and in the Great Temple I shall be priest of priests, and Psychomech my Oracle. And woe unto him who breaks the Laws of the Lord!"

At this point, as at a signal, the other eleven had risen to their feet, repeating as one voice: "Woe unto him who breaks the Laws of the Lord!" Following which Craig took McClaren by the elbow and drew him up. He smiled at him and nodded knowingly.

"Go home now, Andrew McClaren, and think on the things you have seen and heard. And think well on these things. God will not suffer unbelievers. The choice is yours: accept the faith and be saved, deny it and be cast out to die gibbering, insane, your brain melting in your skull. Say nothing now, but phone me tonight and give me your answer." He turned away from McClaren, spoke to Edward Bragg:

"Take him home—let him ask what questions he will—answer them for him." Then he addressed everyone else. "Ladies, gentlemen, friends . . . you have your work and I have kept you long enough. I too have much to do; there has been an accident, further proof that the plague is indeed upon us and gathering momentum. Only remember: you are the chosen, the Elect!"

As they left the boardroom by an exterior door and went out into PSISAC's massive complex, Craig had these final words for his twelfth and last disciple:

"Andy—welcome!"

Chapter Seven

STONE STOOD ALONE ONCE MORE IN THE NEGLECTED graveyard beside the plot with the white marker. Soaked, he stood there—stood waiting— with the rain plastering his short hair to his head and streaming in a torrent from his chin. Already the waking world was forgotten; this was his world now, as real in its way as the conscious world from which he had so recently fled. And no jot less menacing.

Somber thunder rumbled and threatened overhead, and the occasional flash of lightning scarred the drab sky with golden fire. One such flash was very bright, leaving the mark of its lash seared upon Stone's startled retinas. He closed his dazzled eyes and the flash remained, slowly fading into the darkness behind his eyelids. Fading with it, he glimpsed and tried to hold on to a set of strange symbols whose meanings were forgotten along with the world which spawned them:

*Key and manacles, tower . . . and tree . . . and . . . ?
And what? Something else?*

Like a man rising up from sleep and seeking to remember a dream, Stone sought to remember the waking world. But just like a dream, it was gone. A pointless exercise anyway, meaningless. Better simply to stand by the grave in the rain and wait.

But wait for what?

It seemed to Stone that someone had asked him that selfsame question, and recently. But he could not remember who.

The rain came down heavier than ever, but a clinging, clammy rain now, as if a lake of sweat was leaking through the skin of the sky. It was difficult to breathe; a man might drown in rain such as this!

Stone knew he should find shelter from the night and the rain, shelter and warmth—but still he stood there, alone and shivering and stubborn. Stubborn as his father, Richard Garrison, and just as curious. There was a mystery here and he must fathom it. It was important, perhaps the most important thing in the whole wide world.

After some little time, slowly the storm began to abate. The lightning flashed more rarely and less achingly; the thunder rolled and muttered on hills more distant; the slimy flood from the sky turned back into simple rain.

Stone stood in mud up to his ankles. Close by, a shattered headstone offered solid footing. He lifted his right foot like a muddy club and let the ooze slide off in dark, slithering gobs. He placed his freed foot on the slab and leaned his weight upon it, then repeated the motion. His left foot came free with a sucking sound, as if the earth were reluctant to free him.

The rain was reduced to a mere pattering of

droplets now. Heavy clouds scudded low across the sky, like vast luminous bats in the radiance of a thin-horned moon. Stray beams of moonlight found their way into the graveyard, gleaming silver on shattered marble stumps.

Slow as a creeping shadow, an eerie silence fell over the place. A mist crept out of the earth, its knowing tendrils writhing in unnatural languor about the bases of the tumbled headstones and pooling like clotted, scummy milk in small hollows between the plots.

With broken, tottering slabs projecting from the putrid earth like ill-used bones, and the white crawling mist thickening like pus in open sores, the graveyard itself had rapidly taken on the aspect of a sprawling, rotting leprous corpse. Stone crouched down upon his headstone and shuddered—but still he would not leave the place. He knew fear which gnawed at his insides—but still could not flee. Not yet.

He knew in his heart of hearts that what was yet to come would be monstrous—knew that this had all happened before, several times—but that did not satisfy his morbid curiosity.

Morbid? Stone supposed so, but he had to know. He had a purpose now, a way to go. He had . . . a quest. What that quest was he did not quite know, but it had keys. Keys, yes, and one of them—the first one—was right here. It would be worth all the menace to come, whatever that menace might prove to be, just to get his hands on that key.

He straightened up, sighed his resolve, frowned and pursued that last thought.

A key . . . As if the words themselves were "a key," Stone felt his mind unlocked—partially. The merest crack. Through the crack in the door he heard again a conversation remembered of some *other place and time—or a snatch of conversation. Strangely, one of the voices was his own:*

". . . I stood there, soaked to the skin, waiting."

"Waiting?"

"For the undead!"

The undead? Creatures that die only to return and live again by eating the substance of others. Vampires who will not lie still in their graves but must be up and about, pursuing their monstrous—

The door closed again, slammed shut, shocked Stone back to the present, to the graveyard. And here he stood, soaked to the skin, waiting for . . .

. . . From the rain-sodden plot at his feet there came a sucking sound as of many bestial mouths. It was that loathsome sound he had heard when he drew out his feet, except that now it was louder and utterly unsolicited.

Stone's hair stood on end and he gulped air with a sharp, choking inhalation. He cast a horrified glance at the plot before him, at its dark sodden earth—and saw it quaking like a quicksand! His glance was fixed, became a horrified stare; his gaze seemed rooted no less than his suddenly leaden feet.

The steaming, loamy soil of the grave was humping up, cracking open, sliding away from a central bulge which even now thrust itself upward in jerky, shuddery convulsions. The very earth underfoot was on the move, tilting the fallen slab where Stone stood and forcing him to step back, his feet sinking deep in gurgling ooze.

Amidst a concerted squelching and bubbling, still the central eruption of the grave continued and Stone choked and coughed as bubbles burst and escaping gases eddied the seething mist. The air was filled with an incredible stench, with glutinous burstings and gurglings; but then, as the fetor and the awful sounds of suction reached a crescendo, the great bulk of the risen mass separated itself from the earth and stood free over the site of the riven plot. It stood there, huge and completely motionless, as the sodden soil beneath collapsed back in upon itself and water and mist swirled into a depression greater than the original plot itself.

Stone backed away, staggering and floundering in clinging mud.

Gobs of filth fell from the fresh-risen Thing, clots of moldy earth and streams of black water, as gradually its true outlines became visible. A flurry of fresh rain completed the job, washing away sufficient dirt to satisfy Stone's curiosity beyond any further doubt. He knew now who—or what—this undead, this vampire, this risen corpse-thing was. But he did not know why it had returned or what it would do next!

Finally galvanized into activity, Stone underwent an agony of splashing and floundering before he reached firmer ground and at last tumbled out through the tottering gates of the graveyard. From this point on he would have to rely on instinct alone; but at least he had turned the first key, had passed through the first portal of knowledge.

Horror rode on his heels as he ran stumbling through the night. He clambered over a low wall, paused to gulp at the night air and look back—just for a moment.

In the middle of the sundered graveyard, suspended over a lake of mist and gleaming in the thin moonlight, a squat Machine—an intricate thing of metal and plastic and chrome—rested from the labors of its rebirth and felt the currents of the invisible Psychosphere washing over and

*through its being. It was or had been an engine,
a beast, a vehicle, a weapon—all of these things—
but at the moment it was mainly beast. And it had
sentience, of a sort.*

*Stone nodded in the shadow of the wall. "Oh, I
know you," he muttered from under his breath. "I
know you—vampire!"*

*But then, as strange lights began to glow and
pulsate within the bulk of the risen horror, he
turned and fled toward his destiny. Where his feet
would take him, he knew not, but any place would
be better than this. This place was doomed. The
plague was here. To stay here would be . . . madness!*

*A monster was abroad in the innermost dreams
of men . . .*

Stone came awake with a start, sat up, cast about
at once for a familiar landmark. In his first moment of consciousness he had fully expected to
find himself curled up on the padded floor of cell
number 253 at Calm Lawns, but in the next he
remembered his walk with Dr. Gorvitch and
looked instead for the security fence and the
watchtower. None of these things was anywhere
apparent.

Instead, he found himself sitting under a hedge
with coarse grass up to his shoulders. On his
right, a copse of young oaks and ashes stood in
open countryside; on his left, beyond the hedge,
the grass was neatly cropped where a small playground sported a sandy play-pit, swings, a round-
about and a seesaw.

Stone was exhausted: he felt as if he had been
badly beaten. His arms and legs were weak and
trembly and his head ached abominably. He had
recognized the playground immediately, knew

where he was but could hardly credit it. It was almost easier to believe that he had succumbed to the final stages of The Gibbering and was even now a prisoner of his own hallucinations, lost in the long, last madness. How else might he explain his presence here? This place must be all of fifteen miles and more from Calm Lawns . . .

Stone's only half-formed but nevertheless harrowing conclusion, that he *was* now mad, seemed reinforced by an as yet distant, discordant yammer of voices in meaningless conflict; but as his head cleared a little he became aware that this was a far different form of "gibbering." For one thing there was laughter, even joy in it: the glee and excitement of children unable to express their pleasure more coherently.

And so finally, gratefully, he accepted the facts of his whereabouts.

He was in the grounds of the Clayton Institute on the Woodstock Road just outside of Oxford. He'd been here before, with Lynn, helping out with the kids. It seemed ironic, somehow, that he should once have had a measure of control over those retarded, mentally disturbed or disabled, or brain-damaged children: a classic case of the blind leading the blind. He remembered how much he had pitied them . . .

It all seemed about a million years ago but in fact it was less than two. And since then . . . his life destroyed, his mother dead, and this new awareness inside that in fact these kids were the lucky ones. Since they *already* gibbered, in their harmless way, might not their shattered minds be safe from the hideous plague itself? And if not, what would it matter to them? As for the rest of mankind: what had Gorvitch said, about the curve being exponential? It seemed so crazy. Didn't the world know it was on the brink? Wasn't anyone doing anything about it?

But . . . Stone knew it was unwise to dwell too closely upon The Gibbering. In any case, right now he felt in finer mental fettle than he had for . . . for far too long. A pity he could not say the same for his physical condition! Something had really taken it out of him; but it was probably only temporary. His muscles were unused to this freedom; he had spent too long in that bloody awful cell. And it was obvious that during his escape he'd exerted himself to the point of collapse. All of which would account for the way he felt. But as for the escape itself: he could remember nothing past his conversation with Gorvitch. Not even all of that. He must have suffered an attack, somehow contriving to make his escape while it was still in progress. But how in hell would he have gone about that?

He shook his head, tried to work out his thoughts before they dissolved into total chaos or panic. Now that he *was* out, he had better make plans. A plan of action, maybe—contingency plans—before things got bad again.

He was surprised by his own enthusiasm, his last-ditch determination. For if he really faced up to it, surely the whole thing was hopeless—wasn't it?

"Plans," for God's sake! That was a laugh! Not only was he a fugitive—and a potentially dangerous fugitive, at that—but at any moment his own traitor mind might betray him. The first time he lost control and gibbered in public would be the last! So what to do? Where to begin? And what was the meaning of the sudden wild excitement he felt rising inside himself? Or was that, too, just another symptom?

There again, maybe things weren't so bad after all. Gorvitch had thought he was different, and maybe he was. He had escaped, hadn't he?—even if he didn't remember how!

But there were things he *did* remember, and vividly, even if their sources were often obscure. Fixations they might well be—complexes, obsessions? Possibly—but they didn't feel that way. So while he could, for however long he had left before the authorities or The Gibbering caught up with him, Stone would explore the possibilities. Call it a quest. Certainly he had nothing to lose.

Oh, there were things against him (he snorted at the innocence of that last thought, its *naïveté*, its understatement), but just as surely there were things going for him. Some things that he felt reasonably sure of, others he didn't even begin to understand. Like how he got here, for one.

He stood up, brushed leaves and twigs from his clothing and peered through a break in the hedge. Most of the leaves were off the trees now but the hedge was of privet. He would not be seen from the other side.

Beyond the playground an extensive, flat-roofed, single-story building of timber and glass sprawled in gardens of close-cropped grass. A place of trellises and vines and crazy-paving paths, with an aviary to one side and a shallow, willow-shaded fish pond in front. Emerging from a long, open-ended, glass-roofed porch or conservatory, a small crowd of children made their way along one of the paths toward the playground.

It was their distant tumult Stone had almost mistaken for The Gibbering. He looked at the crowd of kids and his heart gave an extra kick inside his chest. Tall in their midst—Snow White with her strange, misshapen, hooting, jabbering dwarves—Lynn smiled and gently chided, reassured and guided her awkward charges along the path. She was one of the few people who ever got through to them. Stone had been another . . .

He knew the routine here: knew that, after "lessons" and weather permitting, the kids were normally allowed half an hour in the playground before the bus came to take them home. The time must therefore be about 4:30 P.M. Lynn usually finished and locked up about five. Sometimes she had help but today she would be on her own. With older children there were sometimes problems, but this was a small bunch and the eldest could be only seven or eight years old.

Stone was at the back of the place. Slowly, carefully, he began to pick his way round to the front. The tall hedge completely surrounded the institute; he should make it without being seen. As he went, he thought some more about the time:

4:30 P.M. Two and a half hours since they'd given him his own clothes and put the manacles on him back in Calm Lawns. Except that Calm Lawns was more than fifteen miles away! Had he run all the way here? Was that possible, over rough, open country? What had guided him? And how about those manacles?

This loss or partial loss of memory, occurring as it did whenever he underwent the mental stress of an attack, was very frustrating. That was the trouble with The Gibbering: he remembered *vivid clarity of thought* on certain subjects—amazing revelations and fleeting glimpses of powers or senses other than the normal five—*awareness* of his own strange identity or destiny—but could *not* remember what these subjects were or where these areas of reasoning and revelation lay. It was like being a novelist who dreams a tremendous plot and wakes excited, only to see the plot fade away and dissolve before he can put pen to paper. Instead of a story, all Stone had left was a couple of vague and ill-defined chapter headings, which in his jumbled mind had now attained the dubious status of fixations. Fixations, yes . . . obsessions. But more than that, he felt that they were clues: keys to a Great Riddle.

It had to do with The Gibbering.

It had to do with his own identity, and with a man called Richard Garrison, whom he believed had been his father.

It had to do with awesome, unbelievable powers.

It had to do with his discovery that he could use an electrical current to knock himself out if things got out of control; and with the fact that this would sometimes bring him strange dreams.

And it had to do with a Machine.

And taking all of these things into consideration, where did he go from there?

He needed a starting place, a jumping-off point. But more than that he needed rest, refuge, if only for tonight.

At the front of the institute, sheltered by the high brick wall which guarded the place from prying, curious eyes, Stone climbed through a narrow break in the hedge and into the grounds proper. No one was about. He could still hear the kids in the playground and knew that Lynn would be right there with them. This was going to be one hell of a shock for her, but right now she was his one hope.

Her car was parked on the gravel drive in front of the institute's sliding glass doors. He knew the car well: a Ford Electron whose propulsion unit ran on converted, satellite-beamed microwave power. It was the perfect symbol of her father's unassailable position with PSISAC, and Stone had been confident of a similar model for his birthday. Why not? Phillip Stone (he could no longer think of him as his father) owned the place, didn't he? But instead of a car he'd ended up with Calm Lawns! Strange that he could find it amusing: it must be his macabre sense of humor.

He moved quickly, quietly across the drive to the back of the car. He and Lynn had used to go everywhere together in that car, and he had driven it and used it almost as much as Lynn herself. Often enough, anyway, to know that the boot had a faulty catch.

Now he'd find out whether or not she'd had it fixed . . .

Chapter Eight

ANDREW McCLAREN PAUSED IN HIS PACING AND stared out through narrow patio windows across the river. The water was gray, almost milky, McClaren wished it was summer again . . . drowsing on the riverbank . . . a little fishing, not bothering whether or not he caught anything. That would be nice.

Summer—it seemed a million years ago. And the next summer? Would he ever see it?

McClaren's mind went back to the drive home, when he and young Edward Bragg had talked about Craig's—proposition? At first McClaren's questions had been guarded, but Bragg was no stranger to this. He understood the older man's reticence and tried to put him at his ease:

"I'm not J. C. Craig's nark, you know. Ask anything you like. Say anything you like. Speak your mind. It doesn't really matter to me. And it doesn't really matter what you believe. You can make your mind up about that later. All that matters is what you tell J.C. you believe."

McClaren had looked at him, tried to catch his eye, but Bragg had kept his attention on the road. "And do *you* believe?" McClaren had asked him. "Do you really see yourself as . . . well, as one of Craig's 'disciples'?"

Bragg was slender and sinewy, smart in his well-cut blue three-piece. Smart, too, in his thinking; an ambitious man. His hands were lean but strong on the steering wheel, his face angular but not unhandsome. His blond hair was fashionably short, brushed forward, and his eyes were keen and cold as blue ice. For jewelry he wore an old-fashioned gold wristwatch with hands, and on his left index finger a wide, filigreed gold ring. Twenty-five or -six years old, he was atypical of his age: a clever, clear-minded opportunist. And he intended to stay that way, through Psychomech.

"Me?" he finally answered. "What do I believe? I believe I'm alive and sane when I should have died a raving lunatic. The Gibbering got to me two years ago, but I'm still here. Or were you asking do I believe J. C. Craig is God's mouthpiece? That's a bit harder to answer. One thing's certain, if J.C. wants me for a sunbeam, I'll shine for him!"

McClaren lit a cigarette and nervously puffed at it. "You're not really saying very much," he grunted.

"You haven't asked me much," Bragg gave in return, "—nothing I can answer, anyway. I mean, when you get right down to it, what the hell is this . . . 'belief'? Look at it this way:

"If this car skidded, went off the road and hit a tree, and you took a header through the windscreen and lay there cut to pieces and bleeding like a stuck pig . . . would you pray?"

"I've always thought there was a God," McClaren answered. "So, yes, I suppose I'd pray."

"Sure you would," Bragg nodded. "Most of us would, whether we believe or not. We just wouldn't take any chances, that's all. But prayers or none, if someone didn't find you pretty quick and get some good fresh blood into you, you'd die. And dying, you'd probably think: 'well, so much for God!' "

"Now that really *is* blasphemy!" McClaren growled.

Bragg ignored him. "But what if you lived? Suppose someone did find you and saved your life—would that increase your faith in God? Or would you later forget your prayers and simply consider yourself lucky?"

"I don't know what you're getting at," McClaren frowned, beginning to feel confused and angry.

"You don't?" the other's eyebrows went up. "Then I'll tell you. When The Gibbering hit me I knew it was all over. I *knew* it! There wasn't so much of it about then, but I'd seen samples and I was scared. Scared?—it was like feeling the straitjacket on me already, like listening to them digging my grave! And I prayed. My first attack was so bad it was nearly my last. Like Belcher, one of our laborers who went mad and copped his lot while you were on the machine, I might easily have killed myself. But . . . somebody bashed me on the head and while I was out cold J. C. Craig got hold of me. I woke up sane and I've stayed sane, with Craig's help. And I'm still alive and kicking. So while common sense might tell me J.C.'s a megalomaniac, a religious nutcase, self-preservation tells me to keep my trap shut!"

McClaren nodded, said: "Son, you've had a bit more time to think about this than I have—two years' more time—but I can't help thinking you're a very greedy, self-serving, very callous man. That goes for all of you—you 'disciples'!" He sat up and leaned closer to the younger man, his voice suddenly urgent. "I mean, Craig's got a machine back there that's a cure for The Gibbering! The world is going mad and he can save it—and he's doing nothing about it. Nothing at all. A prophet of the Lord? The man's possessed of devils!"

Now Bragg grinned. "That's more like it," he said. "It's how we all feel the first day, before we've worked it out for ourselves."

"What?" McClaren was trying hard to understand. "What is there to work out?"

"See, I'm a bit more privileged than you," Bragg said, "—at PSISAC, I mean. I've been a member of Craig's team for a long time, as you've pointed out. So let me put you straight on one or two things . . .

"Yes, J.C. has built a machine to beat The Gibbering—or at least to hold it at bay. One machine—you might call it his life's work. Do you know what he admitted to me one time? Most of his patents, his money, resulted as spin-offs from Psychomech. That's how long he's been tinkering with it, improving it, getting it right. One machine, and the first treatment takes something over two hours. Now tell me this: do you know how many people there are in the world? How many gibberers?"

Bragg glanced at McClaren out of the corner of his eye. The older man had slumped back into his seat. He was beginning to see.

Again Bragg grinned, however wryly. "*Now* you're thinking," he said, "but think a little deeper. Let me help you. Would you understand what I meant if I told you the plague was now of epidemic proportions, its curve exponential? Do you understand the domino principle?"

McClaren shook his head.

"Okay, I'll explain. Take some dominoes—a lot of dominoes—and stand them on end so that if you knock down the first it takes two with it, each one of which knocks over two more." He tapped figures into the car's dashboard calculator. "Let's say for simplicity that each domino or set of dominoes takes a half-second to fall. Question? How many will fall in . . . oh, shall we say five seconds?"

McClaren gave it only a moment's consideration. He was in no mood for this sort of thing. "Quite a few, I suppose. Fifty, maybe?"

"Better check your stores tomorrow, Andy," Bragg grinned. "You're no mathematician, that's for sure. Your answer's about a thousand too few!"

McClaren grimaced, shook his head in exasperation, sputtered: "But what the hell has all this to do with—"

"Everything!" Bragg snapped, cutting him short. Every trace of humor had disappeared from his face and voice now. "We're dominoes, Andy! You and me and everyone else in the world. And The Gibbering is knocking us over. But Craig has found a way to cheat. He's fixed it so that when *we* get knocked over we spring right back up again!"

McClaren slumped deeper into his seat. "This domino thing," he finally said. "Is it really as bad as that? A man goes mad one day, two men the next, then four, and so on?"

"No," Bragg answered, "because if it was *that*

bad we'd all be raving inside five weeks. That's right, all five billions of us. The whole world! That's how quick it mounts up. I only used those figures as an illustration. But it's *going* to be that bad, and soon. Here are some more figures for you, except that these came out of PSISAC's computer:

"As far as we can work it out, it started about ten years ago—but slowly. The Gibbering wasn't really noticed among all the other forms of madness. Then it started to become dominant, began to absorb the others into itself, and in the last five years it's really taken off. At the end of 1999 it was claiming maybe a thousand people every month worldwide. But . . . no one was much worried. Gibberers die, remember? They don't live long enough to clog up the works. Maybe eighteen months if they're *unlucky*, less depending upon how lucky they are . . .

"But then—out of the blue—suddenly we were dominoes. The 1,000 a month became 2,000 became 4,000—and so on for about a year. Came the turn of the century, we had one hundred thousand gibberers! Another year and most of that lot were dead, but the curve was bending more viciously still. As if they came out of nowhere, like mushrooms on foggy mornings, suddenly we were face to face with half-a-million maniacs.

"Listen, I won't bore you to death. No need to, for if you don't join Craig's little coven you're as good as dead anyway. I'll just give you the facts. The curve can't bend much further. The world only has five billion people, and that's not enough. It's now the end of October. Seven days from now, one person in fifteen will be gibbering right across the world. A week after that, one in three. And the next day . . . ?"

They sat in silence for long moments, then McClaren gave himself a little shake—or was it a shudder?—and noticed for the first time that Bragg had stopped the car outside his home.

Bragg asked him, "Can I come in? I could use a coffee and we can talk some more. For a little while, anyway. I want to make sure you've got the idea. See, Craig won't go short of a twelfth disciple if you drop out. He'll be able to take his pick from the five or six we'll have in PSISAC tomorrow!"

Climbing wearily out of the car, McClaren had answered, "You'd better come in . . ."

That had been maybe one hour and forty-five minutes ago, and Bragg had stayed for some fifteen minutes. All the while as they talked, McClaren had paced the floor; the younger man had sat smoking and drinking coffee.

"Only thirteen people in all," McClaren had stated incredulously. "Thirteen out of the seven or eight thousand at PSISAC, maybe out of the whole country. Craig and his twelve. Thirteen survivors. Bloody thirteen! Unlucky for some . . ."

"Fourteen," Bragg corrected him. "Don't forget his daughter."

"But what about the other . . . disciples?" McClaren asked. "Don't they have families?"

"J.C.'s no fool," said Bragg. "And if he is, his God isn't. The Ellis woman's a divorcee, no kids. And the other old bag is a spinster. I'm single; so are you; so are the Jackson brothers from the assembly line. Then there's Carling, the tech from Computers. His wife is dead. Again, no family. Pollock from Security is married, but he can't stand his wife. No family. Two other guys are divorced. And there's Cowan, the micro-tech. His wife ran off with her boss. Can't say I blame her much. They still work in Micros, all three of them, and by now she's probably started to wonder why her old man keeps grinning at her—like he was waiting for something funny to happen, you know? I bet he grins at his boss a lot, too!" Bragg gave a harsh laugh which gradually tapered off. "So you see, Andy, there's no internal feuding about who should be saved and who shouldn't. No problem at all."

No problem! McClaren wanted to cry. Was this the sort of callous animal he could look forward to spending the rest of his life with? This . . . "disciple"? No, Bragg had had it more nearly right when he called Craig's bunch a coven.

But things were falling into place now in McClaren's mind. Pieces in a puzzle which had bothered him for some time and was only now slotting itself together and making sense.

Recently he had had to make room in his stores for great coils of hessian-wrapped barbed wire. Now what the hell would PSISAC want with that? A small, windowless security building, massively and hastily constructed, had been completed inside and adjacent to the main gate; and McClaren had heard rumors of the delivery of certain crated items sounding suspiciously like arms and ammunition. The canteens were vastly overstocked with food and drink, their freezers and storage rooms crammed full. It was as if the giant complex prepared for siege . . .

No, it wasn't "as if" anything. That was it exactly.

McClaren stopped pacing, faced Bragg where he sat. "You said we have only two more weeks?"

The other nodded. "The computers say fifteen days."

"But in the last week PSISAC will be completely disrupted. People will be going crazy left, right and center!"

Bragg shook his head. "PSISAC closes down nine days from now. We keep on Security Section at half-strength for two more days. After that—" he shrugged, "—from then on there's just us."

"But how will PSISAC run? Who will man . . . the . . ." McClaren stammered to a halt. Suddenly he saw it all vividly. Bragg recognized the look on his face and nodded in confirmation, satisfied now that the other understood.

"There'll be nothing to man, Andy," he said softly, after a moment. "PSISAC makes expensive toys for civilized man. PSISAC powers many of civilized man's games, keeps him warm, lets him communicate and helps him live a full, happy life. But in the *absence* of civilized man . . . ? PSISAC becomes a fortress, looks after itself. At the end no one will get in, and no one will be allowed out—not until it's all over. Outside, the gibberers will take care of each other. Some of the stronger ones will survive—even for their full term, as long as eighteen months, maybe—but they won't come near PSISAC. If they do, well, they won't live to tell about it.

"And a year from now, eighteen months maximum, then we'll all get to go out and see what's left . . ."

After that, Bragg had given McClaren a headset like the ones he had seen in the boardroom. He had quickly explained something of its function, reminded McClaren to give J. C. Craig a call, and left. And McClaren had paced and paced, and a good many more pieces of the jigsaw had fallen into place.

PSISAC drew its power from the sun, as did most of the world these days. Radiation from the sun was gathered by vast, mile-wide, paper-thin panels of solar cells spreading out like glittering petals from the centers of strange, mechanical flowers: the power satellites which whirled around the Earth in orbits a thousand miles high. PSISAC's satellites beamed down microwave energy, which was then converted into electricity and piped out to consumers. In the event of a shutdown, even PSISAC's smallest converter would be more than sufficient to power the complex itself.

Then there was the question of food. Supplies sufficient for seven thousand people for a fortnight must last a mere handful almost a quarter of a century—except that long before then Craig's coven would have inherited the entire Earth!

As for protection; PSISAC was already almost a hundred percent secure. With the new armory full of weapons—and not just dart-guns—and the entire complex surrounded with a barbed wire trim along the top of its walls . . . the place would be virtually impregnable! And if in addition an electrical current was passed through the wire . . .

So that was the real meaning behind Craig's prattle about Noah's ark. Craig's cauldron, more like!

McClaren was forty-seven years old. Seeing little of value in women, he had never really bothered with them. He did not have what most men would call "a normal sex drive." But then, neither did he have a great deal of time for men. All his life he had been a loner, avoiding the company and the authority of other men, disinclined toward the claustrophobia of the herd and its subservience to leaders. Instead he had sought the quiet life. His job had been easy and had made for little contact with his fellows; his self-contained bachelor chalet on the banks of the river had been a haven, where he bothered no one and no one bothered him. Well, that was all over now . . . or was it?

While McClaren could hardly be said to "love his neighbor," still in his way he had been a believer, had considered the Bible's ten commandments good ones. It seemed to him that J. C. Craig—this patently megalomaniac, self-styled "prophet of God"—was a living negation of most if not all of those commandments. The man *would* kill, *had* killed, if only by default. He *had* made and worshipped a "graven image," the machine called Psychomech. He was *not* meek, by no means meek, and yet saw himself as the rightful heir to Earth. And not only would the real meek lose their inheritance, but they would lose their minds and their lives, too.

Above all else, that last was the one factor which guided McClaren's decision. With his own ears he had heard the Ellis woman say that Psychomech had cured her no less than three years ago, or at least that the machine had halted and continued to hold in abeyance her otherwise inevitable descent into idiocy. And how many other poor souls might Craig's warped genius have saved since then, who through his negligence had raved and died? The world was a desert where Craig ruled the one oasis—and kept all the water for himself and his "disciples"!

That was the way it was and there seemed precious little that Andrew McClaren could do about it. Go to the authorities? Craig would simply shake his head sadly and accuse him of gibbering. Then he'd take back the headset Bragg had given him— and without that McClaren *would* gibber!

No, he could do nothing to stop Craig and his

cronies, but that didn't mean he had to be party to what they were doing.

Now he took up the headset and looked at it. At least he could thank Craig for this. However paradoxically, it seemed that the man's megalomania had made him naïve as a child. Certainly in this respect. For in simple terms Bragg had explained that the device was an extension of Psychomech, a remote receiver for the greater machine's curative broadcasts.

Whenever McClaren sensed an oncoming attack, he must simply press a button on the chrome headband and put the device on his head. It would then send out a continuous signal and alert Psychomech to his distress. No matter where McClaren was in the world, Psychomech would then pinpoint his position precisely. The machine's life- and mind-saving frequencies would be instantly transmitted to the headset via PSISAC's satellites; McClaren could take a tranquilizer and relax while Psychomech entered and squeezed The Gibbering back out of his mind.

The machine's response would be no less automatic than switching on a radio or dialing a telephone number. So . . . why should McClaren remain with PSISAC? Why affiliate himself with Craig and his followers at all? There were still wild, wide open places in the world, plenty of them. And they would be wilder and wider still when this was all over. And if one day Craig and his gang should come looking for McClaren, they'd find him ready and waiting— and God help them then!

According to Bragg, the world outside PSISAC must soon come to an end—but would it? Man might very well come to an end, but the world would surely endure. Indeed the world would very likely prosper in Man's absence; Nature would take charge once more and return the land to its former natural beauty and wholesomeness.

What would be the penalties if McClaren ran? To his understanding, one only. Alone, he would soon have to face a world filled with maniacs. But forewarned is forearmed and the chaos would not last for very long. With a little luck and a positive plan for survival, he was sure he could come through it.

Doubtless Craig would be disappointed when McClaren failed to show at PSISAC tomorrow, but what would he be able to do about it? Nothing! He would have more than enough on his mind without concerning himself too much with a failed disciple. Odds were he'd simply cut his losses and seek another follower from the new day's crop of potential gibberers. Bragg had said it would be as easy as that . . .

McClaren began to formulate a plan for the morning:

First he would drive into Oxford, draw out all of his money from the bank and close his account. Since money would be worthless in a few days, he might as well use it while he could. A large, powerful car would top his list of priorities, following which he'd need weapons. Shotguns should be easy to get hold of—for "hunting" purposes—and if he could purchase smaller handguns, then he would. He might have to pay over the odds for weapons at short notice, but again, money was no longer of any importance. Then he must find himself a hideaway, a retreat, a place easily fortified, and stock it with life's essentials.

He began to grow excited at the prospects he now found opening in his mind. Perhaps the world wouldn't be such a hard place after all. Perhaps—

McClaren's phone rang . . .

Chapter Nine

MCCLAREN STARED AT HIS TELEPHONE AS IF IT WERE a rattlesnake, his eyes fixed upon it where it clamored for attention. Who would that be? And why now? He had so much to think about, so much to do. Plans to make, and—

It kept on ringing, seeming to get more insistent with each ring.

He picked it up, his scalp tingling as he recognized J. C. Craig's voice and it asked, "Andy? Is that you, Andy?"

"Yes—er, yes, sir, Mr. Craig," he finally stammered. "McClaren here."

"Have you made up your mind, Andy?" Craig's voice was soft, solicitous. "I've been waiting for your call."

"Oh, yes, sir. Yes, I have. And I was just . . . just about to call you. Except I thought you meant later, sir." While he answered, his brain raced, searching for the right words. Words to allay any suspicions or doubts Craig might have.

"And your decision?"

"Why, of course, sir! I mean yes, certainly I want to, er, embrace the faith. Oh, I'm a God-fearing man, sir! There's no other way, I say. Just . . . just tell me what I must do."

There was a pause and McClaren's heart skipped a beat, but then Craig said: "Simply come in and see me tomorrow, early. It's Saturday so we'll have plenty of privacy; there are probably still a good many things you'd like me to explain. And of course, as we get closer to the time, there'll be work for you . . ."

"Fine, sir. I'll be in good and early, then."

"And Andy—"

"Yes?"

"Better if you don't leave your place tonight. After that initial attack of yours, you're liable for others at very short notice. And I value you highly, Andy. Did you perhaps have plans to go out?"

"Oh—no—sir—" McClaren lied, gulping between each word and silently cursing himself for a fool. "No, I wasn't planning on going anywhere."

"Good! You are one of mine now, Andy—one of God's chosen—and you must learn absolute obedience. This is an order, then: you will stay home tonight, and so keep yourself safe."

"I will sir. You can be sure of that."

"Fine. And be sure to keep your headset close to hand. No one knows where or when The Gibbering will strike next."

"Yes, of course. Thank you, sir."

"I'll see you in the morning, then. Goodnight, Andy."

"Goodnight, sir," said McClaren, his hand trembling as he put the phone down. Then he collapsed into a chair, thanking providence that he'd never had his phone video-linked!

But in any case Craig suspected something, McClaren was sure of it. The man had found him out, had guessed he wanted none of it. What would Craig do now? Send someone round to take back the headset?

"No!" McClaren gasped out loud, panic working his limbs, causing him to spring up and run through the house. At first his panic was blind, but in a moment or two he got it under control. After that . . . he gathered up only those things which were absolutely necessary:

Banker's ID tag, keys to his car, loose cash. And a pocket radio—he must have that, if only to keep up with the news. While there still *was* news. And the headset, of course.

Five minutes later he was in his tiny car, headed north. He rarely ran the car these days, even preferred to walk to work. Work, *hah*! That was a thing of the past. But the car was a sturdy little thing. Too small by far, but it still had guts. He only used it on Sundays now, to drive into the country. The country, yes—and that was where he would go now. Head for Yorkshire. Plenty of good places to hide away up there. Lonely old places on the moors. Their owners wouldn't need them, not in a week or so, anyway.

In less than ten minutes he was on the new Oxford-Sheffield eight-laner. By tonight he would be completely beyond Craig's reach, and a week from now no one would care anyway. Gradually his mind settled down again. He started to think clearly, recommenced making plans.

Beside him on the passenger seat the headset

was a comfort, his one link with sanity. It formed a friendly chrome and yellow plastic blur on the periphery of his vision . . .

James Christopher Craig glanced at the old pendulum clock on the wall of his study and checked the time. 6:15 P.M. Lynn was late, probably picking up some bits and pieces in Oxford. The stores stayed open late Friday night, so that people could shop for the long weekend. Craig got up and went to the window.

Situated on the Dome's perimeter, Craig's study was a strange hybrid of old and new. The "window" he stood beside formed an entire wall, from which he could look out at the mighty complex he had made his home; but the other three walls were paneled in old English oak, where books leaned in dusty rosewood shelves and a lifetime's collection of *objets d'art* was scattered on tiny tables and in carved corner niches.

And side by side with the musty books, bric-à-brac and things of the old world, were those symbols of the new which seemed to Craig almost to bear his personal signature: a video-phone, a 3-D TV screen set flush in the middle of a wall full of antique books, and self-adjusting lighting which kept visibility in the study to that precise level of brightness best suited to Craig's eyes. It was rich, yes—but wasn't that only fitting for the man God had chosen as the instrument of His will here on Earth?

Almost all of PSISAC's employees had left the complex now. A couple of techs would be carrying out final checks on the main core—and of course Security would be there, guarding PSISAC through the night and weekend—but apart from them and the converter shift-workers the place was empty. The gate guard would let Lynn in when she came home, but before then Craig had something to do. It was time he checked on McClaren.

Only forty-five minutes had gone by since he talked to the man, and in that time he had given plenty of thought to their conversation. He had not liked the way it had gone. Too easy, somehow—like a forced smile. McClaren had seemed too eager too soon. And he had been nervous. Perhaps that was only natural, considering his attack earlier in the day. Perhaps—and perhaps not. Craig's call might just have tipped the scales one way or the other. If McClaren was going to run, then by now he should be running.

Craig crossed the floor back to his desk, picked up the handset of his video-phone and keyed McClaren's home number. The phone rang . . . and rang . . . and rang.

Craig's mouth tightened, his nostrils flaring. He stared at the video-phone's flat, slender screen where it sat atop his desk showing a blank, swirling grayness. He knew of course that McClaren did not have video—just an old-fashioned telephone—but still the swirling grayness seemed somehow significant and strangely permanent. And the phone in his hand went on ringing.

Craig's knuckles slowly turned white where they held the handset to his ear. He let the number ring for two long minutes, then carefully replaced the handset in its cradle and lifted his hand to his furrowed brow. His face worked for a moment, angry blotches of red showing on his cheeks beneath the gray, swept-back tufts of his temples. Then he smiled, however grimly and lopsidedly.

He made his way to the elevator and was carried to the ground floor. There he passed quickly and quietly through the garage area and into Psychomech, the steel doors closing behind him. Making his way toward the center, where the throne's metal and polished leather gleamed bright in Psychomech's pilot lights, he sighed loudly and began to talk to himself:

"Lord, I have erred. I fear that one of my disciples—a man I myself chose to serve me, just as I serve you—is a traitor. Woe is me, Lord, for this is my Gethsemane. Ah, but have I not learned from the trials of your own true son? McClaren is not the first Judas, Lord, but certainly he shall be the last."

At the foot of the dais Craig bowed his head and remained motionless for long moments. Then he turned to one side, reached into the wall of machinery and drew out a computer keyboard on a swivel arm. He stared at it for a second or two, then tapped out information and a question on the white plastic keys:

ANDREW McCLAREN
HEADSET 12
LOCATION?

Dim lights began to glow in the heart of the machine, complementing the pilots, and needles twitched minutely on a thousand dials. There was the merest whirring as of tiny wings. A small screen flickered into life level with Craig's eyes. Psychomech was coming awake, searching. It would not take long.

Craig waited . . .

No sooner had the steel doors closed on Craig than his daughter's car purred quietly up to the Dome along the private approach lane from the main gate. A scanner read the car's number plate, checked the girl's face through the windscreen, and the metal garage doors pivoted up and back in a yawning welcome. As interior lights flickered on, she drove in.

She parked the car, got out and went to the elevator, tapped her personal code into its lock. Inside the lock a latch clicked open, the door concertinaed to one side.

Moments later Lynn Craig stepped out of the elevator into the central area of the living level, calling out, "Dad? Dad?" She cocked her head and listened for an answer but none came. She hummed a tune to herself as she went through to her living room cum study and tossed down books, a string bag, daily newspapers and some small items of groceries into the wide lap of an easy chair. Then she stopped humming and pursed her lips.

It was unusual that her father wasn't here to meet her. He liked to see her off in the mornings and home at night. Perhaps he was swimming. She crossed to a renovated, refitted 19th Century rolltop bureau, pressed intercom buttons marked POOL, GARDENS and SOLARIUM, and said: "Dad? Are you up there?"

Silence . . .

The place was too quiet. Not unnaturally quiet, but after her hectic day (they all seemed hectic nowadays, and she liked it that way) it was as if she had suddenly been struck deaf. She switched on her 3-D TV, caught an item of the news—something about The Gibbering being on the increase again, about the introduction of new measures that required immediate reporting of all cases; apparently parents were loath to take action where their own children were concerned, had even started to hide them away—then switched channels to a quiz show.

That was when she remembered how earlier, when she had phoned her father from the institute, he had said something about an accident at the complex. Something about the main converter. She sighed. He was probably down there now with a gaggle of white-coated technicians, putting things back to rights. Why couldn't he work normal hours like ordinary men?

She frowned. Why couldn't he do *anything* like ordinary men! But no, that was unfair. He wasn't ordinary, that was why. He was J. C. Craig, Managing Director of PSISAC, and PSISAC was his life. And yet . . . there was something more than that. Something deep inside him, some secret thing. And just lately it had been far more apparent . . .

Suddenly the TV annoyed her: the gabble of voices engaged in quick-fire questions and answers. She switched it off.

It seemed warm in the Dome tonight, either that or she was just plain irritable. She frowned.

Funny how she always thought of this place as "the Dome." Her home for half of her life, still "the Dome" seemed more appropriate. She supposed she should consider herself lucky to live in such a place, in such luxury, but her frown deepened for all that. She had *used* to consider herself lucky—very much so and about many things—but that had all come to an end eighteen months ago.

Briefly, fleetingly, she allowed herself to picture Richard Stone as he had been then. But . . . that was no good. He wasn't that way now, would never be that way again. And as her father kept reminding her, she was very young and there was plenty of time for her yet.

Sighing, she flopped down on a huge recliner that dwarfed her spreadeagled figure. Plenty of time . . .

Time heals all wounds. And true enough, as the days went by she thought of Richard less and less. Or perhaps it was that the futility of her thoughts became more and more apparent.

She shook he head, clearing away the mood of cloying poignancy which suddenly threatened her, the loneliness creeping like a miasma from stagnant wells of memory. Angry with herself, she bounced to her feet and snatched up the groceries, whisking them away to the kitchen.

On the way she detoured and peeped into her father's study. There was an empty plate on his desk, a scattering of crumbs and a few small chicken bones; also, a mug with coffee grounds thick in its bottom. He wouldn't be wanting food tonight. Good! She wasn't hungry herself and relished not having to cook. But on the other hand she felt a little guilty; her father rarely ate a cooked meal these days.

Loneliness was creeping again. And the Dome wasn't just warm, it was clammy. She would take a shower!

She put the groceries away, went back to her own rooms and into the bathroom. While the shower made its automatic adjustment to Lynn's personal preference of temperature, she slipped out of her clothes and gave her naked body a minute, almost clinical inspection in the bathroom's full-length mirror.

She was twenty years old but looked more like seventeen. Her figure was tall and slender, rounded where it should be. As befitted her youth, there was very little sag to her breasts; her buttocks were firm and taut. Richard (*again* Richard) had used to say she had a boyish bottom; and she had used to laugh and ask how the hell would he know?—or did he perhaps have some dark secret?

Again she forced him from her mind.

She gave her head a shake and her chestnut hair bounced on her shoulders; she smiled and the mirror reflected the darkness of her eyes, the perfect white of her teeth like a bar of light set in her tanned face. Turning, she looked back over her shoulder, checking that her tan was deep and even. Finally she was satisfied. She had lost weight since . . . over the last eighteen months, but was now putting it on again. That was something she must watch. It wouldn't do to look heavy and ungainly on the beach next summer.

The beach . . .

Suddenly she was bitter, snatching back the shower curtain angrily and stepping quickly into the hissing cascade, catching her breath in a gasp as the water hit her . . . but in the next moment relaxing gratefully and feeling her tensions streaming away from her along with the sweetly stinging water.

The beach. Actually, she wouldn't care if she never saw a beach again. It just wouldn't be the same. Not now . . .

After the car stopped, Stone had waited three full minutes before he moved. Minutes that seemed like hours, until he felt he *must* move or seize up altogether. Then, easing the boot lid up a couple of inches, he had checked that the garage was empty. The lights had gone out automatically as soon as Lynn entered the elevator, but still there was a little natural light in the place. Not much, sufficient that Stone could make out the outlines of the concrete support pillars. Sitting up, he waited until orientation was complete, then climbed stiffly, awkwardly out of the boot and eased the lid down until it clicked shut.

Less than thirty yards away, J. C. Craig stood with his head as yet bowed in the heart of the machine, but massive steel walls and doors separated the two men and neither knew of the other's proximity. And so, while Craig offered up silent obeisance before his oracle, Stone shuffled and stamped in darkness and flexed his aching muscles, allowing himself the luxury of a single, quiet groan as cramp momentarily threatened his legs. Then, gritting his teeth, he moved painfully to the front door.

Finding the driver's window open, he put his hand inside and fumbled around for a second until he found the keys. Pocketing them, he turned and picked his way carefully to the elevator. Now he would discover if anything else had changed while he had been . . . away. He had used to be a regular visitor here, had even had his own ID code by which the Dome had known him. Would it know him now, or had his code been erased? He paused for a single moment before the elevator. If his code was no longer acceptable, would the Dome see him as an intruder?

He tapped the number into the lock, sighed as he heard that once-familiar *click* and the elevator's door obligingly folded away.

Seconds later, ascending toward the living level, a nervous tic caused Stone's left eye to start jumping. He controlled it, tensing himself as the extra weight went out of his legs and the door sighed open. So far so good. Now the game was to find Lynn before her father found him. Most certainly before that! Stone had no proof but he had always suspected that J. C. Craig wasn't too keen on him. If he hadn't been called Stone, his and Lynn's friendship would have been stepped on before it ever got started. And now? What father would take kindly to an escaped lunatic come visiting his daughter?

Mercifully Lynn's and her father's rooms were on opposite sides of the Dome. If she wasn't in her rooms, Stone would simply hide himself away there and wait for her. If she was in, then they'd see what they would see. And if he bumped into her father first . . . Well, he could only keep his fingers crossed on that one.

Silently, listening to the pounding of his own heart, Stone made his way across deep-pile carpeting and into Lynn's rooms. She didn't appear to be there but her string bag and a collapsed stack of books lay on a chair, and the cushions on her huge recliner had been thrown about a little.

Stone passed down a short corridor toward her bedroom. The door was open, the room quiet and in darkness; but a light shone out from beneath the door of the room opposite. The bathroom.

Stone's heart pounded louder still. He could hear the hiss of the shower now, knew that she would be in there, arms upraised, curving her body and craning her neck to accept the soothing spray, letting the water touch every inch of her lovely body. He knew it because he had seen it, often. They had used to make love in the shower.

The thought of it was vivid, erotic, persistent. God, how they had used to make love! Like young animals coupling—wanting everything—tasting, feeling, lusting after everything. Since the first time, when both of them were just seventeen, they had never missed an opportunity. And nothing had been taboo. Here in the Dome on those rare occasions when her father was away; down at the house in Sussex; out in the open countryside, wherever the grass was long or the trees shady. And yet it had been more than just their youth and their lust, there had been something else.

Stone had known two other girls before Lynn, and both in the same summer, but with them it had been . . . well, it hadn't really been anything. With Lynn, it was a fire, an inferno—it was love. Or it had been.

Stone's jaw tightened. Love? And how many times had he seen her since . . . since then? How many times had she visited him?

Was that why he had come here, to find out? A night's sanctuary was all he thought he wanted, wasn't it? Or was it that he really wanted to see a certain look in her eyes, a look which would write *finis* on all they had ever looked forward to and dreamed of doing together? *Finis* on the life they had planned.

No, that was too bitter. He *had* come here for sanctuary, yes—but there was another reason, too. And that was to tell her that there was hope yet, that he wasn't nearly ready to be written off. Something inside him told him there was an answer to all this, and that he was the only one who could find it. He wanted Lynn to know that, that was all, and he wanted her to wait for him. If he was wrong . . . the wait wouldn't be too long. But if he was right—

—Suddenly Stone reeled, clapped his hands to his head, drew breath in a hissing, agonized gasp. He ground his teeth together to keep from crying out, went weak at the knees as bolt after bolt of

searing fire lanced through his skull. It was as if
someone had slid a white-hot needle into his
brain and was jiggling it about. Someone who tittered and sniggered and laughed demoniacally.

And not just one someone. No, for there were
many of them, an army of them. Coming out of
nowhere . . . dancing in his head like tiny imps
. . . leaping and cavorting around his brain,
stinging it with their barbed, burning needles . . .
sacking the beleaguered city of his psyche.

And all of them gibbering, gibbering, gibbering!

*Oh, Jesus—God—Christ almighty! Oh my great
merciful God—not now! Please, not now!*

But God was not listening, or perhaps the wrong
god was listening . . .

Down below in the room of the machine, the
screen before J. C. Craig's face was now filled with
symbols and numbers. Some of the figures were
static, unchanging, others were fluid as quicksil-
ver and changed with each passing fraction of a
second. Craig had studied the figures for many
minutes, reading them as surely as the pages of
a book. They told him that he had been right
about Andrew McClaren.

Psychomech's lights were brighter, pulsing with
strange colors, semi-sentient as they struck almost stroboscopic patterns. The machine seemed
arched over Craig like a great indolent cat,
stretching and purring for the moment but ready
at a second's notice to snarl and pit and scratch.
For, cruel as a cat, Psychomech had seen the
quarry; the mouse was out in the open, but the
machine was in no hurry. It would strike only
when Craig, the master, commanded it.

Beads of sweat gleamed like iridescent pearls

on Craig's brow as he watched the screen. His eyes were unblinking as he absentmindedly dabbed the beads away with a damp handkerchief. Oh, McClaren was running all right, scurrying north as fast as he could go. Well, it was his funeral.

Craig reached out a hand toward the computer keyboard, and with a nightmare grin on his clammy face he prepared to unsheath Psychomech's claws . . .

Chapter Ten

EDWARD BRAGG'S EXPLANATION OF THE HEADSET'S functions had been, if not a downright lie, deliberately vague and simplistic—as McClaren was about to discover. Certainly the sets were extensions of Psychomech, and what little Bragg had said of them was largely true, but he had not nearly said enough. He had *not* said, for instance, that even without use of the alert button on the headband, still each set was a micro-transmitter, a "bug" whose signal Psychomech constantly tracked. And that was only one of the things Bragg had omitted to mention.

McClaren was not aware, for example, that the aberrant mental patterns of The Gibbering were different for every mind invaded—as different as individual sets of fingerprints—and that Psychomech recorded those patterns with better than photographic accuracy. Nor did he know that they could be reproduced. But indeed that was part of

Psychomech's function: to drive the sick mind to the very brink of collapse, the edge of insanity— and then while it teetered and threatened to cave in, to shore it up and feed it those energies necessary to combat and overcome the mechanically-induced terrors of the id.

McClaren was now some sixty-eight miles north of Oxford, crossing Leicestershire and heading for Derby. Beside him on the passenger seat the headset jiggled and moved with the motion of the car, but there was other activity which was quite invisible. Tracking McClaren's tiny vehicle, locked-in on the headset, a needle-thin beam of energy from the skies had activated the micro-converters in the earphones, setting up between them a flux whose configuration was McClaren's aberrant pattern.

As the satellite-transmitted beam intensified, so the tiny cores of ultra-tough Herculite alloy were obliged to expand the flux until it overlapped the perimeter of the headset and began to permeate the entire interior of the car—including McClaren himself. And as if from nowhere, in his head, suddenly he heard the first distant tinkling of bells.

The start of the thing exactly duplicated his experience of the morning, so that he broke into a cold sweat as he applied the car's brakes, and pulled into a layby. There he switched off the engine and sat for a moment in comparative silence, tensely aware of his own blood's pounding, his eyes darting left to right in utter terror and hideous expectancy. And—

—Yes, there it was again, and louder now: the sound of the bells in his head, jingling on the pennants of the babbling mindhorde army where it marched to the attack! McClaren knew only too well how swiftly that monotonous clamor could expand to break down the walls of his psyche, letting in the baying warriors of lunacy, but still he took time to switch on the car's interior light and wind down his window.

Cool air rushed in and turned his fevered brow to ice. The roar of evening traffic on the dark, eight-lane motorway seemed strangely muted, drowned out by the rapidly rising tumult from within. Hope and pray as he might, McClaren could no longer doubt it. The thing was almost upon him.

He snatched up the headset, fumblingly found and pressed the button on the headband, fitted the device to his skull . . .

On the instant, Psychomech reacted, changed the configuration. A bland, harmless flux washed through McClaren's mind like a soothing salve laid gently on a raw wound. He groaned, sighed, drew deep drafts of air and finally sobbed—only to laugh, however shakily, in the very next moment. It worked! The thing really did work!

Then, as the exhaustion of all the day's tensions and terrors at last caught up with him, he lay back in his seat and warily, shudderingly closed his eyes. How good it would be simply to sleep here, to stretch out in the car for an hour or two and let the world outside go roaring by, like the traffic on the motorway.

He stirred himself up. No, it wouldn't do to sleep. Not now. Not here. He must get as far north as he could, find a hotel for the night in Sheffield, maybe.

With the headset seated firmly upon his head, McClaren started up his car and pulled carefully out into the stream of traffic.

Under the night sky, the mouse was on the move again . . .

* * *

In the Dome, in the corridor between Lynn Craig's bedroom and her bathroom, Richard Stone slowly uncurled from his fetal knot and lay twitching and moaning where he had crumbled. The attack had lasted for mere seconds—maybe as little as half a minute—but it had been utterly savage in its intensity. And Stone had been helpless. Much longer and he knew he would have died. It had left him no room to fight, and he had had very little left to fight with. So perhaps God had been listening after all . . .

Anyway, it was over, done with for now, and Stone was left sick as a dog. His Adam's apple was working involuntarily as his gorge began to rise. Clammy in his own sweat and stinking of fear, he somehow got to his feet, opened and staggered in through the bathroom door.

Lynn was still in the shower, reluctantly finishing off. Her voice was low as she hummed some old familiar tune to herself, lost in the sheer pleasure of the hissing, laving water. The first she knew of his presence on the other side of the curtain were the animal sounds of his retching as he coughed and choked and heaved up his sickness into the toilet. Then the humming died on her lips and she held her breath, listening.

The water of the shower continued to hiss all about her but the other sound was gone now. Then there came a groan and Lynn was aware of movement beyond the curtain.

She queried: "Dad?" and drew back the curtain a little, poking her head out. "Dad, is that—"

Stone was stooped over a sink, its fountain jetting into his mouth, sluicing away vomit. He was a deathly gray, swaying and trembling uncontrollably when he turned his face to stare at her.

"Richard!" she gasped, her mouth falling open. "Richard? But how—?"

"Sh-*shower!*" he whispered hoarsely. He staggered toward the shallow well of the shower, arms outstretched. Lynn caught him instinctively, propped him against the wall.

"You want a shower?" Her wide eyes were questioning, trying hard to understand.

"Cold," he answered. "Tired. Hungry . . ." He lay back against the wall, let her hold him there, shivered like a leaf in a gale.

She stepped fully out of the shower and unmindful of her nudity tugged at his jacket, fought to get it off. He *was* bitterly cold, his flesh like ice. "Hungry? But you've just been sick!" she told him, helping him lower himself to the tiled floor.

"Sick, yes," he nodded, his eyes mud-colored in the pale dough of his face. "Sick from The Gibbering!"

She had him almost naked now, but stopped tugging at his clothes the moment he said those words. In that same instant the facts of what she was doing came to her. She was stripping naked a certified madman in her own bathroom; a man who by all rights should be dead now, and who must certainly be in the final, terminal stage of the mind-plague!

He saw the look on her face, managed a harsh, barking laugh. "Oh, yes," he growled, nodding. "All of that. But Lynn, I'm different. I can—" (he finally crawled free of his clothing) "—I can *beat* it! And here I am to . . . prove it."

"Beat it?" she stared at him incredulously, backing away now, aware of her stark nakedness—and of his. "Beat The Gibbering? But Richard, no one has ever—"

"But I *will!*" he cut her off. "I got this . . . this

far, didn't I?" He used the bowl of the toilet to drag himself upright, stumbled toward the still hissing shower.

Again, instinctively, she went to him, helped him into the shower. If anything he was even colder now. Shock, she supposed. Reaction to . . . to what? Had he suffered an attack here? Again it was as if he read her mind:

"Yes," he nodded, his Adam's apple jerking. "A moment ago."

Then he was under the shower, gasping, clawing at the walls to hold himself upright. And in that moment Lynn gave up any pretensions to common sense and helped him sit down, then sat down with him and hugged him close.

Gradually his shuddering subsided, color creeping back into the marble of his face and form. "That was a bad one," he said, holding her tightly.

She laughed quietly, perhaps a little hysterically, into his shoulder. "You'd better start somewhere," she said, "and tell me all about it. Tell me everything."

He took her face in his hands, held her away from him, looked at her. He was seated in one corner of the shower well, his legs widespread. She kneeled between them, her hands on his shoulders. The water hissed down, streaming from their chins. "You believe me?" he said. "That I've beaten it?"

"You got this far, didn't you?" she repeated his own words of a few minutes ago. "I want to believe you. More than anything else, I want that."

He hugged her to him, his flesh trembling as before, but no longer from the icy cold of shock. "You want me to tell you?"

"Yes—no! First let's get you properly warm and dry. Then tell me."

Both of them naked as babes, she helped him through to her bedroom and flopped him down still wet through upon her bed. She got him a towel and he managed to sit up, began toweling groggily at his hair.

"Hey," he said, "how about a sandwich? Maybe a beer?"

She shook her head to the last. "Fruit juice," she said. "But you have to stay right here—with the light out—till I get back. My father's not home right now, but he could be back any time."

He chuckled wearily and flopped back on the pillows. "I promise I won't move," he said. "Shit, I don't think I could!"

"I'll be two minutes," she said, putting the light out as she went.

She was five minutes, and while she got him food she worked some of it out. Back in her bedroom with the light on again, she said: "I thought the car was a bit sluggish tonight. And it was funny on corners, too. You were in that tricky boot, eh?"

He nodded. "What a waste, so late in the day: to discover a way you could have been smuggling me in all this time!" Then he sobered. "I didn't know how you'd react. I couldn't take any chances. And I needed somewhere to stay for the night." Between sentences he tore at a chicken leg and gulped at pineapple juice.

She shook her head in a fresh flood of wonderment, touched his shoulder almost as if she expected him to vanish, hardly dared take her eyes off him. "I'm not the kind who believes in miracles," she finally said. "You'd better tell me all about it."

"I do a trick with electricity," he began. "When it comes on—when I start to gibber—I give myself a jolt. The heavier the better—just so it's not a killer! That does it, knocks me out. Then . . . I dream. Hell, *weird* dreams! But somehow they mean something. I mean, they help me to see things, know things . . ." He shrugged. "So that's one way."

"I'm not sure I understand," she said, looking blank. "But go on anyway."

"Who understands?" he asked. "Okay, another way: I swear a lot."

"You what?" she thought he was joking.

"If the attack isn't too bad, I can hide it—bury it, sort of—under a barrage of curse words. I do it in my head. I've found that if I make a lot of noise up there, my own noise, my swearing, it's like I don't leave any room for them."

"Them?"

"The voices. The chuckling, sniggering, idiot voices. The Gibbering . . ."

"Oh!"

"And I suspect there's another way. But this one's not so hot and I haven't tried it yet. And I don't think I want to." He frowned and turned his face away.

"You may as well tell me," she prompted.

"Violence!" he said. "I have this idea that sheer physical violence would be as good, maybe better, than the mental violence of my cursing. I think that's what makes them do the things they do—the gibberers, I mean. They try to work it off with violence, but they go over the top. That's why so many of them kill themselves . . ."

"Oh!" she said again, quietly. And then: "You know, I think I understand that."

"You do?"

She nodded. "The kids I work with. You've seen them. Sometimes when they hurt themselves—or when they can't make me understand something, when they're frustrated—then they become violent. Not all of them, but some. Afterward, it's like they've worked it out of their systems."

"Yes, something like that," he said, rubbing at his eyes. "Jesus, I'm tired!"

"And you look it," she told him, taking his plate and glass and covering him with a soft blanket. "Why don't you get some sleep. But before you do, how did you get out of . . . out of that place?"

He turned his strange yellow eyes full upon her. "Damned if I know," he said, shaking his head. "It was during an attack. Afterward I found myself outside the playground at the Clayton Institute. I only hope I wasn't . . ." He paused, chewed his lip.

"Violent?" she finished it for him.

"Lynn," he took her hands, "What I'm trying to do is important."

"Of course it is," she said.

He shook his head impatiently. "More than that, bigger than that. It's not just for me, or us. It's the world, Lynn . . ." Looking into his eyes, she knew he told the truth. At least as he saw it.

"Tell me more about it tomorrow," she said. And added: "I still love you, you know?"

"I hoped you would," he said, kissing her.

Gently but firmly she pushed him back until his head hit the pillows.

A moment later he was asleep . . .

In the room of the machine, J. C. Craig shook his head sadly and decided to end it. He had demonstrated to McClaren Psychomech's mastery over The Gibbering, had given the man plenty of time to think about it and every opportunity to turn back, and still the traitor fled north. Soon he would reach Sheffield and leave the motorway. It must be done before then.

Craig sighed and shook his head again; there was so little time now, else things might be different. But even as late as this, with the holocaust so close, still he could not take the chance that McClaren would remain silent.

For the last forty minutes Craig had been pacing the floor of the fantastic "tunnel" of machinery between the steel doors and the central dais, but now he paused and turned once more to the computer display screen. A single glance told him that indeed McClaren continued to race north.

He cleared a corner of the screen and typed up:

HEADSET 12
MAXIMUM LOAD?

Psychomech answered,

0.0000525 M/WAVE

Craig ordered:

TESTING:
IMPLEMENT OVERLOAD

Psychomech,

SPECIFY LOAD?

Craig, after a moment's thought:

WHAT LOAD WOULD CAUSE
DISINTEGRATION OF THE CORES?

Psychomech,

0-0525 M/WAVE

Craig:

IMPLEMENT

The beam tracking McClaren's car immediately thickened, went from needle-slim to pencil-thick. Power sufficient to propel the car itself, if it had been equipped with a converter engine, surged into the cores at McClaren's temples. Under pressure a thousand times too great, they melted, disintegrated in a micro-second, and twin clouds of white-hot Herculite shrapnel were sucked into the suddenly seething flux—which of course had its center in McClaren's brain.

He was dead before his mouth fell open and said, "Ach-ak-ak-*ak*!" Dead before his body jerked ramrod straight and slammed the driving seat back, shearing its bolts and tearing it loose from the floor.

The car's engine roared as his dead foot vibrated where it drove the accelerator flat on the floor. His dead hands flopped from the wheel and played flutteringly with the air in front of his sightless eyes. Then—

—It was as if someone had dropped a bomb on the motorway.

The car seemed to give a leap, cut across from the third lane, into and across the fourth, bumped against and slid along the central barrier in a shower of sparks. A moment later it smashed into a stanchion, somersaulted into the southbound lanes and landed right side up in the path of a pair of mighty night-freighters.

The giant articulated trucks were only allowed on the motorways at night, and then confined to the two outer lanes. Each one was twelve feet wide and a hundred long; their tires alone were taller than McClaren's car. Racing neck and neck, one was just about to overtake the other when the tiny blue weekender bounced down in front of them and skidded at them side-on. At a combined speed of one hundred and thirty miles per hour, they met.

The juggernauts shared McClaren's car between them. One took the front, the other the rear. They gobbled it up, dragged it under, tore it apart and set it explosively afire, and flushed it out the back in a confetti of blazing plastic and crumpled metal. Cars and trucks behind howled their protests in a blaring of horns and a screaming of brakes as flaming debris lit up the night. A lone tire went burning and bounding along the hardstanding, vaulted a fence and disappeared into an orchard.

The mouse had been taken; Psychomech's bloodied claws retracted into their sheaths; the paw was withdrawn.

Andrew McClaren, probationer disciple (failed), was no more . . .

Craig cleared the screen. He typed up:

GOD IS GOOD
HE IS MERCIFUL
HIS RETRIBUTION WAS SWIFT

Psychomech said nothing.
Craig typed,

DO YOU STILL SEEK FOR THE LORD MY
GOD?

Psychomech:

I SEEK HIM

Craig,

AND HAVE YOU FOUND HIM?

Psychomech, after the merest pause:

NO

But He's out there somewhere, Craig told himself. *Oh, my God—why will You not speak to me
here and now, as You do in my dreams? Why have
You forsaken me? Speak and tell me how I may
serve You . . .*
He asked the machine:

WHEN WILL HE SPEAK TO ME?

Again the pause—

WHEN I FIND HIM

"Then *find* Him!" Craig shouted out loud.
Sweat dripped from his chin; his eyes were
black holes cut in a white paper face; and suddenly he was afraid. Too much!—he had gone too
far. One must not question the ways of the Lord.
He staggered, covered his eyes. Something
slithered on his mind. Something hissed! Blind-
worms of madness burned in his brain. His hands

flew back to the keyboard, and with trembling fingers he typed:

CRAIG

TREATMENT

Stumbling, his head throbbing, he climbed the steps of the dais and almost fell into the throne. "Oh my Lord God," he mouthed, foam flecking the corners of his mouth, "Oh God, save me now. Give me strength, Lord. The hosts of hell are upon me—the serpent coils himself around my brain! *Get thee behind me, Satan!*"

Not one but a thousand snakes were in Craig's head. They crawled, writhed, squirmed and pulsated in his skull—and they hissed, hissed, *hissed*!

Then, slowly, they lifted up their flat, evil heads and their jaws gaped. Forked tongues salivated in Craig's mind, dripped burning acid. They stopped hissing, poised themselves to strike . . .

"No!—No!—*No!*" Craig screamed.

With precious little time to spare, micromotors tilted the metal skull cap forward and down on his head; the U-shaped bracket turned on its jointed arm and trapped his neck, holding up his jaw; the wrist and ankle clamps snapped shut on his limbs.

And at last he felt the hated sting of the anesthetic needles, now welcome, following which he slipped swiftly down whirling funnels of darkness; so that he knew nothing whatever of the other needles, sensors and electrodes where they clasped themselves to him, probing and penetrating. Now he knew only that there was a war to be waged, and that with Psychomech's help he would win and rise up again renewed.

And so J. C. Craig slept and commenced dreaming his artificial, curative dreams. And while he dreamed so, Psychomech, not unmindful of its duties, tuned in to the singing of the Psychosphere and continued to search for God . . .

Stone had been asleep for little over half an hour by the time Lynn got through tidying up. Her emotions and loyalties were in conflict and in fact her "tidying up" had simply consisted of finding a few odd things to do while she explored her own thoughts and feelings.

The problem was that she really did still love Richard Stone and knew she probably always would. So what to do about it? He was a known, self-confessed madman—periodically at least— and by now his escape was doubtless noted and various authorities alerted. But he was Richard, too, and that made all the difference. She sensed that he was important beyond her love for him, perhaps more important than even he suspected, and her heart went out to him in his fix. But how could she help?

Obviously her father must not find him, and that was another point of loyalty. Oh, they had fooled J. C. Craig before—often, during the course of their love affair—but then it had been different . . . Of course, she *should* turn him in to the authorities, was already at risk for not having done so; but she couldn't bear the thought of that.

She shook her head angrily. No, this was no good; in her own mind she was complicating matters. The essence of the thing was simple: her action (or, more properly, inaction) would not be a betrayal of her father or society in general but a symbol of her trust in Richard. And of her love for him. She *would* help him, if only to let him sleep here and then smuggle him out again. Even without her emotional involvement she owed him that much, for old times if for nothing else.

She left a note for her father, saying she had had a busy day, was tired and going to bed early. This was true. Also, it meant that she would not have to face him when he returned. Where she was concerned he was intensely perceptive; she would not have to tell him lies.

All done, Lynn returned to her bedroom and sat in her dressing gown looking at the sleeper. She had used to look at him like this . . . before. After lovemaking, especially if their sex had been very active, he would sleep like a baby, smiling. He was smiling now—and yet somehow managing to look worried at the same time—and there were new, permanent furrows in his brow which belied his youth. He had had a hard time of it . . .

Almost automatically, without any real conscious thought, Lynn slipped out of her garment and into bed with him. Carefully, so as not to waken him, she cradled him, giving comfort. He reminded her so much of one of her poor children, of any one of them. Alone in a world which didn't understand him, which found him alien. Their minds were different, that was all. They thought at a tangent, or their streams of thought were broken by white water or submerged in swirling potholes. But Richard had a chance. He believed his flow was resurgent, that it would find the way back to the surface and emerge as a fresh, clear spring.

She reached out and switched off the light, rocked him as she would a sick child. And she

was surprised and a little amused—and a little
sad—when she felt him grow slowly erect against
her belly. That, too, was something she had
known before.

His arms crept round her . . .

He mumbled something in his sleep, shook his
head with a strange urgency . . .

His erection became more insistent and he
hugged her tighter . . .

With her eyes closed and her head against his
chest, she smiled and pushed him gently away
. . . but he mumbled again, and this time she listened. His words came clearer, guttural with
sleep, obscene and full of raw animal hatred:

"Fucking, cunting, slimy arse-licking, wanking-
whoringbastardbastard*bastard*! Your mother was
dead and your father fucked her and you're the
bastard son of a scumsucking cancer-ridden zombie! Garrison, you ghoul! GarrisonGarrison-
Garrison! Oh, you fuck-pig! Your monstrous mind's
away adventuring now, and here am I mired in
madness! Bastardbastard*bastard*!"

Oh my dear God! she thought, her body freezing solid, her flesh cold in a moment. She opened
her eyes, stared at him.

In the darkness his eyes were closed—but she
could swear that behind lids suddenly transpar-
ent golden amoebas throbbed and pulsated!

She would have jerked away from him but he
clutched her tighter still. He was asleep, but even
asleep he fought whatever it was that invaded his
mind. His cursing was his way of doing battle with
the thing, he had told her that much. But there
was another way, too. Violence!

He tightened his grip more yet, crushed her to
him.

"Richard!" she gasped. *"Richard!"*

He was working his body against her, one hand bunching her hair into a vicious knot, and cursing, cursing, cursing. A combination of two methods of resistance. "Ri-*chard*!" she cried again, drawing back her hand, forming a hard little fist and striking him in the mouth.

No good. He was dead to the world. Like a man who cycles all day and continues to pedal in his sleep, Richard Stone would go on fighting this thing until he won or was defeated. But he would never give in. And Lynn desperately wanted him to win.

She sobbed and sank her nails into his shoulders, tearing at him. Her tears—not of terror but anguish, for him—were hot in the curve of his neck where she bit him. "You want violence, my love?" she whispered in his ear. "Then you shall have it. It's a game two can play."

She opened her body to him, drew him in, curled herself up on him and clawed at his back. There was little of strength left in him, but what there was he now expended. She gave him blow for blow, bite for bite, rode with him and against him, goaded and defied him. Their coupling was primal. They raped each other.

And again . . .

And again . . .

And again . . .

Part

II

Suzy was coming home. Home to Earth.

From halfway across the unimaginably vast Psychosphere, she was returning to the world of men. Earth was her birthplace and called to her with a voice loud and clear. Earth was the bright place of her limited canine memories, shining like a beacon in the mirror of her mind. And this was part of the reason why she came.

Her journey . . . but what use to describe it, except in the simplest terms?

Few men could truly conceive of it and none could visualize it. Easy to say: "halfway across the unimaginably vast Psychosphere," but by definition impossible to imagine.

We might nevertheless attempt the simplest illustration:

Go out one night when the stars are bright and look up into the sky. Choose the furthest star. Keep looking at it and go there—in the merest moment—and keep looking in the same direction. And choose the furthest star; and so on. Do it and keep doing it for a billion years, and then for ten billion years. Keep doing it for twice as long as the Milky Way galaxy has existed. Go so far so fast that the light of stars you left behind can never, ever catch up with you. And you will have taken one step into the Psychosphere, a single pace into infinity. One pace in a walk that would take you forever . . .

And Suzy was coming home across half of forever.

As for her master:

Richard Allan Garrison, or the Being which once was Garrison, was going the other way. There were so many things to do, places to see, sentiences to meet and talk to. He would not be lonely without Suzy. He had with him the other masters, Schroeder and Koenig, or the Beings which once were Schroeder and Koenig. And the wonders they had known were immeasurable, and yet only a fraction of those they were yet to know. They would go on . . . forever! And forever for them would be forever, for they were immortal.

They could not hunger for they feasted on the energy of stars, nor thirst for they drank from the very font of space and time. And even if they would, perhaps they could not return. They were not lost in relation to Earth, no, for no one is lost until he is threatened, and nothing could threaten them. More truly, Earth was lost in relation to them.

But not in relation to Suzy. Neither the Earth nor Suzy were lost, only a very long way apart . . .

After she left, the Garrison Being called to her once or twice, as a man calls his dog across the green valleys of Earth, and she had paused and whined and looked back through the nebulas, the galaxies like daisies in a field. But he did not need her any longer and she knew it. He had companionship, more than she. Nor could she protect him. From what?

And so she had gone, and Garrison had let her go. And after a while he had stopped calling.

Garrison had stopped, but Someone Else had started. Or perhaps the New Someone had been calling for a long time and Suzy had only just heard and recognized His call.

Whichever, the closer she drew to the homeworld, the louder she heard it. Someone needed. Someone was lost—and frightened! A man, of flesh and blood. A man of Garrison's flesh and blood. A child of Garrison!

Already she could feel His hand upon her head, hear His voice saying, "Good girl, good girl!" And these were feelings she had not felt, and words she had not heard, for a long, long time.

This was worth immortality.

This was her destiny.

And so Suzy came home . . .

Day One

PHILLIP STONE JERKED AWAKE AND PEERED ABOUT FOR whatever it was that had woken him. Within arm's reach, an empty whisky bottle stood on a bedside table. Stone groaned and blinked his eyes, which flashed internal warning lights in his head. He knew he deserved his hangover but resented it anyway, and in spite of it he was glad to be awake. His dream had been weird and disturbing, but already it was fading. A pity the same could not be said of the buzzing from his videophone!

Stone forgot the dream, reached out of bed and picked up his phone. As soon as the handset left its cradle, the face of James Christopher Craig snapped into sharp focus on the screen at the foot of Stone's bed. Without so much as a good morning, Craig's voice snapped in Stone's ear, "Phillip, your boy's been here—and he's run off with Lynn!"

"What?" Stone absorbed the information, sat up straight in his bed. Then his shoulders slumped and he sagged a little. "Oh, Jesus!" he said, partly in answer to Craig and partly in respect of his throbbing head. He had half-hoped that last night's call from Calm Lawns had been part of his nightmare; now that hope was shattered. "How did he get in?" Stone said the first thing that came into his mind.

Craig looked daggers at him and his voice became a hiss. "How he got in, what he bloody did here and how he then got out aren't subjects for a video-phone conversation!" He took a deep breath. "Phillip, I can see you're in no fit state, but I want to see you—up here—today."

Stone growled in the back of his throat and sat up straighter. "Jimmy," he said, "we've been friends for a long time, but whatever this is all about it's not my fault. And what the hell do you mean, you want to see me? So come and see me! My place is your place, always has been. Only thing I'd ask: don't use that tone of voice with me. The way I feel right now, I might just come right through this screen at you!"

Craig's face was chalk white. His jaw tightened. "Maybe you didn't hear me. I have a right to be angry. Your boy's got Lynn!"

Stone rang for Mary, yelled, *"Coffee!"* at the top of his voice, groaned and put a hand to his head. "Got her?" he repeated Craig. "Took her by force, you mean? Kidnapped her?"

Craig shook his head impatiently, waved his hands. "He's *taken* her," he said, "isn't that enough? Look, will you come?"

"Hell, Jimmy, I'm only just awake!" Stone protested. "Why don't you come down here? And anyway, what can I do?"

"Well, for one thing, you could show a little more concern!"

Craig's face was beginning to work. Stone wondered: are those tears in the corners of his eyes? He sighed, rubbed the stubble on his chin. He would achieve nothing fighting with Craig, not while he was as emotional as this. "Okay," he said, "I'll come. I'll be there at two, maybe 2:30 this afternoon. Will that be all right?"

"Thanks," Craig snapped, nodding sharply. "It's good to know you care so much!"

The screen went blank before Stone could answer.

Stone's housekeeper came in with his coffee in time to hear his vivid curse as he slammed the phone back into its cradle. She tut-tutted, put the coffee on a side table and handed him the morning paper. "And good morning to you, Mr. Stone!" she said. He grunted something unintelligible after her as she left.

Still angry, he snatched up the paper. Drinking his coffee, he began to read. The front page carried a headline article on Moonbase II, something about a failed sabotage attempt by a gibberer. Stone frowned, he had somehow imagined the moon might be immune, that its distance might somehow isolate it. He turned pages, found other articles on the mind-plague inside. Then he spotted something about PSISAC and his jaw dropped. The story concerned the death of a laborer called Belcher, and something about a near-disaster at the main converter. Craig must be in a bad way if he hadn't mentioned this!

Stone found his son's story on page three, one and a half inches of a single column lost among a host of more important items. Stone was glad: it would hardly be noticed. He nevertheless read it through and picked up a few facts which were new to him. It was worse than last night's phone call had led him to believe; apparently a guard had managed to get himself killed, and there had been considerable fire damage to the security fence and a watchtower. Stone was relieved to note that none of this was ascribed to Richard; it had been a fault in the electrified fence, apparently.

Then there was a word about Dr. Günter Gorvitch which explained why Stone had not been able to speak to him last night: namely that the man was now an inmate in his own institute! Stone shook his head in bewilderment. Was everybody going crazy?

According to Stone's bedside digital, it was 9:15. He got up, reeled for a moment and made a resolve about his drinking. Shaving, he got angry again: why the hell couldn't the world leave him alone to get on with his gradual disintegration?

Fifteen minutes later he stormed out of the house and took Richard's car. He had been driving it since the accident. A few more minutes saw him on his way to Oxfordshire and PSISAC . . .

Stone had told Craig he would be there between two and 2:30. Well, so he'd be early. He wound down his window and drank in the damp morning air. November in a day or two . . . God, the world looked bleak! It was—how long?—since he had called at PSISAC. How long since he'd done anything worthwhile? Maybe Jimmy Craig had done him a favor, getting him worked like that. Something inside him, something that had not stirred for many a year, told him it was time he got a grip on himself. His life really had started to roll downhill, and he had simply been rolling with it.

Grief? Yes, he'd had that . . . But disinterest? Old age creeping on? The hell with that! Things had happened, were happening even now, and so far he'd ignored them. What was wrong with him? Where was his old curiosity?

He put his foot down and the car leaped forward, eating up the miles . . .

Whatever the source of Stone's new urgency or vitality, he quickly discovered how much it had sharpened his perceptions. The minor road he used was well known to him, it had not changed in years—and yet now he discovered that indeed there had been changes, alterations. Subtle, but definite. He discovered, too, that he was on the wrong road! Well, not exactly the *wrong* road, but it would certainly take him a mile or two out of his way.

Cresting a rise in what was now little more than a country lane, Stone pulled the car over onto the grass verge, stopped the engine and got out. A stand of tall trees and a high stone wall sheltered him from a wind that gusted at the tops of the trees and tossed whirling dervishes of leaves about. He crouched against the wall, took out and lighted a cigarette.

Then he rested his elbows on the wall, drew deeply on his cigarette, gazed across the fields. Over there—just . . . *there*—that was where Gareth Wyatt had lived. Wyatt? Stone raised his eyebrows. What the hell . . . ?

Was that why he had come this way today, because suddenly he'd remembered Wyatt? At least twenty years had gone by since that name had last crossed his mind, so why should he remember it now? Something to do with one of his cases when he was with MI6, before he and Vicki got married? Probably—but what had prodded it to the surface of his memory?

The scene beyond the wall was of a shallow valley with a brook, a sprawling copse, and a fenced off property of seven or eight acres. There was a road running parallel with the brook. From the road, a drive led past a tiny dilapidated gatehouse into weed-grown gardens, terminating in front of a large, roughly rectangular area of ground naked of all except rank grasses and thistles. A house had stood there once, the home of Gareth Wyatt. It had never been proved, but at one time MI6 had believed that Wyatt had sheltered the Nazi Otto Krippner here . . .

Wyatt and Krippner. Already the importance of these names was receding, Stone's recollection of them fading. He shrugged, turned up the collar of his coat. His memory wasn't what it had used to be. Actually, there were a couple of years back there that he couldn't remember at all, or at best only very vaguely. His and Vicki's meeting and falling in love really must have been something: a whirlwind romance, it had whirled everything away including memory. Or at best the memories were blurred, as viewed through smoke . . .

Stone growled, stubbed out his cigarette, went back to the car.

Richard's car.

Not bad, but a young man's car, really. Stone had become far too sedate for this sort of thing. His style these days was big and quiet and comfortable. He smiled wryly. He had been going to get Richard one of those beamed-power models like Lynn Craig's, but—

"Maudlin old bastard!" Stone cursed himself

out loud, climbing into the car and starting up the engine. And: "You can't live in the past, Phillip, my boy. What's gone is gone. What's ahead is still to be. Live for that."

Later, as he got back onto a major road near Reading, he noticed another of those strange prefabricated buildings, as yet incomplete, set back from the road behind a hastily erected timber fence. Part of the fence had fallen, allowing Stone a mainly unrestricted view of the work in progress behind it. From what he could see, it seemed like the new building had been forsaken; around its windowless hulk, a team of men and machines hammered metal stakes into the earth, stretching coils of barbed wire between them and around a huge perimeter. The building itself would seem to have become nothing more than a sort of reception hall or entrance opening into the greater enclosure.

There was something about this construction and the activity in progress about it which chilled Stone in some indefinable way, striking him as obscene. He frowned, then jerked alert as the driver of the car behind gave him a blast on his horn, hastening him on.

Five minutes later it came to him what his feeling of revulsion had been: simply that he had subconsciously recognized the shape of the half-built prefab as being the same as the main building at Calm Lawns.

So they were putting up an asylum, fine—but what was this thing with the barbed wire? And come to think of it, that was what he had found different about the country road back in Sussex. In his mind's eye he pictured that road again: the woods it skirted, with new slip roads winding away into foreboding copses where brand new notices proclaimed that this was "Private Property" or "Government Property." And half-glimpsed through the cover of nearly naked trees, those gaunt unfinished buildings and cheaply constructed enclosures . . .

Arriving at PSISAC just before 11:00 A.M., Stone's gloomy frame of mind was hardly improved by what he found going on there. He stopped at the main gate, leaned on his horn until one of the day-shift security men came scurrying from where a repair team was installing a new barrier across the entrance.

The man was stocky and red-haired, not too smart in his dress, a bit red in the face. It had not been a good morning and he was in no mood to take any sort of abuse from impatient visitors. He failed to recognize Stone, shouted "Hold your horses, chum! Where's the bloody fire? Can't you see we have a problem here?"

Stone got out of the car. Huge, he towered over the man, glared down at him. "What does the PS in PSISAC stand for?" he snapped. "And what in hell's going on here?" He stared at the road where splinters of red- and yellow-painted timber from the old barrier had been swept to one side. The barrier itself, in two lengths with splintered ends, lay on the pavement. The barrier's light metal housing pillars had been knocked out of skew.

The redhead winced. Now he recognized Stone, straightened himself up, touched the peak of his cap. "Sorry, sir," he said. "It's been one of those days."

"That doesn't excuse unnecessary belligerence, and it doesn't answer my question," Stone growled. "I own most of this place and I want to know what happened to my barrier."

The man's eyes grew round. "You don't know, sir? I mean—"

Stone sighed. "I wouldn't ask if I knew," he said.

"I'll get you the report, sir," the man turned toward the security control building.

"Hold it!" Stone grabbed his shoulder. "Can't you just *tell* me?" He couldn't believe the other's stupidity—or was it something else? Perhaps a natural reluctance? "Was it a delivery truck? A drunk driver?"

The other shook his head. "A car, sir. Lynn Craig's car."

Stone's eyebrows went up. His next question was more cautious. "Was she alone?"

"No, sir." The man turned his face away.

Stone nodded. "Get me the report—and get those people out of my way while you're about it! I'm going in."

Inside the complex, he drove straight to Craig's office on the perimeter of the Dome. Outside the office door another security man was alert, efficient. He carried a dart rifle, touched his hand to his cap as Stone approached. But as Stone went to open the door the man got in the way. He was broad-shouldered, blunt-featured; his eyes were narrow slits of ice in a scarred, hard face. "Sorry, sir, Mr. Craig's out."

"That's okay," said Stone, "I'll wait for him."

He reached for the door again, and again the man intruded—but this time his hand fell on Stone's arm. "Mr. Craig's orders . . . sir," he said, and his voice held a warning.

Stone looked at him for a moment in disbelief, looked at the man's hand where it lay on his arm. "You do know who I am?"

"Yes, sir, Mr. Stone. Yes, I do." The man's face was blank.

Stone nodded, stepped back a single pace. "Get out of my fucking way," he said, his voice a growl that seemed to come right through the wall of his throat.

The man moved, but not out of the way. Stone's training of so many years ago—his training and the deadly practical use he had so often made of it—stood him in good stead. Close quarter combat as taught by MI6—a sort of military martial art—had been Stone's special forte.

Even as the dart rifle swung toward him, he grabbed it by barrel and stock and jerked it down horizontally across his own belly, already tightened and prepared to receive it. This served to pull the security man toward him, bringing his face close. Without pause Stone butted him, simultaneously kneeing him in the groin. The man gagged and spat teeth, let go of the rifle and tried to both straighten up and fold up at the same time. He was beginning to curl as Stone jerked the body of the rifle up into his throat, just hard enough to finish the job without killing him. The man's head jerked back and struck a doorpost, but his eyes had already glazed over.

Before the man could topple, Stone grabbed an arm, bent at the knees, drew him across his shoulders. He opened Craig's office door and went in, kicked the door shut behind him, straightened up and let the guard fall. The man hit the hard floor like a sack of nuts and bolts. Still carrying the rifle, Stone crossed to Craig's huge desk, phoned First Aid.

When he got an answer he glanced once at the pretty female face on the screen and said, "Miss, do *you* know me?"

"Yes, Mr. Stone. Good morning, sir!"

Stone smiled, feigned delighted surprise. "Good morning to you," he said. "Civilization at last!"

"Sir?"

"Young lady, I'm in Mr. Craig's office. There's a man here who used to work for PSISAC." He looked across the floor, read the guard's name from a tag over his left breast pocket. "Conti, worked for Security."

"Oh, yes, of course," the girl said, looking puzzled. "But surely Mr. Conti is still with Security, sir?"

"No," Stone shook his head, "he just retired. Send a couple of men round here with a stretcher, will you? He's had an accident."

"Yes, sir. At once, sir!" she was gone.

Stone phoned Pay Office, told them: "Conti, from Security—he's finished here. Give him three months' pay and strike him from the payroll." Then he sat on Craig's desk and read the gate guard's report.

Just before 6:00 A.M. Lynn Craig's car had approached the gate from inside the complex. The barrier had of course been down. The man in the control room was one Geoff Bellamy. He was young and under instruction, but his supervisor-instructor was answering the calls of nature. Normally the barrier would have been lifted at once, as soon as Miss Craig's car was recognized, but for some reason Bellamy had delayed lifting the barrier and gone out to the car instead. Bellamy had later been unable to explain his reason for this course of action.

Approaching the car he had seen a person crouching in the front passenger seat. As soon as this person knew he had been seen, he spoke to Miss Craig and she backed the car away maybe twenty or twenty-five yards. Then she had charged the barrier.

Bellamy had been forced to leap out of the way; the car had crashed the barrier and driven off; Bellamy had reported the matter to his supervisor.

As for the couple in the car: the girl was definitely Lynn Craig. She seemed to have some bruises and was wearing dark spectacles. The man had looked in no better condition; other than that, his description fitted Richard Stone perfectly.

Stone scanned the report again, put it down and looked out of Craig's office window. A gang of laborers dressed in overalls and heavy industrial gauntlets were rolling huge coils of barbed wire toward the perimeter of the complex. Stone stared, frowned, scratched his chin. More barbed wire? Here at PSISAC?

There was a knock at the door and a pair of medics came in with a stretcher. "He fell over," Stone told them as they loaded Conti onto their stretcher. The unconscious man was groaning, showing signs of coming to. "After you've patched him up, take him to Pay Office. They have something for him. Then get him the hell off the complex. And you can tell Security from me that I don't want him back!"

When they had gone he toyed with one of Craig's desk pens and idly glanced around the office. Again those feelings stirred in him, feelings from long ago. He had started to note odd details (of which there seemed to be a surfeit around here!) and add things up. The picture didn't amount to much as yet, didn't even make sense, but something was beginning to take shape . . .

Stone shook his head, wondered what had got

into him. He had known and trusted Jimmy Craig for twenty years, knew him *that* well. Why, Craig's daughter and his son had been crazy about each other!

Crazy, yes . . . Stone snorted his frustration.

But the guard, Conti . . . why?

Stone glanced at his watch: 11:15. Should he walk around the complex, talk to people, ask questions? Or might he be better employed seeking his answers right here? Conti must have been guarding something.

Craig's great desk was of metal, had three drawers at each side. On the left they were empty. On the right the top drawer was open, the other two locked. Stone stuck his hand into the top drawer palm-up. The keys were there, stuck to the top with a small magnet. It was an old trick.

He unlocked the middle drawer: empty.

The bottom drawer contained files. Board meetings, inspection reports, efficiency statements, executive personnel, discipline . . .

Discipline? Stone looked at that one again. The title was scrawled on the cover in biro, in Craig's bad handwriting. It looked more like "Disciples." Stone opened it, expecting to find discipline reports. There was a single sheet of paper inside listing twelve names, with dates alongside each name. Stone checked the dates. Only twelve cases of ill discipline in three years? In a place this big? That was damn good!

He looked at the names, saw that Conti's was one of them. Stone could understand that. But Bragg? Stone knew Bragg, was well aware that the man was a go-getter—also that he stood tall in Jimmy Craig's esteem. He thought about it and frowned, then shrugged. If he wasn't careful this frown of his was likely to become a permanent feature!

He glanced again at the list. The last name was dated only yesterday. Andrew McClaren. But the name had been lined out. Some minor discourtesy which Craig had doubtless had second thoughts about. Stone shrugged again, put down the file and picked up another. This one said "Mind-plague." He opened it.

Names and dates again, about ninety of them . . . Stone's flesh crawled. Ninety gibberers? In how long? Four years. But that was something a little short of two percent of the entire workforce. That was pretty bad. Stone hadn't realized that things were nearly that bad. He wondered if it was representative of the country as a whole. Couldn't be, surely?

Couldn't it? The Gibbering had taken two of his, hadn't it? And some of the things that had happened since then . . . maybe Stone himself was going mad!

Another file said "Government Communiqués." Inside were letters—all of them stamped "Restricted: Managing Director's Eyes only"—from the Ministry of Health, the Home Office, Medcen, and . . . the Ministry of Mental Health and Care Coordination? Stone had never even heard of that one! He began to read the letters ("communiqués") and as the minutes passed his face grew stonier and his frown ever deeper.

It still didn't make a lot of sense, but this was part of it, he knew. And whatever it was, it was big.

And it was nightmarish . . .

At 12:30 J. C. Craig appeared. He came in through the door like a whirlwind. Stone was in his chair,

his feet up on the desk, hands clasped behind his
head. He appeared to be sleeping but jerked
awake as Craig entered.

Craig's face was white; he was furious. "Phillip,
that man Conti. I ordered him to stay here and
let no one into my office while I was away. He—"

"—Was bloody rude, obstructive, threatening!"
Stone cut in. "I don't let people point guns at me,
not even tranquilizer guns. Not him, you, nobody!
So he no longer works here."

Craig bit his lip, came over to the desk. Stone
sat up, put his feet on the floor. The desk was just
the way he had found it when he entered: all of
the files were back in their places, the drawers
locked, the keys in their secret place.

"Conti is a trusted employee," Craig began
again.

"Was!" said Stone. He was tempted to add: *and
if he's so trusted why is he in your disciplinary
file?*—but that would be to give too much away.

"I personally found him very trustworthy,"
Craig ranted, "and now his shift foreman tells me
that Conti intends to take legal action—against
you!"

Stone shrugged. "In that case I'll stop his sev-
erance money."

"You can't go round striking employees!" Craig
burst out.

"And I won't have employees threatening me!"
Stone shouted back, coming to his feet. "That guy
was dangerous. He had thug written all over him.
What the hell's got into you, Jimmy?"

Stone had hit a raw nerve there and he saw it
at once. Craig immediately went on the defensive. "Got into me?" he blurted. "I don't know
what you mean! And in any case—"

"In any case, that's not what I'm here for,"

Stone held up his hands, cooling things down. "Look, Jimmy," he continued in a calmer tone, "we've both had bad mornings, that much is obvious. Me, I've had a couple of bad years! A lot of things have gone wrong—they're still going wrong—but we'll get nowhere shouting at each other. Okay, I'll tell you about Conti.

"He wouldn't let me in here. I mean, who am I? I only *own* the fucking place, that's all! So I spoke to him a bit sharply and he started to point his rifle at me. I find that quite incredible! I mean, who did the idiot think he was?—and what kind of orders did he have that he should—"

It was Craig's turn to cut in: "But you don't see what—"

"I saw enough!"

They stood and glared at each other for long moments, then Craig's shoulders slumped a little and he said, "Okay, let it be. I agree, he was over the top. Anyway, there are more important things."

Stone nodded. "That's what I'm here for, so that you can tell me about them."

Craig controlled his breathing for a second or two, got a firmer grip of himself. Finally he said: "Look, I know it's not your fault, but there is something you might be able to help with. You know what I'm talking about."

"Yes, I do," Stone nodded again, "but I still don't see what I can do."

"Let's go up into the Dome," Craig suggested, "have a drink, talk about it."

"That sounds good," Stone agreed. Perhaps there were other things Craig would eventually get around to telling him, once he had the big one off his chest.

Craig led the way out of his office and through

a boardroom where he locked an interior door. They passed through the garage area of the Dome to the elevator. As they went Craig explained: "My nerves are walking a tightrope. I'm just back from Oxford, the police."

"About this morning?" Stone asked.

Craig looked at him. "This morning and last night," he said pointedly.

Stone refused to rise to the bait. "You had to go and see them?" he said. "I'd have thought they'd come here?"

Craig looked uncomfortable. "No," he shook his head, "they were too busy. They have a lot of cases on."

Yes, Stone silently agreed, *nut cases! Last night's crop of gibberers . . .*

"I thought crime was on the decline?" he said out loud.

"Eh? Oh, so it is—but they get their bad periods the same as anyone else." He did not mention The Gibbering.

They left the elevator and went through into Lynn's rooms. Here Craig became agitated again. He took out a crumpled piece of paper from his pocket, handed it to Stone. They stood together in the middle of Lynn's living room while Stone read it out aloud:

"Dear Dad—

"I have to go away for a while. I don't know how long. But I won't lie to you, I'm going with Richard Stone. He thinks he can find an answer to the mind-plague. I think he can, too. Don't let the state of my bedroom worry you—we slept a little later than I planned and I don't have time to tidy up.

I'm sorry about this, Dad, but I love Richard very much . . .

"I love you, too—

Lynn."

Stone looked up.

Craig was on the verge of tears. "I could have stopped it last night," he groaned. "Your boy must have come in with Lynn, in her car. Someone in Security will pay for this! But . . . I was busy. When I got in there was a note. She'd had a big day; she was tired; would I please not disturb her. I thought it was a bit funny, but I'd had my own problems. Then, this morning—this . . ."

He led the way to Lynn's bedroom, continuing, "Don't touch anything. The police will be round later."

The bedroom itself seemed pretty much undisturbed, but the bed was a shambles. Stone stood over it, looked down. There was a little blood on both pillows, one of which had burst at the seam. More blood marked the sheets, which were badly torn. And there were other, lighter stains everywhere. Craig pointed an unsteady finger:

"You know what *that* is?" he almost sobbed. "*I* know what it is—and I still can't credit it! Your son must have balls like a bull!"

"Jimmy," Stone took his arm, "you must have known they were lovers? I mean, you know . . . before?"

"Before?" Craig snatched his arm free. "You mean before they took the crazy bastard away? No, I didn't know, and I don't want to know now. How did the idiot break loose, that's what I want to know? And why did he have to come back here?"

Stone went white and his eyes grew hot. If anyone else—anyone in the world—had spoken to him like that . . .

"That's my son you're talking about, Jimmy," he said.

"And it's my daughter!" the other cried.

Stone gritted his teeth, tried to placate him. "Look, she'll be okay, I'm sure."

"Oh, yes? Is that so?" Craig stamped out of the room. His voice came back to Stone: "She'll be okay, safe? Man, it's not just some daft young lad we're talking about. Richard is a bloody gibberer! How can you say she'll be safe?"

Stone clenched his fists, looked again at the bed. Then he followed Craig to his study.

Craig had never been a heavy drinker and he had stopped drinking altogether many years ago, but now he poured himself a stiff drink and offered Stone one. They both collapsed into easy chairs.

"Yes, he's a gibberer," Stone agreed, "but he's still my son. I can't see him hurting her."

"You saw the bed."

"I saw it—and I've seen worse. Were you never young?"

"What?" the other half-laughed, half-sobbed. "Are you going to tell me my daughter was party to . . . to *that*? Yes, I was young—but I was never a raving bloody lunatic!"

Stone stood up slowly, his voice dangerous when he said: *"So why act like one now?"*

Craig shook his head, waved his arms, burst into tears. "You don't *understand!*" he sobbed. "Look, everything was going so well for so long. I thought Lynn had got him out of her system. Now this. And things haven't been easy for me here at PSISAC, on the contrary. So much to do, so many points to watch, things to arrange. And so little—" he checked himself, but Stone knew he had been about to say "time." So little time.

"You have to excuse me," Craig turned his face away, wiped his eyes. "I'm pretty much distraught."

"Hell, I can understand that," Stone answered. "I just hadn't realized that things were getting on top of you so much. Here at PSISAC, I mean."

Craig looked at him through red-rimmed eyes. "PSISAC? You only own the place. I *run* it! What would you know about it? You haven't been near the place in six months! There's a fortnightly board meeting, but you haven't put in an appearance since . . ."

"Since Vicki died?" Stone finished for him. "Yes, that's true. We've all had our problems, Jimmy." He sat down again, stared at Craig over steepled fingers.

"Jimmy, I read something in the morning paper about the main converter. An accident? Something about this bloke Belcher? Now what was all that about?"

Craig told him—told him also that he had now stationed security men in all sensitive areas. Then he stood up, straightened his shoulders, offered Stone his hand. "See?" he said. "And that's only one incident. Things haven't been easy. And this thing with your boy and Lynn, that was the last straw. That's all."

Stone deliberately ignored the other's hand, pretended he hadn't seen it, looked away. "Maybe you could use a week or two off," he said. "There's nothing here I can't look after for a couple of weeks—until you're your old self again. What do you say?" He watched the other's face.

The change was immediate. Craig tried to appear relaxed, poured more drinks, said, "Now that really would be going to extremes! Hey, there's nothing wrong with me! I've just been working off steam, that's all. And anyway, I'm sure everything will run smoothly from here on."

Stone pretended to think about it. "Maybe," he said, grudgingly, "but—"

Craig forced a smile, slapped him on the shoulder, said: "Look, Phil, I'm sorry. I mean, you're quite right, I've been letting things get me down. Well, that's over now. And anyway I didn't ask you up here to moan on about PSISAC—this place is my life, you know that! But there is one thing you can do for me."

"You only have to ask," Stone grunted.

"Your boy, Richard—he has money of his own?"

"He had, but no longer. I transferred his money to my account. It was no good to him in there. He agreed to it one visiting day, signed the papers. Why do you ask?"

Craig let his breath out in a sigh, smiled relievedly. "Lynn has some money," he said. "Not a lot. She never needed it. He can't run far on what's in her account. I just want your word that you won't help him, that's all."

Help *him*? Or did Craig mean help them? It seemed to Stone they were in it together. He looked at the other, tried to read behind his eyes. He had thought he knew this man but now wasn't nearly so sure. "Help him? Of course not," he said. *But you'd have him shot on sight, wouldn't you!*

Again Craig showed his relief. "Of course you wouldn't. I mean, the sooner they catch him the better," he said. "And anyway, they've legislated now. It's against the law to harbor or assist gibberers . . ."

"Yes, I know," Stone nodded, never taking his

eyes off the other's face. Then: "Hey, listen, I have to go. I have things to do in Oxford—a few things to buy. But is there anything else you want to tell me before I go? Any problems? Anything at all that I should know about?" He stood up, acted casual.

Craig pretended to think about it for a moment, said, "Nothing I can't handle. No, nothing at all, really. Anyway, let's hope this all gets cleared up quickly, eh? Without any more fuss and bother."

Stone nodded. "Yes, let's hope so."

Craig saw him down to the car, sat in it with him to the main gate. There he got out, shook hands with Stone through the window, waved him out through the makeshift barrier. On the other side Stone wiped his hand down his trouser leg. It had felt like shaking hands with a snake!

Driving away he glanced in his rearview—then looked again.

The man Conti was in the control room, stared out of a window after him. He was still in uniform, and he had a dart rifle in his hands . . .

Stone did not drive into Oxford but at once returned home. He was awake now—for the first time in longer than he cared to remember, really awake—and his awareness of the world about him was as near total as it could be for any one man. He counted five barbed wire enclosures or compounds on his route back to Sussex (two of them complete with skeletal watchtowers!) and saw more ambulances and police vehicles on the road than he could ever remember seeing before. He was obliged to slow down and crawl around the scenes of two serious traffic accidents, on what seemed to him perfectly safe stretches of road; in Woking a man ran through heavy traffic directly in front of Stone's car, crossed the pavement and bounded screaming headlong through a plate glass window; just outside Guildford a woman danced in glee in front of her blazing house, fought off her neighbors and worshiped the roaring flames . . .

. . . It was a relief to get home.

But even there Stone was not allowed a moment's relaxation. Entering his study he saw that the indicator light on his Ansaphone was winking; when he lifted the phone from its cradle he was electrified to discover his son's voice—and saner than it had sounded for a long time—with this message for him:

"Dad, by now you'll know I'm out. And you might know that Lynn Craig is with me. But we have a problem. We have no money, or very little. There are places I have to go and things I must do—but I can't go anywhere or do anything without cash. So . . . I'm relying on you. Listen, and I'll try to explain something of what it's all about— which will be difficult for I'm not even sure myself. And then I'll ask you to do something for me.

"First, The Gibbering. Everyone knows it's on the increase but no one knows how bad the problem is. Or if they do know, they've hushed it up. But *I* know because Dr. Gorvitch told me . . .

"I remember that in one of your old atlases there's a graph of world population from the 1600s to the present. The years go bottom to top, the population figures go from the center to the side. The thing is shaped like a great, overhanging mushroom. It was frightening in its time, but as we now know it didn't work out that way. The point I'm making is this: The Gibbering *is* working out that way, and it is much more frightening!

"Now this is the strange bit: I think I might be able to find the answer to it! The only thing is, I don't know how much time I have left to do it. Lynn will help me, and I think—I hope—you will, too. If you won't . . . then I'm sunk before I get started. But if you want to give it a try, this is what you do:

"I know you bank with the World Bank. That's fine, you can simply speak to any London branch. I'm in London now and I can get to any branch you care to name. Tell them to open an account for me in an alias I'll give you in a minute. Transfer in a lump sum from your own account, the bigger the better. That's all I'm asking . . .

" 'All!' I mean, I know it's a hell of a lot—but I also believe a hell of a lot swings on it. Anyway, Dad, I'll call you again about 2:30 and you can tell me which branch to go to for my banker's ID tag. Of course, you're supposed to report all this to the authorities, I know that, but . . .

"I mean, you *could* fix it for someone to be waiting for me. So . . . I suppose I just have to trust you.

"Oh, and obviously I don't want to use my own name, so you'll have to fix it for me to sign under a pseudonym, the alias I mentioned . . ."

Then he told Stone the alias he wanted to use and the call was over.

Stone checked the time, 2:05 P.M. He drank coffee and thought about it. Not that there was much to consider. Five minutes later he put through a call to the main branch of the World Bank in Cornhill Street in the city. Then, all done, he sat smoking for ten minutes until Richard's call came through. "Dad?"

"Yes, it's me, son." He glanced at the screen but it was simply a gray, meaningless swirl.

"Dad—" Richard's voice broke a little, "I don't want to stay on the phone too long. Did you—?"

"Yes," Stone also felt choked up, "of course I did. Go to World Bank Central in Cornhill Street. They're expecting you."

"Dad, I—"

"Save it, son. I know. And son—?"

"Yes?"

"Some of the things you said in your earlier call made a lot of sense. For one thing, you're dead right about The Gibbering. It's going wild. So maybe you're right about other things, too. However it goes, it strikes me you—we—don't have a lot to lose. So . . ."

"Dad?"

"Well, give it all you've got, son."

"Thanks, Dad." He sounded an awful long way away. Suddenly Stone wanted to delay his departure. "Richard, I want you to know . . . that . . ."

"Go on?"

"Nothing. But do yourself a big favor. However things go, stay out of Old Man Craig's hair. Things are going to get bad and I've a feeling he won't much care how he pays his debts—if you know what I mean. Also, take care of Lynn."

Richard snorted, just a little derisively. "That last's a tall order. Will you settle for this: we'll take care of each other?"

"It's a deal," Stone answered.

After that there didn't seem much more to say, but both of them hung on for a little while. When finally he put down his phone, Stone fancied Richard had done so, too . . .

All matters of finance, where they pertained to Phillip Stone, were routed through his accountant. This was automatic; the World Bank computer simply relayed the information onward. Each time he moved or used cash, each time he produced his banker's ID tag—whether he was buying a box of cigars or a street of houses—she, his accountant, got word of it. It had been that way for so long that Stone no longer even thought about it. But the fact of the matter was that this forgotten lady worked in the Pay Office at PSISAC, where Stone's account was just a mass of numbers in one of the company's computers. Or should have been . . .

When J. C. Craig answered his phone at 3:15 he got a face that was well known to him on his screen, and a tense female voice that told him: "You were right, sir. He's made arrangements to transfer half a million to a new account."

Craig took a sharp breath, leaned closer to the screen. "In whose name?" he snapped. "Richard Stone's?"

She drew back a little. "Hardly that, sir!"

Craig frowned, said, "No—no of course not. Whose, then? What's the lunatic calling himself?"

She bit her lip, looked uncomfortable.

"Well?"

"You won't like it, sir."

Craig was astonished. "Is the account in my daughter's name?" he made a guess. "No? Well, come on—*what does he call himself?*"

She gulped, blurted, "Garrison, sir. Richard Garrison!"

"*What?*" Craig half-stood up, eased down slowly again into his chair, stared at the screen wide-eyed. His fingertips were white on the top of his desk. That name . . . anathema!

But of course, what else would he call himself? Craig cursed under his breath, cursed himself for a fool that he hadn't guessed it immediately. It was so obvious!

At a time like this, out of the blue, spawned of madness and sent to defile, dismay and confuse—who else *but* Garrison? The antichrist himself, come to confront the one true prophet of the Lord in the last great battle—and come in the guise of Richard Stone, now Richard Garrison!

After long seconds, controlling himself as best he could, Craig finally said: "Thank you, Miss Ellis," and he carefully put the phone down . . .

Day Two

I T WAS THE EARLIEST PHILLIP STONE HAD BEEN OUT OF
bed in six months. His housekeeper brought
him coffee at 6:30, as he had ordered the night
before, and by 7:00 A.M. he was up and about. He
showered, ate a small breakfast, then retired to
his study and remained there, waiting. Mary,
dumpy and homely, reservedly concerned, looked
in on him once or twice without disturbing him,
brought him more coffee and was delighted to
note that he had not yet mixed himself anything
stronger.

While Stone waited, he sat in an easy chair and
contemplated a sheet of paper on which was
scrawled a list of three names and a single word:

Richard Garrison.
Gareth Wyatt.
Vicki Maler.
Blind.

The list was simply a visual aid for the use of
the rather special visitor he was expecting; Stone
hoped it would be the key to unlock a great mystery. A mystery or a Pandora's Box, one of the
two.

The reasoning, or lack of reasoning, behind the
list was . . . something Stone did not even want
to think about. It was the logic of lunacy. It was
his poor wife's logic in those awful moments before she died; his son's logic during that last
nightmare visit to Calm Lawns. Both of them had
said things which were quite insane, and yet the
things they had said were undeniably connected.

Moreover, and however impossibly, Miles Likeman during his impromptu visit had seemed
almost to corroborate most of Vicki's macabre—
ramblings? But here Stone shuddered and thrust
that part of it out of his mind. And even doing so,
he wondered: *what else has been shut out, or
driven out, of my head?*

What was it he had been trying to recall? What
were those niggling half-memories tugging so
desperately in the back of his mind, which just
refused to bring them together? Were they really
as important as he suspected? Or were they after
all only a new form—his own special manifestation—of The Gibbering? If so then there was no
hope for Stone and he must follow his two loved
ones into madness; along with the entire world,
if what he had read in that file in Craig's office
was anything to go by.

He thought about that file, about its contents—
and about the results of those contents as he had
seen them in action during his brief visit to the
complex yesterday morning. What most astounded
Stone about the file was that he had been kept in
total ignorance of it. He had not known it even

existed; but for his own natural curiosity, he would not know even now! It had been kept from him deliberately, and the more he thought about it the more certain he became of the reason.

As it happened his reasoning was faulty, if only through lack of information; but even so it was not wholly incorrect.

Stone had seen examples of a sort of militarism at the complex, and not alone in the ugly shape of Conti. How many more bully boys did Craig have protecting his interests, he wondered? Then there had been that gang of men with their coils of barbed wire. Quite unthinkable, under normal circumstances, for a gang of that size to be working on a Saturday morning—and the same might well be said of those workmen he had seen at the enclosure near Reading. But at PSISAC . . . what else could Craig be doing if not fortifying the place?—while there was still time and while he still held a measure of control.

As to why he did these things: the file had held the answer to that. It had explained a good many things, not the least of them being the rapid expansion of those prefabricated buildings and compounds. For those oh-so-secret "Government Communiqués" had all concerned themselves with one thing: the restriction of information, "in the Greater Public Interest."

The world was going mad and the authorities did not want the world to know it.

It made sense, in a terrifying sort of way. To broadcast this thing, to make it public knowledge, would result in widespread chaos, anarchy, universal horror. That would come anyway, but in its own time. Pointless, totally irresponsible and deadly dangerous to hasten the terror. It

must be contained as long as humanly possible—
then as long as inhumanly possible—and after
that . . .

As to why Craig should be involved, why he
should have been given access to this information, that was simple. For one thing he was a
trusted servant of the State; more important far,
he was the man who ran PSISAC. The Government
knew PSISAC's potential, knew that if even the
tiniest fraction of a percentage of PSISAC's energies had been channelled in a certain direction—
the collection and processing of mind-plague
data—then that Craig could easily have found out
the truth for himself. And what if he had chosen
to be noisy about it? No, better by far to have him
in on it and to use him, use PSISAC, to whatever
advantage remained.

Toward the end, of course, when things began
to speed up, PSISAC's facilities would be invaluable. Why, the computers would be able to figure
out the exact moment when the sane must begin
to slaughter the insane out of hand. Oh, yes, it
would come to that! There would be no other way.
Stone shuddered again. Those compounds would
be like . . . like slaughterhouses!

Meanwhile, of course, Craig was there to deflect
inquiries, to deny the use of his computers and
their data-gathering and -correlating facilities to
inquisitive outsiders. So that by the time the
world finally woke up to the terror, it would be all
over bar the shouting. Or rather, The Gibbering.
And of course the shooting.

Yes, it had a lunatic logic, Stone had to admit—
and yet there was something out of kilter somewhere. Something with his own reasoning. Just
what it was escaped him for the moment, but—

His thoughts were suddenly interrupted. It was

8:30 already and Stone's visitor was here, this most important visitor from Harley Street. Mary's voice and that of one other—a deep, powerful male voice—brought him to his feet as the door of his study opened. "Mr. Gill, sir," said Mary, ushering him in.

He was short, fat, dark and very hairy. He was also the top man in his field, which was that of remedial psychiatric hypnotism.

"Albert Gill?" Stone took Gill's warm, fat hand. "I'm Phillip Stone. How do you do?"

"I do very well," boomed the other, "though not as well as you, I fancy!"

Stone warmed to him at once, sat him down, offered him a drink. "Ah! Thank you, no, Mr. Stone. Under the influence, I'd never get you under the 'fluence, as it were. And I'd appreciate it if you didn't, either."

"I wasn't going to," said Stone. "Fact is, I've been doing too much of it just lately—not that that has anything to do with your being here."

"Good!" Gill smiled. "And if I might further hasten you, I'd like to get down to it right away. My reason for being here, I mean. After all, you're the only one who knows that reason, aren't you?"

"Well, yes—"

"—And therefore, if you don't mind, I'd like you to start by telling me all about it—er, without the assistance of hypnotism, I mean. At least at this stage."

Stone smiled wryly. "You don't waste any time, do you?"

"Time is money," said Gill, "a fact with which you're well acquainted, I'm sure."

"I'm paying for your time," Stone reminded him.

"8:30 on a Sunday morning? I'll say you are, sir! Maybe you'd like to tell me why?"

"Why now, you mean? Why I'm in such a hurry?" Stone shook his head. "No, I can't tell you that." *It might jeopardize my case!*

"Hmm! Well, then, you were going to tell me all about your reasons for wanting this scan done."

"Scan?"

"Yes—of your past."

Stone sighed. "I don't know *all* about it," he said. "But I can try to tell you something. At least I can tell you why I *think* it's necessary. It's really as simple as this: I *think* I've been brainwashed!"

Gill's expression, of total curiosity or absorption, changed not a flicker. "When?" he asked.

Stone became cautious. "About . . . twenty years ago."

"Are you telling me or asking me?"

"Twenty years ago—if it happened at all."

Gill stared at him, tugged at a pouting lower lip, said, "Explain."

Stone nodded. "I wasn't always well-off," he began. "I made a living where I could. For some time I was a member of MI6—that's when there was a need for such an organization. I was brainwashed by the Russians, later by the Chinese. On both occasions our boys sorted it out, filled in the blank spaces, straightened out the kinks. The point I'm making is that there *were* blank spaces and kinks, and I knew it. That is to say, until I was 'rehabilitated,' as they used to have it, I knew that something was wrong with me. There was partial amnesia, there were fuzzy areas in my mind, blank spots in my thinking. Dents had been put in my loyalty, and I had fears I never knew before and couldn't explain. In short, there was this general feeling that someone had been rum-

maging in my brain and had done a spot of house-
clearing. Yes, and that he'd left a little junk behind, too."

"Yes, yes," Gill nodded, "I see. And now you
have these feelings again. But after twenty years?
Isn't that strange?"

"Right," Stone agreed, "it's damn strange. The
way I see it—*if* I really was got at all those years
ago—is like this: whoever did it to me was a real
expert, top man. The job he did was so good that
I hadn't the slightest recollection of it. Recently,
however, I've become aware that there are certain misty areas in my memory. Nothing much,
and nothing I would previously worry about."

"So why are you worried now?"

"Ah!" Stone answered. "Well, that's another
area I'm not willing to go into."

"That makes two areas you won't go into," Gill
slapped his knees. "Which in turn means I'm not
sure I can continue with your case."

"Then you don't get paid," Stone was blunt and
straight to the point.

"Good argument!" Gill beamed. "Very well, go
on."

Stone shrugged. "That's it. Now I want you to
hypnotize me and see if I really was got at. If so,
I want you to put back what was taken out, untie
the knots, do a bit of spring cleaning."

"I might not be able to."

"I want you to try."

"And am I to work without a single clue?"

"Ah!" Stone said again. "Here I *can* help." He
handed Gill his list.

After glancing at it for a moment, Gill said:
"And where would you suggest I start?"

"Maybe twenty-one, twenty-two years ago? And
come forward from there. Like I said, I was with

MI6. I did some minder jobs in London, one in Paris. I remember those clearly. Start there."

Gill thought about it for a moment, said, "Very well." He stood up. "I left my things in the hall."

"Do you need a hand?" Stone asked him. They went to the door together.

"No, no. I travel light and I work the same way." He stepped out into the hall and picked up a tape recorder and a briefcase, returned to the study. While he prepared the tape recorder he talked:

"You know, Mr. Stone, you really do interest me. I mean, money isn't everything. If I wasn't interested I really would refuse your case. It wouldn't be the first time."

"So what makes me so fascinating?"

"Simple! If what you say of your past is true—and of course I have no reason to doubt it—then your mind has been a veritable playpen for all sorts of unpleasant people. It will be quite fascinating, even enlightening, to see what they scrawled on the walls, as it were."

Stone wondered if his first appraisal of Gill hadn't been off a little. "Morbid curiosity?" he said.

"Yes," Gill agreed, "decidedly. But you see, the more I learn from treating you, the more use I'll be to the next poor fellow who needs me! When it comes to the human mind, Mr. Stone, we will never know enough. I merely seek to improve myself, that is all. And perhaps man's knowledge in general."

He opened his briefcase, took out a small, dish-shaped mirror on a tripod which he stood on Stone's desk. Finally he produced a hypodermic syringe. "Where are you most comfortable?" he asked.

"Right here in this chair," Stone answered, seating himself.

"Fine!" Gill aligned the tripod, adjusted the angle of its legs, peered owlishly along a sight. "There!" he finally said, switching the thing on. The mirror began to throw out concentric circles of pulsing purple light.

Stone blinked, shielded his eyes for a moment, then relaxed and stared into the heart of the display. It was not at all unpleasant; its repetition was rather soporific, really. Which was exactly as it should be. Gill took his pulse, made adjustments to the device; it now kept time with Stone's heartbeat.

"After a while," the hypnotist explained, his voice suddenly a lot deeper, "—using just this device and my own voice—I'll be able to speed you up or slow you down just as I wish. What do you think of that, eh?"

Stone nodded. "And the needle?"

"Saves us a lot of hard work. Oil on the turbulent waters of your mind, as it were. Do you have any allergies?"

"No."

"Excellent!" Gill's voice was a deep, slow drone now. "Roll up your sleeve, Mr. Stone. Fine!" He stood over Stone, smiled. "Now just relax. This will only take a moment. There! And you didn't . . . even feel . . . that . . . did . . . you?"

Stone tried to answer, thought he made it, couldn't be sure. After a while he said: "Where am I?"

"Nowhere!" he heard Gill's deep, dark voice answer him. "You're just drifting. Drifting back, back, back. Don't worry, we'll soon be there."

Drifting.

Down a long misty tunnel lit with purple bands

of nebulous light. Floating with the current. Back, back, back . . .

"Soon be there," said Stone to no one in particular, and the tunnel echoed him:

"Soon be there . . . soon be there . . . soon be there there there *there there* . . ."

Then everything went dark.

After going to the World Bank, Richard and Lynn had ditched the car, bought themselves some new clothes and returned to their central London hotel. The car had been a dead giveaway and Richard had worried about it; he had known that by now the police must be looking for it.

A little hasty cosmetic work on their faces (Lynn's fancy dark-lensed spectacles helped her a lot) had more or less disguised the ravages of the night before; the raw red bites on Richard's neck had disappeared under dressings and the collar of his new polo-neck, Lynn's black eye was hidden, her bruises buried under powder and paint.

With the onset of evening, while he felt vastly improved over the previous day, still Richard had been very wan and tired. For all that their day had been successful, both of them were edgy and a little hag-ridden.

After a meal taken in their rooms they had read newspapers, watched 3-D TV, paid special attention to all news items. In a way it had been a little disappointing to discover only one small newspaper item relating to Richard's escape, but that single report had contained several disturbing hints—of a fire, damage to property, the death of a guard—all of which were quite bewildering to Richard, who remembered no slightest detail of them.

Other than that, however, there was nothing; in the main the world seemed to have forgotten Richard's escape in a welter of far more serious troubles, most of which seemed to have their roots in the mind-plague. Nowhere could they find mention of what Lynn had felt certain would be reported as her "kidnapping." That was the way her father would have seen and reported it, she was sure—and that despite her note to the contrary. But . . . nothing. Well, that was all to the good.

As the night drew on, with no definite plan in mind or clue as to what tomorrow would bring, they had tried to relax. Despite her own anxieties, Lynn had not pressed Richard for answers to her many questions; she had known he did not have the answers. Instead she had tried to keep him calm, hugging him now and then and generally reassuring him. And with every passing moment she was aware that she sat on a time bomb, knew that sooner or later he would—or could—explode again into madness. He knew it, too . . .

They had not made love.

In the old days Lynn would have been just as aggressive as Richard, but after last night she knew she could use her sex as a weapon against the demon inside him. She had therefore been relieved when finally he stretched himself out on his bed, smoked a last cigarette and fell asleep before the crumpled butt was cold. Not that she would have refused him; rather that she thought it best to conserve her own sexual energies against a great future need.

When she had known he was soundly asleep, then she too had undressed and got into her bed. And there she had lain in the darkness, listening to him tossing and turning in the night, mumbling words she couldn't quite make out. It would have been very easy for her then to get up, go downstairs and call for the police.

Physically easy, emotionally . . . impossible.

But finally Richard lay quietly, his breathing deep and even, and then too Lynn had fallen asleep. She had been surprised, just before she drifted off, how very easy it was . . .

That had been last night, the end of Day One of their time together.

Coming awake, Lynn saw the dim light of a new day entering their room, saw too that Richard was already up. "Morning," he said, yawning. "It's nearly nine o'clock. Breakfast is on its way, and we've a long way to go."

Confused at first, she repeated him: "Go?" Then she sat up. "Go where?"

"You'll see. Come on, up you get. Time is wasting."

In the bathroom she threw cold water on her face, cleaned her teeth, glared at her black eye. The color had come out in all its overripe ugliness. Richard caught her looking at it and came into the bathroom.

"You should see my back," he said consolingly. "It's formed scabs! I look like I've been whipped." They faced each other for a moment, both of them frowning—and then she was in his arms. The clouds—of sleep, worry, uncertainty—seemed to lift a little.

"It wasn't exactly how I would have had you make love to me," she said.

"No," he wryly agreed. "We'll have to stop mating like that!"

She laughed—it felt like her first real laugh in years—and hugged him again. This was the old

Richard, the one she had loved so very much. Suddenly she was ashamed that last night she could even have considered giving him up.

When the knock came on their door a moment later, and a muffled voice announcing, "Breakfast!" Lynn automatically moved to answer it. Richard caught her elbow, handed her dark spectacles to her.

"Ihre Sonnenbrille, mein Schatz!"

And later, while they made the most of a very substantial meal, she asked: *"Sonnenbrille?* Why have you gone all German?"

He continued eating, but a frown had settled itself on his face. "I told you about my weird dreams?"

"A little."

"Well, last night I dreamed again. I remember very little of what it was about, except that it was very special."

"Special?"

"Yes. See, ordinary dreams are just so much mish-mash, the junk information your mind tucks away in the hope it will find a use for it later. Also, you get a lot of your emotions and anxieties thrown in. All of which comes out in your dreams, tangled up and distorted and unreal. Later, when you're awake, you *know* it was unreal. Well, sometimes mine are real; and I know it just as surely. Oh, they're still tangled up, their meanings are hidden, but they do have meanings. Do you understand?"

"I'm trying to. You mean they're prophetic? You can see the future in them?"

"Future, present, past—" he shrugged, "—I only know they're real." He grew impatient, with himself as much as with her. "Just take my word for it, okay? Anyway, last night I dreamed about a dog, a car, and mountains—and a stone arch over a gateway. And all of these were pretty strong symbols, I can tell you."

She waited but he appeared to be through. "The car is easy," she shrugged, sipping her coffee. "We dumped it yesterday."

He shook his head. "This car was a big Mercedes, silver. One of the old models, maybe 1990."

"Oh. And the mountains?"

"There were pines, little villages with chalet houses and wooden-beamed hotels, overhanging roofs, creaking signs displaying jugs of beer and beaming, round-faced drinkers. And there were ski slopes."

"You recognized all of this?"

"No, I've often been in Germany with the old folks—but never in the Harz."

"The Harz Mountains?" She finished eating, drank down her coffee. "How do you know that? It could have been . . . the Swiss Alps!"

His frown grew deeper. "Yes, oddly enough it just could have been Switzerland . . ." He paused between mouthfuls of eggs. "But . . . it wasn't." The frown lifted. "It was the Harz. I just know it. My mother always used to say how much she loved the Harz. Strange, because we never got to go there together . . ."

"All right," said Lynn, "it was the Harz. What about the dog?"

"Bitch, really. A Doberman pinscher. Black. Beautiful creature."

"I always thought you didn't like dogs?"

"Who said I liked 'em?"

"Well you seem to have liked this one!"

He looked at her curiously. "Funny that, isn't it?"

Lynn had the picture now. "Okay—car, mountains, dog—all German. I see, I think!"

"Right," he said. "Hence *Sonnenbrille*: I was just catching up with my Kraut, that's all. I used to be good at it in school."

"You haven't mentioned the archway."

"No, I was leaving that till last. It was just an archway, in stone, set back from the road. There was a name on it but . . . I have difficulty with names in dreams. I can never seem to see them. Anyway, ivy had crept across the face of the arch and obscured it. A pity, because it's really that name that interests me. I have to know what it was . . ."

"And so we're going to Germany?"

"*Natürlich!*"

"Naturally?" Suddenly Lynn's voice was a little too high; she was anxious and it showed on her face, in the roundness of her eyes. "Richard, sooner or later they're going to catch up with us, or you'll give yourself away, or—" He crushed her close. "That's why I'm trying to make light of it now," he said, his tone serious once more. "God, Lynn, my main concern isn't for me, not any longer! Not even for the world—though if I can keep it going I'll give it a try. No, it's for you—it's about hurting you!" He released her. "Anyway, they haven't caught up yet, and maybe they won't. Things are getting hot out there," he nodded toward the window. "The world has more on its mind right now than little old me. I have a feeling that if we can make it safely out of England, we'll be free to get on with it."

"Get on with—?"

"I have to track it down!" he said. "Whatever *it* is. Look, old Gorvitch at the asylum knew I was different. I know it, too. You know it, or you wouldn't be with me. So does—" (he almost said Phillip Stone, changed it to) "—my father. If he didn't I'd be in a straitjacket right now; he'd have had them trap me at the bank. Actually, he's a bit of a dark horse . . ."

"Oh? How do you mean?"

"When I spoke to him yesterday—I don't know—I sort of got this feeling he knows more about things than he's saying. There was something in his voice . . ." He paused, came back to the present:

"Anyway, I have to start somewhere, and that somewhere is the Harz."

She nodded and began to pack a suitcase brought with them from the Dome. He stopped her. "Lynn, you don't have to come with me. I'm not depending on it, you know."

"I know," she answered. "But if the world really is going to go bang, then I'd like to be with you when it does it."

He sighed, nodded. "Okay—but there may well be times when it's dangerous. When *I'm* dangerous. To you, I mean."

"Like the other night?" she lowered her eyebrows, tried to look stern. "I can't stand it."

"Maybe, and maybe not quite like that. I don't know."

"Then I'll just have to take my chances," she said, and he was satisfied.

While she finished packing their few belongings, he took a wire coat hanger from the wardrobe. It had been left behind by some previous guest: a cheap modern thing, formed of one length of fairly thick-gauge wire, the ends capped with small plastic balls. For no special reason, absentmindedly, he pulled the balls free, grunting a little with the exertion. The ends of the wire were sharply pointed.

He thought again about the potential violence bottled inside him, quiescent for the moment; thought of Lynn's vulnerability. And looking at the wire in his hand he had an idea. With a little effort he was able to bend the wire around the fingers of a clenched fist until the pointed ends stuck out like fangs. When he was through he had what looked like a very ugly knuckleduster.

"What on Earth—?" said Lynn when she saw what he had made.

"It's not what it looks like," he said, slipping it from his hand and tossing it into the suitcase, "It's a safety device. I'll explain later, or maybe demonstrate—but you'd better hope I don't have to!"

Ten minutes later they booked out of the hotel and took a taxi to Charing Cross, and within an hour they were on the Chunnel train heading for Calais . . .

10:30 A.M.

Phillip Stone gradually became aware that it was all over. Strange, because he had hardly been aware of it starting, and certainly he remembered nothing of it. If he had expected a flood of fresh memories, a sharpening of the focus of his mind's eye, then he was disappointed. There had not even been the snap of Gill's fingers to bring him out of it; merely the feeling that he had risen slowly from sleep and was only now fully awake.

He blinked his eyes, sat up in his chair, looked all about his study. Only the shadows on the walls, cast by a bleary sun's motion beyond bay windows, had changed.

Gill sat watching him, hands folded over his

rounded waistcoat, expression neutral. He had poured himself a liberal brandy, was smoking one of Stone's special slim panatellas. The tape recorder had been closed up; it stood with Gill's briefcase on the floor looking perfectly innocuous.

"Make yourself at home!" said Stone, pouring himself a cup of coffee from a freshly steaming jug where it stood on a small table close at hand. "What's mine is yours—including my unknown past, I hope?"

The other merely smiled, nodded. "I thought you might like a coffee . . . your housekeeper is most obliging." He sat up, leaned closer, peered into each of Stone's eyes in turn. "No ill effects?"

Stone fingered his neck. "Dry throat," he answered. "That seems to be all so far."

"Me too," said Gill. "All that talking, you see. Headache?"

"No," Stone shook his head.

"Congratulations!" said the other wryly. "It seems you have come out of it better than I!"

Stone lit a cigarette, drew deeply upon it and said, "Well?"

"Well?"

"Did you get anything?"

"A little," Gill put pills on his tongue, swilled them down with brandy, pulled a face. "It was—a fair session."

"So?" said Stone.

"Ah!" Gill stood up. "You expect me to tell you—"

"Look!" Stone was annoyed now. "No games, right?" He too stood up, towering over the fat man. Then he swayed a little, grabbed the chair for support.

"Careful!" Gill cautioned. "You may be dizzy for a moment or two. It will pass."

Stone sat down again. "What did you get?" he growled.

Gill sighed. "Mr. Stone, I fully appreciate that you're in a hurry. You've made that more than plain. But if you want the job done properly you'll just have to be patient. This was only the first session. It may take as many as six or seven!"

"What?" Stone protested. "When we spoke on the phone yesterday you said two or three."

"That was before I knew how complicated it would be."

"Complicated? Is it? How complicated?"

"Very! You were right about this much: your mind really has been played about with. Indeed, it's difficult to sort out the facts from the fiction!"

"Fiction?"

Gill chuckled. "Well, yes. That's about the only way I can describe it: fiction. Certainly there are things in your head that didn't happen. And perhaps—just perhaps, mind you—that's why you don't want to remember them: because you *know* they can't possibly be real!"

Stone was perplexed. "That doesn't sound like implanted information to me. Not if it isn't at least feasible . . ."

"Then what else could it be?"

Stone frowned, shrugged. "You're the expert."

"I would like to think so. We shall see."

His frustrations mounting, Stone demanded: "So when will you be able to tell me about it?"

"After the last session, of course."

"But if you've found something already, why can't you tell me about it?"

Gill sighed. "Right, I'll tell you what I've done. Not what I've discovered, only what I've done. Us-

ing one of the names on your list—that of Vicki
Maler, your late wife, I see—I've started to break
down your resistance. That is, I've started to get
at the things you either can't remember or have
been ordered to forget. But I've only just
scratched the surface, really. And your mind is
throwing all sorts of obstacles in my way: the 'fictions' I was talking about. Clear so far?"

"So far, yes."

"Well, if I now divulge to your conscious self
what small amount of information I've managed
to drag out of your subconscious self—"

"I might use it to change the picture?"

"Exactly! And that would only make it harder
for me. In short, I don't want you wondering
about it and perhaps jumping to wrong conclu-
sions which will only create more garbage for me
to sort through! You know, Mr. Stone, my sort of
work is easier to perform than to explain. But . . .
let me try a different approach:

"If I say to you, in connection with your wife,
'murder,' what does that conjure?"

Stone's mind whirled. Vicki? Murder? What the
hell—? Then he relaxed, grinned. His reactions
had been exactly what Gill was looking for: confusion! "No," he shook his head. "Vicki could
never have murdered anyone."

"Hold on, Mr. Stone—whoah!" Gill held up his
hands. "I said no such thing, made no such accusation."

Stone frowned. "But . . . who would ever have
wanted to murder her? I mean she—"

"I didn't say that either," Gill cut in. And more
quietly: "And I'm sorry I used such a blunt instrument to drive my point home . . ."

Stone slowly nodded.

"You see what I mean?" Gill said. "You see how

much the human mind can make of a single word? Oh, an emotive word, I admit—but just a word for all that."

Stone saw. "You've made your point," he growled. "If you tell me what's on that tape now, you'll probably have to start all over again tomorrow. I see."

He sat silently for a moment or two more, then glanced at Gill with a new expression on his face. "So why don't we speed things up? Why don't we carry straight on this afternoon? Look, have lunch here, and then—"

Gill laughed, but without malice. "No, no, *no!* That drug I used is all right in small, spaced-out doses, but—"

"I'll chance it!"

"Doubtless you would—but there are such things as ethics, Mr. Stone. And please don't sour the issue by offering me more money. It's my way or not at all." He picked up his briefcase and tape recorder.

Stone was not finished. "You said there were things in my mind that didn't happen. Fictions. But how can you be sure? Maybe they did happen, fantastic or not! Christ, if you only knew some of the fantastic things that have happened to me—and recently!"

Gill moved past him, out into the hall. Stone followed him, aggressive now. At the main door Gill turned, shaking his head. "Fictions," he insisted. "They did *not* happen, I assure you." He let himself out.

"But—"

"Same time tomorrow, Mr. Stone?" He got into his car, slammed the door, wound down the window. He started the engine.

Stone gave it one last shot: "What . . . what *sort* of fictions?"

"Really, Mr. Stone!" Gill chided. "Fantastic fictions, to use your own word—ridiculous fictions! Why, if I honestly thought they could be anything else, then I should hire a psychiatrist myself!"

At noon that Sunday James Christopher Craig called his disciples together and assembled them around the conference table in the boardroom beneath the Dome, and in all eleven of their minds one question was uppermost: what had prompted this unprecedented action? It was, after all, Sunday. Apart from a handful of converter techs, the usual Security shift and the gangs of men erecting barbed wire atop PSISAC's walls, the place was at a standstill. So what had prompted Craig to call them all in like this?

They did not have to wait long for an answer.

As soon as they were seated Craig went to his accustomed place and stood at the head of the table. For long moments he stood there, staring at each face in turn, before finally speaking:

"My friends—my disciples—the time draws closer and there is still work to be done. There have been certain . . . complications and there will probably be more; all such are sent to try us. In the coming week things will seem to continue much as normal here at PSISAC, but they will not be normal. This is PSISAC's final week as an industrial and manufacturing complex and power relay station; next Thursday we begin to shut down. Yes, only four days from now . . .

"On Thursday, when the rest of the workers go to their homes, you will remain here. This will be your place from that time onward. Over the weekend until Tuesday, Security will be double-staffed.

Each one of you will be responsible for his own section of security men. They will be armed with their usual anesthetic weapons; you yourselves will be . . . armed.

"Cases of mind-plague will occur ever more frequently, the computers have confirmed it. Until Thursday such cases will be dealt with in the prescribed manner. After Thursday, all victims will be put outside the walls. The only alternative would be to kill them, for by then the world outside this oasis will be in the first stages of turmoil and it is unlikely that we will be able to call on any of the usual services. The asylums will have been packed to capacity, even the compounds will be filling up.

"By Sunday, seven days from now, the authorities—whatever shall remain of them—will have ordered the extermination of all sufferers from mind-plague. It will be the only way; the few will no longer have the capacity to care for the many. Even here in PSISAC you will be safe only so long as you are vigilant. Even your squads of security men will be infected; you will shoot dead each man in his turn as he is taken!"

He looked at them where they sat riveted by his words. To all of them it was obvious that a change had taken place in Craig. A power seemed contained in him, in his eyes—but barely contained. He burned with the old fervor they knew so well, but its fire had now become a furnace that roared in him. They could doubt the truth of his words and the reasoning behind them, but not the sincerity with which they were spoken. Perhaps he saw their innermost feelings reflected in their eyes, for now he smiled a benign, understanding, almost fatherly smile.

"I know what you are thinking," he said, "and

yes it is monstrous. But it is also the Lord's decree. He has brought The Gibbering to lay waste to the world, to deny that is to deny Him! Ah!—possibly you are also wondering, how may so few overcome so many? I will tell you:

"There will be no concerted attack upon PSISAC: gibberers are gibberers, they have neither logic nor loyalties. Oh, there may well be small groups who band together in their mutual madness and threaten the walls, and some may even contrive to break through." He smiled sadly and shook his head. "Poor demented souls, we shall not fear them. All of PSISAC's surveillance devices shall be put to the task of discovering them; they shall be destroyed even as they attack us, eliminated even as they batter at our walls and doors. As for the walls themselves: they may not be climbed, the barbed wire barriers will be electrified . . .

"Wednesday week, ten days from now, the external world will be in complete and utter chaos! Men will kill men out of hand, by whatever means available. Gangs of lunatics will rape, mutilate, murder, loot, burn, destroy. All of men's works will go up in flames—the Lord's will be done! If any forces of law and order survive, these will turn mercilessly upon the madmen while they may, before they themselves go down in madness. And that will be the time when we must be most vigilant. By then PSISAC will have been recognized as a refuge, perhaps the only refuge.

"Special armaments will be mounted at the main gate, which will itself have been extensively fortified. *Nothing* shall be allowed to enter that gate! Your only orders will be the orders I myself issue—no police, no officials, no self-proclaimed 'authority' shall enter—any attempted forced en-

try will be met with destruction!" Craig paused
... and after a while continued in a lower but
more intense tone:

"However, and for all that this basic plan remains unchanged, there is now a complication.
On the one hand I blame myself that I did not
foresee it, but on the other I take it as a sign from
the Lord God Himself that indeed I walk in His
ways! For how better may I give you proof that
indeed I am his prophet, if not by this which has
come to pass?

"Oh, yea—for well I know that there are those
among you even now beset by doubts!" He glared
at them. "Even *now*, you doubt! Very well, perhaps one of your own may convince you." He
turned his burning gaze upon Dorothy Ellis. "Miss
Ellis? If you please . . ."

She stood up, self-conscious in a forward sort
of way and full of her own importance. Well she
might be, for of all of them gathered here she
alone knew for certain that Craig spoke the truth.
"Yes," she said, "I do have something to say. And
I confess that I have had my doubts . . . but no
longer." She took a deep breath. "You know
where I work and what I do. The source of my
information is the master accounts computer,
which is a machine and therefore cannot lie. It
can only be mistaken if its input is incorrect, and
here that is not the case." She paused, took another breath and said: "Garrison the antichrist is
real, he has come! His guise is that of Richard
Stone, son of the man who owns PSISAC!" The
other ten sat frozen and stared at her, then began
frowning and glancing at each other.

"Explain," said Craig. "Tell them what has happened."

She did. She told them about the World Bank,

and about Phillip Stone's transfer of a huge sum of money into his son's account in the alias of Richard Garrison. And she finished with: "Mr. Craig knew nothing of this until I told him. I only know it is true because I am Phillip Stone's accountant. I myself took the information from the computer. Any who doubt it can come and see for themselves. Garrison, in the guise of Richard Stone, has come among us!"

Craig waved her into her chair, banged his fist upon the table, pointed at them each in turn where they sat with their own thoughts. His pointing finger, his entire body trembled with his passion. "And how often have I spoken to you of this Garrison, this fallen angel? And is it not an unwritten, unspoken law that no man of that name or any name like it shall be employed here? Have I not singled out every man of that name in all the counties around and investigated them to their very roots? I have!—and did you think it was for nothing? It was *not* for nothing, but it was in vain. The one who has come against me is no stranger. He was and is known to me. And to my daughter!

"Yes, Richard Stone is the one, son of a man I once called friend. And he has come from the pit, come out of madness, to confound us in the very hour of our triumph." Craig moaned now, seeming to slump down into himself.

"The antichrist is here," he finally continued, "and has taken my daughter from me, whom I treasure more than life. My Lynn, hostage of the devil!" Craig was close to tears, his face white and working as he fought to control himself. But his burning eyes blazed through the pallor and the fervor that drove him bore him up, drawing him erect.

"How then may I be avenged?" he croaked when he was able. And then more strongly: "How may I *strike him* and regain my daughter? How may I even know his whereabouts from moment to moment? And remember that with each passing moment she not only suffers his torments but might also fall prey to the mind-plague! Am I simply to give her up? Is he to go free and come against us when he will? No!

"This is my plan:

"As you all know, PSISAC has performed certain favors for the present government of this land. This was to our advantage: they wished certain secrets kept and it suited us to keep them. Ah!—but now in return I have asked a small favor of my own, and it has been agreed. The World Bank has given PSISAC a permanent computer link to the account of one Richard Garrison!" he spat the words out. "Each time the antichrist uses that account I shall know of it at once. At those precise moments of time, I shall know his exact whereabouts—and through him I shall find and take back my daughter!

"For just as Garrison is an agent of Evil, I am the prophet of the Lord. And shall Evil triumph over Good? Never!

"However . . . I personally may not go forth for my work is here. Nor am I so foolish as to expect assistance from any rapidly disintegrating external authority. Police? They seek him, yes—but what would they do with him except protect him? He would live—live to escape again, perhaps, and to strike us, again and again and again! Well, he must not live but die, and the sooner the better . . .

"Who then am I to entrust with this great work of retribution, and who shall be rewarded when it is done?" He gazed about the table, his eyes misty-red with fire and unshed tears.

The first man on his feet was Bragg. "I'll go," he said.

Craig dabbed at his eyes. "Ever faithful," he nodded. "Yes, I knew you would be first."

Conti was next. Painfully he stood up, his broken face puffed and swollen and his eyes cold with hatred. "Stone's son?" his purple lips grunted through an oval of white dressing and tape. "Let him call himself what he likes. Any son of *that* pig's bastard is a dead man when I find him!"

"Good!" Craig's voice seemed to throb. "Excellent!" His eyes swept the table.

The Jackson twins from Assembly came to their feet next. They were awkward about it, grinning a little and glancing at each other shiftily.

"Yes," Craig nodded, "you two will do, I think . . ." He scanned the rest of the faces.

The flat-chested spinster, Miss Emma Tyler, was next and last to rise. If Craig was surprised he did not show it. "Good," he nodded his approval. "A mature woman has certain advantages, yes."

No one else moved but Craig seemed satisfied. The six who remained seated shuffled a little uncomfortably, holding their breath until he said: "Very well, five of you. You shall go forth at once, and—"

Bragg made a motion with his hand, attracted Craig's attention. "Sir, until we return only six will remain to see things through—and to protect you, of course."

"I have taken that into account," Craig answered. "But it's a good point and deserves an answer. Let me tell you my intentions. In the unlikely event that your mission has not been completed by the time PSISAC is to close down, then

I shall recruit others from the workforce here. There will be no lack of them."

Conti, still standing, said: "There were to have been only twelve of us."

"At the end," Craig answered, "there shall be only twelve. The Lord shall see to that. It is in His hands."

Conti stared at him cold-eyed. "Natural wastage'?" he growled.

Craig sighed and answered: "Mr. Conti, I know only this: the Lord has given me my disciples. He giveth and He taketh away . . ."

Conti nodded and asked no more, but Bragg said: "You mentioned a reward?"

"Indeed," Craig nodded. "To him who brings me my daughter unharmed and before she has suffered the embrace of The Gibbering, great rewards. He shall be a ruler in the land. And to him who rids me of this dark angel Garrison . . . he may ask of me what he will. And to all who set out upon this enterprise, my eternal gratitude. They shall not be forgotten when the world is ours, by the grace of God."

The five on their feet looked at each other, perhaps appraisingly, but made no comment.

"Very well," Craig said. "Go, make whatever preparations you will. But do not delay. Time wears thin. And remember—it's a foolish man who goes against the devil expecting easy victory. This Stone, this Garrison, this creature *is of the pit*! His breath is brimstone, his touch poison, his words lies. Give him no quarter—kill him before he kills you!"

"Where can we find him?" asked Conti. "Do you have any leads?"

"Miss Ellis?" said Craig.

"Yes, sir," she said. She stood up and turned to

the others. "He purchased railway tickets at Charing Cross this morning. The value of the tickets is a direct indication of his destination: Calais, France. You can start looking for him there."

As they left the boardroom Craig called after them, "One last thing: don't fail me. God is almighty—and I am his instrument!"

Suzy was, after all, only a dog; but since she was looking for someone there was a definite advantage in that. And canine instincts which had led her back home across half of forever were unlikely to fail her when it came down to a small globe no more than eight thousand miles right through.

In the moments before her actual materialization, of course, she was something more than a dog, but only in scope. Not in her loyalty and affection, nor even in her intelligence. Of her species she had been unique: she had traveled further, faster than any other dog in Creation—but she had not known it. She had known only that she was with her master, and that where he went, she went. She had been a dog lifted to the highest level of canine expectation and beyond it—a dog immortal, indestructible, a dog of the Psychosphere—but never aware of it beyond the certainty that until an END came, she would obey and love, and be companion to Him. Even END had been an uncertain concept. Remembering no beginning and never having been told of one, and in any case being without the equipment to accept such a fact, there had really been only NOW. And of course a promised tomorrow. And instinct.

And it was her instinct that told her that when she became a dog again—a dog and nothing more—then that she would have forsaken forever that Other place in which her master now dwelled. Which was why, before she took that final step, before at last she bounded irrevocably from an immundane to a merely mundane existence, she stopped one last time and looked back. And perhaps in that one fleeting moment of time, if Garrison had chosen to call her, if she had heard His voice calling across the numberless epochs and light-years and kalpas of the Psychosphere, perhaps she never would have returned to the world of men, where all life has a beginning and an end.

But she had heard no such call, only a lesser call from the very vaults of her being. The call of a man who was flesh of her master's flesh, and who now needed her more than He did.

At that point in time she had no physical attributes whatsoever, but she was still a dog. She whined questioningly into the Psychosphere, pricked up her ears and listened. She sniffed as only a dog can, putting aside the scents of stars and the odors of whirling galaxies, narrowing her field from the macro almost to the microcosmic. She sought blood of the blood she had known, the acrid odor—a certain odor—of sweat. There would be something in his walk, his talk. He would look . . . so!

She found him, fastened her focus upon him, read him: his past, his present, even a little of his future. She could go to him now—go to him directly—but . . . what if he should reject her? Unthinkable! Better if he came to her.

She would go then . . . to a place where he was yet to be, and soon he would come there and find her.

Suzy materialized on a street in Avesnes, outside a small *bistro*, not far off the main Calais-Luxembourg ten-laner. It was raining, 5:15 P.M., and a cat sat washing its paws beneath the restaurant's raised porch, having failed to note Suzy's arrival.

Suzy was delirious!

She knew now what she had missed without ever having known that she missed it. The *smells!*—the *feelings!*—the *rain!*—even the cat . . . She could see the Tom through the wooden treads of the two steps up to the porch. He was dry and she would soon be wet. Unless the situation changed.

She moved him out of there in a snarling and spitting rush and a mouthful of fur, glared after him and curled herself up in the place he had warmed for her, then lay vigilant, tongue lolling, gazing out into the street.

And she was satisfied. Her new master was on his way to her. She would not have long to wait . . .

The Jackson twins, Darren and Michael, were not among the brightest of J. C. Craig's disciples. Indeed they had barely the intelligence to hold down their jobs on the assembly line, which involved nothing more complicated than clipping viewing screens into their frames and fixing internal antennae. Almost immediately after the meeting and without concerning themselves with such problems as backup, contact and control, they had simply taken off for France.

They had gone in their own car, a beaten-up old Ford with more mileage on its clock than a PSISAC satellite, almost breaking down in the Chunnel and not getting into Calais until 4:30 P.M. They had put the car into a filling station cum auto repair shop just in time to see the place close down for the day; a new exhaust could not be fitted until the morning. Of course that would mean paying double, for work would not normally be considered on a Monday. But since they were English and in a hurry . . . with a little luck they should be on their way well before noon.

Then they had booked into a hotel, phoned PSISAC and got the latest on Richard Stone alias Garrison. He had paid big money to buy himself transport from a used-car lot only two hundred yards down the road from their hotel. Again they were out of luck: when they got there the place was closed, for of course it was Sunday. They did, however, find the proprietor's name, address and telephone number on a plate on the lot's locked iron gates, and when they got back to their hotel called him on the phone. Fortunately he spoke English.

Yes, M. Dupont told them, he had sold a car to their friend the Englishman Garrison, an old but very reliable metallic-silver Mercedes. Garrison, too, had called Dupont, making him an offer for the car that he could not refuse even on a Sunday. Dupont had personally gone down to his used-car lot and opened up; that had been, oh, maybe two and a half hours ago. Garrison had seemed a most reasonable young gentleman, and his young woman had been very attractive for all that she wore dark spectacles and looked a little pale. Perhaps the Jacksons were also desperately in need of a motorcar?

They had been tempted at that, and only sheer stupidity had stopped them from taking Dupont up on his offer. It had not yet dawned on them that inside a week money would be worthless, nor indeed that for the present PSISAC would foot any bills they cared to accrue. And so, with regret, they had turned Dupont down: but they did have sufficient brains between them to ask him if he knew where Garrison had been heading. Germany, Dupont had told them: he was going via Luxembourg and then heading for Kassel, ten-laners all the way.

And that had been that. The Jacksons had been stuck until morning. They had spent most of the evening and night in the bar of their hotel, as a result of which they were up later on the following morning than they had desired to be . . .

Emma Tyler and Donald Conti had played it somewhat differently. They had waited at PSISAC until Dorothy Ellis relayed to them word of Stone's car purchase. By then Craig had decided it would be better if the blowsy Miss Ellis stayed on at the complex as a permanent contact for his five field agents; which was as well, for by 6:30 P.M. there was more news of Stone. It appeared that he did not intend to use cash at all but was living and traveling solely on his banker's ID tag, which would of course make it far easier to keep track of him. This time he had used his tag to pay for a meal for two at a *bistro* in Avesnes.

Using a touring map of the Continent, the Tyler woman and Conti had come to the conclusion that Stone could only be heading down the main ten-laner for Luxembourg. They had telephoned through a booking for two single rooms at the Luxembourg Hilton, and using Tyler's car had started out together. That had been her suggestion, to which Conti had acceded after only a moment's thought. Why not? Perhaps it would be as well to work as a team. Later, if it didn't work out, he could always ditch her. He probably would anyway.

Taking turns in driving, they had made Luxembourg by 1:00 A.M. Monday morning . . .

* * *

Edward Bragg was the thinker. He had been with
Conti and Tyler when the computer coughed up
the cost of Stone's meal in Avesnes, but while
they were reading their map he was doing some
deep thinking. The result of which was that when
they took off he stayed on at PSISAC.

In fact he slept there (if "slept" is the right
word) with Dorothy Ellis, who had had a bed put
into her accounts office in Pay and Records. She
would doubtless be questioned about the bed
come Tuesday morning, when the rest of the General and Pay Office staff came in—and just as
surely there would be the usual lewd remarks—
but she would explain that there were special accounts she was working on for Mr. Craig. Past
Thursday when PSISAC closed down for the last
time, there would be no one to ask questions anyway.

Meanwhile it had seemed a shame to waste the
bed by merely sleeping in it, especially since
Bragg had intimated he might be interested in
her when all of this was over. And of Craig's mot-
ley gang of disciples, certainly Bragg was the
most appealing. To Dorothy Ellis, anyway.

Staying on at the complex had been a good
move on Bragg's part, and not alone for the sex
. . . though he wasn't complaining about that.
Maybe it was the tension in him—in both of
them—but their lovemaking had been especially
good. It had been good . . . and it had been interrupted.

By 00:30 A.M. Miss Ellis's adroit and practiced
hands and large-nippled breasts had teased an
erection in Bragg for the fourth time in as many
hours, which was good going considering that
between them they had consumed a liter bottle

of vodka. She had been on the point of lowering herself onto him when her personal computer *bleeped* for attention where it sat atop her large desk. Since she had linked it to the main accounts machine with instructions covering incoming information in respect of Richard Garrison's World Bank account only, that could mean only one thing: at half-past midnight, somewhere on the Continent, Stone was once again using his banker's ID tag.

Bragg's hard had wilted before she was off the bed, and by the time she had fixed the new information on Permanent Display he was into his trousers and looking over her naked shoulder. This was what he had been waiting for: triangulation of a sort. He would now know a) Stone's location—possibly for the rest of the night—or b) his temporary location en route to his destination. In the case of b), at least Bragg would be able to observe the trend.

And b) it appeared to be: Stone had bought— was buying—petrol at a filling station on the main ten-laner at Frizlar twenty-five miles from Kassel in West Germany. Bragg knew the Continent well, especially Germany where he had toured. He needed no map to tell him that if Stone were to keep going in a fairly straight line, he could be in Berlin in just four more hours. But no, for he had bought only fifteen liters of petrol.

So, was he just topping-up, or was he simply buying enough to see him safely into Kassel? Bragg didn't know Stone's habits; some men buy just sufficient fuel for their immediate needs. And then again Lynn Craig might be driving; they could well be sharing the effort between them . . .

Bragg soured a little at the thought of the two of them together out there in the night. Being in

Old Man Craig's closest confidence, he knew of course that however the old boy twisted the fact, still the girl had gone off with Stone of her own free will. A pity, that.

Bragg made up his mind. He would go by air.

He had already packed one small suitcase, plus a briefcase containing a dart pistol and an ex-Army Browning 9mm automatic from the armory. Travel restrictions, including checks on hand luggage, had more or less disappeared ten years ago with the rapid decline in crime and terrorism; he should have no trouble getting the guns through. Now he got Dorothy Ellis to phone ahead and book him a seat on a flight for Berlin out of Gatwick—there was a plane at 2:30—and while she was doing that he set off for the airport in a company car.

By 1:45 he had parked the car, was drinking coffee and smoking a cigarette while he waited for his flight to be called. Sitting there in the passenger lounge, he turned things over in his mind. It was Old Man Craig's "reward" that especially interested him. And if the opposition was anything to go by, he should have little trouble claiming it. He thought of Craig's promise that, "He may ask of me what he will." Well, Bragg already knew what he would ask of him. Yes, indeed.

Despite anything he might have said to Dorothy Ellis, Bragg's prize would be Lynn Craig herself!

Day Three

PLAGUE! THE WORD WAS PART OF EVERY HEADLINE IN every newspaper across the face of the globe. Fifty percent of all news items, in every form of the media, concerned themselves with it; one person in fifty now suffered from it. One hundred million gibberers worldwide!

Most of the world coped, for in fact and however paradoxically the figures were *not* enormous. Not on the astronomical scale of 21st Century statistics. One in fifty? A drop in the ocean. After all, one person in *ten* suffered some crippling disability. One person in *five* was over the age of sixty. One in *four* was Chinese and one in *three* illiterate, and that last despite every advance the world had made in the sixty years since the last great war.

But the mind-plague figures were different, and world governments knew it. While The Gibbering itself could not be hidden, its rate of increase certainly could and must be. So far the general populace was not aware of the size of the problem—or those individuals who were had been told to forget it—but a minority was becoming curious, and occasionally vociferous, if not yet hysterical.

Papers were still the most popular news medium. Evidence of the still limited but swelling clamor of protest could most easily be found in the newspapers, usually accompanied by details of the worst cases. For example:

Tokyo Times:

In the early hours of the morning, a maniac jammed the elevators in the Osaki Tower Block of flats overlooking Kanagawa monorail station and spilled ten gallons of kerosene in and around all the ground-floor doors and entrances. He then set fire to the building. In the ensuing inferno seven hundred and twenty persons are believed to have died, many of them crushed on the stairs or broken from leaping out of high windows. As people fled the building, some of them in their blazing nightclothes, the lunatic was waiting for them and killed as many as seventeen with a ceremonial Samurai sword before police could shoot him dead.

Tang Asai Oshito, Premier of the Nipponese Nation, will today review the general situation. It is reported that one of the items under discussion will be a system of rewards for persons offering information on suspected mind-plaguers.

On Shikoku Island police have been involved in two running gun battles with so-called "vigilante groups" who are alleged to have murdered suspect mind-plaguers on sight.

New York Times (Daniel Dunstable's "Action Now!" column):

With that sublime egocentric stupidity we've all apparently come to know, love, trust and suffer so much under which characterizes the minds of a certain White House sub-species known as and inhabiting the Office of American Affairs, the President of these United States today told Congress that a solution for the mind-plague which continues to devalue our lives will soon be found.

I for one am glad to hear it!

When pressed for details, the President remarked that "the best brains in the world are working on it." Well good for them, Mr. President, sir, but this columnist is here to tell you that some of the best brains in the world are *suffering* from it! And so those of them who *do* still have their marbles had better scramble pretty damn quick!

As for evidence of this claim of a just-around-the-corner miracle cure: we've heard rumors (just rumors, mind you) of "inoculative injections." Wazzat? A jab to prevent you from catching lunacy? We can't crack the common cold but we're on the verge of discovering a cure for cuckoos? Something "more momentous than penicillin"? Like maybe funnycillin? As my six-month old son might have it when he can speak—*if* he's still sane by then—"aw, come off of it, Mr. President!"

And the plethora of hypothetical and hyper-comical "causes" are funnier than any hyped-up gooney-baloney "cure" could ever be!

To name a few: Monsters from outer space. Radiations from the Earth's core. The commies are coming (*that* old chestnut!). The release of radioactive gases from all that atomic waste we junked in the sea those seventy long years ago. Consumption of contaminated grape- or seaweed-wine. Excessive atmospheric lead and/or microwave radiation. And—wait for it—inbreeding!

Inbreeding?

Mr. President, twenty years ago my brother (we are sons of an English father and an American mother) married a nationalized Armenian model whose father was White Russian and whose mother was Australian. They have three children, one boy and two girls. My dear brother will forgive me for using his (and my) family to illustrate a point, I know. But just a week ago one of his little girls started gibbering.

Now, this columnist really isn't aware what goes on behind locked doors up there in the Office of American Affairs, but we sure ain't doing a hell of a lot of inbreeding out here!

For Christ's sake, what's going on!? I mean, whatever happened to the good old American Way of Life? The other day, driving in the city, I counted a straight dozen traffic accidents all caused by maniacs. In the last week there have been twenty (count 'em, *twenty*!) cases of arson by mind-plaguers right here in the city. Whatever happened to the straight-from-the-shoulder, dyed-in-the-wool, all-American mugger? At least we knew why they did the things they did: because they were just plain mean! But maniacs? Or maybe we should get the muggers back to handle the crazies?

What the hell, there's never a mugger around when you need one . . .

Daily Mail:

Mrs. Evangeline Moffat, President of CLAMP (the Committee of Ladies Against Mind-Plague), lays the blame for worsening plague figures directly at the feet of the incumbent Tory Government. Amongst those especially selected for a tongue-lashing today are Arnold Hillier, Minister for the Environment, George Cubbit of Social Amenities and Welfare, and Charles Ingram, previously something in Health but now Minister for the recently formed and oddly-named Ministry of Health and Care Coordination.

Mrs. Moffat's principal claim is that mind-plague is inherent in all of us, but only manifests itself or is triggered in us by exposure to our increasingly technical world. In the '70s and '80s this used to be called "future shock." She further claims that it should now be possible to discover potential plaguers at birth, and states that all high-risk cases in children must be kept separate from cities and areas of high technology, preferably growing up on small farms or in wilder country regions more in touch with the natural order of things.

Arnold Hillier is said to approve of much of what Mrs. Moffat proposes: Charles Ingram has been criticized for calling her arguments "so much twaddle."

Das Bremener (and later syndicated throughout Germany):

Herr Doktor Ludwig Künstler of the Bremen Institute for Psychiatric Studies today expressed his opinion that the mind-plague is contagious. "One mind-plaguer," he is reported as saying, "may contaminate as many as twenty of his fellows. Close proximity is quite sufficient to transfer the plague, and any prolonged contact is fatal."

It has long been suspected that this might be the case, but Dr. Künstler now says he has definite proof. "The actual seed of the madness is an organism which breeds in the carrier's brain," says the Herr Doktor. "But only in living brains, and particularly those of Middle Eastern or Asiatic origin or nationality. Regrettably, I can only advise that all gibberers are put out of their misery like the hopelessly sick animals they are as soon as their condition becomes apparent. This is the only solution . . ."

These papers, however, were not yet out. They would not appear until the morning, and as yet it was only the middle of the night.

1:45 A.M., and the big silver Mercedes had passed through Göttingen's nighted streets in the direction of Bad Harzberg. The car was climbing now and beyond its windows the German night was cold. Stars were ice-bright where they dusted a clear sky. Beside Stone, curled down a little into her seat, Lynn was soundly asleep, replenishing herself. All of her worries and fears had finally caught up with her, now she was sleeping them off.

While he drove, Richard's mind went back over the events of the last couple of days:

His escape from Calm Lawns, of which he still remembered nothing . . . The recruiting of Lynn to his aid and cause, and the terrifying way in which that had been accomplished . . . Phillip Stone's unstinting assistance and the fact that he seemed to know something about all of this . . . His own dream of last night—about a car and a dog and mountains, and an enigmatic stone arch—and the almost frightening way in which, quite literally, all the major points of that dream were now reality. All, that is, with the exception of the stone arch and its all-important, unknown legend.

He and Lynn had been en route by taxi from the Chunnel terminal to a hotel when they passed the used-car lot. Vastly sprawling, the compound had contained every conceivable model, but Stone had had eyes for only one: the very car he was now driving. Getting hold of the proprietor of the lot and clinching the deal had been a mere formality; the outcome had been decided from the moment he saw the big silver Merc sitting there, just begging for an owner. In something less than an hour and a half it had belonged to Stone. It had been as easy as that.

Then he and Lynn had found a place to eat a sandwich and drink a little coffee—paid for in loose change, like the taxi, for they had changed what little cash they had to francs at the terminal—and after freshening up they had been on their way again. But that had only been the start of it.

The most astonishing thing had taken place in Avesnes, when they had left the ten-laner to answer the call of nature and eat a more substantial meal. They had left the *bistro* at about 6:30 P.M. and returned to where the car was parked. And there, sitting on the big Merc's bonnet—

Right now Suzy was in the back, directly behind Richard where he sat on the left at the wheel. Twice she had tried to climb over into the front, between him and Lynn, and twice he'd ordered her back. It seemed that the great black bitch just couldn't get close enough to him. And oddly enough Richard, who had never in all his life had much time for dogs, didn't mind a bit!

There she sat now, up on her haunches, her great paws on the top of the backrest, her muzzle close to the back of Richard's head. Occasionally she would mutter and grumble, give a small, almost inaudible whine and lick his ear, but he was used to her now. Funny, but he had been "used to her" almost from the word go. And she to him. It was as if they were old friends.

Again he let his thoughts drift back to Avesnes:

The car had been in a side alley just off the street with the *bistro*. Night had fallen an hour or more ago, just as they were arriving; it had stopped raining but the light was bad. It was Lynn who had spotted the big Doberman first, and she had clutched at Richard's arm, hanging on to him as they cautiously approached the car. Then—

The moment had been something magical. Lynn had begun to voice her alarm but Richard had hushed her, putting her behind him and out of harm's way. But he had somehow known there was nothing to fear. And he had gone up to the bonnet of the car, his face level with that of the dog where she sat waiting in the darkness. Her eyes had been like yellow beacons, reflected in the mirror-silver of the car's bonnet, and she had quivered as she gazed at Richard—but not from the chill of evening or any ordinary sort of fever.

For long moments they had simply looked at one another, and finally the bitch had lifted a forepaw and uttered a low, querying whimper. Déjà vu?—Richard knew nothing of that—but suddenly he knew the dog.

"Suzy?" the word was out before he knew it, spoken softly into her face without conscious volition. He had not known where the name came from, knew nothing except that beyond any shadow of a doubt it was *her* name. And then the dam had broken.

It had been just as fantastic for Lynn, even a little frightening, for she was witness to a meeting of old friends who had never before met! And what joy there had been in it!

As Richard had spoken the dog's name, down she came off the bonnet of the car and up onto her hind legs, drowning him in her saliva and her love and her sheer happiness. And after showering him with her adoration, then she had turned her attention to Lynn.

"Lynn Craig," Richard had said then, "meet, er . . . Suzy!"

This time it had been different: not exactly stiff-legged, but a more cautious inspection, certainly. Suzy had sniffed Lynn's skirt, her hands, finally standing on her hind legs again to offer one tentative lick to her nose. And yes, Richard's scent was on her, she could only belong to him. And so she too was to be cared for, protected, treasured.

"Your black Doberman bitch," Lynn had finally stuttered out the words as Richard let Suzy into the back of the car. She felt the *frisson* of the encounter, a sense of wonder at this rapid unrolling of Richard's dream. She was watching it come true. "But how?" she wanted to know. "What does it all mean?"

"Means we're on the right track," he answered as they got into the car. "We have the Merc and the dog—or rather, she has us!—and all we have to do now is get up into the mountains."

"And find your archway?"

"Right."

And that had been that, Suzy had become one of them . . .

Down in the room of the Machine beneath the Dome, surrounded by its steel and concrete skull, the brain which was Psychomech lay almost su-

pine but not entirely inactive. Indeed activity was constantly present—as it had been for many, many years—but on a different level of machine-consciousness. Psychomech was only ever truly "awake" when Craig communicated with the brain or used it to boost his own resistance to The Gibbering, or employed it in the initial treatment of his disciples; all of which were comparatively rare occurrences. Other than these, the Machine had no other function save one. But that was one which went on unceasingly and would continue to do so until an answer was found.

Namely, Psychomech searched for God. James Christopher Craig had told the Machine all it knew and understood of God, and he had ordered the search. Psychomech could not question Craig's authority, could only obey. But since Craig was God's prophet, who could possibly know Him and His ways better than Craig?

As for the Machine's terms of reference: Psychomech searched for a Unique Being whose attributes would set him aside from all other beings in the Universe. What were these attributes?

God was manlike, for He had made men in His own image. Therefore Psychomech sought an anthropomorphite—a man with the powers of a god.

God was omniscient. Knowing all, He knew Psychomech searched. He would not be "found" until He wanted to be. But search Psychomech must for Craig had ordered it.

God was almighty, invincible, unchanging. Try as one might, one could neither harm God nor alter His being.

God was good but He could also be wrathful! Stricken, He might well strike back—devastatingly!

How, then, to find Him? Answer: by elimination. Anthropomorphic: His mind was like a man's

mind. Psychomech knew about those. There were
five billion of them, and all of them had fear-
centers.

Omniscient: knowing He was sought and not yet
desiring to be found, He might disguise Himself
from Psychomech. He might hide among the five
billion, going in the guise of one of them.

But the minds of men were not unchangeable,
not impregnable, and not invincible. Men could be
changed and they could be hurt. Therefore find a
manlike mind which resisted interference, which
survived when others succumbed, which would
grow angry and fight back if one applied too much
pressure—and you would find God.

And so, down in the room of the Machine, Psychomech sent out its machine-thoughts into the
Psychosphere and explored the minds of men,
searching for God. There was no hurry: God would
be found in His own good time; but because Craig
had ordered it, so the process of elimination went
on. In fact it was a process of which Craig stood
in total ignorance; he had not instructed Psychomech in the method to be used in its search, had
merely ordered that the Machine "find God." And
so the Machine searched, and so it eliminated.

As for those eliminated . . . they gibbered!

2:15 A.M. and Lynn slept on. She had earlier demanded a share of the driving, if only to lighten
Richard's burden, but so far that had not been
necessary. He was tired now, yes, but he was sure
he could hold out to Bad Harzberg. Pointless to
wake her now, so close to journey's end.

About ten miles back, just this side of Göttingen where Stone had left the ten-laner for the
lesser roads to the mountains, he had passed a
small motel. Because he was weary he had failed

to see the place until it was behind him, and then he had not cared to turn around and go back for his unremitting sense of urgency continued to drive him on. Now he wished he *had* stopped there; it might be difficult to find anywhere else at this hour of the night.

In the back seat Suzy had been restless for a little while, whining, growling and pawing his shoulder, but Stone had ignored her. He was simply too weary to care now. If she peed in the car it would be his fault.

He thought he heard something, a whispered word, and turned his head to look at Lynn's face in the glow of the dashboard lights. Had she murmured something just then, voiced some irritable protest in her sleep? No, for her chin rested on her forearm and her mouth was firmly closed. Perhaps it had been Suzy then, panting in his ear.

A sound in his ear . . . *or in his mind?*

The whispering came again, the suggestion of a snigger, and this time there was no mistaking it. It sent goose-flesh marching across his shoulders and down his spine. At the same moment Suzy howled, began pawing frantically at his shoulders, the back of his neck, sank her teeth into the padding of his jacket at the shoulder. She had known before him and he had paid no heed to her warnings.

Jesus! Oh Christ, no!

Richard applied the brakes, pulled off the rising road onto a wide grass verge and stilled the engine. Over his shoulder he said a sharp "No!" to Suzy, who at once crouched back from him.

"Lynn!" he grabbed the girl beside him and shook her. "Lynn, for God's sake!"

The whispering was louder—a babble which only he could hear, rising to match his own frantic shouting—rising above Lynn's shocked exclamation as she came fighting awake. "Wha—!" she threw his arms away. "Who? Richard, I was asleep and I—"

She saw his face. *"Oh, no!"*

"Run!" he told her. "Out of the car and run. I can hold it down for a little while, but after that I—"

"Run?" she repeated him, still trying to orientate. "Where to? I can't just leave you."

Oh you bastard bastard bastard! He tore at the door catch on his side. *Why now, why here in the middle of nowhere? Of all the fucking, whoring, screwing bloody luck!*

He yanked open the door, fell out into the night, crawled in the grass. Suzy was over the back of his seat and out after him in a flash, whining loudly as she went to him where he crawled blindly in darkness and shook his head, trying to dislodge the horrors clambering over his brain. Their whispering was now like the roaring of mad worlds reeling about alien stars—whispers that howled!

Lynn had a hand to her mouth, her teeth clamped on the first knuckles. "Oh, Richard— *Richard!*"

She leaned across his seat, stared out of the open door into a darkness beyond which pines were silhouetted against a steeply sloping horizon. The grass was long, bending in a night breeze and brushing against the bottom of the car door.

Richard was cursing out loud now, his verbal obscenities rapidly rising to a babbling and incoherent shriek—

Following which—nothing . . .

"Richard? *Richard!*"

The grass was moving again. He came flopping through it, still on his hands and knees. Lynn looked at him, at his face in the light of the stars, and screamed!

His face writhed. He sucked at air like a vacuum cleaner, his lips forming a tube of flesh that siphoned and slobbered in their need. Air, oxygen, fuel for his lungs, energy for the frantically jerking and vibrating muscles of his arms, his legs, his shoulders and torso—and his face! And those golden amoeba eyes writhing in that face like bright yellow coals at the heart of a fire, while the flesh of his brow, his cheeks, chin and neck contorted and fluttered bonelessly, like the rubber mask of an astronaut under a force of many Gs.

This was The Gibbering in all its horror—or rather, this was the result of trying to contain it. For still Richard had not given in—not yet, not quite—but he felt the madness mounting in him and knew that soon he must release it one way or the other.

"K-k-k—" he choked out the sound, sent it hissing from his mouth in a froth of foam. One letter, but it was as if she saw the entire word written in his pulsing eyes.

"Keys? Car keys!" she snatched them from the ignition.

"B-b-b—" he pointed a writhing, thrashing arm toward the rear of the car, his head wobbling like a jelly on his jerking shoulders. She understood, had seemed to *hear* the entire word spoken in her head. Boot—the boot of the car! She scrambled out of her door, staggered along her side of the car to the boot, inserted the key. The lid lifted.

Richard came crawling, sweat streaming from him, babbling and writhing through the grass.

Suzy was with him, tugging at him, dragging him. He clawed himself half upright, and still mouthing violent curses fell inside. She lifted his spastically kicking left leg in after him, slammed the lid down.

Then she went down on her knees in the night-damp grass and hugged Suzy to her where the great black bitch whined and trembled. "Oh, Suzy!" Lynn sobbed, gulping at the cold night air. "Oh, Suzy, Suzy, Suzy!"

And inside the boot—safe now from the possible consequences of his madness, from the harm he could do to others, but still not safe from himself—Richard Stone at last gave vent to all his pent fury, his caged frustration. Even muffled, the sound of it was terrible. Lynn stayed where she was, kneeling, praying, until it was all over . . .

For most of the rest of that day—the third in what might well prove to be Man's final fortnight—Dorothy Ellis' accounts computer at PSISAC would remain silent. For the time being Stone spent no more money, and therefore he disappeared.

In Berlin Edward Bragg would wait at the Neu Tempelhof Hotel, dividing his time between dozing in an armchair in the resident's lounge, smoking plastic-tipped Kiel cigars, and drinking coffee and schnapps—the latter not to excess. He would remain there for some twelve hours, putting through the occasional call to PSISAC and growing ever more impatient, until a little after 3:30 P.M. when at last the call he waited for would come through.

Then, angry with himself that he had been wrong, he would catch the first available jet-copter shuttle to Hanover.

As for Emma Tyler and Donald Conti:

Upon their arrival at the Hilton in Luxembourg, she had got in touch with PSISAC and been told that it looked like Stone was en route for Berlin, that within the last hour he had bought petrol midway along the Luxembourg/Kassel/Berlin ten-laner. While she was on the phone, Conti had gone up to see their rooms. It was a pleasure for him just to get away from her, if only for a few minutes. He had felt that he traveled not with a middle-aged spinster but with another man, one whose thoughts and emotions were blacker and deeper far than Conti's own.

When he had come down again she was gone, as was her car and his small suitcase. It seemed she had come to the same conclusion: that their partnership wasn't going to work. Or perhaps this had been her plan in the first place: to strand him, leaving him without means in the middle of the night in a foreign country. But he was not without means. He spoke excellent French and German; his banker's ID tag was safe in his pocket; PSISAC was there to back him to the hilt. His embarrassment would only be temporary. Hers might later prove permanent.

But obviously she had learned something. Conti phoned PSISAC, received the same information. Putting down the telephone he shrugged, so what? Stone was safe from all of them until he actually stopped running. And no one was better informed than anyone else as to when that would be.

Conti was no fatalist but he knew how to face up to facts. The bar was open but the hotel in general was about as lively as a morgue. He was on his own and without transport in the early hours of a Monday morning. There was no way he could improve his situation until daylight. So . . .

he bought a half-bottle of brandy, went up to his room and drank it, undressed and fell into bed. And there he lay making his plans until he fell asleep.

Plans for Richard Stone and for Lynn Craig.

Yes, and interesting plans for Miss Emma Tyler, too . . .

As for the Jackson twins: for all that they had made a bad start, still they would come closest. By 2:30 P.M. they would be in Kassel, where finally they would be obliged to trade their car in. Worn out from an 85 mph dash along four hundred miles of ten-laner, their vehicle would at last give up the ghost. PSISAC would pay the balance, pay also for their rooms at the Lindenhof Hotel. By then they would be fully in the picture where they stood with regard to expenses.

Geographically, however, they still would not realize where they stood in relation to Richard Stone, alias Garrison. Like the other four, they would have to wait until a little after 3:30 P.M. for that information. Only then would the Jacksons learn that their quarry was less than twenty-five miles away . . .

Stone was back in the badlands of nightmare.

Victim of horror in both conscious and subconscious worlds alike, he had quit one only to find himself mired in the other. And once again this world was now the real world, more valid than that other. Like many vivid dreamers, while he slept his knowledge of a waking existence took the form of only the most fragmentary memories, his dreams totally absorbed him.

He was no longer alone.

He had no recollection of where they came from or when (for it seemed that years had gone by since he witnessed the bomb-birth of the undead horror on the night of the rain and the mist), but he now had companions. A girl and a dog ran with him, fleeing from what had now emerged as a universal, omnipotent terror which hunted men across the hollow shell of this dead and crumbling world as men had once stalked stags.

Except that "fled," which creates an impression of headlong flight, is not the word Stone would have used. No, for their flight was anything but headlong; they had neither the energy nor the will for that. They were weary, stumbling ankle deep through gurgling mud as the rain came down in sheets from a cloud-black sky. Behind them lay a morass, leprously spotted with the leaden glint of brooding lakes and potholes where the water was deeper. At some time in the dim and distant past that swamp had been a valley where men had made their homes, for in places skeletons of crumbling brickwork still stuck up from it like bones from a shattered grave.

Beyond the swamp, distant hills rose to meet the lowering sky along a gray and desolate horizon. There were balefires on those hills, where lunatics leaped and cavorted and worshiped their mad god, welcoming him with the blazing beacons of their homes and villages. The fires were a sure sign that he came—that dead-alive Thing from beyond the grave, that zombie-corpse of steel and chrome and plastic—for fire was ever his harbinger. Oh, yes, he came, would always come, until the entire world went down in shrieking madness.

But for the present the trio of man, girl and dog had stolen a march on the monster, had left him beyond the hills, feasting on the brains of those he had found hiding there. Stone knew that it was merely a respite and nothing more, but still he was grateful for it. It seemed that he had been running for a very long time, and he was weary to his bones.

At least he was no longer alone. The girl was with him, and the dog, too. And yet . . .

On the one hand he was glad of their company, their love, but on the other he felt only guilt. The dog was safe, for the monster fed on men, not dogs. But the girl . . . she would not be here if not for Stone. Because of him, she was threatened. Oh, that threat would have come soon enough, even without him, but with him it could only come sooner. For the mad god pursued Stone relentlessly, for what purpose and to what end he could not imagine. So far he had managed to elude the thing, but for how much longer?

Now they came up out of the mud onto higher ground. The storm was almost over and the rain had turned to a drizzle. Behind them the marsh was beginning to scum over with a mist that thickened from moment to moment. Rain and mud and mist: it seemed that the world was made of them.

There were trees ahead, a wood, and in the heart of the wood a light shining out, beckoning them on. The light had the warm glow of a fire, the flickering effect of dancing, warming flames.

Suddenly Stone realized how fatigued and hungry he was, how hungry the girl and dog must be. Hungry not only for food and warmth—hungry for peace, safety and shelter—starved of sanity and contact with wholesome, untainted minds. And as the mist swirled up and obscured the far hills and the drowned plain, so the fugitives moved more quickly through the limp and dripping trees toward the fire.

There was a clearing. A tarpaulin had been stretched over poles, was roped at its corners and *pegged to the ground, forming a shelter. A central hole let out the smoke from the fire; beneath, a spit turned and meat sizzled and gave off mouth-watering aromas. Crouched beneath the tarpaulin with their backs to the silent, tree-shrouded trio, a half-dozen thin and ragged people, adults and ur-chins alike, sheltered and warmed themselves and watched the meat turning on its spit. The man who worked it was old, his back hunched, hands like claws where they turned the wooden handle. The meat he cooked would feed a tribe, let alone this starveling handful.*

Stone and his two edged closer, the mist rising and closing in behind them.

Then—

It was as if, suddenly, an electric current had passed through the very air. The dog's hackles rose; the girl drew air in a sharp hiss; Stone felt his flesh crawl as at the touch of something unseen, some-thing unclean. His eyes felt hot as they stared at the wire-bound and almost completely cooked form of a blackened, steaming, red-dripping, recently-alive human being!

And starting in horror, his weight shifted on a dry branch—which snapped with a report like a gunshot.

The group at the fire sprang up, turned—

Their faces were grinning masks of madness—

The mad god had overtaken the trio, was here even now!

Stone and his two whirled—and crouched back!

Coming at them through the trees, looming up out of the mist, a great squat throbbing brain of chrome and blue metal and colored plastic floated in air; a thing of pulsating lights and crackling energies, which trailed broken cables and fraying rubber conduits behind it like mummy-wrappings as it bore down upon them. It was . . . a mechanical anemone from some alien, sunless sea. A monstrous machine-mind risen up from the pits of some robot hell!

They sprang away, all three, turned and fought with the mad people, who jabbered and shrieked and tried to hold them there. Stone and the dog broke free but the girl was grabbed, hurled down directly in the path of the advancing horror.

Its cables were like tentacles now; they snaked down, coiled about her, lifted her up and into the monster's very body. The mad god ate her!—and at once spat her out. Of course, for the vampire didn't eat people—only their brains!

Stone flung himself down beside her where she lay crumpled on the steaming earth. She opened her eyes and looked at him—looked through him!

Then the dog was howling like a banshee and frenziedly tugging at his arm, dragging him back from the mindless thing which had been a lovely young girl. And the dog was right, there was no helping her now. Cables groped for him but he danced aside; broken conduits lashed at his legs but he leaped high, avoiding them. Then he was beyond the monster's reach.

A moment later Stone and the dog were fleeing through the trees and the mist and the nightmare, and behind them the girl laughed and bayed and screamed and sang . . . and gibbered!

Stone jerked awake.

He snapped upright in his bed, almost cried out in unexpected, unaccustomed pain. Gritting his teeth, he slumped back down into his pillows. He was drenched in sweat, shuddering in his sheets. But a moment later he knew that it had been only a dream, a nightmare, and that already it was fading, slipping from his mind. He tried to hold it there, then changed his mind and let it go. He had the essence of it and that was enough . . . who needed more of a thing like that?

With his heart still thudding like a trip hammer in his chest, slowly Stone came out of his shock. He was okay now. It was all right. It had been a nightmare, just one of his bloody awful nightmares.

"Just" a nightmare?—or one of *those* nightmares? Lord, let it not be one of them. Let it not be prophetic.

He released the sheets where he clutched them to his chest, forced the shuddering out of his limbs, and as his terror subsided he looked all about the room. It wasn't much to look at.

Daylight—even sunlight—came in through windows with lace curtains drawn across them. The room was small, contained only a bed, two chairs, a table and an old-fashioned TV. There were two curtained recesses in the wall opposite the bed; one was a shower unit, the other a toilet. Very austere. A hospital room, perhaps? Hot on its heels, that last thought conjured another: or was this some place where they put you while they checked your credentials for the madhouse?

Stone began to get out of bed, saw the bandages on his hands and knees and knew what it was that hurt so much. Also, there was a large square dressing taped on his forehead, interfering a little with his vision. Carefully, he stood up, felt the skin of his knees crack where it was trying to heal. He had obviously given himself something of a rough time. But not too rough, thank God!

The door opened and Lynn came in, Suzy with her. The dog came straight to him, whined worriedly, thrust her muzzle into his bandaged hands

and adored him with huge soft eyes. Lynn sighed
her relief, closed the door behind her, burst into
tears.

"I told you it could get rough," he said, his
voice gritty from a throat and mouth like twin
deserts. "Maybe even rougher than this. We don't
know yet."

She came over, clasped him, made him sit down
on the edge of the bed. "What do you remember
of it?" she eventually asked through her tears.

He tried to comfort her, patted her back, clumsily kissed her neck. "I remember thinking I had
to get into the boot of the car," he shrugged.
"And I suppose I must have made it."

"Yes, you did. And for twenty minutes or more
you sounded like—"

"Like a madman? Yes," he nodded. "Then?"

"When you were quiet . . . I didn't know what to
do. A couple of cars passed, then one stopped
and the driver asked if I was in trouble. I said I
was just tired or something and asked if he knew
a place with rooms. He told me I'd passed a motel
only fifteen kilometers back; I said thanks, I
would go there. When he saw I was okay he drove
off.

"Then I opened the boot and somehow got you
out. Your hands were bleeding where you'd torn
your nails and knuckles, your forehead had a big
bruise, and you'd banged up your knees a bit. The
boot is lined with thick rubber or it could have
been worse. Good job there were no tools in
there."

He nodded. "I got the idea from traveling in the
boot of your car," he told her. "That's two rough
rides I've had! But go on."

"I bundled you into the car—or rather dragged,
pushed and heaved you in—and drove back here.

The desk clerk is an old man. He was half-asleep, a little deaf, not too bright. I took this room, came back to the car and got you. You were dead on your feet but you actually managed to walk—to stumble, anyway! I told the old man you'd had a little accident, but he wasn't that much interested. Anyway, I made sure he didn't get too good a look at you.

"He didn't like the idea of Suzy, though. No dogs allowed! I told him we'd pay for her along with our bill before we left, and that there'd be something extra in it for him too. That did the trick.

"Then I slept, too, but only for three or four hours. This morning about 9:00 I had breakfast and fed Suzy, since when I've sat beside you. I thought it was a good idea to let you sleep it off. Then . . . I suppose I must have nodded off. About an hour ago I woke up but you were still sleeping. So I went out for a breath of fresh air—and here I am back again.

"But Richard, the air is so clear up here and it's been such a lovely day—weather-wise, anyway! So sunny—and warm, too. To the northeast, the mountains are so clear and bright . . .

"Oh, Richard . . . !"

She was sobbing again, crumpling up in his arms. And that hurt worse than his cuts and bruises. He dabbed her tears away with a corner of a sheet, comforting her as best he could.

He still looked and felt groggy, but his mind was ticking over once more. When she had herself under control, he said: "So today is Monday, and . . . time?"

"About 2:30."

"—And this is a motel just east of Göttingen."

He looked at the bandages criss-crossing his knuckles. "What am I like under these?"

"Your hands are a mess, the skin all laid back," she told him. "Lucky you didn't break any bones. Lucky, too, that you were wearing your old things. I've dumped them. They were so bloody!"

"My knees don't feel too bad."

"They're okay. You skinned them a little. The right one has a large soft lump."

"Forehead?"

"Grazed, bruised. A bump might come up, but I don't think so. You didn't have a lot of room to move in there."

"I know," he grunted. "Like a steel straitjacket! Well, my hands and knees can stay bandaged, but the sticking plaster has to go. You can hide the bruise with your powder and paint. But not only can't I see straight with this padding on my brow, I can't even think straight! First, though, the three 'S'es."

"The what?"

"Shower and shave," he said, testing his stubble with the back of his wrist. "You can guess the third one."

"Oh!" Lynn nodded. "But what's the hurry?"

"Daylight," he answered. "I want to get up into the Harz, today. Bad Harzberg or Braunlage, or maybe St. Andreasberg. We're nearly there—twenty miles or so."

"But you should rest!" she protested, fluttering her hands.

"I *have* rested, and too long."

"But you've just suffered an attack, and—"

"I've just *recovered* from an attack—and we don't know when the next one will be!" He turned his strange eyes on her. "Time, Lynn. It's all a matter of time. We may not have enough of it."

She gave in, nodded. "Okay."

He ripped the dressing from his forehead and managed not to wince. "Is it okay?"

She looked at it. "I can fix it."

"Do we have fresh bandages?"

"There's a first aid kit in the car," she told him. "It's standard equipment over here."

"That's right," he nodded. "I remember seeing it on the floor in the back. Good!" He carefully unwrapped his bandages, sniffed disgustedly at his raw wounds and gingerly inspected them, then went and showered.

After the laving water had taken something of the sting out of his sore places, he called: "Hey, and I'm hungry! We'll get into the mountains proper and eat there. Should be no problem getting rooms this time of year. Skiing season doesn't get underway for six or seven weeks yet."

"I thought you'd never been in the Harz before?"

"I haven't," he answered, carefully soaping himself. He frowned through the streaming water. "Must have read about it."

"Richard, there's something I wish you'd explain . . ."

He switched the shower off, came out dripping. "What's that?" he asked.

Patting him dry with a towel, she said: "Back there where you had your attack, something happened. It was really very strange. As strange as anything else that has happened."

"Oh?"

"You tried to say 'keys' but couldn't make it—tried to say 'boot,' too. But I knew what you were saying anyway—that I was to take the keys and open the boot. I mean, I just *knew* it—in my mind."

He looked serious for a moment, then shook his head and grinned. "Maybe you're telepathic!" Lynn's expression remained the same.

"Not me, Richard," she said. "You! You put the words there in my head. You couldn't say them, so you found another way . . ."

While she went to the car for the first aid kit, he thought about what she had said. Back at Calm Lawns during his "chats" with Gorvitch, he had sometimes felt that if he really tried he could make the doctor do whatever he wanted him to. He'd used to get this feeling when an attack was imminent, when he was under pressure. But of course he had never really put it to the test, because that was crazy . . .

Wasn't it?

Twenty minutes later, wearing fresh bandages and with his face tidied up as best Lynn could manage, Stone paid the bill and they left . . .

Dorothy Ellis passed the information on: Garrison had used his banker's ID tag to pay a bill in a small hotel near Göttingen.

By 4:00 P.M. Edward Bragg was on a jet-copter shuttle to Hanover. Less than an hour later he hired himself a brand new Opel Komet equipped with a radio-telephone and by 5:00 he was heading south for Hildesheim.

Some time before that, however, Darren and Michael Jackson had already visited Herr Fischer's motel. There they had learned that the English Herr and his lady had set off just a little while ago for Bad Harzberg . . . or was it Braunlage? Yes, yes, it was Braunlage! Herr Fischer could not be mistaken—he had heard them mention the place by name. Braunlage, yes . . .

Old Rudi Fischer could hardly know it, but he

had done the fugitives a great favor. Stone had settled for St. Andreasberg.

Conti stayed right where he was, in Magdeburg. Things were working out just fine. From his point of view Stone was still running, and if things didn't change he was going to run right into Don Conti!

Miss Emma Tyler also stayed where she was—at a hotel in Kassel. She might have gone to Göttingen but as she was about to leave there had been a complication. Now she would have to wait until later. For the moment she must simply wear her headset, lie here on her hotel bed and be still, and let Psychomech fill her head with those soothing mind-patterns which alone could keep her safe and sane . . .

Day Four

L AST NIGHT RICHARD STONE HAD EATEN LIKE THREE men—a massive *Zigeunerschnitzel* heaped with mushrooms in a thick, dark sauce: a side plate of potato salad with sliced, pickled cucumber; a pudding of gateau with a rich, fresh cream topping; all washed down with coffee and two steins of Schultheis beer, and night-capped with a double Asbach Uralt from its distinctive cobwebbed bottle—and yet this morning he put paid to his breakfast like a man half-starved!

Lynn watched him enviously as he burned his way through a large oval plate of eggs and bacon and a pot of steaming coffee. By comparison she had eaten like a bird, but her envy was not of his appetite but his obvious enjoyment. Were it not for his bandages and patched up forehead—and of course her own memories of the last few days— she would swear this was that very same man she had known back there at the beginning of time, when the world was young and beautiful and The Gibbering was something people only ever spoke of in hushed whispers.

He *looked* so well this morning! The bags had disappeared from under his fascinating eyes, which were especially bright; his face had a good color to it; even his walk (given that his knees were sore) had a spring in it she hadn't seen since . . . hadn't really expected to see again. All in all it was uplifting. For the first time she felt they had a real chance. Other men taken by the mind-plague were dead by now, but Richard looked almost reborn.

"It's the freedom!" he told her. "At least, I think that's what it is. After Calm Lawns the sense of sheer freedom is . . . a knockout! It's great. And up here in the mountains—the air—the food," he winked at her leeringly, "—the sex!"

She remembered last night:

She herself had driven the car up into the mountains from the motel; Richard's hands had been too painful. Before 4:30 they had been in St. Andreasberg. The light on the peaks had been wonderful and she had well been able to imagine what they must look like decked with snow, but for now everything was green and the town had looked almost unreal in its olde-worlde, fairy tale beauty. It was the very place of Richard's dream: chalet-style buildings, overhanging roofs, timbered houses and wooden signs over pub doorways—everything was as he had described it.

But on a higher slope, way up on a spur overlooking the town on one side and a wide gorge or pass on the other, they had spotted their paradise hotel: a large three-story affair with a log porch, wooden-railed balconies, white walls and dark wooden beams. A scaled-up Swiss chalet, standing at the top of a winding road that climbed up from the town and along the steep contours of the spur to a white-railed car park. With the sun's last rays glancing off its windows, the place had seemed almost to smile at them.

And indeed the Schweitzerhof had proved to be popular, where most of the rooms were booked up in advance right across the winter season. But their luck had been in: there would be spare rooms for five weeks yet, until the early birds got here looking for the first snow. And so the Schweitzerhof had welcomed them with open arms.

Having booked in they had ordered their meal, and while they waited to be called went out onto a deep, wide balcony to sit on pine benches and look down on the town as the light drew dim and the mountains turned steel blue . . .

Then there had been their meal—and afterward they had let Suzy go for a run, and when she was through fed her on finest steak and a bowl of sweet water, putting her in the car for the night in a nest of worn-out blankets, for the hotel did not cater to dogs—and finally it had been time for bed.

Because of Richard's condition, Lynn had been the aggressor; she had taken both the initiative and pity on him in their lovemaking. She had been gentle, careful—she had not wanted to hurt him more than he hurt already, or further harm those places which still ached from their last frenzied coupling—and the tenderness of her touch, and the heat of her sweet young body, had combined to make it that much more exquisite. She had loved him with her hands, her mouth, with her body and all of herself; and sated at last, finally they had slept like babes . . .

"You're smiling," he said, drawing her back to the present. He had finished eating.

"Oh!" she answered. "Do I do it so rarely, then?"

"This last couple of days, yes," he gave a wry grin. "But that has to be understandable!"

They were downstairs at a table in a glass-fronted dining room with a view of ski slopes where a cable car system stood for the present immobile. Further down the mountain, St. Andreasberg was abustle with townspeople. From where they sat they could also see the car park and the Mercedes. Suzy was up, her face staring at them through a back window. Without taking her eyes off them she lolled her tongue in seeming anticipation of something or other. They were brought to laughter by her expression.

"Good morning," said a gentle, slightly stilted Germanic voice, and they turned their heads to see a smiling gray-haired man in the striped trousers and waistcoat of a waiter standing beside them. "Excuse me, sir, madame," he said, "but is the black, er, *Hündin*—the bitch-dog—in the car there, is she yours?"

"Why, yes," Stone answered, "she's our dog. Is there a problem?"

"Oh, *nein, nein*—but if you wish you may bring her in here, as long as she does not go upstairs. And I may have something good for her from the kitchen, you know."

Lynn smiled. "That's very kind of you," she said. "As long as the owner won't mind . . ."

The man nodded understandingly and patted her shoulder. "Ah! You English. You love your animals, yes? Well, the owner will not mind, be sure. Don't let these clothes fool you, I am the *Wirt* here. Er, how do you say—the proprietor? My name is Herr Gutmann," he bowed. "It is that I like to play my part, and so I sometimes serve—at least until the skiing opens. Then I have all the paperwork."

Stone got to his feet, saying, "I'll fetch Suzy," but Lynn beat him to it.

"You sit!" she told him determinedly. "Let your breakfast settle and take it easy on your knees. I'll get Suzy." She smiled at Herr Gutmann and made for the door.

"Charming," he said, watching her go. "A charming young lady." Then he looked again at Stone: at his bandaged hands, his forehead.

"A little accident," Stone said. "Nothing much."

Still the man stood there. He was maybe fifty, fifty-five, his face tanned by mountain weather and wrinkled with laughter lines. But he was no longer smiling. Instead a frown creased his brow and he seemed puzzled.

"Is there—something?" Stone finally asked.

"Something?" the man seemed miles away. Then he snapped out of it. "Oh! I am sorry. Yes, perhaps there is—something. I saw you come in last night and since then I have tried to place you. Now I think I have it!"

"Sorry," Stone shook his head, "that's not possible. We were never in the Harz before. You must be thinking of someone else."

"Oh, but of course—*natürlich* I am thinking of someone else! But it is really quite—amazing?"

Stone shook his head again. "I'm sorry, I—"

"*Mein Herr*, did I hear you and the lovely lady say 'Suzy'? The dog's name is Suzy?"

"Why, yes."

"And you are called Garrison?"

Stone almost denied it, returned the other's puzzled frown, said, "Yes, but—"

"And does the 'R' before your name stand for Richard?"

Stone was alarmed now. Did the authorities back home know he was in Germany? Had they forwarded a description? Did they know his alias? "Now look here—!"

But no, the *Wirt* was smiling now. He reached over and squeezed Richard's forearm where he rested it on the table. "Then perhaps it is not so strange after all. I read your name in the registry this morning, you see, and when I saw it was Garrison . . . may I sit down?"

"Please do."

He sat, looked at Stone again, leaned back and slapped his thigh. "Was *für ein Zusammenkunft!* A fantastic—how is it—coincidence?"

"I still don't follow you," Stone was mystified.

"Richard Garrison!" the other nodded, chuckled, slapped his thigh again. "Oh, I am sorry, *mein Herr*—but I have you, er, at a disadvantage? Yes? Well, it is simply this: that I believe I knew your father!"

Stone's jaw dropped. "My father?"

"Yes, yes! Oh, you are not just exactly the same, but close enough. Yes, and he too had a black *Hündin*—a girl-dog—who was also Suzy!"

Stone's hair tingled at its roots. Only by the greatest effort of will did he manage to contain himself. He grasped the other's hand. "Herr— Gutmann?"

"*Ja,*" the other nodded, "Klaus Gutmann."

"Herr Gutmann, when was this? When did you know—my father? How well did you know him?"

"Oh, I did not know him well—" Gutmann shrugged. "It was maybe, oh, thirty years ago, when I was just a little older than you."

Lynn was back with Suzy. The Doberman went

to Stone and sat at his feet, put her muzzle in his hands. Lynn had caught the latter part of their conversation; she kept silent, listening. She could tell from Richard's expression that there was something new, something out of the ordinary here.

"Please go on," he urged.

"Well," Gutmann continued, "my father had a business in Eisleben—that's not far from here. He supplied many of the local hotels with foodstuffs. With their . . . *Gemüse?*"

"Their vegetables, yes."

"Vegetables, of course. And he had the contract to supply Herr Schroeder with all—of—" Gutmann paused, gaped at Stone. *"Mein Gott! Ist etwas los?"*

Beneath the table, Suzy whined deep in her throat.

Lynn had taken a third chair from a nearby table. Now she shuffled it closer, clutched at Richard's arm. "Richard, what's wrong?"

All the color had gone out of Stone's face in a single instant of time. His eyes were yellow, huge, staring. He was like . . . like what? A ghost who has seen a man!

"Richard!" Lynn said again, and now he heard her, recognized her tone. She had read something into his actions which was not there, not this time.

"It's okay," he said at last. "I'm all right!" The color began to creep back into his face. He tightened his grip on Gutmann's hand until the German drew back, then released him. "I'm sorry, Herr Gutmann—but you don't know how important this is to me," he said. "That name, Schroeder. Who is he?"

Gutmann had thought for a moment that Stone

was going to be terribly ill. Now, relieved to see
that he was well, he relaxed a little and took a
deep breath. This had become much more than a
simple conversation, and he knew it. His voice
was shaky as he continued: "Oh, everyone in the
Harz knew Thomas Schroeder—or knew of him.
He was a rich man, *very* rich! He had a place not
far from here, maybe ten kilometers. A big place.
When he died it became your father's place, but
he came to the Harz only rarely."

Stone was absorbing all of this as fast as it hit
him. "You mean Richard Garrison—my father—
actually owned a place up here?"

"Property, yes," Gutmann nodded. "It's strange
but I haven't given a thought to those old days
for such a long time. But when I saw you—and of
course the silver car—and your lady with her dark
spectacles. And the *Hündin* . . ." he paused, his
smile nervous. "Why, then everything came back
to me!"

Stone was pale again, Lynn too by now.

"Listen, Herr Gutmann," Stone spoke very
slowly. "This is not only important to me but to
a great many people. Do you believe me?"

"Why, yes!" the *Wirt* answered, his eyes widen-
ing, "if you say so."

"I do," Stone's eyes bored into him. "How did
you connect the car, the dog, myself and the lady
here with Schroeder, my father and all?"

Suddenly it was very thirsty work. "Wait," said
Gutmann. "A moment please." He called over a
serving girl. *"Weinbrand, bitte—dreimal."* When
she had hurried off he turned back to the pair.

"Thomas Schroeder had a Mercedes like yours,"
he said. "His man, Koenig, used to drive it for
him. After Schroeder died, Koenig became companion to your father. At least he left these parts,

and afterward was only ever seen with Richard
Garrison . . ." Suddenly it was Gutmann's turn to
frown. "But . . . you don't know any of this?"

"I never knew my father."

"Ah! I am sorry. Very well, let me go on:

"Soon after Herr Schroeder died, your father
came for a while to the Harz. From that time I
remember the dog. So now, you see, when all of
these things are coming together again, I—"

"And the lady? You mentioned a lady with dark
spectacles?" Stone's voice almost shook with its
tension.

"Oh, yes, but that was while Herr Schroeder
lived. I remember seeing them together at his
place, laughing and splashing in a swimming
pool, and sitting with their feet in the water. I can
see them now. Young people: they looked so good
together, like you and the lady. And I was sorry
for them."

"Sorry for them?"

The *Kellnerin* had brought a tray with three
large brandies. Stone gulped his down without
apology, Gutmann more slowly. Lynn merely held
hers tightly in both hands.

"Of course," said Gutmann. "And your lady too
wears the dark spectacles, you see? Naturally I
was sorry—that they should be so young, Garrison and his lady friend—and both of them blind!"

"Blind!" Stone's mouth formed the word, but it
emerged as a whisper. The glass clutched in his
bandaged hand shattered. To himself he said:
And her name was Vicki Maler—my mother!

No one moved. The three sat as if molded there.
Then Suzy whined worriedly and Gutmann gave a
nervous laugh.

"Blind!" Stone said it again, audibly now, his
voice a croak. "My father, too!"

Yes, blind—but he had seen more than any other man might ever have hoped to see. And out of the blue a thought, a revelation, struck at Stone like a bolt of illuminating lightning:

Great merciful God—I believe I've inherited something from my father! His memories! Those, yes . . . and maybe something more . . .

The mountain road was a good one; its lanes were comfortably wide for all that there were only two, and its surface had plenty of grip. It was the major service road for most of the Harz district, linking lesser tracks and roads to all the towns and villages and offering a first-class route to the mighty ten-laner where it crossed the mountains between Nordhausen and Stasfurt to the southeast. But because of the mountain contours, the road wound tortuously and contained numerous hairpins, which made the going fairly slow.

Just before 11:00 A.M., coming around a bend on a steep, pine-clad slope and along the edge of a high, wide saddle between twin peaks, Stone sensed that they were almost there. Several things alerted him to the fact: memories which could not possibly be his—Suzy's sudden attitude of alert awareness where she sat behind him, her great paws on the back of his seat—the way his pulse picked up for no apparent reason. And where Herr Gutmann's directions had been only vague, Stone's instinct was sure.

"Easy," he told Lynn, who was driving. "Slow right down."

The road skirted the saddle gently. On the right, beyond the width of the oncoming lane, the mountainside fell away for many hundreds of feet down to toy towns and villages whose chimney smoke was blue where it hazed the still, sheltered air. On the left the saddle had a front all of a half-mile wide; it reached back through a belt of pines to a gradually narrowing, gently rising slope between the peaks. Sheltered despite its elevation, the place was like a valley of the sky—a pocket in the mountain's highest folds—which trapped the sunlight, avoided the winds, looked down on the world with a sort of remote disinterest.

But behind the pines the sun struck glinting fire from many bright facets. There were buildings, windows and gleaming domes back there. And now Stone knew for certain that this *was* the place, for he remembered it . . .

"Take the slip road," he said.

"What slip—" Lynn began—a moment before she saw it. Just beyond a kink in the road, a turning into the pines was guarded by a sign which warned:

PRIVAT!
Eintritt Verboten!

Suzy gave a single sharp bark and licked Stone's ear. She whined curiously—knowingly?—as the car turned off the road, past the sign and slipped like a silvered shadow into the belt of pines. Beneath the canopy of the trees, unseen from the road, a high perimeter fence of wire defined the forward facing boundary of the place. Stone pillars draped with a small-leaved variety of ivy loomed up, between which iron gates stood open. The shape of the pillars at their tops, plus low mounds of long tumbled masonry half-buried in pine needles, leaf mold and vines, told their own story of a fallen archway.

"Stop!" Stone heard himself say; and he was halfway out of his door before Lynn could bring

the car properly to a halt. Then she and Suzy
joined in helping him clear away dirt and leaf
mold, and to turn over several of the heavier
chunks of masonry which had fallen face down,
until the original legend could be reconstructed.
Then—

It was not difficult to decipher, neither did it
shock Stone—not after all the other revelations
of the morning. Indeed it was nothing more or
less than he had expected. Nodding, he finally
stood up, stood back from the uncovered evidence. Indisputable evidence that indeed his
dreams had strange meaning.

" 'Garrison's Retreat,' " he repeated the legend
out loud, then looked beyond the gates, where
the drive disappeared into the pines. "And up
there, maybe the answers to all this." He took
Lynn's arm and gave it a squeeze. "We might be
that close!"

They got back in the car, drove on.

In less than fifty yards they came out of the
pines into a large cleared area of many acres that
sloped gently upward into gardens and lawns, beyond which stood those buildings glimpsed from
the road. There were six of them, one central with
the others ringed about it, so that all stood fairly
equidistant. They were symmetrically similar—all
had two stories with the exception of the central
one, which had three—and all were domed, their
domes carrying clusters of solar cells of an outmoded design and manufacture. The domes also
bore large, concave mirrors, which faced more or
less into the sun, though they had obviously
stopped tracking it some years ago. Their angles
were slightly askew and at least one was completely off-target. Between the buildings were
paths, gardens, fountains—even swimming pools—

but the pools were empty now and the fountains no longer spouted.

The drive passed between two of the outer buildings and ended in a graveled area in front of the taller structure. Weeds were coming through the gravel in places, in others it had been blackened by oil drips. No one had turned or changed it in a long time. The place was clearly untended. An upstairs window in the main building was cracked diagonally behind a hanging board; the paintwork was flaking; the doors were nailed shut. But the place as a whole was not quite deserted, not at the moment anyway. A second car stood in one corner of the parking area, and the glass doors of one of the outer buildings stood open. A male figure came walking toward them along a path from the open doors.

The stranger was German, carried a bulky briefcase, looked official—but in an untidy, friendly sort of way. He was young, blond, casually dressed, and he looked mildly surprised. Lynn and Richard got out of the Mercedes, stood waiting for him.

Stone tried to concentrate on what was happening but his mind would not let him. It was too busy elsewhere—elsewhen?

The place was as he had known it would be (no, he had to face it, *as he remembered it*) or as someone else remembered it deep down in *his* mind. There was the pool where Garrison and Vicki had played together, and over there the copse where Schroeder had grown his exotic aphrodisiac mushrooms from the Tibetan Nan Shan. And behind him in the main building, apparently long boarded-up, the bar where he (no, not he, Garrison, *Garrison*) had got drunk more than once on cheap Ligurian and Cyprus brandy. And here—

right here where he stood now, this very spot—
this was where he, Garrison, had first met Suzy.
He had been blind then, with only the vaguest
hope of ever seeing again, but he had "seen"
Suzy . . .

External interruptions would not go away.

"What?" Stone looked up. "Oh, I'm sorry! I was
miles away."

The stranger smiled, "That's all right," and repeated: "You are English, then?"

"Yes," Lynn thought she had better answer,
"we, er—"

"My father used to own this place," Richard cut
in, glad of the opportunity to anchor himself and
not go wandering in pseudo-memories again, at
least not for the moment. "We thought we'd just
look in."

"Your father owned it?" the other's smile
dimmed a little. "I think perhaps you are mistaken. This is the property of Herr Heinrich
Schroeder, who now lives in Berlin. Or rather it
was his property, but recently he sold it to the
State. I am Karl Schmidt of the Department for
the Environment, Hessen area. I am—" he looked
suddenly embarrassed, a little uncertain of himself—"supposed to be here to make an assessment . . ."

"Your English is very good," said Lynn. "You
could pass for an Englishman."

"Thank you," said Schmidt. "I studied at Cam-
bridge." He turned back to Richard. "No, I am
sure you must have the wrong place."

"My father had it before Heinrich Schroeder,"
Richard told him. "He inherited it from Thomas
Schroeder, later gave it back to Heinrich—I think.
My name is Garrison. Richard Garrison."

Lynn looked at him. He sounded as if he really

meant it, as if he believed indisputably that he *was* Richard Garrison, son of Richard Garrison. Or perhaps it was simply that she too had now come to believe.

"Ah!" the other's smile came easier. "Yes, I know the name, I have certain documents." He patted his briefcase. "This place was once 'Garrison's Retreat,' yes?" He stuck out his hand and Richard took it, but gingerly. The other saw the bandages.

"Accident," said Richard.

"Oh? I am sorry."

"So what, er," Richard shrugged awkwardly, "what are you assessing?"

Schmidt laughed ruefully. "To tell the truth, I'm not sure! But if you know this place, maybe you can tell me? It's just the contents of this one building that are causing the problem. How can I decide what they are worth, or what to do with them, until I know what they are?"

"That building?" Richard nodded toward the one with the open doors. "Instruments, machines, observation windows, strange rooms?"

"Yes!" Schmidt was eager. "You understand these things?"

Richard half-nodded, half-shook his head. "I don't know," he said. "Let's go and see."

Lynn went with them, but Suzy was off exploring the grounds. Or perhaps "exploring" is the wrong word. Certainly she looked like she knew where she was going. Anyway, she could look after herself . . .

As soon as he entered the building, Richard felt changed, made small, almost oppressed. It was not that he was afraid; it was fascination more than fear. The air seemed tangible on his shoulders, weighing there. As a child, exploring weedy seaside caves in rocky bays, he had known the same feeling. Like entering the lair of some unknown, unknowable beast.

Except that this was a beast he *did* know . . . now. An esoteric beast. One of mystery and imagination, and of the mind.

Behind hermetic seals, the place was clean as a hospital and had the same feel. Ceramic tiles, plastic paint, thick glass . . . antiseptic.

"You see?" said Schmidt, waving his arms expansively. "A man would have to be psychic to know what all of this is for!"

"Exactly," said Richard, nodding.

"Pardon me?"

"A laboratory," Richard told him. "Upstairs, too. One big laboratory." He felt he knew what was coming, that this conversation had all happened before.

"Laboratory?" Lynn repeated him, her voice echoing.

"A test center."

"To test what?" Schmidt was lost.

"ESP—Extra Sensory Perception. A place to measure the unknown, to sound the unfathomable."

Déjà vu . . . paramnesia . . . I was here before. No, my father was here, Garrison . . .

He wandered through the place and the others followed, their footsteps echoing.

"ESP?" Schmidt repeated him. Even in this area his English was exceptional. "Do you mean . . . parapsychology?"

"Yes."

"And the machines? *Are* they machines?"

"Oh, yes."

"But they have no motors!"

"Of course not. They were designed to harness

the hidden power of the human mind. If they had motors that would be cheating."

"This room, for instance. There is nothing in it. It is only—shaped. Oddly shaped."

"A *Ganzfeld State* room," Richard explained. "To induce maximum ESP receptivity. Empty? No, it's merely in a *Ganzfeld* state."

He opened a door, pointed: "Zenner Cards machine. And those other devices, they're after Rhine. J. B. Rhine. He 'invented' ESP."

And déjà vu? Did he invent that, too?

"And here," said Schmidt. "Look—an empty room, and yet it has electrical apparatus built into the walls. And no visible controls!"

"De-magnetizers," said Richard, "to test teleportation and levitation."

"And these cabinets?"

"TET cubicles: Telepathic Exchange Tests."

"Hah!" Schmidt laughed. "How may one assess?"

"Easy," Richard told him. "Assess it as valueless!"

"What?"

"Rip it all out, destroy it. It has no value."

They left the building. "I think I agree," said Schmidt.

"Good," Richard answered, "and thank you."

"But what for? It is I who should thank you."

Richard shrugged, laughed. "Thanks for the memory!"

Of course, Schmidt failed to understand.

"What will the place be?" Lynn asked. "I mean, what will your government do with it?"

"It will be a sanatorium," Schmidt told her. "For people with sick minds."

"Then it is eminently suitable," Richard nod-

ded, his tone suddenly sour. "Oh, yes, for there'll
be plenty of those . . ."

Back at the car, Suzy was waiting for them.

They did not drive straight back to St. Andreasberg, for first Richard had something he wanted
Lynn to see. He knew the place now as if it had
been part of his life, and there was that which he
"remembered" so vividly that he wanted to check
it out. Therefore, as they passed through the iron
gates on their way out of the grounds, he said:
"Turn left but don't go onto the main road. Just
follow the fence, dead slow, through the trees.
It's a bit of a squeeze in a car this big, but . . .
there!"

They had emerged onto a grassy track running
between the fence and the pines, which Lynn was
obliged to follow at little more than walking pace
until it widened. "Where does this go?" she asked,
picking up a little speed. Her question was totally
innocent, as if Richard should legitimately know
the answer—which of course he did.

"It skirts the fence all the way along the front,
parallel with the road, then turns back into and
over the saddle," he told her. "We actually climb
above those buildings back there, and we'll be
able to look down across the domes. Then we go
across the hump of the saddle to the far side of
the mountain. There, where the drop is sheer for
about a thousand feet, stands a log cabin—a secret place, lost in the trees. It looks out over Hal-
berstadt toward Berlin. In fact on a clear night
you might even be able to see Berlin's lights, almost a hundred and twenty miles away! Certainly
the ten-laner will look marvelous from up there:
all those lights marching away to Berlin. Of
course, there were no ten-laners when my father

had the place built—" he turned his strange eyes on her, "—almost thirty years ago . . ."

The place turned out to be just as he described it. Built of logs and standing in a dense clump of tall pines, its back was supported by massive timber stanchions wedged deep into the rock of the mountain's rim and concreted there. Its front had a railed verandah; its roof sloped gently down from front to rear and was tiled in slate; it was a tiny hideaway no one might ever suspect of being here at all. And by the looks of the place, no one ever had suspected it.

Pine needles were thick on the floorboards of the veranda; the glass had shattered and fallen out where one small frame had warped; the door hung slightly askew where an iron hinge had rusted through. As for the rest of it: the pine was sound and the place was intact. It had suffered little through the years.

They went in.

Lynn busied herself opening windows, letting in some fresh air. The place was gloomy where sunlight barely forced a way in through fly-specked dusty panes. Dust lay thick everywhere, and pine needles had been blown in through the broken window. Beyond the log walls new trees had grown up over the years, shutting out most of the light.

Suzy knew the way. Tail wagging, she passed straight through the main room to a door in the back wall. Richard opened it for her. Out there a sturdily-railed balcony looked out on empty space, where the view was dizzying. A rocking chair, the springs beneath its rockers long since rusted away, faced mutely toward the northeast. But Richard felt that if he listened hard, still he might hear those springs creak . . .

He stood in the doorway, absorbing the feel of the place; but Suzy had already crossed the balcony to stick her head out through the rails. She gave a short, sharp bark, which long seconds later came echoing back . . . and again . . . and again. She looked at Richard expectantly, tail still wagging.

"If you insist," he said smiling, and yelled: "Halloo!"

"Halloo! . . . Halloo! . . . Halloo!"

"I'm not coming out there!" said Lynn at Richard's shoulder.

"It's safe enough," he told her. "Built to last."

"Books!" she said, and he turned back from the door.

Now that there was some light, he saw that she was right. In a corner stood a small bookshelf with two rows of hardbound books. Just seeing them there was enough; he didn't have to go any closer. "All the classic works on ESP," he said. Lynn didn't answer, simply replaced the dusty volume she had been looking at.

Richard let his gaze slowly wander over the rest of the room, making himself familiar with its contents . . . again?

In the center of the floor stood a large pot-bellied stove, its iron flue rising through the ceiling. Its door was open and there were sticks in there, some protruding: a fire just waiting to be lit. Double windows on three sides opened outward, except the empty, warped frame which had jammed. A large cupboard, its door open, stood empty. The walls and ceiling were of varnished, knotty-pine boards, but dusty now. A thick carpet of pine needles on the floor close to the broken window . . . grass had taken root in them, even a tiny creeper . . . moss turning the sill green where it was starting to invade the room.

There was a small wooden table, a couple of old easy chairs, some crockery and a pair of old-fashioned oil lamps on a shelf. That was it. "Wouldn't take much to fix it up," he said.

Lynn gave a little shiver. "Can we go now?"

He was surprised. "Don't you like it?"

"I *might* like it," she answered, "if it wasn't perched on the edge of eternity! Anyway, it's full of ghosts!"

He snorted. "Well *I* like it."

"Well of course," she said. "You would, wouldn't you—Richard Garrison?"

And later, driving back down from the place through the trees to the road, she promised herself that as soon as they were able she was going to have a long and searching conversation with this man—this sometimes-stranger—whom she loved so much. There were things in his head that he had not told her about, which seemed hardly fair. After all, she was as much caught up in it now as he was . . .

The Merc was running on air when Lynn stopped to fill up at the garage in St. Andreasberg before returning to the hotel proper.

Darren Jackson, watching the big car through binoculars where he sat with his brother on a wooden bench against the front wall of the Schweitzerhof, grunted softly as it rolled away from the filling station and began climbing again along the hairpins. "Here they come," he said, "They were at the garage some time, so I reckon she filled her right up."

"For a long run?" Michael took the glasses from him. "Or just to be on the safe side?"

"Search me," said Darren, "but it makes no difference anyway. Even if they take off right now we can't lose them—we'll be right on their tails. What's more important is this: buying petrol like that, now the whole gang will know they're here."

"Right," Michael nodded, finding the car and focusing the glasses upon it. "And I suppose that means we have to move pretty quickly, eh?"

"Quicker than that!" Darren grunted. "Tonight at the very latest, because tomorrow this place will be crawling with our goddamned brother disciples—and a sister!"

"Right!" said Michael again.

"Also it's Tuesday. Day after tomorrow, Craig closes down PSISAC. I'd like to be back there by then. The world will be going crazy."

"It is now," said Michael, "except that you don't notice it so bad up here. But down in the cities . . ." He let the sentence ride.

The Jacksons were twin sons of a backward Oxford girl and the unknown tramp who took advantage of her some twenty-eight years ago. They neither knew this nor cared. They had been brought up in an orphanage, where even as small children they had quickly earned a bad reputation for shifty, devious ways. Twelve years ago the State had found them work at PSISAC; from general laborers they had moved up to assembly-line workers, but it had taken them most of ten years to achieve even that. Their fellow workers had no time for them (though nothing was proven they had been labeled as light-fingered and untrustworthy), and no woman of the factory floor would go near them. They had bad mouths and could not keep their hands to themselves.

None of this had ever reached the ears of Management, however, for the boys on the shop floor had their own ways of dealing with things. The Jacksons had been worked over several times outside of working hours, not that this had taught them anything. If J. C. Craig had known, then he would never have sent them to bring back his daughter. But he had not known . . .

As twins they were identical: long-faced, shifty-eyed, lank- and sandy-haired, and deeply pocked from long bouts of teenage acne. Heavy-browed and pallid, gangling and awkward, they were gray, gloomy figures. They knew no friends but each other and wanted none. As for their membership of Craig's order: when this was all over and the mind-plague had reduced mankind to scattered, nomadic tribes, then would be time enough to see about that.

As the Mercedes entered the car park, the Jacksons left their bench and went indoors, taking seats in the reception area where they hid their faces behind newspapers. It was exactly 2:30 P.M. by the hotel clock when the pair they watched entered and went in to sit for a late lunch. But as Lynn and Richard passed from reception into the dining room she saw them, caught a single glimpse of Michael Jackson's face as he folded his newspaper and stared after her. Then he had turned his face away, and she was through the door—but the *feel* of his eyes on her remained, so that she gave a little shiver as she took her seat beside Richard.

She might have mentioned it to him then, but he was already busy ordering and anyway, she was probably wrong. It was simply that she thought she recognized the pair. Well, and she probably did: they may well have been there the night before, and she perhaps remembered them from then. In any case, after their light meal when they passed through reception to go upstairs, the gray strangers were no longer there. A fact for which Lynn was very glad, without quite knowing why.

Up in their room Lynn and Richard showered together and made love in the stinging water, just as they had used to. Then she had wanted to sleep, and though he did not think himself tired, still he joined her in their double bed and they fell asleep in each other's arms. The sun was just going down when they awakened. Feeling good, they wrapped blankets around themselves and went out onto their balcony to watch the mountains turning blue as evening's shadows started to creep.

"Richard," she said, when they were close in the twilight, "when are you going to tell me what you've learned? I know there's something, for you've been quiet and lost in thought ever since Schmidt took us into that ESP place. So what is it? I'm part of this too, you know."

He looked at her in the light of the first stars. "I'm not sure you'll believe me," he said. "Maybe I don't quite believe myself. It's all very fantastic."

"Fantastic?" she gave a little laugh. "Have you just noticed? Richard, it has been fantastic for quite a few days now! I'm even getting used to it."

"Well," he went on the defensive, "that's not the only reason I've been quiet. See, I haven't quite got it all sorted out myself yet."

"Then just give it to me the way you see it," she begged. "Please?"

He shrugged. "All right, if that's what you want. It might help if I can get it all out. But where do I start?"

"At the beginning?"

"You already know that. I've told you about Dr. Gorvitch at Calm Lawns—how he thought I was different from other gibberers—and you know that my father trusts me . . . Phillip Stone, I mean."

"Yes," she snuggled closer, "start there. What is it that makes you so sure that this Richard Garrison person was your real father?"

He frowned. "Well, it's like this, Lynn. It's as if there were two of me . . ." He sighed and turned his face away. "How the hell am I supposed to explain what I don't really understand myself? I mean, I'm here now because I don't understand, because I'm tracking it down, because I'm *trying* to understand!"

"But so am I, Richard, so please go on."

He sighed again. "The ordinary me, the one you know, is just the same as everybody else. I feel the same things, see the same things, know the same things as you or anyone else does. This is me now, the ordinary one, telling you all this."

She nodded. "That's fine. I understand that. So?"

His voice sank lower. "The other me is . . . very much different. It's as if he lives deep down inside me."

"Sort of Jekyll and Hyde."

"Yes," he said—then shook his head. "Hell, no! He's not evil, this other—just different. Let me put it this way: you saw all of that junk up there in the mountains, in that building Schmidt showed us?"

"Yes. Does that have something to do with it?"

"Oh, yes. Yes, it does."

"But you told Schmidt that all of that stuff was valueless, 'junk' as you've just called it . . ."

"That's right," he answered, "to anyone who doesn't understand it."

"But you do?"

He shook his head. "No, but my father did—and so does the *other* me. Lynn, you know how we inherit some of the features of our parents? I mean, like you got your mother's eyes and your old man's walk?"

"Yes," she said.

"Well, I'm the same. I got my mother's slim hands and her small ears. But from my father—"

"Yes?"

"From him I got a lot more, and I'm only just beginning to learn about it. You see, the things I got from him don't show. They're down inside me, with the *other* me. Richard Garrison wasn't an ordinary man, and the things he's passed on to me—things more in my psyche, my mind, than in my blood—well, they aren't ordinary either. They are what make me different. And I won't kid you, I'm frightened of them . . ."

"What sort of things?" she asked after a little while.

He nodded ruefully. "I saw that one coming, and I walked right into it—but this is where I get stuck. I don't know what sort of things. They're subconscious things. Sometimes I dream them, and with a little luck I remember what I dreamed; and at other times—"

"Yes?"

"They come—with The Gibbering. It's as if, when *I* can't fight back, *he* fights back for me. My father—or what he put in me. When I'm under stress, I get strength from within. That's why I'm still alive when other gibberers are dead and forgotten."

She nodded. "Let's see if I'm getting it. Your

father, Richard Garrison, was psychic. Maybe that's the wrong word. Let's say instead that he could make those machines in that building work. He was good at ESP. He had extra sensory powers."

"Yes."

"How do you know that?"

He was growing exasperated. "But I've *told* you!" he growled. "I know because I'm psychic too. I inherited it from him. Lynn, I knew it the moment I went into that building—and before today I didn't even know who J. B. Rhine was. I never even heard of him! As for TET cubicles and Zenner Cards—!" He shook his head.

She was silent for long moments, then said: "How about Suzy? How do you explain her? I know you dreamed about her, but that's not what I mean. Herr Gutmann said your father also had a black bitch called Suzy."

"I can't explain her," he shook his head. "She has me beat. I mean, it's too fantastic to be a coincidence, and yet I can't see what else it can be. Let's face it, my father's Suzy would be more than thirty years old by now!"

Lynn nodded slowly. "Yes," she agreed. "I suppose we'd better skip Suzy." Then: "Okay, last question. When we first started out, you said this wasn't only important to you but to the entire world. How did you mean?"

"Isn't it obvious?" he answered. "If I can beat the mind-plague, maybe others can do it too—maybe all of them." He looked out over the lights of St. Andreasberg, the lights of the world.

She stared at him, and his eyes were like a cat's where he looked out over the valley. Suddenly cold, she snuggled closer still. "Most girls would run screaming from you," she said, "and yet I only seem to love you more. Maybe I'm abnormal, too!"

She felt him relax and his arm crept around her, squeezing her. He smiled and gave a little snort. "Birds of a feather?" He kissed her.

"You know something?" she kissed him back. "Your eyes are really weird at night."

"Oh, yes," he said, "that, too. That's something else I got from my father." And with that the smile quickly faded on his face. "And that's probably the weirdest thing of all, because according to Herr Gutmann, Richard Garrison was blind . . ."

An hour later they went down to the bar and sat at a small table with their drinks. Herr Gutmann was helping at the bar when they entered. He smiled at them and bade them, *"Guten abend,"* but it seemed he had gone off Richard. A little while later he left the bar and another barman took his place.

It was then, too, that Lynn spotted the two sour-faced men from the reception area earlier that day. She pointed them out to Richard, but they were already on their way out of the room. He only caught a glimpse of them. "What about them?" he asked.

She explained about earlier. "The way one of them looked at me made my flesh creep," she said. "And why would they be wearing dark spectacles? I mean, in the evening? They weren't wearing them earlier."

"But you're wearing dark specs too," he shrugged. "So why shouldn't they?"

"Mine are to hide my black eye," she said. "So what's their excuse? Is it supposed to be a disguise? And if so, why? Also, I think I've seen them before."

"Oh, where?"

"I don't know. I've been thinking about it on and off ever since I woke up. It's just that . . . but no, that would be too much of a coincidence."

"What would?" Richard sighed.

"PSISAC," she said. "I have the feeling I've seen them at PSISAC."

Now he was interested. "But you're not sure?"

She shook her head. "No, it's just the way that one looked at me. Someone looked at me like that once at PSISAC, when I was with my father one day out in the complex."

Richard downed his drink and stood up. "Come on, let's walk Suzy. In the morning we'll get out of here."

"Oh, Richard. What a shame. I mean I really do like—"

Now he spoke more harshly, but under his breath so that no one else could hear. "We'd be moving on anyway," he told her. "But if those two are really from PSISAC—well, as you say, that's much too much of a coincidence."

"You think that maybe my father sent them?"

"Possibly. I don't know what I think, but I certainly don't like it. Maybe we should move on tonight."

They went to the bar where Richard had already ordered a steak from the kitchen, and the barman passed him a paper parcel and a deep bowl of water. Richard thanked him, led the way out of the Schweitzerhof to the car park. They let Suzy out of the Mercedes and watched her wolf her food, and Lynn remarked: "Her appetite is almost as good as yours!"

Richard grinned. "Well if it's as good as yours I hope there are no boy dogs around!" And before she could answer, he said to Suzy, "Rabbits, Suzy—*Rabbits*!"

She gave a bark, squeezed her way through the three-bar fence, ran off down the slope between the dwarf pines and across the grass, following a zigzag, tail-wagging course toward the town.

"Will she be all right?" Lynn asked.

"Oh, yes, don't worry about Suzy," he told her. "Come on, we'll follow the road down a little way. We're going short on exercise, you and I."

It was chilly now but they were wearing their warmest clothes; not that they had a lot to choose from. Richard wore a vest under his polo-neck, and a jacket; Lynn had on a woolen trouser-suit and a pullover over the top, wearing the collar on the outside. Hands in pockets, arms linked, they walked the winding road. A car passed them, flashing its headlights in a friendly manner, on its way up to the hotel.

Another car came from behind, also flashing, but this one was pulling up as it drew level. They turned toward it, were momentarily blinded by its lights. It stopped and doors sprang open. Two figures confronted them in the night.

"You!" Lynn gasped.

Michael Jackson had a gun with a silencer. He pointed it at Richard. "Goodbye, Mr. 'Garrison'!" he said. The gun spat a small jet of fire, went *plop!*—and Richard was knocked back off the edge of the road and down into the grass.

At the same time, as Lynn drew breath to scream, Darren Jackson grabbed her and slapped a gloved hand over her face. He squeezed her mouth, crushing her lips as he bent her head viciously backward. A moment later and he had dragged her into the back of the car. Somewhere far off in the night Suzy barked inquiringly.

"Hurry!" Darren called out, his voice hushed but urgent. "Finish him off!"

Michael aimed his gun into the darkness. A figure came halfway to its feet in the long grass at the side of the road.

"Hurry, for fuck's sake!" Darren called again. "There's a car coming!"

The figure in the grass stumbled and croaked an inarticulate protest. Michael was panicked. His hand shook as he squeezed the trigger. *Plop!— plop!*—and the stumbling figure was knocked down again.

"Quick!" Darren called.

Michael stepped into the road, into the driving seat, slammed his door. He put the gun in the glove compartment. His hands shook as he took the steering wheel, put the car in gear. Then they were moving.

"Not too fast!" Darren cautioned. "Drive normally. Take it easy." In the back he shifted his grip on Lynn's face and heard her sob. The sound of women crying always did something to Darren. It made him feel strong, potent. "You take it easy, too," he said. "Give me a hard time and I'll break your fucking neck!" He held her tightly, aware of her woman's shape against his.

Tits like melons! he thought. *And just as sweet. Oh, sweet lord! And couldn't I just?*

The first bullet had broken Richard's right collarbone and passed out the back of his shoulder. The second had scored a shallow groove along his rib cage on the right. But the third had lodged in him, three inches over his heart. He was a dead man, or should have been. But he had inherited more of his father than even he had guessed.

At first he crawled, then got up and staggered,

and finally he *ran* back to the Schweitzerhof. Halfway there Suzy joined him, whining as she sniffed
the blood that dripped where he stumbled and
swayed.

It was a miracle that no one saw them go
through the porch and into the reception area.
The desk clerk was out for the moment, the stairs
free for Richard as he slid up the wall to the corridor leading to his and Lynn's first-floor room.

Lynn! And where was she now? And who were
those two who had her?

Suzy went with her master all the way into the
dark room, watched him anxiously, whining as
he tipped the contents of the suitcase out onto
the floor. He left a trail of blood and he knew it; he
must surely be dying and he knew that too. The
pain was unbelievable; it threatened to black him
out; it was a white-hot poker in his chest, his
heart. But it was also something to fight. And
God, his father had been a fighter!

His pulse was speeding up, his heart hammering behind his ribs. The final burst, perhaps, before it ground to a halt.

He fell to the floor and in the darkness found
what he wanted. In his hand, the wire knuckleduster, its points sharp as the devil's horns. He
crawled to the TV set, found the cable. Suzy
growled, danced in her anxiety. She licked his
face, his blood where it stained the room's carpet.

"Away, Suzy!" he whispered hoarsely. "Away,
over there—*go!*"

She went, sat whining, shivering, watching him.

He squeezed his fingers through the coils of the
wire device, located the cable again and stabbed
one prong right through it. He was starting to
black out . . . the pain . . . the room was spinning.

He caught the other prong between the numb thumb and forefinger of his flopping left hand, positioned it over the cable—

—And leaned his weight on it.

The jolt of electricity snapped his body out as rigid as a pole. The stink of roasting flesh instantly wafted into the air as his fingers began to blacken where they held the smoking conductor. For one, two, three seconds he lay there, his body stretched out straight, vibrating. Then he released his grip and was shot away across the room.

But as he flew so he rose up off the floor, came to a halt in a horizontal position in the center of the room. And slowly spinning like a human fan, there he stayed.

His legs were open wide; his arms stood out straight from his shoulders; he formed a five-pointed star, slowly turning, unsupported, in mid-air. And the room was no longer dark but lit with the strange soft glow of his body. Suzy continued to whine low in her throat, her forelegs stiff and the hair of her body risen; but she sat still, never taking her eyes off him for a second.

His rate of rotation slowed, stopped. He turned through ninety degrees until he was vertical, stood there on air inches from the door. His entire face and body had a St. Elmo's fire glow in the darkness—but his eyes when he opened them were golden!

Suzy had seen eyes like these before and was unafraid. She waited impatiently as those eyes sought her out, as their golden beams reached out and touched her with their warmth.

SUZY. GO, FIND LYNN. BRING HER TO ME. BRING HER TO THE CABIN. AND SUZY, THOSE MEN . . . THEY ARE OUR ENEMIES!

The golden fire from his eyes intensified. Something passed from him to her, from man to dog. She leaped for the windows. Mid-leap, the windows opened, banged back on their hinges, and the great black bitch was through. But out in the cold mountain air it was not a dog that came plummeting down through the night. *Nothing* fell from that high balcony, nothing at all—but a dark cloud flowed over the valley. A nebulous cloud with the shape of a vast hound, whose paws were big as houses where they loped over St. Andreasberg's rooftops . . .

When Suzy had gone, Richard's body turned back through ninety degrees to the horizontal position. His legs came together and his arms slowly closed to the sides; his eyes closed: much of his body's glow faded until his luminosity left him a mere outline. Then he too sped out through the open windows . . . away and out into the night.

The desk clerk, Georg Stuker, had been slowly, methodically checking the security of the cars in the hotel parking lot when Richard and Suzy had entered the Schweitzerhof. He had taken his time, smoked a cigarette as he worked. The hotel was quiet tonight, only a handful of people in the bar, nothing much happening. It was good to get out from behind the desk for a few minutes. But as he was finishing and turned to go back inside—

Gravel crunched behind him, the unmistakable sound of a car's tires freewheeling. Stuker whirled. He had seen no one in the car park. What did this mean? Then his jaw dropped and his eyes bugged. A silver Mercedes was rolling directly toward him!

Stuker leaped out of the way, skidded on the

gravel and went down on one knee. He yelled out after the car as it glided by. He cursed vividly as only a German can, yelled again. Couldn't the driver hear him? Why didn't the madman put his lights on?

The car turned toward the exit, passed between Stuker and the hotel. The hotel's lights shone clearly through its windows. Stuker stopped yelling, snatched back his breath. The car was empty—there was no one in it!

Its lights came on as it turned out of the car park and its engine roared into life.

Stuker was enraged. Someone thought to make a fool of him! He ran after the car a little way, caught up, crouched down and stared hard. Empty! There was definitely no driver! An empty car was driving itself down the road toward St. Andreasberg!

"I am doomed!" Stuker groaned out loud. He clasped his head in both hands, spat out his cigarette. "The mind-plague!" He staggered into the hotel through the porch, came to a frozen halt halfway to his desk. His eyes went to the floor, grew round as marbles in his head. He saw the swath of fresh blood where it patterned the carpeting and climbed the stairs.

"*Mein Gott!*" he croaked. And a moment later, ashen-faced, he was screaming for help.

"Herr Gutmann!" he cried. "Herr Gutmann! *Oh, mein Gott, mein Gott! Mord!—Mord!—Mord!*"

Michael Jackson drove the big square Fiat through the night at a speed just a few kilometers over the limit. He knew he had to control his excitement, which always ran high after violence. And certainly tonight had been violent. Remembering the way he had cold-bloodedly stood there and killed a man, he shuddered in strange pleasure.

"Christ, the way I knocked him down!" he said, glancing over his shoulder.

In the back, his brother chuckled. "Dead as a doornail," he said. "You stretched him out in the grass like a fallen tree!" He looked down at Lynn where he held her head in his lap. She lay on her back, her legs sprawled along the back seat. Her right arm was trapped under his left leg, the other arm was jammed down between her and him. He took his hand off her face, said: " 'Fraid your boyfriend's a goner, love."

"You bastards!" she sobbed. "Murderers! I'll see you dead!"

"Orders is orders, love," said Michael from the front.

"Whose orders, you swine?" she spat.

"Wouldn't you just like to know?" Darren mocked. He moved a little where he sat, freed his erection where it was trapped awkwardly in his trousers. He let his left hand ride up a little where it crossed her midriff. His thumb touched the swell of her right breast. She struggled and started to sob again but he leaned down, put his mouth over hers and sucked at her. She was nearly sick.

When he drew back she spat out saliva, sobbed and screamed until she was hoarse. The brothers laughed, and Darren's hand was more determined where it explored her breast.

"Where are you taking me?" she demanded. "And you—*you . . . take your filthy hands off me!*"

"Here, our Darren!" said Michael, his voice gently chiding. "What are you doing back there then?"

"God, couldn't I just?" the other answered, his voice husky.

"You all randy, then?" asked Michael.

"Randy? Jesus!"

"My father will have the skin off you," Lynn sobbed unashamedly. "He'll cut your hearts out!"

"Your fucking daddy-dear sent us, sweetheart," said Darren softly.

She froze. *"What?"*

"It's right, love," Michael agreed. "He said we was to knock over the Stone kid and bring you back home to him."

Darren switched on soft, internal lights. He looked down into her astonished, unbelieving face. "Eh? You don't believe it: Well, it's true enough." He laughed and got his hand up under the pullover, began unbuttoning her trouser-suit top.

She struggled again. "I don't . . . don't *believe* you!" she snarled. "And did he say you were to maul and molest me? He'll *kill* you for this!"

Michael looked over his shoulder again, saw what his brother was doing. "Better cool it," he warned, his voice a croak. "You're getting me all worked up."

"God, look at that mouth," Darren ignored him. "Jesus, I could fuck her face!" He yanked up her pullover, tore open the front of her trouser-suit, ripped her brassière loose.

"Swine!" Lynn sobbed helplessly. "The first responsible person I see, I'll—" Darren dipped his head, sucked her right nipple into his mouth.

Michael applied his brakes, pulled off the road beneath an overhang of night-black trees. He looked into the back, licked his lips. His brother's mouth worked at the girl's breasts; his left hand was down inside her trousers; his right arm was across her face, stifling her sobbing. "Jesus!" breathed Michael.

Darren looked up. "We'll never take her back, you know," he husked. "She'll yell copper every chance she gets. And if we did get her back, what about her old man?" He took his hand out of her trousers, yanked open his fly. His stiff penis lolled out against her face.

"What'll we tell old Craig?" Michael asked, reaching between the front seats to squeeze Lynn's wet breasts.

"Tell him Stone had already killed her when we nailed him. Tell him we forced it out of the bastard before you shot him."

"Yeah!" said Michael. "I like it!"

"Come on, sweetheart," said Darren, clasping Lynn's chin. He grunted as he strained to hold her writhing body still. "Turn your sweet little mouth this way a bit."

"No!" said Michael. "Not here in the car. Too confined. If we open the boot we can have her there, with her legs sticking out. There's a light in the boot, too, so we can see what we're doing."

"Me first," the other grunted. "I want her mouth."

"No!" Michael snapped again. "Me first. You've been having your fun. I want her up the front. *Then* you can have her face—and after that I'll have her up the back!"

Lynn could hear all of this and could hardly believe her own ears. Half an hour ago there had been hope for everything. Now there was only horror. They literally stripped her in the car, tore her clothes from her. Terrified, she knew she was going to die. What could possibly save her? And anyway, Richard was dead, killed by these two monsters, so what was left for her? But surely she didn't have to go this way?

"You wouldn't kill me!" she whimpered, which only drove them to greater frenzy. "Have me if you must, but let me go—*please*!"

"Wouldn't we kill you, little Miss Craig? Wouldn't we?" said Michael, his voice a hoarse bark. "Well, we would, see. First we're going to fuck you with our little guns—and then our Darren's going to fuck you with my big gun—plop! plop! *plop!*"

"Can I?" Darren giggled. "It's only fair. You shot him, so I'll shoot her—and I know just where to do it!"

They dragged her naked from the car, opened the boot and thrust her headlong into musty darkness. A moment later and the boot light came on, illuminating her nudity—and their animal bestiality. As Michael went to mount her, she cried again: "You wouldn't kill me!" But she knew they would.

Strength came to her from somewhere. Her hand snaked out, opened the side of Michael's face in four scarlet lines. He cursed and fell back. Her sweat helped her slip from Darren's grasp. She ran along a ditch beside the road, screaming. They were on her in a moment. She tripped and fell, was dragged down into shallow, icy water.

Michael positioned himself between her legs, began to come down on her. His breath came in great foul *whooshes* into her face. "Come on," he gasped to his brother who was crouching over her. "Have the cow's face!"

Something huge, black, of awesome strength, incredible weight, came down on the car twenty-five yards away. It came down out of the sky, between the trees, a black column that crushed the car flat as if it were a matchbox under a boot. And like a box full of matches, the car exploded, lighting the night in a searing flash of igniting petrol, blasting back the darkness in a livid tongue of light and flame.

The Jacksons looked, saw—froze!

A black shape blotted out the stars. Golden eyes as big as doors fixed them in their glare. Teeth like logs gleamed white in a snarl high as the trees. And a growl like thunder rumbled all about them!

Suzy's head came down. She snapped at Darren where he came upright, the gun he carried falling useless from nerveless fingers. He had time for a grunt but not a scream as her teeth met through his waist and severed him, flinging his halves aside. Michael screamed, but only for a second. Then Suzy picked him up, shook him as a ferret shakes a rat, ground his skull and his chest and his body to a pulp and hurled him high over the pines in a welter of blood and entrails.

Then—

Lynn had fainted before ever she could see the cause of the explosion of the night-black phantom come to save her. Now Suzy's great moist tongue licked her once, head to toe, warm as a blanket. Her unconscious form was taken up in a mouth soft now as pillows, and Suzy's great head lifted.

She sniffed the air, searched out and found her master. She bounded high and wide . . . and the trees and the blazing car and the horror shrank into insignificance behind her . . .

Lynn came awake with a frantic lashing of her naked arms and legs. She cried out, thrust something wet away from her face, huddled down into

herself to hide her nakedness. Suzy whined at her,
barked, peered with great soft eyes. Lynn looked
fearfully about for her attackers, felt the bed of
pine needles under her . . . saw where she was.
There was no explaining it; for a moment her
mind reeled and she almost fainted again. Then
Suzy crept closer, her tail fanning left and right.

"Oh, Suzy, Suzy!" Lynn cried. She clutched the
bitch to her, the only sane thing in a mad world,
stared beyond her at the cabin. And her eyes grew
round in the night and her lips parted in a gasp
at what she saw.

The cabin was as before, except that now the
door stood open and a light shone out from
within. A soft, bluish light that filled the doorway
and windows with its not quite electric radiance.
The roof, the eaves, the veranda and corner
posts—all were outlined in foxfire. Unflickering,
steady as the glow of a dim electric lamp, the
light was strangely cold and not at all reassuring.

Beginning to shiver, Lynn looked down at her
body and touched herself all over. She seemed
unharmed. Bruised perhaps, but that was all. She
did not *feel* unclean, not as she would if . . . but
what of those terrible men? She scrambled up,
reeled, clutched at a veranda post and steadied
herself.

Suzy coughed out a little bark, backed up the
steps onto the veranda, turned to the door. She
looked back at Lynn, wagged her tail. Lynn followed, swayed, grabbed at a doorpost. She looked
into the cabin.

A moment later and she had thrown herself inside, was clutching at Richard's glowing body
where it hung suspended in air above the table.
Then she realized that it *was* suspended!

She backed away into a corner, her hand to her

mouth. His head turned, his shuttered eyes opened a crack. Golden light bathed his drawn face, washed out from him and touched her. His mouth remained closed, moved not at all, but—

LYNN. DON'T BE FRIGHTENED. STAY WITH ME. SUZY WILL . . . PROTECT . . . The voice in her mind grew faint, tailed off. His eyes closed and his face turned upward again.

"Oh my God my God my God!" Lynn gasped, shuddering in every limb. But Suzy was there, unafraid, and Richard was . . . alive?

Alive, yes! She could not—hardly dared to— believe it. She was mad or going mad. The terrors of the night had snapped her mind's last thread of sanity.

LYNN . . . LYNN . . . LYNN, the voice in her head was a whisper now, a receding echo. LOVE . . . LOVE . . . LOVE . . .

"Oh, and I love you too!" she cried. She made to go to him, cowered back. She could not, was not able. Not yet.

Cold with terror, and naturally cold, she hugged herself. There would be a frost tonight. What was she to do?

BLANKETS . . . CAR.

Was the car here? She went out onto the veranda. Under the pines to one side of the cabin, a dull glint of silver in the starlight. She collected Suzy's blankets from the back of the Mercedes and went back indoors.

FIRE.

She found matches on the shelf with the crockery and oil lamps; the matches were dry, and by some miracle they still worked! She dropped a flaring match into the potbellied stove, closed the door. A moment later and a warm glow told her that the fire had taken. Things were looking better.

But Richard, floating like that . . . !

She began to shiver again, wrapped a blanket around herself, dragged the door shut. Feeling a little easier—having mainly accustomed herself to the situation—she looked about the cabin. She took down the oil lamps, shook them, heard oil sloshing in their squat bodies. Lifting a glass chimney, she lit a wick crisp as paper and watched it start to draw the oil. Then she lowered the chimney and lit the second lamp.

What with the glow from the crackling fire in the stove, and the yellow light of the lamps, Richard's own peculiar radiance seemed damped down a little. It didn't frighten her so much. Lynn began to breathe a little easier; her heart's thudding slowed beneath her ribs. She swallowed hard once or twice, looked about the room again. The old armchairs had large square cushions for seats and backs. They had gone a little moldy underneath but were still serviceable if you weren't too particular. She had neither time nor circumstances to be particular. She stripped the chairs down, lay the cushions on the floor lengthwise and draped them with a blanket.

Gulping, she then approached Richard's body where it floated motionless above the table. She touched him. His flesh was icy cold—cold as the tomb itself!

"Richard," she said. "Please! I can't stand seeing you doing . . . *that*!"

His gaunt face changed not at all, his eyes remained closed—but slowly his body moved, floated over to the makeshift bed, lowered itself until the cushions took its weight.

"Oh, thank God!" Lynn breathed. "Thank God!"

She took up the edges of the blanket and folded them over him. The blue glow was contained, only his cadaverous face remained lit by that eerie foxfire.

The bed she had made for him was too long. She pulled out the bottom cushion and tossed it onto one of the chairs. The cabin was beginning to warm up, the flue of the potbellied stove started to glow red at its bottom. Suzy curled herself up close to the stove, but her eyes continued to watch Richard across her paws, never wavering.

Lynn dragged the chair with the cushion close to the warmth, flung herself down in it. She warmed her feet in the curl of Suzy's body for a moment, then jumped up again. "God, oh God! What am I *doing*? I have to get a doctor . . ."

NO!

She started, turned toward him where he lay unmoving, his eyes closed in his pale, sunken, blue-glowing face. "Richard, I *have* to get a doctor or you'll die!"

NO.

"But—"

I HAVE TO REST. NOT TALK—REST! STAY. WATCH. NO . . . DOCTOR . . .

"Richard, I'm frightened!" She began to cry, flopped into her chair.

SLEEP.

"Oh, sleep, sleep!" she giggled hysterically. "How can I possibly sleep? I—"

SLEEP. This time he ordered it.

And at once she slept.

And Suzy kept watch . . .

In the middle of the night Lynn awakened. The oil lamps burned on; the fire was low; Suzy had not moved, nor Richard. His face was still bathed in blue light. He lived.

She had noticed a small stack of moss-grown logs close to the veranda. They had been cut for the stove. Now she went out and brought an armful in, piling them quietly on the floor. The last two logs went straight into the stove. Then Lynn sat down again and Suzy uncurled herself, came and put her head in her lap. The bitch looked at her questioningly.

"I think so," Lynn said. "I think he'll be all right."

The new logs in the stove hissed, crackled, took flame.

The hissing continued.

Suzy whined, her soft eyes going to Richard.

Lynn looked, too.

The hissing did not come from the stove. A puff of smoke drifted up from the blanket where it covered Richard's chest.

Lynn was up and across the room in three jumps. She jerked back the blanket . . .

The smoke curled from his jacket near the top pocket. She opened his jacket with fingers that shook, jerked up his polo-neck, his vest. She forced the garments up under his armpits. High on his chest was a hole in the center of a circular blue bruise. The smoke came from there.

Holding his clothes up under his chin, she watched, her eyes riveted on the bullet hole in his chest, her mouth open. The hissing grew louder. Something bubbled up, filled the hole, started to flow over. It looked like mercury. Lynn touched it with a trembling forefinger. It burned!

She snatched back her finger. A thin trickle of

molten lead ran across Richard's rib cage, smoked where it dripped on the blanket beneath him, puddling there as it cooled. His ribs were unmarked. The blue bruise was fading even as she watched, the hole sealing over.

The *other* Richard was taking care of him . . .

Day Five

DAILY MIRROR:

SHOCK FIGURES!

More than 1,600,000 people, men, women and children, in the British Isles, now suffer from the so-called and so far incurable "mind-plague." The number is not known exactly, but reliable sources have it that the problem is now of epidemic proportions. The government has been lobbied to give an accurate assessment of the situation, but so far it would appear they are taking a softly-softly approach.

New offices in Whitehall have been opened where staff studies in "Statistics and Strategy" are said to be proceeding satisfactorily, but no further information is yet available. Mr. Charles Ingram, Minister for Mental Health and Care Coordination, could not be drawn on the subject. There are however rumors of the imminent fruition of a long-term joint U.K.-U.S.A. project for a "cure" or "prevention" in the form of an oral immunization similar to the birth pill of the mid-20th Century. It is believed that final tests are now in progress . . .

Tokyo Times:

Tang Asai Oshito, Nipponese Head of State, has now approved the organization of vigilante groups for the protection of the populace from mind-plaguers. These "V-Groups" will be organized through local government; recruitment and swearing-in will commence today at police stations throughout the Nipponese Nation, on all four major islands and lesser islets. The principal aim will be to confine gibberers in pre-determined secure areas, and to keep them there under guard. These are of course emergency measures only, and as conditions change so procedures may be altered to suit new situations. Total support for government policies is anticipated; after today, anyone found to be harboring mentally diseased persons will be liable to the most severe punishment . . .

The Organ (Johannesburg):

Violence is flaring again along borders unmanned for more than ten years. So-called "refugees" are flooding the country from the plague-pits of the North. The mind-plague has come among us and all white South Africans must surely recognize its source. *The Organ* makes no bones about it and will speak out as of old: the time for action is *now*!

In order to stem the flood of potential pest-carriers, our President, Mr. Joachim van Hechler, has ordered a thin red line of paramilitary volunteers in support of the much run-down and hardpressed regular forces already setting up along the northern approaches—and this journalist for one stands firm behind a right and proper course of defensive action.

However:

Black mind-plague enclosures in the very heart of our homeland are steadily approaching saturation point; empty only a week ago, they are now beginning to overflow! We have already witnessed the results of a mass breakout in Odendaalsrus—where last evening 9,000 blacks raped, looted and murdered their way through a predominantly white township, killing as many of their own as they did of ours—and while yet the horror of this sinks in, we cannot help but conjecture upon the results of similar disasters taking place in the major cities.

If more need be said, then let it be this:

The mind-plague is incurable; the Black Condition is unchangeable and always has been, despite certain government policies of the last fifteen years; the answer is simple and obvious to all but blind men and fools. We are breeding horror! Each enclosure and stockade is a running sore whose pus can only infect us all.

In the old days men knew how to deal with such matters and were unafraid. You could treat a village for dysentery, but plague-towns were put to the torch! And is this plague any different?

The Organ speaks out, before it is too late, and asks this question:

Where are today's torch-bearers?

Watchdog! (U.S.A.):

THE PILL: PURE POISON?

Acting on allegations so serious that they could not be ignored, the owners and editors of this weekly journal last night took unprecedented steps in their on-going fight for the freedom of the spoken and printed word. This followed the covert approach to these offices yesterday of a senior chemist from the recently established and Government-funded Yonkers Institute for Mind-Plague Studies, who came to us with a story so terrifying in its implications that we ordered an immediate investigation.

But while our reporters were stonewalled at Yonkers—while our tele- and video-phone switchboard turned red-hot from our largely ignored and unanswered outgoing calls—and while Professor Lon Zebber himself (our informer) was being arrested by FBI agents at his home in White Plains and removed to parts unknown, our own chemists were already working on the samples we had been given.

Their findings were such that despite threats from sources we cannot at this moment of time reveal, we changed our newsprint overnight to bring you this article; and our readers are asked to forgive us if the quality of this leader is not of our usual high standard. But you may now judge for yourself whether or not it was worth it.

The alleged "pill" they are working on at Yonkers is not a pill at all—not as we were led to believe—but it will certainly cure The Gibbering. Indeed, it will "cure" just about anything! Naturally we are loath to give the names of our team of chemists (suffice it to say that their credentials are impeccable) but the results of their analysis of the pill *must* be made public at once!

And then all you readers, just like us *Watch-*

dogs, will want to know the answers too—and we mean right now!

Quote: "What this stuff is," (say our scientists, after working halfway through the night) "is simply a very efficient poison. It could be manufactured in the form of pills, certainly—or as a liquid, even as a gas. Whichever, it's a sure-fire killer!"

And they went on to say: "Do you remember Hitler, the gas chambers? Well, World War II is some way back now, but if we had to name this stuff we think we'd take a lead from what was done over there in Germany all those years ago— except that this stuff is far superior to anything the Nazis ever had. What would we call it? Would you believe, 'Zyklon C . . .'?"

Which is why *Watchdog* asks, as will every single one of its 200,000 readers: *What the hell is going on here?*"

Phillip Stone stopped reading and tossed his newspaper aside. It was the *Mail*, and probably as conservative as ever. He suspected that the figures were in fact far more serious than was being reported. 1,600,000? That sounded on the low side to him, and his mind went back to the files he had seen in J. C. Craig's office three days ago. That had been Sunday, and already it was Wednesday.

His video-phone interrupted his train of thought, buzzing determinedly.

Stone was not in a good mood. Following long-established habits, which came into play quite automatically whenever he was having an off period, he left his end of the two-way vision system "off" until he knew who he was speaking to. Why should he let some complete stranger gawp at him like he was a monkey in a glass cage? And conversely, why should *he* have to look at some stranger's ugly mug?

His mood was dictated by the fact that he had been "let down," and he fully expected that the caller would be Albert Gill with some totally unacceptable excuse for not keeping their morning appointment. Gill was the most infuriating man! This was to have been their fourth—and possibly their last—session, but the psychiatrist was already more than an hour late. It was particularly galling because he had promised that this time it would all come together: finally, he would be able to tell Stone what he wanted to know.

Actually, Stone had scarcely believed him. It had seemed to him that Gill was stalling, that he was finding it more difficult to fathom Stone's mind than he had anticipated. The tubby little psychiatrist had seemed to grow more confused from day to day; the answers he was getting seemed to confirm something, but not what he wanted them to confirm; the fantastic "fictions" in Stone's subconscious mind were stronger, or had been more strongly implanted, than the real facts he was trying to dig out.

Paradoxically enough, Stone was just sufficiently contrary to enjoy Gill's confusion; the complexities of the case had taken a lot of the initial wind out of the psychiatrist's sails. On the other hand, Stone was more than ever aware of the passage of time. His sense of urgency had been increasing with every session, but Gill had stuck to his guns and refused to tell him a single thing until it could all be laid out for him, cut and dried. Infuriating!

Urgency, conflicting emotions, frustration—in combination, they were explanation enough for Stone's mood. But when the voice on his phone introduced itself as that of Police Sergeant Weston at the Dorking police station. . . .

Stone had respect for the law. He had been a lawman himself—of sorts—once over. He switched vision "on" and sat back, staring half-apprehensively at the screen. This could be anything, but there were certain things it was more likely to be. For instance, something to do with Richard.

The gray smog of hazy lines snapped into sharp focus; background detail was mainly lost but the face on the viewscreen came up sharp-etched. "Weston, sir," that face repeated, unsmilingly. "Good morning—and thanks for vision. It helps to be able to see who you're talking to."

"There are conflicting opinions on that, Sergeant," said Stone. "Often it hinges on the subject of the conversation. I'm Stone, Phillip Stone. What can I do for you?"

Weston was maybe twenty-eight or -nine, looked solidly reliable, highly intelligent. While still youthful, his face was nevertheless strained, overworked, worried. A young face and mind rapidly growing old. All the services were suffering. The Gibbering was stretching them like so much warm putty. Police, fire, prisons, hospitals . . . asylums. Even the Armed Forces. Stone snorted at that last thought: "Armed Forces," that was a laugh! In his day they had been forces—and forces to be reckoned with, at that. But now they had become so run-down as to be little more than government auxiliaries.

The face on Stone's screen frowned. Weston must think his derision—which had obviously showed on his face—was directed at him. Well, let him think it! "Did you want something, Sergeant?" Stone asked again.

"Yes, sir, possibly," Weston answered, leaning back a little way and out of focus, turning his head to look at something off-screen, then coming back again. But at least this had given Stone the chance to check out the other's smart blue uniform with its three stripes, complete with bright whistle-chain disappearing into top left-hand pocket. Weston's movement had been quite deliberate: while ostensibly he sought something, he had displayed his badge of office, the regalia of his authority. It didn't faze Stone at all.

"Mr. Albert Gill," said Weston. "A friend of yours, sir?"

That *did* faze him.

"I know him professionally," said Stone, sitting up straighter. "Why?"

"Appointment with you this morning, sir?"

"He had, yes—and he's late!" Stone's heart gave a lurch. He was counting on Gill. A great deal might be counting on Gill. What was all of this? Weston saw the query on his face and didn't keep him waiting.

"I'm sorry, Mr. Stone," he said, "but I'm afraid he's not going to make it."

Oh, Christ! What now? "Something's happened?"

"Accident, sir. Went off the road. I'm afraid he's knocked himself about rather badly."

"But he's alive?"

"Oh, yes, he'll live—but it was a close one. He's in hospital here in Dorking. Broken neck."

"Good Lord!" Stone chewed his lip. "A long job, then? When will I be able to see him?"

"Visit, you mean?" Weston's gaze was even. "You're not . . . related, sir?"

Stone had had that question asked him before. His heart sank.

"You're telling me I should get myself a new psychiatrist, right?"

Weston nodded.

"Mind-plague?"

Again the nod.

Stone slumped down. "How did you get hold of me?"

"Appointment book in Mr. Gill's pocket," Weston answered. "He had your appointment down for today at 8:30—your name and address, too."

"Yes, of course. Sergeant, about the accident—"

"We're calling it an accident, naturally," Weston cut in. "We haven't had time yet to decide on categories for mind-plague cases. Crimes? Acts of God. It's difficult . . ."

"I can see it would be," said Stone. "But the car—was it a write-off?"

"No, not at all. We're having it towed in for a mechanic's check and report. Have to get things right, you know? Sort of what came first, The Gibbering or the crash? But from what we know, it seems he must have suffered an attack while driving. He began to swerve the lanes—other drivers had to avoid him—and then he just ran out of road. Not going too fast. Jumped a ditch and turned over. He was wearing a seat belt, of course. He got caught up in it. It was probably his own weight that broke his neck . . ."

"But the car's okay?"

Weston nodded, frowned. "You have an interest in that car?"

"There may be some of my things in it, that's all."

"Oh?"

"Yes. A handful of tape recordings."

"Ah! Well if that's so, you'll get them back in due time."

"How long is due time?"

"When we're through checking the car over—and when I can spare the time to arrange—"

"Sergeant, those tapes are very important to me. Very. If you could speed it up I'd be greatly in your debt."

Weston stared at him, sensed his urgency. "Well now, sir, I—"

"Look," Stone said. "The tapes are Gill's recordings of my case. Now then, I'm an influential man. Those tapes aren't the sort of things I would want falling into just anybody's hands. Personal stuff, you know?"

Weston nodded, his eyes narrowing a little. "I see, sir."

Stone wasn't at all sure he did see. "You probably know that I'm *the* Phillip Stone" (he didn't really like to do this, but what the hell?—Weston had shown him *his* authority, hadn't he?) "PSISAC's Phillip Stone?"

The policeman's eyes widened out again. "No, I hadn't—"

"Well you should do your homework," said Stone, "for I am. Now obviously I'll get my tapes back sooner or later, but I'd prefer sooner. And I *would* be grateful. The constable who delivers them to me here at home can collect a check for any charity you care to mention. Or if you're pushed for a man I can collect them myself. All right?"

"Ah! Well, sir, I'm not at all sure—"

Stone ran out of patience. "Well if *you're* not sure," he snapped, "I'd better speak to someone who is! What's your Chief Inspector's number? Or don't you have a CI in Dorking? Okay, so I'll speak to the Chief Constable. Thanks for calling me." He made as if to end the call.

"Wait!" said Weston. He could see from Stone's face that he wasn't bluffing. And anyway—Phillip Stone? He must be worth millions! He could make life really difficult for a body.

Weston smiled at Stone, however tightly. "That won't be necessary, sir," he said. "You can consider it done—ASAP."

"Good!" Stone sat back.

"Policeman's Widow Fund, sir?" Weston had been impressed, not intimidated.

"Eh? Oh, yes. Certainly. Very worthy. A thousand?"

Weston's eyes grew round. He was even more impressed. "Well, sir, I should think that will do very—"

"Thanks," said Stone, terminating both conversation and call.

"Mary, coffee!" he yelled, standing up.

She was next door, called back: "In there?"

"In the grounds," he lowered his voice a little. "Just give me a whistle."

"Right you are."

He went outdoors, walked through the dreary November garden to the perimeter wall. He was glad now that the place was no bigger. Small, really, for what he could afford. Some acres, nothing much. But it had always been big enough for him and Vicki. And Richard . . .

The wall was of stone; quite massy, though broken down in places. Grown with moss and grass, the breaks had seemed to add to the charm of the place. Now they were a worry. Still, with his reinforcements, it shouldn't matter too much. The workmen were getting on with the job very well, a whole gang of them with their iron stakes and steel netting. He caught the foreman's eyes, called him over.

"How long, do you reckon?"

The man was squat-bodied, with great calloused hands like old and well-used hammers. He pushed his helmet to the back of his head, scratched his nose. "Tomorrow noon," he grunted. "*If* there are no more absentees!"

"Oh?"

"Yers. I calls 'em absentees, anyway. Two more this mornin', Chief. We started Monday wiv a baker's dozen, and nar we're darn ter nine! Bloody Gibbering!"

"All four of them?"

"Yers," the other nodded, "reckon so. World's gone bleedin' crackers, Chief!"

"That certainly seems the case," Stone wryly agreed.

Now the foreman scratched his forehead. "Anyway, what's the idea of all this?" he waved his hand, broadly indicating the tall wire enclosure they were throwing up around the house and grounds. "You expectin' World War III or something?"

"Or something," Stone nodded, grinning—but his grin was pure camouflage and quickly fell from his face. "Anyway, you'd better take on more men, just to be on the safe side. Work late if you have to. Double time after 4:00 P.M.—and something extra in it for you personally if you get done by midday tomorrow. Call it a hundred?"

"An 'undred?" the other's grin was genuine through and through. "No sweat, Chief! I'd finish it on me own for a ton!" He turned and went back to work, began barking harsh, urgent instructions.

Good! Stone said to himself. And: *what's good enough for J. C. Craig is good enough for me.*

Mary called him from the main door of the

house. Stone heard her voice over the renewed clanging of sledgehammers, the grunting and coarse, muttered oaths of the workmen, and the roaring of a small truck's motor as it was used to stretch out the tough wire-netting between stanchions.

Walking back down the drive to the house, he found himself once more thinking about Richard. What was the lad up to right now? he wondered. And Lynn: what sort of a time was it for her? Brave girl, that. Open as a book. Pity the same thing couldn't be said for her father . . .

Stone had worried about the fugitives constantly since Saturday; and yet, for all that they had been gone four days, Jimmy Craig hadn't brought it up again. That bothered Stone. In fact, he had had no contact with Craig or PSISAC since Saturday.

Suddenly the thing which had been bothering him—that elusive something in the back of his mind—sprang forward into sharp relief. Of course! Now why hadn't he thought to ask himself that question before? Too much on his mind, he supposed. But after all, you can't expect to get the right answers if you don't ask the right questions—and the big question was this:

Wasn't J. C. Craig aware that he, too, was just as much a candidate for the mind-plague as anyone else? And yet up there at PSISAC he was turning the complex into a refuge, a fortress. It seemed utterly futile . . . didn't it? What use to be master of a mad castle? And yourself mad to boot?

But on the other hand . . . well, here was he, Phillip Stone, doing exactly the same thing. Taking a leaf from Craig's book. It was like everything else, he supposed: you never think it's going to happen to you. And yet . . .

He shook his head to clear it, chewed his lip harder, stood watching the work proceeding while he drank his coffee. He would dearly love to go back up to PSISAC and start asking questions—and demanding answers! And yet something warned him that that would be an extremely dangerous course of action. No, he would stay away from the place—for now, anyway.

But sooner or later, he promised himself—if there was to be any later at all—J. C. Craig was going to have a hell of a lot of explaining to do!

At that very moment, the subject of Phillip Stone's silent conjecturing had just received a video-call of his own from the Continent. Up in his rooms in the Dome, J. C. Craig sat at his desk and waited for the screen to shift into focus on Edward Bragg's expressionless face, then leaned forward and snapped:

"Edward—what news?"

"Some," said the other, nervously, "—but none of it very good."

Craig saw now that Bragg's blank expression was more the result of shock than of impassivity. He caught his breath, let it out in an explosion of words:

"What's that you say? Bad news? Tell me, quickly—what's happened? What of Lynn?"

Bragg held up his hands. "Give me a chance!" And after a moment: "It seems that the Jackson brothers found them first," he said.

"Yes? Well, go on?" Craig could barely contain himself.

"The Jacksons found them, and the Jacksons are dead!" Bragg told him. "Both of them."

His voice had a tinny edge to it and there was a lot of static, which showed up on the screen as well as in the audio. Craig made as if to adjust his set but the other stopped him: "This is a car-video," Bragg said, "and I'm in a bit of a hollow between hills. You can't expect any better reception from here. The main thing is that you can hear me okay."

"Yes, yes, I hear you!" Craig snapped. And more calmly, almost pleadingly: "Edward, what about Lynn?"

Bragg's mouth tightened a little. "As far as I'm aware she's all right," he said. "That is, there's no evidence yet to say she isn't . . . but you'd better let me tell it the way I know it."

"Then get on with it!" Craig bit his lip, clenched his fists.

"Listen!" Bragg suddenly snarled—and immediately controlled himself. "I'm sorry, sir, but it's no good you sitting there nice and safe at PSISAC, yelling at me and getting all frustrated. I'm the one who's up against a bloody murderous maniac!"

Craig's jaw dropped, not at Bragg's tone but at the implications of what he had said. "Garrison murdered them?" he gasped. "He murdered the Jacksons?"

Bragg nodded his confirmation. "Yes, he did. That's the way I see it, anyway. But don't ask me how he did it."

"But I am asking you! Please go on."

Bragg nodded. "Very well. I'm near a little place called Duderstadt. I heard it on the local morning news that there'd been a traffic accident of some sort or other—an accident, anyway. The two people involved were thought to be English tourists. Since I was close to the scene of the . . . the thing,

I motored straight round here. I told the local police I might know the two dead people—said I'd had drinks with a couple of English people last night—and they let me see the bodies."

"And it was the Jacksons?"

"Right. Sir, they were in a hell of a mess! Christ only knows what Stone, er, Garrison, did to them!"

"Don't take the Lord's name in vain!" Craig snapped. And, "Explain."

"One of them was crushed from his thighs up. Not flattened—sort of scrunched up, as if a hippo had closed its mouth on him. The other—" Bragg pulled a face.

"Yes?" The corner of Craig's mouth had started to twitch.

"He was chopped in half, right across his middle. The two halves weren't even close together, and his guts were slopped between them . . ."

Craig groaned. "Power of the antichrist!" he breathed. "What else?"

"They had been driving a Fiat—a big square job. At least, I suppose it was their car. It was crushed, burned out."

"Crushed? Burned?"

"Yes, as if a building fell on it. There were tire tracks where it pulled off the road and under some trees, and then . . . just crushed. It was pressed into the ground to its belly—roof caved in, windows all smashed or popped out—and gutted with fire."

"Edward, listen," Craig was frantic now. "You *have* to find my daughter. Find her and—"

"I'm not finished," said Bragg.

Craig didn't like his tone of voice, guessed that something even more unpleasant was yet to come. "Then go on and finish," he said.

"In a ditch close by, there were some items of torn clothing. Trouser-suit, pullover top, underclothes, shoes—the lot. It was a woman's gear. The shoes were definitely Lynn's. I've seen her wearing them . . ."

Craig's face drained of blood. "What . . . what are you telling me?" his voice was a croak.

"I suppose I'm telling you not to get your hopes up too high," Bragg answered.

"But you said she was all right! You said—"

"I said there's no evidence yet to say she *isn't* all right! There's no body, is there?"

Slowly Craig's head bowed. He covered his face with his hands and began to sob.

"Sir," Bragg said, less harshly now, "it may not be as bad as it looks. Don't give in. I haven't."

"No, of course not," Craig's voice was muffled, racked with his sobbing. "We must never give in. Do you have any leads?"

"He has to be up in these mountains somewhere. I've heard rumors of some weird occurrences in St. Andreasberg—and Garrison bought petrol there yesterday. I'd be there now but I suffered a couple of bad attacks. Anyway, I'm going now."

Finally Craig looked up, dried away the tears from hollow, red-rimmed eyes. "Then I must wish you Godspeed," he said. "I shall pray for you, Edward."

Mad as a hatter! Bragg thought. *This one gibbers as a matter of course!* Out loud he asked: "What of the others? Any word from them?"

"Not from Conti, no. But he's close-mouthed, that one. The Tyler woman says she has a good lead, but she was speaking to Miss Ellis, not to me personally. She didn't say what her lead was."

"Then I'll speak to Dorothy Ellis next," Bragg nodded.

"Yes, fine. But waste no time, Edward. Time is precious now. And spare no effort."

"One more thing . . . sir," said Bragg.

"Yes?"

It was now or never, Bragg decided. "If I carry this off—if I can find and kill Garrison, and bring your daughter home to you—there's something I want."

"Anything, anything. Haven't I said as much?"

"I want her."

"What?" Craig's face took on a startled expression, rapidly turning to astonishment. "You want—?"

"I want Lynn, your daughter. Her hand in marriage. In the new world—in *our* new world."

Craig's face darkened. Slowly he began to rise from behind his desk. His face was working furiously now, growing more mobile with each passing second.

"Who else will there be for her?" Bragg gabbled defensively. "And am I not one of yours? I've admired her for a long time—from a distance, of course. Or would you let her go off with someone else—someone like Garrison, perhaps? Some undeserving outsider, survivor of the holocaust?"

His words, however blunt, made sense. Craig listened to him, breathed deeply, slowly sat down again. He forced the nervous twitchings of his face to immobility, held himself in a tight grip. And finally he spoke:

"Bring her to me, unharmed—and let her tell me herself that you killed Garrison the antichrist—and then let her tell me that she wants you, and you shall have her."

Bragg considered it and found his chances fair.

If Lynn still lived, she must surely be terrified of Stone by now. How many times had he gibbered, Bragg wondered, since the little fool ran off with him? And as he had pointed out to Craig, who else would there be for her when all of this was over? In the event that it failed to work out the way Bragg saw it, well, he could always think of something else. In any case, the New Order would be far better suited to younger men; and surely the New World would be a world for strong men, and not doddering old fools like Craig. It would be a simple matter to trim the religious trappings once this so-called "prophet" was gone, and certainly he would not last long—not with Bragg there to help him on his way out. By which time Lynn Craig would be Bragg's whether she liked the idea or not. And so:

"I agree," he said . . .

This time Lynn woke up starving.

She came awake slowly, her eyelashes gummed down from heavy sleeping. Her mouth was very dry and clammy, her back stiff from the awkward position in which she half-reclined; but her sleep had been too deep and she emerged from it fuzzy in her mind . . . and hungry. That was her first waking thought: how very hungry she felt.

Richard's eating yesterday would have fueled a Rugby XI, but she had been much more restrained. Now she wished that she, too, had tucked in. She yawned, smiled as she remembered Richard with his heaped plates, and dragged her eyes half-open. The cabin was full of a dim daylight . . .

Cabin?

Suddenly Lynn knew where she was, remembered everything.

She started out of her chair, all of her senses jangling with the sudden clamor of alarm bells, like gears clashing in a dry gearbox. She stumbled, pins and needles numbing her thighs and buttocks, her arms stiffly windmilling as her legs refused to move. And trembling, she leaned on the table, got her heart and her breathing under control as she looked all about and completed orientation. Suzy came to her, tail wagging as Lynn worked first one leg, then the other, getting the blood flowing again.

Her head was clearing rapidly now, terror flooding in to color the gray wash of blurred memory. If she ever had to live through a night like that again . . . well, it would be too soon! Automatically she went to check her watch, only to find that it was no longer on her wrist. She had not seen it since those men attacked her. Obviously, in their animal haste, they had stripped her of the watch, too. Oh, well—it had never kept the right time anyway.

She supposed it must be, oh, 10:00 or 11:00 A.M. at a guess. Outside the windows, while the day was not particularly bright, it was nevertheless broad daylight; the fire in the stove had burned itself away to a small heap of dull red embers, and that despite the fact that she remembered automatically stoking it on several occasions throughout the night; the cabin was cold again and a draft swept in from the door where it hung slightly askew. Lynn had *really* slept this time; she must have needed it.

She thought again of the men who had attacked her, their awful *faces* as they mauled her . . . then cast them from her mind. More important far was the fact that she had escaped them— or had been rescued—or a combination of the two. She supposed she would have to wait for an explanation of that. Perhaps Richard would be able to tell her what happened, eventually.

Fully awake now, she dropped a few splinters of wood and dry bark into the stove, then some heavier fragments, finally two of the thinner logs. Then she went to Richard.

He lay exactly as she had last seen him, flat on his back, face up, the blanket's edges folded over him. But the blue glow was much less in evidence and his face seemed to have filled out a little, losing most of its cadaverous hollowness. Sliding her hand under the blanket and inside his jacket, Lynn felt for and found a heartbeat, slow but certain, faint but unfaltering. And she noted that last night's icy chill was off him now; he was warm, or very nearly so.

Sighing, she tucked her blanket robe under her and sat beside him cross-legged for a few moments, gently using her fingertips to smooth out the lines in his forehead. Suzy sat, too, tongue lolling.

"Are you hungry, too?" Lynn asked the dog.

For answer, Suzy got up and went to the door. She sniffed at the gap where the draft came in.

"You want to go for a run?" Lynn guessed. She got up, dragged the door open a little way. Suzy barked her thanks, squeezed through the gap and went bounding off, tail wagging.

Lynn looked out after her for a moment. The day was cold and gray. Gray clouds boiled slowly by overhead, seeming very low in the sky. Lynn hoped it would not rain. It would be hateful if—

FOOD, said Richard's voice in her head, the hollow, unspoken "sound" of it causing her to start.

She turned to look at him. He lay perfectly still, his eyes closed as before. "You're hungry?"

NO. BUT YOU ARE. AND SUZY.

"I can wait. Suzy can catch herself a rabbit."

SHE'S NO GOOD AT IT (a mental shake of his head).

"Then we'll both have to wait."

NO.

"But what can I do?" she shrugged helplessly, thinking: *thank God no one can see me talking to myself!*

NOT YOU. ME.

"You? You can just lie there and get well! Don't go worrying about—"

Her words tailed off, the sentence forgotten as the blue glow returned, stronger than before, clothing his form in a cold neon glare. It lasted only for a second, maybe two—then switched itself off like a light.

FOOD, came his voice again in her mind, but fainter now, fading . . .

Lynn *smelled* the change first, the sudden difference in the atmosphere of the place, and the smell set her mouth instantly to watering. Then, slowly turning away from Richard where he lay, feeling her flesh charged with a tingle of eerie anticipation, she scanned the room. The difference was not hard to find. Her eyes were drawn immediately, as by magnetism, to the table—which was set!

It was set exactly as Richard would set it: with a tiny tablecloth bearing the Schweitzerhof motif—Schweitzerhof crockery, consisting of a deep bowl of something dark, hot and steamy, and a small oval plate of fresh sliced bread thickly buttered, *and* a pot of coffee and a tiny cup and saucer—and Schweitzerhof cutlery, each piece stamped with a distinctive "S" on its handle. There was even a napkin and a glass of crystal clear mountain water. But all of it untidy, haphazard, just *put* on the table in any old position. And the tablecloth off-center, so that one corner overlapped the table's rim. No question as to whose hand, or mind, had been at work here!

Moving closer to the table, Lynn felt dazed—as if her brain was momentarily anesthetized—so that she very nearly stepped in a bowl of water where it stood upon the floor beside a fresh steak big as a small plate. He had forgotten nothing, no one.

She collapsed into her chair, giggled half-hysterically, stared at the table, the meal. And she was complaining about the layout!

For long minutes she simply sat like that and stared, her mouth unashamedly gaping, before she dared to touch anything. But then—

Well, she could look at it—or she could eat it. Perhaps she had better do that, before it disappeared back where it had come from!

She was halfway down the bowl of oxtail soup—which tasted as good as only the Germans can make it—when Suzy returned disappointed from her hunting. Richard had been right: she was not very good at it. But how the great bitch's eyes lit up when she saw her steak and bowl of water! And after that it was simply a contest to see who could get finished first . . .

Later, finally spurred into action by a thought which had worried her in all her waking moments ever since last night—and despite the fact that she knew she should not disturb him—Lynn approached Richard again and sat by him on the floor.

"Richard," she said, speaking directly to or at him and watching his face intently. "I was right about those men. They came from PSISAC. But I can't believe my father would order you killed. I know I got away from them—for which you were probably responsible—but I'm worried about them finding us again, even up here."

THEY WON'T, his thoughts were definite on that, very final. Lynn shivered as their coldness touched her.

"But what if they do? And maybe there were more than just two of them. Suppose there are others?"

OTHERS? (Did his eyelids flicker there for a moment?)

Suzy gave a nervous whine and crept closer, trying to get her nose wedged under Lynn's arm.

OTHERS . . . Richard's mental voice in Lynn's mind was more thoughtful now. And even as she watched, so the blue glow returned to suffuse his features, the outline of his body beneath the blanket's folds. She quickly edged back from him, Suzy too, until they came up against the table.

The blue glow became intense, frighteningly so. Lynn could see Richard's body—every last detail of it—glaring right through clothes, blanket and all. And a moment later . . . *she could see his bones!*

His entire skeletal structure stood out clear as an X-ray beneath translucent flesh, and the glow was so dazzling now that Lynn had to turn her eyes away. She did so gratefully, waiting with bated breath and peering through half-shuttered eyes at the opposite wall until the glow slowly subsided and shrank back down into him.

Then she gulped air and turned to look at him again. At Richard, and at the cabin. Nothing seemed to have changed . . . or had it?

Was it darker?

Suzy uttered a thin, keening whine like a knife-edge of ice drawn across the strings of some strange instrument. Lynn knew enough about Suzy now to heed her instincts. Indeed something had changed. And yes, it *was* darker. She turned to the door which opened on the high balcony, stepped toward it—

NO! A warning.

She hesitated. "I mustn't go out?"

NO . . . YES . . . JUST LOOK.

Very carefully, she opened the door a fraction. She looked.

Starlight blazed out there. The heavens were afire with constellations Lynn had never guessed existed. But the fact that it was night when it should be day—and the fact that the stars lit the sky like bright beacons, brighter than she had ever seen them—and also the fact that the air was utterly stirless . . . these things were not the reasons for her reaction, which was quickly to close the door and slip quietly to the floor in a numbing paralysis, but formed only part of it. The reason *itself* was something entirely different.

It was simply that Richard had taken one very short pace out across the great gulf of the Psychosphere, and he had taken Lynn, Suzy, even the cabin, with him. One thing was certain: no one from PSISAC would ever find them here.

Lynn had seen stars before, marching in the sky, but there had always been a horizon to shut them off. She had never before seen them marching across, and down, and *under* the sky! She had never before looked *down* on stars from above!

Wherever, whenever she was now, Lynn knew that it was very far away from any mere mountaintop in the Harz. But beyond that her mind simply refused to conjecture . . .

* * *

There were just two of them again—man and beast, two against terror—and still they fled before the advance of the mad god. Of how far they had come—of the endless miles sped beneath their weary feet—Garrison remembered little, only that the way had been long and lonesome and horrible. Horror was come upon the world, whose people screamed and laughed and danced and died, and the mad god would soon reign supreme over all. But not yet over Garrison.

Garrison . . .

The name tasted strange on his tongue. And yet he knew it was his name. Richard Garrison, son of Garrison. And Suzy, that same faithful Suzy who had served his father even as she now served him. As friend and companion . . . and familiar spirit. But that had been in another world, another time, and men had been mostly sane then. Now there was only this world and this world was mad.

Garrison sighed, paused and looked back.

They were climbing now, man and dog, and behind and far below them lay foothills clad in green trees and shrubs and wild grasses. There were rivers, too, threading their ways like silver ribbons to distant lakes and oceans; but up here there was only cold stone and dizzy overhangs, and on rare occasions a wind-blasted pine. Higher still, a snowline turned the craggy uplands white, and distant peaks were shrouded in puffy clouds.

Still, it were perhaps better to look forward: to the heights still to be climbed, the fields of treacherous snow still to be crossed. Forward and not back: for back there lay only horror and death. Garrison was too well aware of the rising columns of smoke that dotted and smudged the rearward horizon, knew only too well the meaning of those burning towns. They simply signaled the monster's inexorable pursuit, telling mutely of how the mind-beast followed him still and burned a path across all the world and all the minds of men.

And so Garrison and the dog climbed, and the mountain went up dizzyingly, and the world fell away behind . . .

Presently they came to a false summit where the way ahead lay flat for some little distance before the mountain climbed again, sheer to its roof. Perhaps they could go around, follow the base of the cliff to the far side of the range. Perhaps, and perhaps not.

But then, moving forward again through crisp, shallow snow and wrapping his tattered clothes around him against the bite of a freezing wind, Garrison saw ahead the great dome of some dark cave in the face of the cliff. A cave, yes, but in no way natural. Its curving wall was too regular, too smooth, and deep within were distant lights. There was life here, life!

And maybe even sanity.

Garrison hurried forward, entered and led the way down a long straight tunnel cut through the very rock. No cave but a tunnel, and lights ahead and the promise of life! Now the walls were tiled, clinical in their sterile austerity, and now the tiles were coated in ice. Deeper, and the ice thickened, and the way became bitter cold where massive icicles descended like stalactites from the high dome of the ceiling.

But the deeper Garrison went the stranger the tunnel became; for now he saw that it was indeed a true cave, a mighty ice cavern which stretched windingly ahead; and yet lit with bright neons which glowed in its ceiling and turned the ice a glassy blue. And here began numbered niches in

*the walls, where frozen trolleys stood immobile,
bearing great steel tubes like metal coffins in endless procession all along the length of the cavern
on both sides. And beneath the feet of man and
dog, the ice was slick over gleaming steel rails
which narrowed into the distance and led the pair
on into the heart of the mountain.*

*Suzy did not like the place and she showed it,
yelping occasionally and whining pitifully as she
slunk along in her master's neon-cast shadow. Nor
was Garrison of a mind to argue with her canine
premonitions; though why she was so afraid of
those niches with their trolleys and tubes, and
what it was that made her cling so desperately
close to his side he could not hazard.*

*But where were the people he had so longed to
find here? Where the life?*

*They had come a long way into the ice cavern
when suddenly Garrison snatched a chill breath of
air and skidded to an abrupt halt. Above a certain
niche he had seen a number—the number 2139—
which in some inexplicable way held meaning for
him. He went to the niche readily enough, and
Suzy behind him . . . but she slinking and snarling
all the way. He dragged out the frost-rimed trolley
and its tube, and the dog backed off barking, all
of her fur standing up as if it, too, was frozen.*

*The tube was hinged horizontally along its
length, and a faint crack showed where the two
halves might be separated. Chromium hasps
locked it and kept its contents secure.*

Its contents?

*There was a curving glass window toward one
end of the tube, and Garrison rubbed and scraped
at the frost, breathing on the window and trying
to see inside. Was that the outline of a head and
shoulders in there? A face?*

Then he saw the small, frosted metal oval and breathed on that instead. The plate was of brass and bore a name etched between a pair of fixing screws—a name and a date. He read them:

Vicki Maler: 1973.

His mother!

Now Garrison's hands scrabbled at the frozen hasps, snapped them back on stiff sprung hinges. The tube cracked open, its lid hissing up and back on slender pneumatic pistons. He looked . . . but cryogenic gases were gushing out dense as the thickest mist to rime his face, so that he must shut his stinging eyes against them. When the hissing stopped, he opened his frosted lids a crack and looked again. And at the last, simultaneous with Suzy's scream of horror, his disbelieving eyes bulged fully open.

His mother seemed to break at the waist in an explosion of icy crystals; jerked stiffly upright in her tomb of man-made ice. Her face was sheathed in it, but as she came erect so the sheath cracked like a glassy eggshell and fell from her in a cascade of smoking shards and splinters. And she turned her face toward her son.

Then Richard joined Suzy in her screaming and snatched himself back from what he had done. His mother laughed at him until her laughter became a tormented shrieking. Her mouth fell open like a wooden puppet's and her tongue lolled out, writhing. With it came the flopping tendrils of something from within, a living, cancerous mass that groped and quivered where it slopped its anemone tentacles to hang like a beard from her chin.

And still she laughed and gibbered—while her shriveled hands clutched at the rim of the tube and *scrabbled there dementedly—while leprous living stuff burst from her nostrils and her ears and groped hideously—laughed until, with a sound like exploding puffballs, suddenly her blind eyes caved in upon the pulsing pus behind them!*

Even as Garrison watched, petrified, the thing ate her from within, until she crumbled shrieking into herself and slopped back down into her tomb. And after that—

After that there was only flight. Flight from the horror in the tube, from the ice cavern, from the entire world of his nightmares. A frenzied, leaping, floating hag-ridden flight which sent him crashing through all the barriers of the subconscious world, screaming his terror over and over again into the waking world of men . . .

Lynn came out of her own dreams—vague, formless wanderings with no real substance to them—with the sound of Richard's screaming and Suzy's howling dinning in her ears. She had put the spare cushion on the floor beside him, lain her blanket half on top, stretched herself out and turned the blanket over herself. That had been later, when she was used to the idea of being . . . somewhere else. And some little time after that, Suzy had crept in between them, and then all three had slept.

Suzy's weariness was born mainly of boredom, there was nothing else to do; (obviously, while they were "here," she could not go "out": the cold spaces between the stars were now as inimical to her as they were to all mortal life; this cabin-bubble which the *other* Richard sustained marked the boundary between the "safe and known" and the "deadly unknowable.") Lynn had slept for somewhat similar reasons, but also because she was exhausted; if not physically exhausted, certainly mentally. She had asked her mind to accept too much. And Richard: he had slept—actually slept—because true sleep was the transitional stage which would lead to renewal of *his* control over his "repaired" body.

And now his body had been repaired and he *was* back in control, if control was the right word. For this time, because of the nature of his nightmare and his final plunge back to the relative safety of the waking world, he was really in a bad way.

He lay there beside Lynn with his eyes screwed shut, as if fearing to open them, "running" still and screaming himself hoarse, his heels drumming on the floor and his arms wildly pumping. Suzy got the worst of it and was quick to be out of the way, by which time Lynn was fully awake and trying to pin Richard's arms down. The look on his face as he jerked and shuddered and screamed (she had never heard a man scream before, not like this) was almost as bad as anything she had yet seen, which made her fear for a moment that in fact this must be the onset of another attack.

"Richard!" she cried, throwing her weight on him while Suzy danced about and generally got in the way. "Richard, it's me, Lynn!"

"Oh, Mother!" he yelled in his terror. "Oh, Ma, Ma, *Ma*!"

She wrapped him in her arms and rocked him, and when his breath stopped catching in his throat crushed his head to her breasts and stroked him, saying: "There, there, there!" And: "It's Lynn, it's only Lynn."

"Oh, Lynn! It was . . . *horrible*!"

It chilled her to see the way he looked at her now, his strange eyes round as saucers in a face chalk-white and quivering. After all he had been through, and all he had known, a mere nightmare was horrible? It *must* have been!

"You dreamed about your mother?" she said.

"God, yes! Yes, yes . . ."

He got up, not at all stiffly but shivering dreadfully, and went to the stove. The fire was almost dead again; it threw up a few fitful sparks from dull embers as Richard haphazardly piled in logs through the stove's door.

"Do you want to tell me about it?"

"No, Lynn, no. It's not for telling."

"But it was only a dream," she reminded him gently, going to him and hugging him close.

"Not 'only,' " he answered, frowning. "No, it was more than that." He reached down absent-mindedly and patted Suzy's head with a trembling hand where she wagged her tail uncertainly and gazed up at him.

"A dream, a nightmare—a 'premonition,' " Lynn shrugged. "At least you were asleep. My nightmares have all been waking ones! It's been one long nightmare, Richard, ever since last night." She glanced out of a window, saw slow-moving clouds in an early evening sky and thought: *Oh, thank God! Thank God for that, at least!*

"Not a premonition, either," he said, still frowning. "More a memory—but not *my* memory. Anyway, it's over now."

Then he thought about what she had said. "Last night?" He looked about the cabin, his eyes seeming to focus at last, seeing her for the first time. The dream had fully receded now, taking its place among all of his dreams in the ghost places of his mind. He could remember it for its sheer horror . . . but it was over now and he knew it had been unreal. He had not *really* been there. Not yet, anyway . . .

"What about last night?" he asked, his mind going again to what she had said about waking nightmares. He looked at her nakedness, pulled her to him. The strength in his arms was real, normal; he felt little the worse for wear, despite—

"I was shot!" he gasped.

She nodded. "Three times."

"My God!" His hand flew to his collarbone, paused, touched the spot gingerly. "And here—?" he felt the area over his left breast.

"And your side," she reminded him. "There are bullet holes and blood all over your clothes."

He tore off his jacket, dragged his polo-neck and vest up over his head and off all in one movement. While he examined himself, Lynn took the polo-neck and separated it from his vest. "May I?" she said, pulling it on.

"Yes, of course," he murmured, holding up his jacket and peering through the holes. And: "This hole looks . . . burned?"

She nodded. "Hot lead."

He snorted, "Hell, a bullet's not *that* hot! And anyway, it moves too fast to—" But he paused when he saw her shaking her head.

"Not just hot," she corrected him, "molten!"

He looked blank.

"How much do you remember, Richard?" She arranged cushions on chairs, wrapped her legs and feet in a blanket and plumped down in the chair closest to the stove.

He too sat down, warming himself, pulling his jacket over his naked shoulders. He was frowning again, concentrating. But then he shook his head. "Nothing. Only that I was shot. Two men in a car. They grabbed you, shot me. And then nothing.

No, wait!" His eyes opened wider. "I remember running back to the Schweitzerhof. I knew I was dying—"

She took his hands, which were shaking, but his grip was strong; he grimaced as he said again, "Jesus, Lynn—I was really dying!"

"I thought you *were* dead!" she said. "What else do you remember?"

"I got the pronged thing—the knuckleduster—on my hand, and I rammed the prongs through the TV cable."

"You did what?" her frown matched his own.

"That's the third way," he explained, "don't you remember? I curse, I get violent, or I give myself an electric shock."

"But surely that's only when you're about to suffer an attack?" Lynn was completely baffled.

He nodded. "I thought so too. Anyway, I did it. And that's all I remember." He looked at her, managed a wry smile, touched his shoulder and chest again and shook his head in complete bafflement. "Now you'd better tell me what you know about all of this, before I have a stroke trying to work it out for myself!"

She told him all she knew:

About the two men, twin brothers who worked at PSISAC (she did not know their names, except that one of them had called the other Darren); something of her ordeal in their car; her "escape" as she saw it, and how she must have made her way through the night all the way to the cabin; of finding Suzy here, then Richard himself, and of everything else that had happened. She left very little out and took most of an hour to tell it.

"It was the *other* you," she finished. "It was what your father passed down to you."

Through it all he had not once interrupted her.

Now that she was done he shook his head, slumped down into himself. "You're sure that you haven't been dreaming too?"

"You've seen the burns in your clothes where the lead came out of you," she said. She got up, went across to his blanket and pried free a blob of lead. "Look at this. This was a bullet! And that crockery and cutlery there on the shelf: all Schweitzerhof stuff. Check it if you wish."

He merely glanced at the shelf, took the small leaden blob from her fingers and weighed it in the palm of his hand. "No," he said, "I don't really doubt a single thing you've told me, Lynn. Of course I don't. Actually, I'm half-glad I don't remember any of it." Then his expression turned angry. "But as if we haven't enough on our hands, now we have to worry about those two thugs!"

"No," she said, "I don't think so. You seemed pretty sure they wouldn't bother us anymore. I mean, when you were like . . . that."

"But your father may have sent more of them."

Now Lynn got angry. "We're still not sure he *did* send them!" she snapped. "I just can't believe that he—"

"Who else if not your old man?" Richard cut in, no less harshly. "Anyway, they told you he sent them."

"But not to kill you, surely?" she was on the verge of tears.

He drew his chair close and hugged her. "You mean everything to him, Lynn," he said. "I've always known that. And in his eyes I'm just a gibberer, a bloody lunatic. Hell, in a few more days it won't matter one way or the other! Mind-plaguers will be killing themselves off left, right and center . . ."

"But *he* doesn't know that," she protested. "I

mean, I can understand him wanting to know I'm safe and all, but—"

"Wait!" Richard held her back from him, gazed at her in something like astonishment, as if she had suddenly slapped him in the face or spat at him. "What did you say just then?"

She stared back at him. "I said I can understand him wanting me back, and—"

"No, before that."

"Before that?" she frowned. "I said he doesn't know the world's going mad: that people will soon be killing themselves, each other, everybody. That there'll be mind-plaguers running amok all over the place."

Richard's expression stayed the same and she was puzzled, worried by it. "Well, he doesn't, does he?"

"He shouldn't," Richard finally said, his voice much quieter. "But what if he does? That would explain his wanting you back right away—even his not caring a twopenny toss what happens to me!"

"But how could he know?"

He shook his head. "I've no idea. Maybe we'll find out eventually."

They came to a silent, mutual decision to leave it at that. "So what's next?" she asked.

"Next?" he stood up, yawning, stretched. "Next, I'm hungry! And if I don't pay a call I'll burst—and you and Suzy, too, by your looks. So first we'll settle those little problems. Then . . . well, it's too late today to buy fresh clothes, so that's for the morning—following which we'll be on our way south. As for tonight: we're probably safest right where we are. I don't think there's anyone else in the world who knows about this place."

"South?" she repeated him, "Tomorrow? What's south?"

"Switzerland," he answered, "that's what's south. Schloss Zonigen—" and he paused. Even saying those words, that name, he had not known where they or the idea behind them came from. Yes, he had—from his dream, his nightmare. From someone else's past.

"Schloss Zonigen?" she said, shaking her head. "I never heard of it."

"No," he slowly answered, "me neither, until just a moment ago. But now I know where it is, and what it is. I was there in my dream. It's one of those cryogenic suspension places, where rich, dead people are quick-frozen in the hope that a cure will be discovered for whichever illness killed them. That's where we're going. We have to."

She touched his face, waited for the faraway expression to go out of it. "But why?"

"Because . . . because it's the next stop along the way," he said, coming back down to earth. "I have this feeling that if I can just see that place, maybe all of this will come together."

She looked at him suspiciously. "You know more than you're telling me," she accused.

He grinned and drew her close, said: "No, I don't. Really I don't, Lynn. It's just a feeling, that's all." But over her shoulder the grin slipped from his face in a moment.

How could he possibly tell her why he had to go to Schloss Zonigen? If he even tried it, she'd be convinced that there was really no longer any hope for him! Even after everything else she had accepted, still this would be too much. No, he couldn't tell her.

Not that Schloss Zonigen was where, ten years before he was born, they had laid his mother to rest in a tube of freezing gas deep in the glacial ice . . . the *first* time she died!

Without her clothes, Lynn was unable to accompany Richard when he went off in the Mercedes to find food and drink for them. In any event, he had something of a problem himself, mainly because of the state of his own clothing. His trousers were not so bad, a little creased now but surprisingly clean, but his jacket was bloody. Fortunately the jacket was of a brown color and the blood-stains did not show too much, but the bullet holes did. Lynn solved most of the problem by suggesting that he wear his polo-neck backward, and by pinning a pine sprig just under his left jacket lapel, in the German fashion, to hide his bullet hole there. As for the tear between neck and shoulder: an eight inch wide strip torn from the edge of a blanket, worn as a loose scarf, covered that. The hole at the side of the jacket was scarcely noticeable. With his stubble of beard he still looked something of a rogue, but he would get by.

Then, leaving Suzy behind for Lynn's protection, and keeping his lights dipped as much as possible as he maneuvered the uneven surface, he drove the car slowly down the trail toward the main road. In two or three difficult places he had to use his full headlights, for it was that time of evening before darkness has fully fallen, when the light is strange and plays tricks with the eyes. But at last he got down to the belt of pines fronting Garrison's Retreat, and through them, out onto the slip road.

There, deeming it foolish to go back into St. Andreasberg, he turned left and headed for Wernigeroder maybe fifteen kilometers away across what had once been the East German border. The road was good and all downhill, and he made the town in a little less than ten minutes. Fortunately it had a branch of the World Bank with a night-cash system, where he was able to dial in his personal number, hold his ID tag to the scanner for verification and draw the standard three hundred deutsche marks in crisp fifties.

Then back to a *Schnell Imbiss* where the service bar opened into the main street for a small bucket of potato salad, *bratwursts*, cold *schnitzel*, a chicken fresh-roasted on a spit over charcoal, several large bottles of mineral water and two cans of Dortmunder Actien beer. The grubby-looking *Wirt* was good enough to fill a plastic container from the back of the Mercedes with two gallons of fresh water.

And so back into the mountains proper.

In all, the round trip had taken him a little over fifty minutes, and it had been doubly successful in that he had spotted several ladies' outfitters in Wernigeroder where in the morning he could buy clothes for Lynn. Moreover, he was back at the cabin long before the chicken and *bratwursts* in their thermal wrappers could begin to get cold . . .

Those were the simple criteria upon which Richard reckoned the value of his brief excursion. In another way it had been far less than profitable, but of this he as yet knew nothing. For as he had descended along the saddle's rim and through the flanking pines—especially where he had been obliged to use full beam—and when he had returned, climbing up and over the saddle's hump again, his to and froing had not gone unobserved.

Earlier in the day Emma Tyler had spoken to a somewhat puzzled and bitter Herr Gutmann, whose splendid hotel was now the center of a frightening and largely unexplained mystery. She might have explained something of it for him, but she preferred to listen; and from him she had learned interesting things indeed about this Garrison and his young lady who had gone off without paying their bill and left their room in such terrible disarray. And his information had been so useful that Miss Tyler had insisted upon paying the truant pair's costs, against which Gutmann had pleaded not at all.

Since then, and before darkness set in, she too had visited Garrison's retreat and read the legend of the tumbled arch, and she too had driven in through the iron gates to enter the one-time hideaway of Thomas Schroeder. And there she had been, in the tricky half-shade of twilight, when Richard's flashing lights had sent their beams swinging along the downward slopes and cutting through the pines; and at the gates she had waited until he returned, standing not fifteen feet away behind one of the gate's columns as he drove past her in his big silver car. And her eyes had been not at all friendly, and her gaze more than a little calculating, as she watched his red and orange rear lights out of sight and up through the wooded belt . . .

During the last twelve to fifteen hours:

In South Africa all white men between the ages of eighteen and thirty-five had been mobilized, issued with weapons. Sections of territory with clearly defined boundaries had been placed under their partial control, areas of responsibility wherein they would work in close liaison with the police. Their orders were simple: gibberers—black gibberers—were to be shot on sight or notification. This was not information which should reach the outside world, the South African press and other news media would remain silent on the subject. Nor would there be any talk tomorrow, *none*, about the black mind-plague enclosures, which overnight would be seen to have become mysteriously depleted of inmates and in many cases entirely emptied. For the present, white gibberers would be dealt with as before, until the situation either changed for the better or became more desperate yet, when further measures might have to be taken.

Along the northern borders a barricade of men, machines and weapons kept watch; no one was to be allowed over those borders from the north without very good reason for being there; alleged "refugees" were to be turned back or killed, depending upon their degree of insistence; white travelers must be completely screened before admittance . . .

In the East, two million cyanide capsules of British manufacture had been flown in a special container aircraft from Hong Kong to Tokyo. Their cost was only a small fraction of a percent of that of the Hiroshima and Nagasaki bombs; but their cost in human lives, albeit irreparably damaged lives, would be far greater. Nippon had started to poison the worst of her mind-plaguer sons.

In Australia the left-wing government had been overthrown. Certain members of the new regime were said to have conclusive proof that the Aborigines were plague-carriers. Large gangs of drunken, fear-crazed locals were shooting premen by the score in all their reservations and protectorates. Social and civil rights improvements of twenty years' standing were erased in a matter of hours. No one opposed the carnage.

Recently prosperous Poland appeared to be preparing for war on her neighbors . . .

In Russia, a large suburb of Moscow had been burning uncontrolled for a day and a night in an inferno which threatened to rival the Great Fire of London. According to a Kremlin press release, the U.S.S.R. was *not* being inundated with mind-plague—cases had numbered a mere handful. An old curtain, albeit with many a moth hole, was slowly closing once more across half-forgotten frontiers.

In New York in the early hours of the morning there had been a power failure. Gangs of distinct ethnic origins had gathered out of nowhere to battle and vie with each other in looting, destroying, and brutalizing the city's center within a radius of half a mile. In the morning presses there had been accusations of unnecessarily harsh police retaliation and the indiscriminate shooting of over one hundred rabble-rousers and suspected gibberers. Some of the larger organs, however, were seen to applaud.

In most of South America there was utter chaos, particularly in Argentina which had suffered a major coup and was now under the rule of a *junta* of three mind-plaguers. This was hardly surprising: madmen had been in power there before.

In England, parliament had been sitting for four hours and would continue throughout the night; the press had been totally excluded; several ministers would be detained and "removed to a safe place" following the ayes having it on a certain very controversial subject. Tomorrow police nationwide would be issued with special emergency powers . . .

The rest of the world fared no better, most of it far worse. In the main, international relations were seen to be rapidly deteriorating, communications were becoming "very strained."

There had been no contact whatsoever with Moonbase for more than eight hours . . .

At PSISAC that Wednesday evening, J. C. Craig personally inspected the recently completed fortifications and put his disciples, old and new alike, through their drills. All went well, which was all to the good.

The day had been long and hard—especially for Craig, with no further word concerning his daughter, and with pressures steadily mounting—but he and his initiates had somehow struggled through it. The worst of it was over now, the bulk of the preparations completed.

Plainly, though, Craig must now bring forward to tomorrow noon his original plan for closing PSISAC down; and as today's lessons had taught him, even that might be a little on the tight side. For today there had been almost four hundred new mind-plague cases at PSISAC, all of whom bar three—who killed themselves—had been dart-stunned by Security or by Craig's disciples; but patently the thing was now mounting to a crescendo. Which was why, when PSISAC's employees reported for work tomorrow, the great majority of them would be turned away. Only the technicians and a handful of laborers would gain access to the complex, the people whose skills were required to close down and seal off the lesser converters, and muscle to put the finishing touches to the fortifications and secure the main buildings and installations no longer in use.

Then, at noon, the last of these would be sent away and finally PSISAC would come to a standstill—almost. But the main converter would function as before, supplying PSISAC's power—and Psychomech's. To this end Craig had recruited and initiated an ample number of technicians, each of whom now carried the headset insignia of the disciple wherever he or she went in and about the complex.

In all, including the six left behind when Bragg and the others commenced their pursuit of Richard Stone and Lynn Craig, there were now twelve of them at PSISAC. Craig had further ensured that two of the newer members were dog-handlers from Security; and as chance would have it a third, also from Security, was one Geoff Bellamy . . .

Along with the three remaining seekers, all of whom were somewhere out in the Harz Mountains, that would appear to make fifteen. Except that Craig had already decided that those three absent members were now expendable—and especially Bragg, contrary to anything he might have been led to believe.

As for PSISAC's fortifications:

The perimeter wall had been fully wired and the main converter could readily supply anything from a few volts of electricity to a sudden jolt massive enough to light a town. Nothing was going to climb over that wall—nothing human.

There were places, however, where the wall in its own structure was weak—where, for instance, internal prefabricated buildings, sheds and warehouses backed onto it—and others where it was overlooked by buildings outside the complex. All such weak areas had been reinforced as best as possible, often with steel plates bolted to the walls within and supported by concrete stanchions, or by large vehicles and bulky machinery strategically parked or positioned. And on top of the wall where it was overlooked and wherever entry might conceivably be gained from adjacent buildings, there were platforms where machine-guns had been mounted behind hastily erected sandbag barriers.

To complement all of this, Craig had arranged batteries of surveillance devices (which PSISAC had on occasion manufactured), linking a network of screens and alarms to three control centers arranged in a triangle about the Dome. From there he would be able to witness for himself any attempted break-in and personally supervise all defensive actions. A pool of PSISAC runabouts—speedy, battery-driven three-wheelers—had been split three ways for the use of the control centers, to enable rapid deployment of firepower to any trouble spot. There would also be a complement of three guard dogs kenneled in the immediate vicinity of each control center. Craig's ten men and two women were armed to the teeth.

As to why he had considered all of this necessary:

Craig had long considered it a likelihood that certain local-dwelling "authorities" and "VIPs"—government ministers, officials and the like, who were in the know, and their families—might in the last event seek entry into his ark; which was now borne out in the contents of several recent government "communiqués" laying down procedures should Craig be required to make PSISAC available. But God had decreed that all except the chosen were to drown in His deluge of madness, and J. C. Craig was His one true prophet on Earth. No, any so-called authority must seek his refuge elsewhere, in other PSISAC-styled complexes throughout the land, or in those shelters doubt-less laid aside for them; but nowhere else would they be safe. God's hand was set against men, and all the nations of men could not stay His wrath . . .

And so, unlike Noah, J. C. Craig had turned *his* ark into a fortress, and let them try to gain entry who would.

Until which time—

All that remained for him now was to watch and wait. To watch the madness fall upon the land in all its raging torrent, and to wait for Lynn to come home to him. To these ends, then, he would offer up his prayers: the deliverance of his daughter, the confusion and destruction of his and the Lord's enemies, and to the completion of His work, into whose hands the bulk of the burden must now be given. Yes, the rest of it must now be left to God.

To Him, and—albeit unknown to Craig—to Psychomech . . .

Day Six

WHEN AT 8:15 ON THURSDAY MORNING RICHARD set out again for Wernigeroder, Emma Tyler had already been back at Garrison's Retreat for more than half an hour. Having slept the night at the Schweitzerhof, she had been up at the crack of dawn and back to the place in the high mountains without delay; and as Richard drove away from the place on his own she watched him go, then cast speculative eyes across the hump of the saddle to where a thin column of blue wood smoke rose almost perpendicular into the sky. Then she went and brought her car from where it was hidden in the pines, following the Merc's multiple tracks all the way up to the saddle's crest.

There she once more hid her vehicle away—this time in a thick clump of young trees well off the track—and went the rest of the distance, perhaps a quarter mile, on foot. Gutmann had told her all about "Herr Garrison's *Hündin*," and she was well prepared for Suzy. In any case, dogs had never frightened her—only men.

She was dressed in soft boots, trousers, a blouse and fur-lined jacket, and she carried a shoulder bag. In the bag were weapons, her headset, ID tag and a few small cosmetic items. Also a three-pronged claw, in chromium-plated steel, like a full-sized replica of some cruel eagle's foot . . .

She was maybe a hundred yards from the cabin in the pines where they reared at the very edge of the mountain when she heard Suzy's muffled bark and guessed that the dog had sensed her presence. Crouching down behind a half-buried boulder, she could just see the door of the cabin beneath the trees, kept her eyes fixed upon it until it opened and the girl came out. Tyler recognized her at once as Lynn Craig. The girl looked about, turning her head left and right, then went back inside. But the great black bitch had come out and was even now sniffing the air, obviously suspicious of something.

A moment later and she came loping down the trail, tail swaying, head erect and eyes scanning the ground ahead. Behind her boulder, Tyler now saw how big the animal was and nervously licked her thin lips. She opened her bag and took out a single-shot dart pistol. It was already loaded, ready to fire.

Suzy did not stand a chance. Maybe twenty feet from Tyler's cover she paused, sniffed the air, then crouched back startled as the thin woman rose abruptly into view. Before Suzy could even snarl her surprise Tyler lifted her weapon in both hands, took aim and fired. The gun went *phut!* and sent its dart into Suzy's side, leaving only the tuft of its flight projecting. Suzy yelped once and gave a little leap—then started forward, snarling and baring her fangs. She took perhaps three stiff-legged strides, paused to lick at her side where the dart was fixed, seemed to slump drunkenly for a moment and had to spread her legs wide for support. Then her head bowed, her front legs buckled, and with an almost inaudible whine of distress she toppled over.

Emma Tyler reloaded the pistol, replaced it in her bag, set out for the cabin. Less than a minute later she entered the stand of pines, crept up onto the veranda and looked in through the window with the missing pane.

Lynn was naked, taking a shower in front of the roaring potbellied stove. A plastic container hung from the ceiling at the end of a piece of tough twine, its perforated screw-top sending streams of water over the girl, who scrubbed at herself and tossed her hair beneath the flying spray. Her body gleamed damply, buttocks perfectly shaped, breasts full and proud, legs tapering and wide-spread for balance.

Again Miss Tyler licked her lips. Then—

Hands to her tousled hair, Lynn turned, her eyes half-closed and full of sensuous pleasure at the water's cold, sweet sting. She saw the face at the window—

In another moment Tyler was in through the door and Lynn had snatched up the Schweitzer-hof tablecloth to cover herself. She saw the pistol in the woman's hand, cowered back. "Who—?"

"Just be quiet, Lynn," the spinster said, "and I'll not harm you." She stepped to the center of the room, tore down the improvised "shower" from its twine and stood it right-end up on the floor. "A bit short of amenities, eh?" she commented, her face twitching with a smile.

Lynn's mouth opened even wider. "I know you!" she said. "You work in one of the canteens at PSISAC. Your name is . . . Tyler. Emma Tyler!"

"Right," the other nodded. "And your father has sent me to bring you back—you stupid little whore!"

Lynn gasped, then yelled: "Suzy!—*Suzy!*"

"I warned you to keep quiet," Tyler told her, straightening her arm and pointing the pistol at Lynn's middle, "and I *meant* it! Your dog can't help you. She's fast asleep. And if you make me, then I'll put you to sleep, too."

"But what—?" Lynn began, only to be stopped by:

"*Quiet*, I said! When you're nice and safe and tied up—when I'm happy that you can't do anything silly—then we'll talk." She nodded at the chair nearest the stove. "Sit."

Lynn took a blanket, wrapped it round herself and threw down the tablecloth, and sat. Tyler said, "Good! That's much better. You see, we can either be sensible and talk, or you can simply go to sleep right now and not wake up until you're back in England. It's up to you."

While she was talking she had taken up Lynn's discarded tablecloth and started to tear it into strips. She gave one of them to Lynn, telling her to tie one of her wrists to the arm of the chair.

"I will not!"

"You will, or I'll use this right now!" Tyler rasped, pointing her pistol. "It'll hurt a little, but then you'll fall asleep and that will be that. Well?"

Lynn tied her left wrist to the arm of the chair, Tyler pulling on one end of the binding when she tightened the knot. When it came to the right wrist, Tyler swiftly wrapped a second strip several times around Lynn's wrist and the arm of the chair together, then held one end in her teeth to tie the knot. Not for a moment did her cold eyes leave Lynn's face, and not once did her pistol waver where it pointed at Lynn's middle.

"There," said Tyler finally. She put the pistol on the table with her bag, added a further loop of binding to each of Lynn's wrists. Then she tied her ankles together.

"Now can we talk?" Lynn snapped.

"In a little while," Tyler answered. "First I want to see what you and your mad lover have here." She went to the back door, opened it and looked out onto the railed balcony. The view was dizzying and she quickly turned away from it, leaving the door open. "Not much of a love nest," she said.

"No," said Lynn, "it's not—but it has been somewhere to hide from you people."

"Ah!" Tyler said. "It's a hideaway—for you and your demon lover!" Her voice was now as mean and vicious as a man's when he discovers he's a cuckold.

"You're mad!" Lynn snapped. "Richard's a man—a sick man, yes—but he's no demon."

"Your father says he's the antichrist," Tyler told her. "And if what I've heard about the Jacksons is true, maybe he's right."

"The Jacksons? What are you talking about?" Lynn asked. But the name had struck a chord. Then she tied it together. "Those two men!" she gasped.

Tyler smiled a lopsided smile. "Yes," she nodded, "those two. They were going to take you back too, weren't they? Until your precious little Mr. Richard Stone—or should I say Richard Garrison?—caught up with them!"

"What do you mean?" Lynn's voice was more subdued now.

"What I mean, my dear, is that the Jacksons are dead. And the way they died, only a raving mad beast could have done it!"

Lynn shuddered, and slowly her shoulders slumped. Richard was quite right: the world *was* going mad, and she was a part of it. "Oh my God!" she said.

"Are you saying you didn't know?" Tyler laughed harshly. "Oh, you knew all right—you and the mad swine you sleep with."

Lynn looked up, contemptuous, furious. "You dirty-minded old hag!" she spat. "You've never been in love, have you? Not with a man. What would a lesbian creature like you know about men? You're so dyke you stink of it! And what man would come near your shriveled body? You flat-chested crow!"

Tyler's face went white, twisted in rage, and her hand struck out like the head of a snake. The force of her slap rocked Lynn's head back, left a rising red weal on her face.

"Slut!" Tyler croaked. "You slut!"

Lynn burst into tears.

Tyler reached over and jerked open the loose folds of Lynn's blanket robe, exposing her breasts. "And does he put his mouth on them?" she said. "And does he squeeze them with his hands?"

"At least I have something to squeeze!" Lynn cried.

"Oh, you bitch, you bitch!" Tyler hissed. She made as if to slap Lynn again, then checked herself. "So I'm a lesbian, am I? I'm no lesbian, my dear little whore, though I might well have been." She threw off her coat, yanked open her blouse.

Beneath it she wore no brassière, her tiny breasts were naked. Like small empty sacks, they lay on her chest—and they were deeply, horribly scarred.

Tyler tipped up the contents of her bag onto the table. Her actions were erratic now, her eyes dull and seeming glazed. "I'll tell you about men," she said, staggering a little where she stood by the table. Then her expression changed, became afraid.

She stared at Lynn, her mouth half-open. "Did you say anything then? Did you sing?"

Lynn looked at her in horror. The woman was quite mad. "Sing? Nobody sang. What are you—?"

"No, of course not," Tyler grinned in a sick way, all gums and worn down, yellow teeth. Then she tilted her head on one side a little, held her breath and listened intently for . . . something. Lynn heard nothing; neither did the Tyler woman, apparently.

The vacant look was back in her eyes. "Where were we?" she asked. "Ah, yes—we were talking about men!"

"You're mad," Lynn accused. "You're stark, raving mad! The only difference between you and Richard is that he knows it and is trying to do something about it. But you—"

"Men," said Tyler, quite as if Lynn had not spoken at all. "All about men, yes." She gave her head a shake, as if something irritated her. "You see that claw there on the table? Well, that claw goes with me wherever I go. It's a memento of my youth, you might say, to remind me of when I was your age. To remind me about men and what they can do."

Lynn looked at the table, saw the claw. There was also a second pistol—an automatic weapon and *not* a dart pistol—a portable radio headset of some sort or other, and a few commoner items. The headset reminded Lynn of one she had seen in the rear window of the Jacksons' Fiat, forgotten until this very moment, but she was far more interested in the claw. The thing looked so cruel. A memento of Tyler's youth?

"He used that on me," the madwoman said. "Did this to my breasts. And I was just a young girl like you are now. He liked hurting, you see? And I thought he loved me. Love? From a man? Do you know what he got for this? He got three years. And I got life!" She leaned across the table and glared at Lynn, her thin lips drawing back in a snarl from her ugly teeth.

"What are you going to do?" Lynn whispered, terrified now.

At the sound of her voice the Tyler woman's face grew outraged: her eyes widened in shock, then accusation. "It *is* you! You *were* singing!"

"What?" Lynn gasped. "Why, I only—"

Tyler clapped her hands to her ears, rocked back on her heels. "Stop it!" she screamed. *"Stop singing!"*

Lynn knew she had to free herself and get away from the insane creature—and right now. She knew exactly what was wrong with Tyler: the woman was suffering an attack. She was a gibberer! Desperation lent Lynn strength. She strained to free her hands—and the binding round her right wrist immediately snapped. The cloth was old, thin and dusty. Tyler seemed barely to have noticed. "The singing!" she cried again, clapping at her hands. "Oh, *God*—the singing!" Her trembling hands reached toward the table, groped for the headset.

Lynn thought she was after one of the guns—

or worse, the claw. Her feet were still tied together, but not to the chair. She lifted her legs, kicked at the table with all her strength. It crashed over, spilling its contents to the floor. The guns were heavy and lay more or less where they fell, but the headset was mainly plastic and bounced on its edge, rolling and bounding like a broken hoop. It went out of the open door and across the boards of the balcony, teetered for a moment beneath the bottom rail—then toppled forward and fell from sight.

"No! *No!*" Tyler screamed, scuttling after it like a demented spider, but too late. "Oh, no!" she gasped. "*Noooooo!*" She ran out onto the balcony, looked over the rail, reeled back from it tearing at her stringy hair.

Lynn tore at the binding on her left wrist, tried to drag her hand free. Tyler was back, lashed out at her and knocked her flying, sending Lynn, chair and all crashing to the floor. Lynn's head banged against the hard boards, and she dimly heard Tyler hiss: "You fool—oh, you stupid singing *fool!*"

The woman groped across the floor and found the claw, came back with it clutched in her trembling hand.

She kneeled over Lynn where she lay half-stunned, her left wrist still tied to the chair. "You've finished me," she mouthed. "You and your singing have finished me. But you'll pay!" She held up the claw before Lynn's eyes. Its talons gleamed razor sharp. "Oh, yes, you'll pay. So you know all about men do you? And do you think they'll still want you with your breasts in tatters?"

Lynn saw what was going to happen. She held up her free hand before her, tried to fight Tyler off. The woman's face was a mad white mask now, saliva foaming from the corner of her mouth. She beat Lynn's hand aside, raised the claw—

A shot rang out, deafeningly loud, and a black hole seemed to open in the woman's throat just below her mannish Adam's apple. She dropped the claw, lurched upright. She gurgled, her hands flying to her throat. A splash of scarlet fell on Lynn's thigh.

There came a second shot, striking Tyler dead center between her withered, deep-scarred breasts. Both holes spouted blood as she staggered backward, still gurgling and clawing at the air. And yet again a shot, which slammed into her forehead and blew the back of her head away in a cloud of blood and brains, sending her corpse flying out onto the balcony. Already dead, snuffed out as if she had never been, the small of her back hit the top rail. The top half of her body kept going; she cartwheeled backward and seemed to hang there for a moment against the sky . . . then rushed earthward in a fluttering of her loose blouse. The balcony stood empty, open to air, space and time . . .

A shadow fell in the cabin.

"Richard! Oh Richard!" Lynn sobbed, fighting desperately to hang onto consciousness. "Thank God! Thank—?"

Through eyes which refused to focus, she stared at a blocky figure silhouetted in the doorway. In the shadowy face—which was not Richard's face—eyes like shards of ice stared back at her, void of emotion, chilling her blood in the piercing permafrost of their gaze.

Then, like a scene viewed upon the single frame of a jammed film, the picture turned dark at its edges and grew blurred to Lynn's sight. And in the next moment it slid from view and was replaced by the darkness of oblivion . . .

The girl was out cold.

Donald Conti quickly checked the cabin but found little of interest. He pocketed Emma Tyler's weapons and the keys to her car, then checked the girl's condition again. Out, most definitely; she had given her head a really hard thump on the rough wooden floor. And of course terror had had a lot to do with it, too—terror of Emma Tyler . . .

Conti gave a sardonic grunt as he thought of the Tyler woman.

He had caught up with the spinster last night, when he spotted her car in the Schweitzerhof parking lot. That had meant something of a rough night for him, but he had reckoned it would be worth it.

Conti had earlier boxed clever, using PSISAC's purchasing power to get himself a small, tall-bodied camper-van of the type currently favored on the Continent. Parking it on the opposite side of the car park from Tyler's vehicle, he had simply sat there in the van all night—peering out now and then through a crack in his curtains, nodding, yawning and smoking the occasional cigarette—until dawn had started to show as the very palest stain on the far horizon.

Tired though he had been, still it had not been too hard to stay awake; indeed in other circumstances it might have proved difficult to sleep. There had been a lot of trouble in St. Andreasberg last night, which had helped Conti stay alert. Police sirens blaring intermittently through all the dark hours; a fire at one time, roaring up brightly to bathe the southern quarter of the tiny town in its ruddy glow; mind-plaguers screaming and dancing in the streets by the hour, until the relevant authorities could arrive in heavily armored black vans to drag them away. Oh, yes, things were really starting to get rough now.

And yet still it had seemed a long night, for Conti's patience was now beginning to run a little thin. Having found the woman who double-crossed him, he now desired to be even with her. Oh, he would get her eventually, he had promised himself—even if he must wait till hell froze over—but that had not been necessary. For sure enough, as the birds began to sing and the mist rolled down off the hills, Emma Tyler had put in an appearance.

And so Conti had followed her, keeping well back for the moment and letting her lead him wherever she would. His intention was simply to get her alone somewhere and beat everything she had learned out of her skinny hide before killing her. But as it happened, things were to work out far better than that, better than he could have dreamed.

He had almost missed it when she turned off the road into the pine-fronted saddle between the mountains, but then he had spotted her lights cutting through the trees back from the road; and so he had parked his van on the grass verge close to the slip road, lit himself another cigarette and settled down to watch and wait some more. It had dawned on him by then that perhaps she was closer to the fugitives than he might ever have suspected.

Then, as the light brightened he had seen Richard Stone drive away from the place alone in the big Mercedes; and shortly after that Emma Tyler's car lights had come on again, and she had taken her car creeping up through the misty pines toward the saddle's ridge. And at last Conti had spotted the fire smoke from the cabin, and the rest of the scenario had not been hard to figure out. Tyler was after the girl, for she knew that Stone would be coming back for her.

Conti was a big man and strong. Despite the fact that he had not yet fully recovered from the beating Phillip Stone had given him, still he was very fit. He decided to leave the van where it was and follow the Tyler woman on foot, jogging all the way up through the pines and along the saddle's rim to its crest. In all, the distance was only some three-quarters of a mile, but it was all uphill and over rough ground. Still, a good workout could do little harm, and anyway the van would be difficult in the trees.

He had reached the cabin in plenty of time, had listened to the shouting and Tyler's raving, and then had put an end to the madwoman without giving it a second thought. He owed her it. Besides, she had been about to ruin the girl—which would *not* have stood Conti in good stead with her father!

Now there was only young Stone to deal with, except . . . well, that might not be as easy as it sounded. Certainly it would help if the girl were to oblige and remain unconscious. It would never do to have her coming to at the wrong moment . . .

For long moments Conti stood undecided. Perhaps he should put a dart in the girl. That would be the safest thing—but it would also mark her. If possible, he would like to get her back to her old man completely undamaged. A knockout pill would do the job as surely as a dart; but again, it could well prove dangerous to give her a mickey while she was unconscious.

He tossed the second blanket over her where

she lay, went out to the balcony and looked down. Way, way down there, trees where the sheer drop turned into a steep, scree-littered slope; and somewhere in those trees, the body of Emma Tyler. Miles away, villages and secondary roads all converging on the multibahn, and occasionally a lone chalet, lodge or guesthouse on a hill or at a crossroads. It was Nowhere Land. She wouldn't be found for a long, long time—might never be found at all. After all, in just a few days' time, who would there be to find her? And who would care anyway?

Conti grunted his satisfaction, spat over the rail into space . . . but in the next moment the frown was back on his face.

He was thinking now of what he had learned of the Jacksons' undignified and as yet unexplained joint demise. He had not liked what he heard about it—not at all. That had been a very nasty business, definitely. Not that Conti was against nastiness, on the contrary, but he liked to be on the end dealing it out and not the reverse.

Of course, Old Man Craig was himself crazy, but the more Conti had followed this thing up the more time he had had to think about it; and indeed this Richard Stone kid appeared to be different. As a gibberer he should now be dead; mind-plaguers didn't survive more than a year or eighteen months at best, their brains simply caved in. But not only had Stone ("Garrison") survived, he was actually staying ahead. Or at least had been doing so until now.

Antichrist? No, but . . . well, if he did not have the devil's blood in him, he certainly had his luck! But luck of the devil or not, whatever he had it had just run out on him. He would be coming back here for the girl, and he would find Donald

Conti waiting. And then there would be another score for Conti to settle . . .

Conti left the cabin and jogged back to the ridge. In a small backpack he carried beer, sandwiches, his binoculars and all-important headset. Along his way he spotted Suzy's body, paused and had a closer look. The great black bitch must be with the fugitives, but that was no problem. Darted, she would be out of it for at least a couple of hours.

It was not hard to find Tyler's car; it could only be hidden in the trees, and on his way up Conti had seen her tracks leading off from the deeper trail left by the Mercedes. Using her keys, he checked the dead woman's car over. Maps in the front, large- and small-scale—tough ropes in the back, and a couple of boxes of small caliber ammunition hidden under the seats—a spare can of petrol in the boot, along with tools and jumper leads. Some of it might come in handy.

Conti found a place on the ridge where he could look down on the secluded nest of deserted buildings in their grounds and the main road where it cut across the mountain contours. Seating himself on a boulder, he removed his backpack, drank beer and ate sandwiches. The cold air gave him a good appetite. Then he took his binoculars and studied the road to the northwest where it curved round the mountain and disappeared toward the ten-laner, ultimately toward Berlin.

He thought about what was to come, fixing it in his mind:

When Stone returned, he was unlikely to notice Conti's camper since it stood on the grass verge on the St. Andreasberg side of the slip road. Even if he did see it, he would probably think it belonged to an advance party of skiers up here to map out routes for use when the snows came, and would not give it a second thought. On the other hand when he drove up here, he might just see the body of the dog.

That gave Conti an idea . . .

He went back to the dog, hoisted her limp body up onto his shoulder and walked back to the ridge. There he dumped her in the middle of the tracks, between the deep indentations of tires, where Stone would be sure to spot her as he crested the rise. Then back to Emma Tyler's car for ropes, spare can of petrol . . . and jumper leads.

Jumper leads, yes. Conti ran his tongue over the raw craters in his mouth where his teeth had been, and gently over the jagged stumps of others which were broken. He remembered his pain when he had regained consciousness after Stone's father had worked him over. He couldn't take his revenge on the older man—not for the moment, anyway—but he sure as hell could take it out on the younger one!

And shit—he was to die anyway, wasn't he? Old Man Craig hadn't specified *how* he was to die . . .

In Wernigeroder Richard had drawn a thousand deutsche marks from the World Bank before going on his spending spree. His first purchase had been an overcoat for himself, mainly to cover up his general *déshabillé*, and next a packet of throwaway razors. Then, in a public lavatory he had given himself a quick shave and combed his hair back into a reasonable semblance of its normal brush, before continuing with his list of purchases. The money had lasted just long enough, though maybe there were items he had missed, but he and Lynn could later pick up anything he might have forgotten.

Not only had the money flown but time too, so that it was almost 11:00 A.M. by the time he turned the car into the slip road and threaded it between the pines and onto the now familiar trail. Things were working out well and Richard was pleased with himself. He hummed some half-familiar tune, something from happier days, as the car climbed along the edge of the saddle toward the skyline. But then, cresting the ridge—

Suzy lay where Conti had tossed her. As Richard hurriedly applied his brakes and brought the car to a shuddering stalled halt, the dog lifted her head a fraction, then let it flop back down in the grass. Richard was out of the car in a moment, round to the front, kneeling beside the bitch where she lay sprawled and drugged, her limbs beginning to twitch as life gradually returned to them.

"Suzy!" Richard gasped his concern. "What the hell—?" Then he saw the dart in her side.

Simultaneous with the sudden knowledge that all was far from well here, there came Lynn's cry of warning, echoing down to him from the higher slopes to the right. "*Richard!* . . . Richard! . . . Richard! *Look out!* . . . Look out! . . . Look out!"

Conti, cursing himself that he had not made sure the girl would stay down, came out from cover with the speed and ferocity of a pouncing panther. He had been only thirty feet away, crouched down in a hollow between a pair of sapling spruces, but now he plunged directly to the attack. Richard saw him, a single glimpse of that snarling, bruised and brutal visage, before Conti was on him.

The sheer force of his rush bowled Richard over,

and as he made to scramble to his feet a roundly swinging blow smashed into his left temple and knocked him down again. Following which there was simply nothing he could do . . .

Minutes later and Conti had tied him upright to the bole of a pine, was splashing petrol round his legs and feet in a small circle, gradually working back from him. Groggily Richard sagged in his bonds, shaking his head and trying to piece his shattered senses back together again. Then he heard Conti's voice bellowing up toward the higher slopes, and what the man yelled served to speed his recovery.

"Girl! Lynn Craig! Look, girl, I don't want to have to hurt your boyfriend if I can avoid it. If I *did* want to he'd be dead right now, but I'd prefer to take both of you back alive and let your father do his own dirty work. Do you hear me?"

No answer.

Richard finally lifted his head, gave a grunt as he strained uselessly against the ropes that bound him to the tree. Conti was standing, with the empty petrol can dangling from a huge fist. He grinned as he tossed it away. "Do you want to tell her she'd better come on down? Maybe she'll listen to you."

"Balls!" said Richard, his head throbbing dully where Conti's fist had smashed into it.

Conti grinned again. "You talk hard," he growled, "just like your old man, but you don't pack his punch. He's really dirty, your father, did you know that? It'll be a pleasure to come up against him again some time—but between times I've got you."

"I don't know what you're talking about," Richard answered. "Anyway, what do you want with us?'' He felt like he was speaking round a mouthful of cotton wool.

"I'm going to take you back to England, that's all, like her father wants me to."

"Why does Craig want me dead?'' Richard asked.

His question caught Conti off guard. "Hell, you need to ask that?'' he started to answer. "You call yourself Garrison, and you run off with—'' but there he paused and scowled. Richard knew now that he was right. Lynn's father *did* want him dead. And as soon as his paid thug had his hands on Lynn, his life would be utterly worthless.

"Lynn,'' he croaked, then used his dry tongue to clean his mouth and tried again. "Lynn!'' he shouted, hoping his voice would carry. "You stay wherever you are. He's going to kill me no matter what you do!''

Conti nodded, the grin slipping from his lumpy, damaged face. "Well, that just about does it,'' he said. He looked up into the high places, at the scree- and boulder-strewn slopes where the trees were scanty and spaced out as the mountain climbed to its peak. Was that the flash of a white thigh up there in the trees?

"Girl!'' Conti yelled. "I can't wait around all day. Come down and you have my word I won't hurt him. Stay up there and he's a goner for sure—and then I'll come up after you! What's it to be?'' Another flash of white, maybe a little closer, lower. Was she coming down? Did she think she could somehow tackle him? Conti's grin was back on his face. That should be fun!

He turned back to the youth tied to the tree. "Fun and games time,'' he informed. "You'll see what I mean. Hey, I'll just be a minute. While I'm busy, you just think about the petrol. Can you smell it? Pretty strong, eh? About a gallon and a half, I reckon, round you and that tree . . ."

He went to Tyler's car, drove it back, bumping it carelessly over the rough ground. He parked up close to the trees, stopped the motor, got out and lifted the bonnet. Then he brought out the jumper leads from his backpack and clipped them to the battery's terminals. The leads were quite long; they just reached to Richard, a distance of maybe nine feet.

"Got the idea, son?" Conti drawled. He tore open Richard's trousers, ripping the inside legs away to expose his underpants. He let a clip close slowly on the cotton, trapping the loose skin of Richard's scrotum between its jaws, then the same on the other side. "Do you know the kind of jolt it takes to start a car?" Conti grinned. "You know what'll happen when I turn the key in the ignition?"

"You bastard!" Richard gritted his teeth. "You slimy—"

"Yeah, yeah—all of that," Conti nodded. "Sorry, son, but I've no time for name-calling. Sticks and stones, as they say . . ." He turned his back, stared up into the slopes and cupped his hands to his mouth:

"Lynn Craig—if you don't come down your boyfriend's going to die right now! He's going to burn!"

Burn! . . . Richard shuddered. Yes, he would burn. The petrol fumes were heavy in his nostrils. Already the clips were painful where they held the loose folds of his scrotum. When Conti turned that key, Richard was bound to convulse. The clips were very close together . . . they would make contact . . . there were almost sure to be sparks.

Richard closed his eyes, bit his lip, shook his head. Thinking about it could do no good; this sadist was going to do it anyway.

"Lynn!" he yelled, trying to keep a sob of desperation, of fear, out of his voice. "Stay away!"

"I'll say one thing for you, son," Conti grunted. "You've got guts!"

I may have more than just guts, Richard thought. But if only he could be sure.

Something black moved in the trees close by: Suzy, staggering, shaking her head, falling and getting up again. She did not seem to know where she was going or what she was doing, her body still fighting the drug. But she was nevertheless determined to do something.

Conti could waste no more time. "Your very last chance, girl," he yelled, leaning into Tyler's car on that side away from Richard.

"Are you coming down?"

Nothing.

But there . . . he saw her! Moving between jutting boulders, picking her way from one patch of cover to the next. He could catch her while the kid burned.

"Goodbye, son," Conti softly called—and turned the key.

Richard's scream of agony gouted up to the heavens higher than the tongue of fire which immediately *whooshed* up and engulfed the tree. The heat licked at Conti where he backed off, laughing. Tyler's car's engine had fired first time, was ticking over right now and feeding electricity through the jumper leads. Nothing was visible through the blaze and the wall of heat-haze, but Conti could well imagine his young victim's body blackening while the current convulsed his agonized flesh.

"No—no—*noooo!*" Lynn came running down the slope, tumbling, bouncing, her blanket ripping from her where it caught on sharp rocks poking through the scree.

Conti simply stood, hands on hips, his back to the blaze, and let her come crashing toward him. Then, as the heat became fierce on his back, he moved forward to meet her. It was all over. The chase was done. The prize was his.

A dozen paces away she tripped, flew forward, hit the ground and scrambled to her knees. She looked beyond Conti through horrified, disbelieving eyes. Then—

Her eyes widened, her jaw dropped, she began to back away. Not from Conti, from something else. Already white, her face turned to chalk. There was fear in her eyes, but there was recognition, too.

Whatever it was she saw, it was not merely sickening and horrifying—it was awesome, terrifying! And she had seen it before. Slowly Conti turned, his flesh crawling. Thirty feet away, a great tree and the earth around it blazed—but at the heart of the fire a man-shaped blue glow pulsed like some alien heartbeat!

Conti knew that he witnessed something from outside normal human experience, that there was a power here he could never hope to understand. He, too, backed away, following the girl where she crept, putting distance between himself and the blazing tree with its fearsome burden. But as he went he watched, and what he saw he could not believe.

The blue glow reached out twin pseudopods that followed the cables of the jumper leads to Tyler's car. The car glowed blue for a single moment, seemed to contract a little and shrink down into itself—and exploded!

Conti was picked up and hurled flat, knocked over like a skittle in the blast of hot air that rushed outward from the riven car. Lynn, further away, got to her feet and stumbled for safety. Conti, dazed and disoriented, picked himself up and uselessly dusted himself down, brushed leaves, twigs and dirt from his clothing. And again he looked back.

For a moment longer the pillar of fire blazed—and then was extinguished!

It went out, like a snuffed candle, like a light switched off. The tree was black, smoking—likewise the scorched earth at its foot—but the thing that stood before it was untouched by the heat, unchanged and undamaged by the fire.

The *other* Richard moved forward through smoldering ropes that fell away from him; drifted forward until he stood where Tyler's car lay shattered like a burst egg. But no, he did *not* stand, and Conti began to moan his terror as he saw that the soles of the blue-glowing figure's feet were in fact inches above the ground.

Conti ducked behind a tree, kept watching. He felt sure he had not been seen, was not even certain that this thing which had been Richard Stone could see—but something was happening. The blue glow was pulsating faster, more intensely.

Conti kept trees and bushes between himself and the terror in the smoke, backed away further yet. The figure standing free in air was beginning to move, slowly turning on its own axis like a weight at the end of a thread. Conti gasped and ducked lower as thin golden beams reached out from the apparition's face, from its eyes.

The beams touched the bole of a tree, which

with a series of great cracking reports immediately split lengthwise from its roots to its highest branches, bending over in two halves as if struck and split by lightning. And as the blue-glowing figure turned, so its golden eyes sought fresh targets.

Conti moaned again, clutched at his hammering heart, staggered back from that which he could not comprehend. Trees—great pines, some of them thirty feet and more tall—exploded, shredded down like shattered sticks of celery, were cut through and felled where the golden beams touched, or simply crumbled to piles of gray ash before his disbelieving eyes! And already the man-thing at the heart of the blue glow had turned through three-quarters of a circle.

He's looking for me! Conti told himself. *Oh, sweet Jesus—he's looking for me!*

Galvanized into panic-flight, he stood up, broke cover, ran into the trees—or would have. Except that now he came face to face with something almost equally terrifying.

The black Doberman bitch glared at him through eyes red as hell. Her teeth were drooling ivory daggers in a face twisted into a quivering snarl of sheer hatred. Almost fully recovered from the effect of the drug, Suzy wanted revenge on someone, and Donald Conti looked like the perfect candidate.

He made to snatch out a gun but already she was in the air, flying straight at his face. He threw up his arms and the weapon was knocked from his hand; her teeth sank into and met through his wrist. He screamed, jerked back from her and tripped; she let go of him, made to attack again. He staggered to his feet, turned—

—And crashed through a bush directly into the view of the blue-glowing thing in the smoke!

The golden beams from its eyes instantly flickered toward him. Conti leaped aside, leaped high and wide, danced like a madman as he tried to avoid those beams. But he could not. He drew air to scream again, gave a final wild leap . . . and the scream died in his throat.

His flying figure was trapped in a golden haze, held fast, impossibly suspended over the stony earth in a bubble of golden light. Then the bubble grew dark and its gold was replaced with crimson.

The bubble burst with a soft *pop!*

A scarlet rain descended to earth.

And with the rain, clattering hollowly down, a host of irregular white things large and small, and one round white thing that bounded and rolled where it fell, and grinned vacantly where at last it came to rest.

Suzy sniffed once at the red wet earth, at the pile of freshly flensed bones, and drew back in disgust. Then she ran to find Lynn . . .

The tapes had been delivered by 9:30 A.M. and for two and half hours Phillip Stone had sat and listened to them, hearing his own sleepy voice—prompted now and then by Albert Gill's deep, sonorous tones—telling a tale so fantastic that its message was still sinking in. Unfortunately, it had been just as vague as it was fantastic.

Outside in the grounds of Stone's house, the workmen (only five had turned up, and without their foreman, who would not now be collecting his bonus; who, in any case, would no longer have any use for money) were cleaning up the last of their mess and packing away tools and machinery. But even their hubbub failed to make any real impression on Stone or break through the wall of frustration and bafflement with which he now surrounded himself.

Mary was not here this morning and Stone missed her—Mary and her constant supply of coffee. But last night she had "felt queer," said she wanted to go and see her married daughter and her family in Salisbury. Stone had not liked her looks, but she had known what she wanted: just to see her family, before the waterfalls in her head inundated her mind completely. Harmless old dear: he had called a taxi for her and paid for it, and that was the last he had seen of her. Nor did he expect to see her again.

This morning, up before 8:00, he had watched the morning news (what little detailed news there was, for certainly someone had a tight grip on the media) and had been more than ever aware of the undercurrents of hysteria beneath the gathering tide of unease and downright fear which swept the world. Overnight, even here in England, the thing had seemed to gather an almost physical form to itself.

Oh, for the time being the politicians still held their own against the two-prong attacks of public opinion and reaction, but for how much longer? Soon the pressure would become too great, the politicians themselves would grow afraid. Sheer weight of evidence would speak for itself; cracks would appear in the great Dam of Staunch Reserve; finally the Great British Public would have to be told all. And then watch the deluge break!

Stone remembered the ludicrous "measures to be taken in the event of a nuclear attack" campaign back in the '80s—the government pamphlets telling how to whitewash one's windows to keep out heat and radiation, and how to build indoor shelters using doors, tables and sandbags: as if people kept sandbags in their cupboards, for God's sake!—and guessed that this would be more of the same. Indeed it was here already, though for the most part the advice was proper and intelligent, however cold.

An hourly citizen's advice spot, broadcast on all radio and TV stations, told how to deal with relatives suffering primary mind-plague attacks (and, discreetly, who to speak to about them); advised on avoiding congested traffic, crowds, tubes, buses; warned about the penalties for harboring or concealing gibberers; detailed how to inform on suspects, and to whom, giving contact numbers for the brand new Emergency Mind-plague Control Centers; and so on, etc., etc., etc. . . .

But this was England—Land of the Uncommonly Sane—last bastion of *Homo Phlegmaticus*, down-to-earth man! What of the rest of the world?

Ireland, apparently, was already in the throes of utter nightmare confused by inherent irrationality. All sales of liquor had been banned, likewise smoking in any public place (an eminent Irish doctor had now "established definite links" between smokers, alcoholics and mind-plaguers). It made no difference, apparently, that children, even tiny babies, were going mad. On a far more terrifying level, the United Irish Army was now enforcing a government curfew and arresting and beating anyone caught out in the streets after 8:00 P.M. This latest measure had come into effect only last night, but already there was the case of a military mind-plaguer, an arsonist, putting isolated houses to the torch and shooting "curfew-breakers" as they fled their burning houses.

Ancient feuds, too, had been rekindled, and the IRA marched again as bloodily as of old.

U.S. intelligence had released (and immediately retracted) satellite photographs of mushroom clouds over Poland, to coincide with worldwide seismograph reports of massive concussions in that region. Nothing was confirmed, however, for the initial dearth of reports coming out of Poland had soon become total. The U.S.S.R. had denied any knowledge or connection: Russia's frontiers were being closed and she desired peace and solitude, wishing no further commerce or contact with the outside world as of now—this despite rumors that her rapidly mobilized forces were now marshalled in great strength all along the Chinese border. The Moscow fire still raged completely out of control.

In South Africa all blacks—whether they gibbered or not—were being hunted down like animals and shot on sight; elsewhere in Africa the roles were reversed and whites suffered the same fate. The Human Rights Leaguers who leaked these reports were now ominously silent . . .

In Switzerland some genius had proposed that a "sterile environment" was the only real answer to mind-plague; the Swiss were taking to their nuclear shelters in droves, convinced that they would be safe there. Stone believed differently. *God help them!* he thought.

In Holland, reversing an old, old legend, gibberers had mined the seawalls and let the ocean in, flooding vast areas all along the west coast and drowning hundreds.

South America was said to be in a state of war, apparently internecine.

The U.S.A. was rapidly succumbing to utmost chaos.

No single ray of hope shone from any direction . . .

And here Phillip Stone sat, safe for the moment in his own little bubble of isolation and sanity; and the answers, he was sure, lying somewhere in these tapes, these recorded "memories" of his own past life and the lives of others—*but where?*

Oh, the tapes told a story all right. No doubt about it. And what a story! What they did *not* tell was how it should be read, or who had erased or rearranged it in the first place. And because these "fantastic fictions" had been dug out of Stone's head piecemeal, the story was disjointed—it had gaps, its sections followed neither logical nor chronological patterns. That had to do with the way Gill had gone about it, which in turn had not been his fault but Stone's own. For Stone and no one else had supplied the list of key words, and Gill had merely gone by the list.

Now Phillip Stone looked at that list again:

> *Richard Garrison.*
> *Gareth Wyatt.*
> *Vicki Maler.*
> *Blind.*

On Sunday, Gill had started with Vicki Maler. The tubby little psychiatrist had sent Stone's mind back in time, reaching into his earliest memories of Vicki; and having listened to the recording of that session, Stone knew far more now about his late wife than he—*or she*, he was sure—had ever "remembered" in their lives together. But still it was only "knowing" and "accepting," not truly "remembering" at all; and the acceptance came very hard indeed.

That was the whole problem: he had assumed

that as soon as he had the facts—as soon as his subconscious mind had been sparked into life—then that everything would come back to him. But it had not done so. What had sounded like "fantastic fictions" to Gill sounded no jot less fantastic to Stone. With the exception that he *believed* them to be true. A belief based on one or two peculiar and still unexplained coincidences: Vicki's suddenly remembering that she had been blind, and that she had known a man called Garrison, *her* Richard's real father; and Richard himself making that same allegation—no, stating it for a fact!

Stone felt mental panic setting in, controlled his suddenly whirling thoughts. He must not fly off at tangents. He must not stray from the path of logical examination and evaluation. And above all he must *not* deny these hard come by clues. These tapes were real: what was on them was real, it had happened. How? Why? That must be reckoned as incidental. What mattered was the sanity of the world. And the answer was here . . .

It all had to do with—

Something flashed like a bright light in Stone's mind. A single scene, monochrome, sharply black and white. Not a scene remembered, a scene imagined! Pipes and circuits and conduits and screens and graphs and ticker tapes. Massive. Awesome size and power. Electroencephalograph? Psychic monitor? Psychometer?

Stone screwed up his eyes, forced himself to concentrate . . . but the thing was gone. He had almost had it. A single word—*the* word—on the tip of his tongue, slipping away, now beyond reach.

He was sweating, feeling the urgency building in him, the frustration rising to its peak. He thought again of what he had glimpsed for a split second framed in the mirror of his mind.

Psychometer? Now what the hell was that supposed to mean?

Reluctantly, knowing he had been *that* close, he returned to his original train of thought.

. . . He must accept that the tapes were real, and that the information they held, fragmentary and inconsistent (apparently) was nevertheless real, not fictitious. It had after all been taken from his own subconscious mind, from memories which were still in there and which someone else had tried to erase. So—

Vicki Maler had been blind.

No! His mind denied it.

Stone took a deep breath, sweated, clenched his fists and tried again:

Yes, she *had* been blind. And she *had* loved a man called Richard Garrison, also blind. And yes, this Garrison had controlled strange powers, which he had come by when—

When?

How?

The tapes didn't say. The restrictions that had been placed on Stone's memory in this one respect—in respect of Richard Garrison—were so tightly locked into place that Gill had not even been able to shift them, let alone remove them. Stone *had* the answer all right, deep down inside, but it had been buried there under the tombstone of the dead past. Dead and buried in his mind. R.I.P.

Go back to Vicki:

She had been blind before Stone knew her, some years before he had known her, but somehow she had regained her sight. Also, when The Gibbering took her, she had regained a little—a very tiny part—of *her* memory. So . . . whoever or whatever had wiped Stone's mind clean had also done his/its work on Vicki. And how many others?

Go *back* to Vicki:

She . . . had been in danger, yes. That had been Stone's fault, though not deliberate. He had got her into some sort of big trouble and had to get her out again. And the danger had been in the shape of—

Black—huge—a giant!—neither man nor woman—a beast—

What? Stone grabbed at the fleeting vision. Too late, gone, meaningless. He slammed his fist down on to the top of his desk, shook his head and saw a spray of sweat fly, tried again.

Go back to Monday:

On Monday Gill had dealt with Gareth Wyatt. But here the taped conversation was so confused that Stone was utterly at a loss. It had involved Hitler, or some project Hitler had worked on—and the Nazis, an organization to help German war criminals escape justice and find new lives and identities in the years following World War II—and the destruction of Wyatt's house by unexplained forces—and Wyatt's possession of . . . something. A device?—which had made Wyatt important to Richard Garrison.

A "device," yes—

Massive! Metal, plastic, glass. A computer—no, but a brain—a device to free the brain? A psychic enhancer. A mechanical psychiatrist!

And again the vision faded, the sought-for word vanishing from the tip of his tongue.

Garrison . . . blind.

Vicki . . . blind.

Gareth Wyatt . . . a device.

Did Wyatt have a device which could return sight to blind people?

Vicki had remembered being blind. And she had remembered Richard Garrison, her lover before Stone, *her* Richard's father.

And Garrison had been blind, too. Until—

Until what?

The thing went round in bloody circles!

"Blind, blind, *blind!*" Stone suddenly shouted out loud. His arm moved almost independent of mind, sweeping tapes, cassette recorder and all from the top of his desk. The recorder shattered where it came down on one fragile corner on the floor; the tapes clattered into silence in their plastic cassettes: the room seemed to wait anxiously, breathlessly, for the rest of Stone's outburst. It didn't come. He merely sat there, haggard.

Outside, the workmen had finished and were gone. Stone was left alone in his cocoon of safety, waiting for horror to germinate in his mind, waiting for The Gibbering.

The funny thing, he told himself, *is that I'm blind too—insomuch as I can't see, can't look into my own past.*

"God," he prayed out loud, "show me the light! Let me see. Only let me see. Don't—please *don't*—leave me in the dark like this. Your world is coming to an end and the answer is right here, but I can't see it. God, to whom I've never really prayed before, *please* let there be light!"

But there was no light; those dark places in his mind were as void of it as the great abysses beyond the furthest stars. Someone had spilled ink across a page of his memory, and the blot was jet, black as he River Styx, dark as the ferryman himself.

The ferryman him—

Charon! Charon Gubwa!

The gates opened in Phillip Stone's mind.

His hair moved as under the influence of static electricity.

His flesh crept.

The blood drained from his face, which turned from the darkness of anger and frustration to the pallor of sudden shock.

He felt faint, grasped at consciousness and held on.

He saw the light.

He . . . remembered!

Stone eased himself gently, almost fearfully, back in his chair and let his memories fill themselves in, closing the gaps in his mind—gaps he had never guessed existed until just a few short days ago. And now that the dam had burst his memories were in full flood, and like parched earth his brain soaked itself in them and seemed to sigh as it grew rich with memories that were *true* memories and which had never been fictions, fantastic or otherwise.

For half an hour he sat there, head back, face pale, eyes closed and hands limp on the arms of his chair. He remembered, yes—and uppermost in his returned memory, the voice of Vicki, and the megalomaniac voice of Charon Gubwa:

Gubwa: *". . . Psychomech shall live on. I have made arrangements. The man who built the machine for Garrison will be here tomorrow, and—"*

Vicki: *"Jimmy Craig? You have him, too?"*

Gubwa: *"Indeed! Mr. James Christopher Craig himself. I have him, yes—or will have him. Already I have visited him in his dreams and made certain . . . suggestions? Ah!—and how susceptible, our Mr. Craig."*

Vicki: *"But Jimmy wasn't the builder! Psychomech was built by a man dead now or disappeared. Jimmy only improved on what was already there. He stripped away outmoded parts and replaced them. He—"*

Gubwa: *"I know all of that, Miss Maler. You told me, remember? Well, perhaps you don't. Anyway, I have been in Craig's mind. I told him he has a mission, a Great Mission, which is to build Psychomech again—a mightier, more powerful Psychomech—and this time to build it for me. I told him that with the completion of this marvel, this Oracle, he himself will become a wondrous power in the world. I told him that he had erred in working for Garrison, and that Garrison was a great sinner! But I also said that I would strike Garrison down, and then that Craig—through his work for me—would be redeemed. And I told him that, through Psychomech, one day he would communicate with the One True God himself. Yes, and I shall be that God! Do you see, Miss Maler, do you see?"*

Vicki: *"Yes . . . yes, I see . . ."*

And now Phillip Stone believed that he, too, saw. Not the whole picture, not even now, but most of it.

He sat up, readied himself. He regained something of his old strength, a lot of his old anger. J. C. Craig was lording it up there, safe at PSISAC— safe with a machine which could cure mindplague—watching while the world went crazy!

He video-phoned PSISAC, but Craig's personal number was engaged. He tried the switchboard and after a long wait got a harsh male voice he did not recognize, and no vision at all.

"What's wrong with vision?" he snapped at the swirling gray screen.

"No vision. Sorry, Chief," said the voice.

"Chief?" Stone's voice grew dangerously soft. "This is Phillip Stone," he said in a low growl. "Put me through to Jimmy Craig, right now . . ."

A pause. "He's not accepting calls . . . *Chief!*" The man's insolence was deliberate.

"He'll accept this call," Stone's growl was deeper. "And later, after I've spoken to him, don't be surprised if he wants your balls for door-stops!"

"Look, Stone," the voice answered. "Your name carries no weight up here anymore. In fact it stinks like shit! J.C.'s accepting no calls, and that's—"

"*Psychomech!*" Stone shouted.

"Eh?"

"Tell him I said Psychomech—just that. And tell him he can reach me at home."

Stone put the phone down, sat back once more, got his temper and his thoughts back in order and waited for Craig's call.

He did not have long to wait . . .

2:00 P.M., and Lynn drove the silver Mercedes south, holding steady to seventy miles per hour down the eight-laner she had picked up near Heiligenstadt. Her route would shortly take her past Würzburg and on toward Stuttgart and eventually Zürich. Beside her Suzy sat—or stood—on the front passenger seat, her paws on the backrest, her huge soft eyes peering into the back. And there, under a blanket, the rigid form of Richard lay like a blue-glowing mummy under its shroud.

Lynn deliberately kept her mind from dwelling too much on what had happened back there in the mountains, but in fact she had seen very little of its resolution. When the *other* Richard had begun clearing the area in his search for Conti, she had simply taken shelter behind the largest boulder she could find, staying there until the explosions and other . . . *sounds* were finished. She had not witnessed Conti's death and had been spared discovering his remains; in fact (and not surprisingly) she had remained in a sort of numb condition, inured from further shock, even as she fumblingly dressed herself and prepared to leave the place.

By then, too, Suzy had taken her place in the front of the car, and Richard had . . . *moved* into the back, where Lynn had only to cover him with a torn and disheveled blanket. One other thing had impressed her: the discovery in Conti's backpack of a headset exactly like those belonging to the Jacksons and the Tyler woman. Even in her near mindblasted condition she had known the thing was important: it now rested in the Mercedes' glove compartment.

There had been no . . . *conversation* between Lynn and Richard before or during the journey so far. She had known of his intention to go on to Switzerland and had seen no reason to waste time waiting for him to become himself once more. The decision to start the journey had been hers alone; if he had disapproved, doubtless he would have "said" so. Traffic had been surprisingly light, traffic accidents numerous and too often horrific, the presence of wailing *Polizei* vehicles and ambulances depressing.

At a place called Fulda Lynn had filled up with petrol at a small self-service station, only to discover afterward that the place was deserted. All the doors and windows were wide open, but no sign of an attendant anywhere. Knowing she would later feel guilty if she simply drove away—

knowing, too, that her honesty was time-wasting and would make no difference whatsoever—she nevertheless used Richard's ID tag to pay the bill. The electronic till was working and accepted the payment; her conscience was clear.

What she had not seen, between the public lavatories with their pictorial *Damen* and *Herren* signs, was the ruptured body of an overalls-clad middle-aged man who doubtless was—or had been—the station attendant. His face was purple, eyes like plums, and he lay on his back on a narrow strip of grass framed in a border of late-flowering shrubs. Clenched in his teeth he still held the nozzle of a hissing air hose, its jet causing his cheeks to flutter, and in his now limp right hand the metal trigger . . .

That had been something a little less than an hour ago.

Now, having passed the Würzburg *Ausfahrt*, slowing down to maneuver the scene of yet another accident (an articulated truck had started to mount an embankment before crashing over onto its side; a man, presumably the driver, sat on the door of his cab, singing and laughing while his co-driver tried to coax him down), Lynn found herself flagged down by two police motorcyclists where their bikes were parked across one of the two remaining free lanes.

Her heart pounding, she slowed the car to a standstill and the policemen—looking very military in their smart gray uniforms, motorcycle jodhpurs and boots—came unsmiling to her where she waited. The one on Suzy's side stayed well back, despite the fact that the window was closed, but the other leaned on Lynn's sill and spoke to her in German. She was not particularly practiced in the language.

"I beg your pardon?" she answered politely, smiling nervously. "I'm sorry, my German isn't much good." *Oh, God—please don't let them look in the back!*

"Ah, English!" said the policeman, his stony face relaxing a little. "Where go you, please?"

Lynn was more interested in the other one, who was now peering into the car's rear window. Suzy growled and snapped, watching him anxiously. The sound of the bitch's paws scratching at the glass of her window rasped on Lynn's raw nerves.

"Please?" said the policeman again.

"Oh!" she jumped, startled, and blurted: "We're going to Switzerland."

"Hans!" called the other over the top of the car. *"Hier ist komisch, nein?"*

"Was?" Hans answered, looking up. He took a pace toward the rear and looked in through the back window.

God, oh God! Lynn thought, clenching her teeth. *When they see him glowing like that . . .*

Her policeman came back, frowning beneath the low peak of his cap, his eyes unblinking. "Something is wrong, yes?"

"Wrong? Why, no, of course not. I—"

"Please, under the blanket—what is?"

"My husband!" Lynn blurted out, unthinking. "My man."

The policeman nodded slowly, his eyes unwavering. *"Krank*, him? Sick?"

"No, just tired. We've driven a long . . ." Her mouth dried up.

Hans unbuttoned his gun holster. "Please—I see?"

"Yes, certainly," she said, stalling. "But tell me, why did you stop me?"

"Is new law," he told her with a shrug. "You

hear it not? Not driving alone. Two people in car always."

"Oh! No, I didn't know that. But you see, there *are* two people in this car—so now can I please—"

"See!" he snapped, his impatience showing. "See *now*, please!" He pointed to the rear door catch. "Make open."

His companion had joined him on this side now. Both of them had taken out their guns.

"Suzy, be still!" Lynn whispered. And to Hans: "What are the guns for?"

He looked at her, reached a hand in through her window and round to the back catch, freed it. "Not all sick people laugh like this one," he said, nodding to where the idiot truck driver was getting down off the door of his cab, assisted by his co-driver. "Sometimes they . . . angry. They strong. The law say, if not good, shoot!"

He opened the back door, lowered his head and leaned forward, took the corner of the grubby blanket between thumb and forefinger . . . and jerked it back to reveal Richard's face.

Eyes squeezed tightly shut, Lynn waited. When nothing happened, she opened her eyes the merest fraction and looked.

The expression on the faces of the two policemen was one of uniform shock—but frozen. They moved not a fraction. Their faces were bathed in a golden glow. Richard's eyes were closed, but the gold came right through his eyelids, filling the back of the car with its yellow light. And still the policemen stood there at the open door, leaning slightly forward, frozen in their tracks.

Another moment—and the golden haze was sucked back again through Richard's closed lids and into his eyes. He continued to glow blue.

Hans put the blanket back over his face, straightened up, closed the door. Both policemen stepped back a pace. They smiled at Lynn, holstered their guns, began to walk along the length of the sprawled, toppled trailers toward the cab of the crashed lorry. Hans paused and half-turned, seemingly surprised to see Lynn still sitting there. *"In ordnung!"* he called. "I thanking you."

For a moment longer Lynn remained motionless, numb, scarcely breathing. Then she put the car in gear and moved slowly forward. As she passed them, both policemen came smartly to attention, saluting her. Sitting stiffly at the wheel, she thought: *nice touch, other Richard!*

Then she drove away, and did not look back . . .

At PSISAC, J. C. Craig was still waiting for Phillip Stone to arrive when the call came through from Edward Bragg at the Rastatte Heilbron between Würzburg and Stuttgart. Craig ordered it switched through immediately to his study in the Dome.

"Yes, Edward, what is it?" he asked as soon as the other's face appeared on his screen. "I would hope that this time your news is rather better?"

"It is," Bragg nodded. "Judge for yourself. I have them."

"You *what*?" Craig leaned forward, his face suddenly alive with excitement. A face full of its own madness, Bragg thought, quite separate from The Gibbering. A driving megalomania, a completely misplaced religious fervor. "You've actually got them?"

"Not 'got'—" Bragg answered, "found. I'm onto them. From where I'm sitting now I can actually see them—your daughter, anyway."

"You can see Lynn? She's well? I had almost

given up hope!" Craig breathed. "Oh, well done, Edward!"

"Let me tell you what's happened," Bragg went on, quickly sketching in his last twenty-four hours for Craig.

Not all of them had been good hours, not by a long shot. First his car had broken down on a high mountain road and had to be recovered to Göttingen for repairs. The car was brand new and suffering from teething problems, but despite the fact that he had offered treble the normal wages for the work, still the job had taken most of Wednesday afternoon.

Meanwhile he had learned from Dorothy Ellis at PSISAC that Emma Tyler was now in St. Andreasberg, and that Conti wasn't far behind her. When the garage in Göttingen was finished with his car he had finally driven on to St. Andreasberg and got himself a hotel room, but just when he would have gone on from there to check out all of the local hotels he had suffered another attack. Deeming it unwise to proceed while using his headset, he had waited for the attack to run its course. It had been a long one, lasting well into the dark hours. Then, before proceeding further, he had checked again with PSISAC. Tyler had been in touch, saying that she was now "very close." There had been no word from Conti.

Then, even while Bragg and Dorothy Ellis were talking, she had received word through the computer that "Garrison" had drawn money through a night-cash system at the World Bank in Wernigeroder. The withdrawal had been the standard 300 DM—enough, presumably, to pay for a couple of nights for two at a local inn.

Then Bragg had hit upon an idea. It seemed to him not unlikely that in the near future the fugitives might have to use the bank in Wernigeroder again . . .

Without any further delay he had gone there and kept surveillance on the place, passing a bloody night in a town—indeed in a world—where people seen on the streets long after nightfall were rapidly becoming objects of hostile suspicion. Still, he had remained on watch all through the night until the following morning, when sure enough Richard Stone had returned in a large silver Mercedes to draw more cash. Bragg could have killed him there and then, but that would not lead him to Lynn Craig.

Instead he had tailed Stone on foot during the course of his shopping spree, noting that he bought a good many items of women's clothing, and then had followed him in the car back into the mountains. Uncertain whether or not to go into the saddle between the peaks after him, Bragg had waited, and after maybe half an hour had seen a fire up near the skyline. There had been explosions of some sort of other, but then the activity had died down and Bragg had continued to wait. Just before noon Lynn had driven the big Mercedes out onto the road and headed back toward Wernigeroder. There had been a huge black dog in the front of the car with her, but no sign of Richard Stone.

Unwilling to lose track of her now (the girl was, after all, the most important prize in the chase) Bragg had followed her onto the eight-laner at Heiligenstadt. He had constantly sought a way to intercept or interrupt her journey but was given no opportunity—while traffic was light a high percentage of it was made up of police vehicles—but in any case she had at last pulled in at this Rastatte near Heilbron. Before that, however, Bragg had twice been stopped by police pointing out that he should not be driving alone. On both occasions they had let him carry on after a warning, but as a result of these interruptions he had only just caught up with Lynn again when she turned into the Rastatte.

But now the payoff: when she had gone into the Rastatte with the dog, Bragg had taken a look inside the Mercedes. In the back, apparently asleep, he had seen Richard Stone—or "Garrison," as Craig kept insisting.

That was all . . .

"You've done a superb job!" Craig told him, eager now and filled with the flush of imminent triumph. "What now? Will you kill him there?"

"No," Bragg shook his head. He stared at Craig's flushed face where it was framed on the car's small screen up beside the rearview mirror. "It's broad daylight and there are too many people about. Wherever they're going, they're sure to hole-up before long. I'll do it then. It will be just another small incident to add to the general chaos. There are gibberers all over the place now. I would guess that maybe one person in every seven or eight has suffered or is about to suffer a primary attack."

"One in seven, coming down to six," Craig nodded. "The computers here confirm it. The curve is bending faster than we allowed, but we're following the trend. Whatever you're going to do, Edward, it had better be tonight. You *must* get Lynn back here tomorrow at the latest. After that . . . you may not get back here at all!"

"Tomorrow it'll be," Bragg nodded. "Tonight, if I can make it. It's as good as done."

"Can I help from this end?"

Bragg thought about it. "Can you get hold of a

jet-copter? Something small, range of about fifteen hundred miles?"

Craig smiled thinly. "Oddly enough, I'm expecting to take delivery of just such an aircraft this
evening."

"And a pilot?"

Craig nodded. "That can also be arranged."

"Okay. When I've got Lynn I'll head for Paris.
You'll get coordinates when I can find a place
suitable for the chopper to land."

"Fine!" Craig rubbed his hands. And: "Edward,"
he said, "I want you to contact me again—not
later than, oh, 11:30 tonight."

"Oh?"

"Progress report. Also to check I have the jet-
copter. Okay?"

"Of course."

"If you fail to contact me, I shall assume something is wrong."

"I see no problem. I'll speak to you from the
car, as I'm doing now." Bragg frowned. "Are you
expecting trouble of some sort?"

"I am thinking of you," Craig told him. "*You*
should be expecting trouble! This Garrison is the
antichrist."

Straight-faced, Bragg shrugged. "God is on our
side," he answered.

Craig slowly nodded. "You're doing a marvelous job, my boy. And believe me, you shall get
your just rewards . . ."

Phillip Stone drove up to PSISAC along roads and
through streets and towns ominously sparse in
moving traffic. The two major motor-roads north
were out of action, hopelessly blocked due to
massive multiple accidents, and barriers had
been erected across their access points; which

would normally mean that the lesser roads were crowded. But on the contrary, the roads were almost empty, where only police vehicles constantly cruised on the lookout for trouble. Every nine or ten miles Stone found himself stopped and questioned by dazed-looking, weary and unshaven mobile patrolmen, who appeared not to have slept for days.

They were no longer polite, these men, and fired their questions and instructions in harsh, staccato machine-gun bursts showing only too clearly the ragged edges of hysteria in orders repeated until they had no meaning and advice offered almost to extinction. They no longer had to *think* about what they said or did; their work in this respect had become automatic. They were indeed automatons: not gibberers themselves—not yet—but slaves of The Gibbering, certainly. After he had been stopped three times, Stone hardly listened to them at all (he was used to listening to men, not babbling robots) but merely caught snatches of their conversation, obtained a general impression of what they were saying or trying to put over:

"Who are you, sir, and where are you . . . ? PSISAC? Ah, you're the top man up there, are you? You're aware of course that . . . mind-plague? Well, fair enough, but if you're planning to drive beyond . . . out of the question. I really would have to advise you . . . gibberers . . . telling people not to drive if they don't have to, you see, and . . . stranded, and the mind-plaguers are . . . very well, Mr. Stone. You'd better be on your . . . but watch out for . . . traffic accidents up there and the road is completely . . . lunatics . . . 'fraid you'll need to avoid . . . gibbering sods . . . no longer possible to . . . mind-plaguers . . . road should be

all right. If you cut across . . . crazy bastards . . .
stick to the wider roads if you can . . . mindless
wankers! . . . And if you get crowds of people trying to . . . *drive right through 'em!* Not deliberately to kill or maim 'em, you understand—but
don't stop whatever you do! . . . bloody dangerous . . . murder . . . may not find all policemen are
as experienced as you'd expect . . . short-staffed
. . . mind-plague . . . hitting us too you see? Oh,
we're recruiting as fast as . . . day and night . . .
shoot the bastards! . . . only way . . . burning and
looting . . . bloody fuckers will do just about . . .
Good luck, sir. And take care!''

A babble, only a babble; and the more you
heard it the more meaningless it all became. In a
way, it was a form of gibbering itself. Stone wondered if he, too, was beginning to sound like
that . . .

And there was another way in which these cus-
todians of the law—these British policemen, always a race apart from the rest of the world's law
enforcement officers—were different now from the
simple policemen Stone was used to; which was
simply that they carried weapons. Each and every
one of them was armed: they wore pistols at their
hips, and over their shoulders were slung sub-
machine-guns of a type Stone himself had used
often enough back in the old days. Sterlings—
street-fighting weapons—deadly at close quar-
ters, and even at a distance in the hands of the
right man. All in all, it told a terrible story . . .

For all that the traffic was light, abandoned vehicles were parked everywhere, in places almost
blocking the roads. The police were doing their
best—moving forsaken cars and trucks to the
sides of the streets and occasionally on to the
pavements, advising drivers to go home, keeping

what traffic there was moving—but it wasn't nearly enough. Accidents (Stone supposed they must still be called accidents) were frequent, where drivers suddenly started to gibber and crashed their vehicles; which meant that wherever the congestion was worst, the roads were littered with broken glass and plastic and bits of twisted metal or chrome. Again there were men clearing rubbish aside, but how long could they hope to go on? One in six gibbered, and the curve was still bending. By tonight it would be one in five, and tomorrow?

If, suddenly, right now, the sun were to come out in the leaden sky and the mind-plague were to go away, still it would be weeks before things were back to normal. But that was not going to happen; things could only get worse. Stone was aware that once he got to PSISAC he might well be there for good. Well, since he owned ninety percent of the damn place, he supposed he might as well be there as anywhere. But of course that was not the reason he was going there.

In fact he was less than sure of the real reason himself, not even now, except that he suspected that what little would remain of humanity when this was all over might very well have its core at PSISAC. Then again, he had a score to settle with J. C. Craig. Craig, who had the answer to The Gibbering in the shape of a machine called Psychomech, and who used it for his own ends only. Oh, yes, that was what really drove Stone on: the thought that Richard might have been saved, even though he wasn't his son, and the thought that Vicki might never have had to die. And how many thousands—how many *millions*—of others? How long ago had Craig built himself this machine? And why had he kept it to himself?

These were some of the questions Stone wanted answered, and the answers were all at PSISAC. When Craig had got back to him earlier he had asked him to come up—had told him he would be safe at PSISAC, had promised to tell him all. Well, maybe he would and maybe he wouldn't, but Stone would never find out back in Sussex. This was the only way. He was aware that he was only one man, and by no means the man he had used to be—aware, too, that this was a straw he clutched at to save himself and what was left of the world from drowning utterly—but he must at least try. Anything was better than sitting on his butt and waiting for madness . . .

Along the way, Goring and Cholsey were burning. Firemen fought a losing battle. Whole streets were ablaze, the fire jumping from block to block, pouring clouds of black smoke and red flame into a sky already dark with November clouds and heavy with rain which refused to come. It was as if God frowned on the world, and perhaps He did. Stone skirted the burning places, aware that time was slipping by, controlling his impatience and frustration as best he might.

Then, almost at the end of his journey, north of Wallingford as he came round a corner—

He saw the idiot maybe fifty yards ahead: a man, leaping out into the middle of the road, laughing as he hurled a brick straight at Stone's windscreen. Stone applied his brakes, ducked . . . the brick smashed through the windscreen and passed over his head into the back in a shower of tiny glass cubes . . . Stone looked up through his collapsing windscreen to see the lunatic drawing back his arm, a second brick gripped in his hand. And civilization flowed out of Phillip Stone like water through a sieve. The car was still moving forward: he moved his foot to the accelerator and rammed it down. The car's engine coughed once and thrust the car forward like a hound un-leashed. It smashed the gibberer down and dragged him under, and as he went Stone saw that he was still laughing. He drove on without looking back . . .

And at last he was there, or as close as he could get in the car. For two hundred yards from PSISAC's main gates, finally the clutter of abandoned ve-hicles in the road was enough to bring him to a halt. He must cover the last few yards on foot.

Among the stranded vehicles were a number of police cars, and others which were some of the finest machines Stone had ever seen. He might expect just such a collection of expensive toys at some millionaire's summer garden party (at one of his own, as they had used to be) and wondered what they were doing here, abandoned. It puzzled him until he got to within fifty yards of the gates.

It was already dark: 4:30 P.M., November, PSISAC, outskirts of Oxford, England. Lighting-up time, and on the horizon parts of Oxford sending up pillars of flame to light up the lowering clouds with shift-ing patterns of red. But no streetlights flickering into life and the street itself dead as a morgue. And the reek of burning heavy in the air . . . and also the reek of death. Then Stone saw that the street *was* a morgue—or at least a slaughter-house.

Between the haphazardly parked cars where they blocked the road, bodies lay in a lattice of limbs and blots of blood. Men and women, there was no distinction. They lay where they had been cut down even as they left their vehicles. Stone saw them, a great many of them, but failed to understand or did not want to. And in the small square of PSISAC's entrance, more bodies sprawled in front of massive concrete blocks and sandbagged fortifications.

And as Stone stumbled numbly forward across a corpse-littered pavement, now a voice began blasting at him from some unseen loudspeaker:

"Halt! Who goes there?"

"What?" he whispered, his stunned mind still trying to grasp all of the implications.

"Come no closer!"

"What?" he raised his voice a little, the single word emerging as a bark.

"State your business!"

"What?" Stone now yelled. He shook his fist at the place: at its walls festooned with barbed wire, its blockhouse, its sandbags, its hidden guns. "This *is* my bloody business!" He opened his arms. "I'm Phillip bloody Stone!"

A pause while Stone stood there, swaying like a wind-blown scarecrow, his shoulders slumped. Then:

"We thought it might be you. Proceed, Mr. Stone. But please hold your arms high, and come slowly."

Stone moved forward, passed in through a gap in the wall of sandbags, was swallowed up in shadow. "Glad you could make it, Mr. Stone," said a voice in the darkness close by, a voice he did not know. A bright spotlight glared suddenly in his face; he hissed his shock, jerked his head back, threw up his hands.

"Secure him!" another voice crackled over a radio link, but this time it was one that Stone knew only too well. "Confine him at once, and don't be too soft with him. He can be quite deadly!"

"Craig!" Stone spat the word out like a curse.

"Oh, yes," the unrecognized voice chuckled

coarsely behind him. "That's our Mr. Craig all right. J.C. himself. He's been waiting for you—Mr. Phillip bloody Stone!"

Stone spun, crouching, his iron hands reaching—but something hard and heavy came out of the darkness and struck him on the side of the head. Then he was falling and the world spinning, and a voice from somewhere was echoing in his head, saying: "That'll hold the big bastard—hold the big bastard—the big bastard—big bastard—bastard, bastard, bastardbastardbastard!"

Bastard! Stone soundlessly agreed, and passed out . . .

J. C. Craig's study in the Dome was now a mass of electronic equipment. He had fixed up remotes to Psychomech two floors directly beneath him—audio and TV links to the three security control cells, the main gate and half-a-dozen other important locations—direct communications with all strategic areas within the complex. He was now the spider at the center of his web, and he enjoyed it.

Yes, and now he had Phillip Stone, the man who sired the antichrist himself out of hell and out of the womb of a woman who had long since paid the price of her sins and gone the way of all mind-plaguers. Just as Stone himself would go—but all in good time. The only thing Craig did not have was his daughter, but that too would come. Then everything would be his: all the power and the glory, the entire world in all its newfound innocence: and God's will be done!

Incredible, Craig thought, that a mere dozen disciples were sufficient to control all of this—all of PSISAC—but indeed they had succeeded well, and this was only the beginning. Of course, as yet they had barely been called upon to flex their muscles, let alone fight, and that might still come; but Craig could see nothing ahead but success. His nostrils were full of the smell of it, and it was sweet. The Lord God was on his side and He was a mighty ally.

Incoming communications from "the Government" in London had grown frantic over the last four or five hours, until Craig had simply ordered that all calls from the City were to be ignored. Let them make what they would of that; let them call until they went blue in the face and died gibbering, but in the end they could only suppose that PSISAC too had fallen, and then they would stop calling.

As for those so-called "authorities"—those local "VIPs" who would seek shelter here—well, they had been arriving at the main gate in a steady trickle ever since noon. At first they had been allowed inside the complex—following which they had quickly been disposed of and their bodies burned in one of the incinerators—but later, as the day had drawn on and the flow increased, then it had become necessary to initiate a new routine. They had been killed as they arrived, picked off like sitting ducks by Craig's marksmen on the wall over the main gate.

There had been no helping these people for they were not of the chosen. Why, Craig had done them a service! Better a bullet than The Gibbering, surely?

Not even the police had posed too much of a problem. When local patrols became too inquisitive, they were simply invited in and shot; and later, when they failed to maintain contact with their base stations, it would simply be assumed that they had either fallen victims to or joined the ranks of the insane. It was as easy as that. The only thing that the corpses outside the main gate lacked was a decent burial, but who was there now to give them that?

Craig thought of all the rotting flesh out there, thought of the whole world rotting. Mercifully winter was fast approaching; though the stench of death would be terrible, still it should not penetrate too far into PSISAC. Buildings, streets and other "sore spots" in the immediate vicinity of the wall could always be put to the torch. Plague (of the more mundane variety) was much less likely than it would have been in summer, and come the spring the problem would have gone away entirely. Along with the rest of the world . . .

These were among Craig's thoughts as he left the Dome and took a runabout, turning the three-wheeler's nose toward PSISAC's recreation area, where Phillip Stone had been dumped in what was once a store for sports equipment. Almost there, Craig's attention was drawn to the sky by the whine of a jet-copter's exhaust and the *chop-chop-chop* of its rotors as it descended toward the edge of a sports field. In the fast-gathering gloom of evening and under a lowering, red-tinged sky, its landing lights blinked like jeweled eyes as it settled, a strange insect of metal and glass, to the blast-flattened grass.

Two of Craig's disciples were there just ahead of him, their weapons at the ready as the rotors slowed and the door in the body of the 'copter slid open. Stepping down from his runabout, Craig watched as a fat man and his equally gross lady clambered out. A scrawny, long-haired youth followed close behind them. The man, Craig now saw, was none other than the Minister for Industry, Sir George Blewett, and the lady was his wife.

The youth with them—normally a surly, ill-disciplined lout but now just a frightened boy—was their son.

Earlier, before he had stopped communications with London, Craig had been told to expect a jet-copter before nightfall, but he had not known who would be in it. As PSISAC's managing director, Craig knew Blewett well; he had had quite a lot of contact with him and thought of him as a pompous fool. Right now, however, while a little dazed, still the man seemed pretty much in control of himself. His wife, on the other hand, was giggling like a schoolgirl and frothing at the mouth. Obviously she was gibbering.

"Craig!" Blewett held onto his hat, came staggering out from under the 'copter as its blades rotated slower yet. "Craig, thank God you're here! My wife needs help. You must do something for her, if only to quiet her down. Are your facilities here in order? Have you got your hospital set up? I imagine there are some of my own people here from London; I'll thank you to take me to them now." He turned to Craig's men:

"You there—help my wife to the hospital."

The 'copter's rotors came to a standstill, its engine whine fading away. Craig's men looked to him for orders. In the sudden quiet he said: "Get the pilot out of there—but don't hurt him! He'll come with me." He took out a pistol.

It had dawned on Blewett that he was being ignored. His face puffed up, grew dark with blood and fury. "Craig! What the hell do you think—?"

"As for these three—" Craig glanced contemptuously at Blewett and his family. The woman was crawling on the grass now, intermittently giggling and meowing like a kitten, grotesque in her hugeness and monstrous in her madness. Craig felt no pity for her. "Kill them," he said.

"What?" Blewett's mouth fell open. He clutched at Craig's arm. "You're . . . *mad!*"

"No," said Craig, shrugging him off, "I'm sane. The rest of the world is mad."

Babbling, then shouting, finally screaming, Blewett and his two were herded away. The boy made a run for it and was shot dead in his tracks. Then they were out of sight round the corner of a building. A moment later and shots rang out, the rattle of automatic fire. Then silence.

The pilot was young, red-haired, wide-eyed and trembling.

"Do you want to live?" Craig asked him. "Do you want to stay sane? If you do I can help you. If you don't you might as well die now." He cocked his weapon.

"I . . . I'll do anything you say," the other blurted.

"Good," Craig nodded. "Then come with me. There's someone I want you to meet. His name is Psychomech . . ."

It was quite dark at the Rastatte Heilbron by the time the fugitives were ready to take to the road once more. Richard had stopped glowing just before Lynn pulled into the place, and he had come awake about two hours after that. For the last half hour they had sat in the car talking.

Lynn had told Richard everything, but again he had been at a complete loss and must simply accept whatever she said. Her own haggard face told him, however, all he needed to know of the truth: that indeed she had gone through every ordeal she recounted, and that the strain of it all was fast catching up with her.

Which was why, as soon as he felt able, he decided they must press on. Time was precious now and they could spare none of it. The world actually teetered on the brink of total lunacy. Even while they were talking a lorry had crossed the central reservation, crashed the barrier and plowed head-on into a coach going the other way. The lorry must have been carrying something volatile, for there had been a tremendous explosion and both vehicles were still blazing furiously. A fire engine had been on the scene almost immediately, and a crowd from the Rastatte's cafeteria had gathered in the car park to watch the show.

Another incident:

Even as all of this was happening, a couple with a small child had got into their car and the man had driven it straight through one of the cafeteria's huge windows into the tables where people were eating inside. Tired policemen were dealing with it right now; but simultaneous with all of this, yet another gibberer had taken a large spanner and was smashing the windows of parked cars. When challenged by a furious owner, he turned on the man and laid him out with a single blow. A policeman, coming out of the cafeteria, took out his pistol and calmly shot the madman dead.

Obviously the fugitives could not stay here . . .

And so, with Richard driving, at last they left the place and continued south; and two hundred yards behind them, having picked up a hitchhiker making his way to Zürich, Bragg clung to their taillights like a leech as they sped into the night.

An hour and a half later, just across the Swiss border in Schaffhausen, Bragg's passenger went mad. This was not an initial attack, far from it. The man had known he was a gibberer and had expected just such an attack; which was made obvious by what he said moments before the thing came over him:

"My friend," (he spoke to Bragg in German), "I am ill. It is coming again and I can't stop it. I must break things, just as my brain is being broken. I am sorry."

With that he had wrenched the car's tiny video-screen from its seating, blowing all the communication fuses, and had commenced to use the screen and its casing as a hammer, battering at the dashboard instruments. Bragg had wasted no time. Pulling over onto the emergency shoulder in a screeching of tires, he had stalled the car, taken out his pistol and shot his passenger through the head. Then he had leaned across the dead but still twitching body, opened the door and kicked the corpse out into the night. Following which it had taken him fifteen minutes to catch up with the silver Mercedes again.

He managed this just in time to follow the runaways when they quit the multibahn for an old six-laner for Berne. Cursing them for going on, still Bragg stuck doggedly to their trail. He had hoped they would stop at Zürich, but no, Zürich was behind them now . . . and now Langenthal . . . and now Burgdorf. And here they started to pick up signs for the Neu Lötschberg Tunnel where it cut through the Alps.

Almost 8:30 P.M. and Bragg was very tired now, but still the couple ran. Through Thun and along the west shore of Thuner See, and up into the Rhône Valley through the Neu Lötschberg Tunnel (which carried both rail and road traffic and which, miraculously, the Swiss authorities had managed to keep open) and along the River Rhône toward Brig. Until finally Bragg no longer really cared where they went but merely tracked the car ahead; so that he was shocked suddenly out of a sort of hypnotic daze when it made an abrupt left turn and began to climb a series of incredible hairpins high into the snow-capped peaks themselves.

At the very top the white pinnacles had been carved by the winds of countless millennia into weird natural battlements like the ramparts of a giant's castle, from which the place had taken the "Schloss" in its name. Not that the frozen, narrow, impossibly winding road climbed to those topmost peaks; it did not, but ended on a sort of windswept plateau whose sides were a nightmare of vertigo, where a cleared space fronted a rock-hewn shrine cut into the heart of the mountain itself. And here, in a large but nevertheless crowded car park, at last the big silver Mercedes came to a welcome halt.

Here too, above a huge façade of stone and glass set flush with the looming cliff, the legend "Schloss Zonigen" had been carved from mountain rock, standing out cold and gaunt in the reflected glow of Bragg's headlights before he switched them off; so that he sat there in darkness, watching as Lynn Craig, her mind-plagued lover and their dog climbed the steps to the entrance and passed within . . .

Schloss Zonigen's administrative area was huge, totally in keeping with the massive natural cave in the face of the looming cliff which housed it. And if at this hour—and at this altitude—Richard had half-feared to find the place deserted, then here he was happily wrong. Very wrong. Indeed, the place seemed almost congested with humanity. At a long marble reception and information desk the pair found a haggard, bleary-eyed clerk who jotted down Richard's details and asked:

"Are you visiting, or do you seek shelter?" He was maybe forty-five, prematurely gray-haired, obviously exhausted. He had been on duty, unrelieved, for quite some time.

"What?" Richard frowned. The man was Swiss and his accent was hard to understand. "I didn't quite follow what you—"

"Ah, you are not aware of the new measures," said the clerk. "I see . . ."

"Look," Richard said, "I'm English, and I'm only here to visit my . . . aunt. My aunt, yes. She was—interred?—she was given a place here thirty years ago, about 1973."

The clerk nodded tiredly. "Very well," he said. "And was her name also Garrison?"

"No, it was Maler. Vicki Maler. She had a number, 2139. Anyway, what are these new measures you mentioned?"

"Ah, yes! The measures," the clerk answered. "They are orders from the Swiss Government." He took out an old ledger while he talked, turned laminated leaves. "Anyone with close relatives at the Schloss is to be offered shelter here. Some fool has said that isolation will ward off The Gibbering! Since this place is isolated, naturally people want to come here." He shrugged. "It is crazy. They go mad here as quickly as they do anywhere else—except that here it is colder!"

"But this place isn't a hotel," said Lynn.

The clerk understood her English. "No, but—" again his shrug, "see for yourself."

Richard and Lynn looked about. The place was

like an airport: people were sprawled everywhere. They were asleep in chairs, stretched on the carpeted floor, huddled in sleeping bags. They were here single, in pairs, whole families of them.

"Two hundred," sighed the clerk, his shoulders drooping wearily, "and tomorrow there will be more of them. But it does not save them." The corners of his mouth turned down and his tone became bitter. "Isolation—*hah!*"

He found what he sought in the ledger and looked up. His eyes were more alert now, questioning. "Niche number 2139 is not occupied," he informed. "It has not been occupied for a long time."

"How long?" Richard asked.

"The records do not say."

"But it was occupied once," Richard's voice was beginning to reveal his desperation. He snatched the book from the clerk's hand, pointed. "See! Alterations. The entry has been whited out. Your master records will be the same."

"If that is so," the man answered, "then it was done a long time ago, and I—"

"But if she's not there," Richard cut him off, "why has the niche been left empty?"

The clerk looked confused, uncomfortable. "I do not know—" and yet again his shrug. "I cannot say. I am only a clerk here. I—"

"For the same reason there's no 13th floor in some skyscrapers," said Richard. "Because that slot—niche number 2139—is strange, unlucky, unnatural!" His eyes were pale yellow ovals whose pupils were blobs of gold which seemed to expand and contract with a life of their own. He stared at the clerk, spoke very slowly and very precisely.

"I know that Vicki Maler is no longer there," he said. "I just want to see the niche."

"But—" the man could not look away from those eyes. "But—"

"I want to see it!"

"Out of the question," said the clerk, his hand reaching like a robot's under the desk, coming up with a pass card. "If you have no one in here, then you may not stay."

"We don't intend to stay," Richard's eyes pulsed. "Only to see."

"No, you must go now," said the clerk, handing over the pass card. His voice was a dull monotone, speaking routine words which his zombie actions denied.

"Of course," said Richard. "Which door takes us into the ice tunnel?"

"You are not allowed—" said the clerk, pointing to a door in the innermost wall.

"Thank you," said Richard. And: "Why don't you sleep? You look so tired."

The clerk's lips framed the word "tired" but made no sound. He slumped down in his chair, closed his eyes. His head lolled.

Richard took Lynn's hand, half-dragged her toward the nominated door. She held back for a moment, then hurried to keep up. Suzy followed at their heels. "Richard," Lynn said, breathlessly, "what did you *do* to him? I mean, it was you this time. It was *you*—not the other you!"

"I know," he said. "I know—but I don't know how. I'm just starting to learn the trick of it, I suppose."

"The trick of what? Of hypnotism? Of those other strange powers?"

He looked at her through eyes almost as normal as her own. "Something like that," he said, "yes. It's always been in me, but I didn't know, that's all." He let go of her arm. "It will be cold in there. You don't have to come."

She shuddered. "It's cold everywhere," she said. "I'll come with you, Richard. I've come this far, so I may as well see it through to the end."

They passed through the door, man, woman and dog, into a small room where a pair of armed, parka-clad attendants stopped them. Richard handed over his pass card, which apparently covered them as a group. One of the attendants took them into a side room, issued parkas, showed them to a second floor. But this door was different: set in a wall of natural rock and hermetically sealed, it hissed when it was opened. Cold air washed out and stung their faces, their eyes. They stepped through and the attendant closed the door behind them.

"Suzy will be cold," said Lynn, herself shivering.

"We won't be here long," Richard told her. "Anyway, Suzy will want to see."

Lynn looked at him. "To see what?"

Richard looked away, turned and led the way down a narrow stone corridor toward a well-lighted space beyond. "She'll want to see where her old mistress was put to rest," he answered over his shoulder, "—*before* Suzy knew her!"

"Richard!" Lynn caught up, clutched at him. Her flesh felt icy, and not alone from the cold. "Sometimes what's in you frightens me."

"Sometimes," he answered, "it frightens me, too."

They came out of the corridor into the great ice tunnel . . .

* * *

Regaining consciousness was one fight Phillip Stone had not meant to get into. It was just too much trouble. But down there in his subconscious mind, some inner self kept prodding at him and yelling in his ear and generally giving him a rough time. He felt like a hopeless drunk whom some fool keeps trying to help and who only wants to lie there and sleep—or die, it really didn't matter which. Except that the busybody bastard wouldn't go away but kept demanding that he wake up, take stock, do something—anything—while there was yet time. The voice in his head was his own, and so was its urgency.

Finally he came out of it.

He had a head like an old football, or at least it felt that way: as if it had been kicked a lot. Whoever had hit him must have used a lead pipe or something. Stone tried to move and found that he could, just. His feet were tied at the ankles, his hands behind his back. And he was facedown on a cold linoleum-covered floor.

A foot, none too particular in its probing, turned him over, the motion accompanied by a grunt as someone put a lot of effort into it. Stone was big and he was heavy. Strip lighting blazed into his eyes as he thudded over on to his back. Groaning, he pulled his head back into the shadow of ceiling-high metal shelving. Shelves, with cricket bats, bails and stumps; rugby strip in PSISAC colors, green and gray; tennis rackets; medicine balls and dumbbells. He was in the sports store. Maybe that was why he'd thought of his throbbing head as a football. Word association: obviously he'd been waking up for some time.

He looked up out of the shadow of the shelves, traced coveralled legs (two pairs) up to workbelts with dull buckles, up to a sub-machine-gun in tense, almost expectant hands on the one side, and arms crossed in front of the body on the other. The one with the gun had a pale, nervous, highly intelligent face. By his looks he might be a PSISAC technician; he wore some sort of headset with cups fitting over his ears.

The other one was J. C. Craig. He too had a headset but it was over his shoulder, passed through the epaulette of his coveralls.

"Can you hear me, Phillip Stone?" Craig asked.

"I hear you," Stone grunted.

Craig took out a pistol, said to the man with him: "Hill, you can go. Wait outside the door."

Hill quickly went down on one knee, tested the ropes at Stone's ankles and wrists, then straightened up and left. He closed the door behind him.

Stone turned his head to one side and spat into the dust beneath the shelves. "Your idea of 'safety,' Jimmy? Safety for who—you or me?"

"For both of us," Craig answered. "I said you'd be safe here, and you are—for now. As safe as you would be anywhere else. Also, while you're here I know you're not shouting your mouth off anywhere else. And so I'm safe, too."

"Shouting my mouth off? About Psychomech, you mean?" Stone said.

Craig looked down at him. Stone's body was in plain view under the white light of the neons, but his face was in shadow. Only the eyes were really visible, and then as diamonds in the darkness: cold, hard and unyielding. They were full of hate, those eyes. Oh, yes—the devil himself was in Phillip Stone.

"Yes," Craig nodded, "about Psychomech. You gave yourself away when you mentioned the machine, Phillip. You see, there's only one possible way you could know about Psychomech—and that's if you're in league with the devil. Which you are."

"The devil?" Stone repeated him. "You mean literally the devil? Old Nick?"

"You know it well enough. Yes, the devil. Hell's master!"

Stone's lips curled in disgust. Crazy, the man was crazy. His face showed it: puffed up and blotched with wild fervor, and eyes like beacons flaring to light the darkness of men's ignorance, and chin held high in the recognition of his own position of supreme importance. Megalomania, certainly—but complicated by religious mania, too!

"So I'm in league with the devil, am I?" Stone sneered. "That's a bit over the top, isn't it? Me— I'd say I was more sinned against than sinner. You've stolen my place; you've built a machine on my property which I know nothing about— which, incidentally, might have saved both my son and my wife—you've had me assaulted and knocked unconscious without just cause, and you've taken me prisoner! And you say *I'm* in league with the devil?" He snorted derisively. "Jimmy, you're a crazy man. You're gibbering, my friend."

"Ah! No," Craig smiled coldly down at him. "In just a few days the entire world may well be gibbering, but not me and not mine. I am the second Noah, Phillip, and PSISAC is my ark. The deluge is coming—indeed, it is almost here—but I shall ride out the storm quite safely."

"Yes," Stone nodded, "you and your animals!"

Craig's smile tightened. "With God's help."

"And with the help of Psychomech? A device which helps you stay sane? Looking at you right now, Jimmy, I wouldn't put too much faith in that machine if I were you."

Craig breathed deeply. "Psychomech has a calming effect on the minds of . . . disturbed people, yes. But that is not its main function."

"Well, that was the main function of the first Psychomech, Jimmy. Its name was a dead give-away. Psychomech: a mechanical psychoanalyst!"

Craig was shaken and Stone could see it. His face twitched nervously; he took an awkward step to the rear; his hand lifted and tremulously touched the headset in his epaulette, as if seeking comfort. And comforted, he quickly recovered.

"Rubbish!" he snapped. "The first machine was an abomination, a thing of darkness. It was Garrison's weapon, his strength in the face of God's wrath! But it could not save him. And you see, once more you condemn yourself—out of your own mouth. You were in it with Garrison, weren't you? Yes, I see it now. You must have been."

"Man," Stone shook his head sadly, "you're really raving! But that's all right, I'll let you rave. Go on, tell me all. After all, that's what you promised me if I came up here. So off you go, get it out of your system."

"Tell you all?" Craig looked about, found a light chair and brought it close to where Stone lay. "Tell you? Collaborate with the devil?" He nodded knowingly. "Now that really would be madness! No!" he shook his head, "I'll say no more. Do you seek to make a fool of me, Phillip? Get thee behind me, Satan!"

"Then I'll tell you," Stone offered, "—or are you too scared to hear me out? What the hell's wrong with you, J.C.? Why are you so frightened of me? Or is it just the truth that frightens you?"

"I know the truth!" Craig blurted.

"The whole truth? I doubt it. I only learned it myself today—and even I don't know all of it. For instance: I don't know why I was made to forget—or who made me forget."

"Forget?" Craig frowned, looked edgy. Stone felt he might be getting somewhere.

"The old days, Jimmy, think back, man. There was you, me, Vicki. You remember that, don't you? Our beginnings? This place was once Miller Micros, and it came down to Vicki, and she gave it to me. But how did Vicki get hold of it? You were a micro-electronic engineer at Miller Micros; how did you suddenly make it to Managing Director? Vicki didn't promote you, and neither did I. Do *you* remember how it all came about? Do you remember anything at all of the days before this place was PSISAC? And what of Garrison? What do you remember of him?"

"Of course I remember," Craig blustered. "I remember . . . everything! As for my position here: I worked for it. What are you trying to say?"

"I'm not sure you do remember, Jimmy," Stone said. "That's what I've been telling you. Personally, I didn't remember until today. Nor did Vicki remember—not until minutes before she died."

"Vicki?" Craig at last cut in. "That whore! You invoke her name here?" He spat on the floor.

"Whore?" Stone's voice was a whisper. His eyes stood out in a suddenly chalky face. He worked furiously at his bonds, struggled and strained against them—uselessly. If he could have broken loose at that moment, then Craig had better use his pistol quickly.

"Whore, yes!" snarled the other. He jumped to

his feet, kicked his chair away. "Didn't you sire the devil's own spawn out of that bitch? Wasn't she mother to that scum of hell you call son—*who now carries Garrison's demon in him?*"

Stone stopped struggling. "What do you know of that?"

"You admit it, then?" Craig's eyes blazed.

"Richard is Garrison's son, yes. I know that now—but how do *you* know it?"

Craig's legs seemed to turn to jelly. "I . . . I did *not* know it!" He stumbled backward until he came up against shelving. "Garrison's *son*? I thought Garrison had merely come back in him, possessed him. But now you tell me he's Garrison's son. Garrison reborn!"

Stone shook his head. "You're not making sense, Jimmy. Garrison reborn? We don't even know if he's dead! Knowing what I now know, I doubt if he *can* die! But come on, tell me—what do you remember of it?"

Craig merely gazed down at him, gulping and blinking nervously. Finally he shook his head. "I'll say nothing. You only seek to confuse me."

"Then I'll tell you what *I* remember, and how I came to remember it." Quickly Stone began to relate what he knew of the story. He mentioned the Nazis, Gareth Wyatt, Krippner and the machine that he built at Wyatt's country home, a machine called Psychomech. He got that far and no further.

While he had talked, Craig had at first blustered and tried to interrupt; then he had become quiet, listening intently and with bated breath; and at last he had seemed to recognize something of the truth in what Stone was telling him. Or perhaps he had started to remember for himself. Stone saw that he was right: whatever had caused his and Vicki's "amnesia" in respect of Garrison and Psychomech, it had also worked on J. C. Craig. Now Craig *was* remembering, but he did not want to!

His eyes had begun to dart about in his face, like trapped animals in a cage, and his limbs had become filled with a wild trembling. Then he saw the way Stone was staring at him . . .

With a great effort of will, Craig forced himself to a semblance of calm; he controlled his fears, whatever they were, and with a breathless, deadly intentness pointed his pistol at Stone's head. "An end to lies," he whispered harshly. His hand was steadier now, but beads of sweat stood out on his brow.

Stone fully believed he was a dead man; but in the next moment Craig once more began peering about in a sort of agitation, almost as if he listened for something he feared. His hand trembled worse than ever; he put the pistol away, snatched the headset from his epaulette and slipped it quickly onto his head.

Stone's sure knowledge of imminent death turned to disgust. "You can't even do your own dirty work, can you?" he growled. "Why didn't you shoot me? That way you might always be safe from the truth!"

"I know the truth already," Craig gasped. "God *is* truth!"

"You know nothing of God," Stone sneered. "Look at you—what would God want with you?"

"Damn you!"

"It's you who are damned, J.C."

Craig managed a laugh, harsh and strangled. Once more he seemed to have regained something of his equilibrium. "Shooting is too good for you," he said. "The waste of a bullet. No, you can gibber like the rest of them. So far you've escaped it; doubtless the devil has protected you. But your master hates failures, Phillip, and you have failed. You, too, shall be taken. The world has another day, maybe two. And when you are taken, then I shall come to you and perhaps you'll confess your sins. Indeed, you'll beg me to hear your confession, and you'll beg me to kill you. And if God decrees it, maybe I will." He turned toward the door.

"J.C. Craig, you mad bastard!" Stone shouted. "Listen to me, J.C.—I have proof, at home. I had myself hypnotized. That's how I know all that I know. I was *made* to remember!"

"Be *quiet!*" Craig was at the door.

"Send someone to my house," Stone begged. "There are tapes there, recordings. The truth is on them, picked out of my mind by an expert. The tapes helped me to remember. They can help you, too."

"Liar!" Craig spat. "All lies. The devil is a great liar."

"A tape recording can't lie, Jimmy—no more than your bloody Psychomech can lie! You're sick, J.C., sick! Maybe you don't gibber, maybe you have beaten that—but you're still sick."

"The world is sick!" Craig cried. "Sick of the evil in men—men such as you and your devil-spawn son. But God will purify. Your son—or Garrison's, it makes no difference—will die, and so will you. He might already be dead, for certainly I've ordered it and prayed for it."

"What?" Stone saw that it was true. "You've done what? Why you mad, blind, bloody fool . . . he's probably the only one who can do anything about all this! Damn you, Craig, *damn you!*"

Stone was raging now, fighting the ropes that held him.

Craig slowly shook his head, his grin awful. "No one can do anything about anything now, Phillip. No one. I'll come to see you later."

"Wait!" Stone yelled. "You're wrong, J.C., wrong. I might die, yes—and the world itself go insane—but don't be too sure about Richard."

On the point of slamming the door behind him, Craig paused. He looked back. "What did you say?"

"Richard is Garrison's son, remember? Yes, and he has Garrison's powers, too . . ."

"Power of the devil!" Craig hissed. "He shall *not* prevail!" He slammed the door, turned and stumbled drunkenly to his runabout, headed it back toward the Dome. Above the vehicle's electric whine he could hear Stone's voice receding:

"The tapes, Craig—send for my tapes and listen to them. Learn the truth, J.C.—for God's sake!"

For God's sake . . . Craig told himself, hunched over the runabout's steering mechanism. *For God's sake* . . . And through the headset, Psychomech laved his mind with calming configurations.

When they were close to niche number 2139 Lynn and Richard held back a little—but Suzy went on. The great ice cavern was very nearly empty of people, a handful only: people who, perhaps having heard The Gibbering for the first time, had come to pay their last respects to those they had loved in life; or perhaps they really were here because they believed that isolation could help them. But no one was near niche 2139; the area was utterly silent.

Acting on her own initiative, Suzy went straight

there. She sat down in front of the vacant slot in the wall of blue ice and looked back at the two where they stood, her eyes shining out at them like small pools of some deep, dark liquid. Her expression was unmistakable: if an animal may know pain of the spirit, then Suzy knew it. She was sad, she knew grief. As Richard moved to join her, she whined, licked his hand, looked to him for comfort. He patted her head, fondled an ear.

"Is this the place?" Lynn asked, her voice echoing softly.

Richard nodded. "This was her place. Empty now, of course. As it has been for more than twenty years. They'll not put another body in there. They don't dare!"

"But why have we come?" Lynn whispered. "Was it necessary?"

"Oh, yes," he answered, "it was." Suddenly dizzy, he leaned against the wall of naked ice. "We had to come, so that I . . . so that I can *feel*!"

Lynn stepped back apace and Suzy joined her. They stood together watching Richard.

He bowed his head, seemed to draw himself down into his bulky parka. He became small and started to sway a little from side to side.

Lynn and the dog backed away further yet.

Richard began to moan and Suzy whined to match the sounds he made. For perhaps a full minute he swayed and moaned beside the ice wall, then gave a gasping cry and lifted his head. His face was drawn and shriveled as a mummy's, eyes closed and cheeks sucked in. He gave another little cry and his legs seemed to buckle beneath him. He slid down the wall, sat crumpled on the floor of the cavern.

Girl and dog sprang to his side, but already he

was shaking his head, struggling to rise. Lynn helped him to his feet.

He was tall again, strength returning as he and the girl began to retrace their steps through vaults of ice. "Is that all?" Lynn asked, her voice hushed.

"That's all," he said.

Suzy ran back, halted at the empty niche. She sat stiffly erect, lifted her head and howled once, long and loud. Then she gave a single bark, sharp and glad, and ran to catch up. She had paid homage, was satisfied; her tail was wagging.

Richard nodded. "Suzy, too," he commented, smiling a wan smile.

"Richard, what do you mean?" Lynn clung to his arm. "What was it back there? What happened?"

"We—Suzy and I—we have been with her for a little while, that's all. Or rather, I was with her and Suzy sensed she was there." His words were clear, spoken here and now, but his eyes seemed to see beyond the caves of ice. They gazed out on all of space and time. "She was put here when she died," he went on, "thirty years ago. And when my father was able, he brought her back to life. He took away her blindness and gave her sight— gave her breath, warmth. He got his power from—" (he frowned, concentrated) "—from a Machine! Oh, there was power in him to begin with, but the Machine expanded it, made it . . . great! That Machine is important. I have to know more about it . . ."

Lynn shook her head, her mouth half-open. She tried desperately to understand. "You mean Richard Garrison came here for her and . . . woke her up, revived her?"

"Woke her up, yes," Richard looked at her. "But

came here—no. He didn't have to come. He simply called her to him, and she went. From here to England. Levitation, teleportation—I don't know how. How did I move the cabin to that place in the stars you told me about? It was the same sort of thing."

Lynn clung to him. "It's so hard to understand. I—"

"Don't try to understand," he stopped her, squeezing her hand and smiling again. Then his smile faded, was replaced by a look of awe. "But . . . she spoke to me."

"What?" Lynn pushed him away to arm's length. "Your mother *spoke* to you?"

Richard nodded. "Yes. We have to go back to England, Lynn. The answer is there. We have to go where she went: to Wyatt's place in the country. And then we have to find Phillip Stone."

"Wyatt's place?" Lynn was hopelessly lost. "Who's Wyatt?"

He shook his head tiredly. "I don't know," he said, "but when I was just a small boy I was out with my father one day—with Phillip Stone—and he said: 'Son, that's Wyatt's house.' We were in the country. I remember it well, because there was no house there at all! That's where we have to go—and then to him, to Phillip Stone. The man I've always called Dad."

Wide-eyed, Lynn asked: "And she, your mother, *told* you all of this? Back there," she vaguely indicated the ice tunnel stretching behind them, "she . . . told you?"

"Yes."

At the door there was a bellpush. They were let out, handed in their parkas, left the cavern-built place and went out into the car park. A large modern car, an Opel Komet, was just leaving as they approached the Mercedes; they were lost in their own thoughts and barely noticed it. The Komet was the only thing that moved in the night—the same car which had been following them for hours—but that was something else they had not noticed. They seemed to have been tired for so long now.

"What now?" Lynn asked when they were seated in the big car, waiting for its motor to warm up and drive the external frost and internal condensation from the windows. "How do we set about getting back home?"

"It's late," Richard answered. "We'll head for Brig or Gletsch, whichever is closest. A night's sleep—a few hours, anyway—and then we're off again. Home, England. A plane would be quicker, out of Zürich, maybe. But it'll have to be tomorrow. Right now I'm dead on my feet."

"Me too," she settled down in her seat, yawned, then sat up again. She brushed hair out of her eyes, brushed at her face. "But I'm not that tired! Maybe it's just that I'm over the top: *too* tired, if you see what I mean. Let me drive. I mean, Zürich can't be that far away. An hour, maybe?"

He shook his head. "More like two! No ten-laners up here, love. No, I'll drive . . . straight to the nearest town." He glanced at her out of the corner of his eye as he slipped the car into gear. "Are you all right?"

"Hmm?"

"Your voice. A bit slurred. A bit jumbled, too. You sounded like you'd had a drink too many just then."

"Did I?"

"You still do. A bit pissed. Know what I mean?"

"Tired, I suppose." She yawned again, brushed away more hair. "Maybe I shouldn't drive after all. Must be the altitude. Does things to your ears. And I'm itchy! Hair on my face, in my eyes."

"Close them," he advised. "Your eyes, I mean. Rest them a bit. Sleep."

"Suzy's hair, maybe," she complained. But as he had suggested, she closed her eyes.

Richard drove carefully down the steep ramps of the mountain-hewn roads. The wind had died away and the night was cold and bright. The stars seemed huge, sparkling in the frozen sky. There might well be black ice on the roads, which made him wary. Almost down, Lynn sat up again.

"Richard?" she said, questioningly. And again, more urgently: *"Richard!"*

He was startled by her cry. His head snapped round and he stared at her. "Lynn?"

Suzy began to whine knowingly, ominously.

"Richard," Lynn brushed frantically at her face, breathlessly, "Richard—what does it feel like?"

"Feel like?" his back was suddenly icy.

"You know, when you . . . when The Gibbering comes?"

"What?"

"The hair—I can hear it growing! It's growing in my head, Richard. It's strangling my brain . . ."

"Oh God, no!" he gasped. "Oh Jesus!—not you, Lynn?"

Suzy growled worriedly, began to bark.

"Quiet, girl!" Richard snapped.

Lynn had curled up in her seat, was quietly sobbing. "It's got me, hasn't it?" she said. "This is it. I have hair in my head, growing there. I can feel it smothering my thoughts, suffocating my mind . . ."

"It'll go away," he said, praying it would. "Just fight it—fight it, Lynn, and hang on. It's your first. Maybe it won't be too bad."

"It *is* bad," she answered, sucking in air.

"Ropes of it coiling in my skull. Soon there'll be no room for my brains!"

Richard guided the big car round the final spur, its headlight beams slicing the night's darkness. On the right, cliffs climbed to the next loop of roadway; on the left a white three-bar fence marked a steep drop of maybe sixty or seventy feet down to a rushing river.

"Can you stop?" Lynn gasped. "I'm going to be sick. Oh, God! My stomach is full of hair. It's growing out of my ears, my nose. It's coming out of me everywhere."

Richard glanced at her in horror, looked back at the road ahead where the Mercedes had just cleared the curve of the spur—and slammed the brakes on. A car was across his lane, the car they'd seen leaving the car park ahead of them. Its driver was in the road, frantically waving his arms.

Tires screaming, the Mercedes jerked to a halt with a few feet to spare. In a moment Lynn was out of her door, slamming it shut behind her. She ran down the steep slope of the road, tripped, flew forward into a shallow ditch where it skirted the foot of the cliff. Richard jerked his door open— but the man from the other car was there, holding it shut. He pushed something in through the gap. Richard saw the menacing barrel of a pistol; his eyes opened wide and he looked at the man's face through the glass of his window. A young face, but chillingly cold—and yet dripping with sweat! The face's owner wore a headset like the one in the glove compartment; the one Lynn had told him about, which he'd scarcely glanced at.

"Wha—?" Richard said.

Before he could close his mouth the gun went *phut!* and released its dart. In the last moment Richard had jerked back. The dart, aimed at his

face, stuck in his shoulder through his jacket and
shirt. Bragg slammed the door shut and leaned
against it.

Richard sat up straighter, dragged the dart out
of his shoulder and threw it down. He grimaced,
tried to throw himself at the door—but already his
arms and legs were useless as lengths of rubber.
All sensation was fleeing his body, limbs, brain.
Bragg held the door shut, watched as the doped
man slumped down between the front seats. He
flopped there, staring, mouth wide open, arms and
legs twitching, fighting to move and failing.

In the back of the car Suzy went mad with rage.
She threw herself again and again at the rear windows, scrambled over the back of the seats into
the front, licked at the face of the man slumped
there. She barked at him frantically, demanding
that he do something. He did nothing.

Bragg reloaded his pistol, ran to the ditch where
Lynn was being sick. He let her finish and shot her
in the thigh. She slumped down in the ditch. He ran
to his car and got in, backed around the Mercedes
and let the Komet roll forward until its hard rubber
bumpers came up against the Merc's rear end. Then
he put the car in first gear and pushed, angling the
Komet so that the Mercedes skidded slowly off the
road and into the fence.

The fence resisted, leaned a little, groaned and
finally gave way in a splintering of timbers. Bragg
pushed harder and felt his wheels starting to spin.
The Mercedes began to topple, slid, grated to a halt;
its underside was hooked on the rim of the drop.
Bragg sweated, pushed harder yet. The Mercedes
went. Bragg applied his brakes and watched the silver car topple. Its rear end stood up, red stoplights
glaring like angry eyes, and in a sort of slow motion
the car descended from sight.

Bragg got out of his car, went to the broken fence. Down below in the darkness he could make out the headlight beams of the doomed car flashing intermittently across the river's surface, slowly turning as the car turned in the current. Its red taillights were still burning, too. The Mercedes was upsidedown, bumping downstream and slowly sinking.

Satisfied, Bragg went to get Lynn.

But something had happened which Bragg had not seen. If he had, perhaps he would not feel so satisfied.

Slumped there between the front seats as the Mercedes tilted and fell toward the river, Richard's strange eyes had gleamed yellow and then gold. Twin golden beams had played for a moment on the passenger's door, and in the instant before the car hit the water that door had shattered outward as from the blast of a bomb! Only then had Richard finally succumbed to the dart's drug, and the rest he had left to Suzy . . .

Across the face of the world one in six people now suffered from mind-plague, and the curve was still bending. At PSISAC, J. C. Craig had kept his vigil; the complex was still his and would remain so. People had their own problems without having to worry about PSISAC. Only a handful more of local "personages" had attempted entry; all of them had been dealt with. Things would appear to be proceeding according to plan—and yet Craig prowled his study in the Dome like a caged tiger.

While his faith had not been toppled, certainly it had started to sway a little. For one thing, Phillip Stone's lies continued to bother him, repeating naggingly in the back of his mind; and for another, Bragg had failed to contact him at the prearranged hour, which seemed to suggest that there was a snag. Of course, Bragg might yet contact him (he was, after all, only fifteen minutes overdue) but each extra minute felt like an hour to Craig, and he did not like it.

Over and over in some inner ear, he kept hearing Phillip Stone's voice telling him to listen to his tape recordings. And some of the other things Stone had said were still stirring faint echoes in Craig's mind, too, memories he would prefer to let lie. Also, there was Stone's warning (no, more than a warning, a definite threat) that Richard Stone was indeed Garrison's reborn, and that he had inherited his father's power. And Stone had touched a soft spot when he talked about Craig's memory, or lack of it, in respect of certain events; for the truth of the matter was that there were areas in Craig's past which he did *not* remember any too clearly.

His rise to power in PSISAC, for example. And while he knew that there had been a man called Garrison—or at least, a devil in the shape of a man, a creature fallen out of God's grace—still he could remember nothing of him except what God had told him in his dreams. That . . . and those memories or doubts which Stone with his lies had stirred back to life.

He thought abut Stone's tapes. Would it hurt any to listen to them? And then he grew angry with himself. No, for they could only be a Satansent ploy!

But what of Lynn? Where was she now? And was she still safe and sane?

And Bragg, the snot-nosed little upstart!

The world going crazy, and Psychomech could at least have saved some of them. A great many of them . . .

"*No!*" Craig shouted his denial. No, for if the Lord had wanted things other than the way they were, then things would *be* otherwise. There was no paradox; God works in mysterious ways!

. . . And was it God's doing, too, that Craig had lost his daughter? A test, perhaps? A trial? Wasn't Abraham required to sacrifice his son, in the land of Moriah? Indeed! But in the end God had spared Isaac, and Abraham had prospered.

Would Craig also prosper? Perhaps he had not prayed enough? Perhaps he was a sinner still?

11:50 and still Bragg had not got through. What if Garrison had beaten him? In which case . . . what of Lynn?

Craig rushed to Psychomech's remotes, his hands trembling over the switches and buttons. He snatched them back, checked himself. No, that was not the way. He must himself go to the room of the Machine; one does not speak to God on the telephone! To a machine, yes—to Psychomech in its secondary role—but not in its first role as God's oracle, God's voice on Earth . . .

"Oracle—*hah*!" Craig found himself blaspheming as the elevator took him down to the garage level. "For ten years I've waited, and for ten years the machine has searched. Searched for Him! And found nothing . . ."

He passed through the garage area and entered Psychomech. Softly the lights pulsed, the machinery hummed and whirred. Craig approached the central dais, bowed his head for a moment in supplication. Then he straightened, reached into the almost solid wall of machinery and drew out the computer keyboard on its swivel arm.

He typed up:

CRAIG TO PSYCHOMECH. WHERE IS GOD?

Psychomech:

I SEEK HIM.

Craig gritted his teeth, took a very deep breath and slowly let it out.

WHY HAVE YOU FAILED TO FIND HIM?

Psychomech:

I HAVE NOT FAILED. HE WILL BE FOUND
WHEN HE DESIRES IT.

Craig:

I DESIRE IT.

But since this was neither a question nor a direct order, Psychomech ignored it.
Craig:

YOU ARE GOD'S ORACLE. THROUGH YOU
HE WILL SPEAK TO ME.

No answer was required.

IS THIS SO?

Psychomech:

YES.

"Yes!" Craig shouted, his eyes blazing. "Yes—except that you're not trying!" Sweat dripped freely from his chin and his hands shook as he typed up:

HAVE YOU MADE EVERY EFFORT?

Psychomech:

TO WHAT END?

"A machine!" Craig snarled. "Just a damned machine . . ." He typed up:

TO FIND GOD.

Psychomech (after a slight pause):

NO.

"Then do so!" Craig shook his fists in rage. He controlled himself with an effort, typed:

DO SO.

No answer was required.

ARE YOU MAKING EVERY EFFORT TO FIND GOD?

Psychomech:

YES.

(All around Craig, unnoticed by him in his extremity of rage and frustration, the Machine's lights glowed brighter and pulsed faster; needles swung over on dials; the whirring and fluttering picked up speed, increased in volume.)
Craig:

WHEN WILL YOU FIND HIM?

Psychomech:

WHEN HE DESIRES IT.

Craig reeled. Sweat dripped from his chin like thin slime. "When He desires it!" he croaked, almost choking on his words. For obviously He did *not* desire it.

Craig threw up his hands, collapsed on the dais steps. He bowed his head, sobbed through his fingers where they clawed at his brow. "Oh, my God—why has Thou forsaken me?"

For answer . . . *a snake hissed in the core of his brain!*

Craig jerked upright, listening intently, his eyes twitching left and right. He groped at the epaulette of his coveralls—but he had left his headset in his study. And again the hissing, and a slithering of scaled, sinuous bodies.

Craig leaped to the keyboard, typed:

CRAIG: TREATMENT.

Ah!—and how they hissed now! Hissed their anger—for they knew he would escape them yet again. Satan's servants, hissing and slithering in his head, dripping their venom on the cringing surface of his brain . . .

He stumbled up the steps of the dais, slumped down into the throne. The throne responded, gave him succor—and for once he was able to ignore the sting of the anesthetic needle. Better that than the sting of those hellish forked tongues in the matrix of his mind . . .

It was midnight exactly, and as Craig sank into a salving subconsciousness, so Psychomech obeyed his command: which was that the Machine spare no effort in its discovery of God. The fact that God would not be found until He desired it was now immaterial. The order was to make every effort.

Psychomech spoke to PSISAC's satellites. Those on the dayside of Earth drew energy from the sun and beamed it to those on the nightside—Psychomech's side—and through them down to PSISAC. Psychomech drew energy from PSISAC's converter. The Machine *drank* energy to power its machine-thoughts, which it now poured out into the Psychosphere. First the world of men must be searched, diligently and with dispatch, and if God was there He might be found. If He could not be found there, then Psychomech must seek afar.

But first: four billion minds to test.

. . . *Make every effort* . . .

. . . *Find God* . . .

Innocent, the Machine monster speeded up its process of elimination. And if Craig were now to ask the right question: WHEN WILL YOU KNOW IF GOD IS IN THE WORLD? then certainly Psychomech could compute the answer. And that horrifying answer would be:

IN SIX HOURS—MAXIMUM . . .

Part

III

Six Hours

BY 12:30 A.M. BRAGG HAD PASSED MULHOUSE ON A modern six-laner and was heading northwest in the general direction of Paris. If J. C. Craig had been awake and checked Bragg's headset location through Psychomech, he would have seen that he was now making for some as yet undecided jet-copter liaison point. Craig was not awake, however, but still deeply asleep and on the point of winning a dream-skirmish with his mind-serpents. The result of the battle had never been in doubt: with Psychomech's help it was one Craig could not lose; but at the same time and however paradoxically, it was also one he could never win—not completely—not as long as the Machine communed with the Psychosphere and searched for God.

So far Bragg had neither the opportunity nor any strong inclination to communicate with PSISAC; there were other things on his mind. It was not that he had forgotten he was supposed to speak to Craig, simply that he believed his personal safety to have priority. And safety was becoming a hard thing to find. First he had wanted to put distance between himself and the scene of his crime (or between himself and the victims of that crime, for there was undeniably that about Richard Stone—alive or dead—which gave Bragg the shudders), and that achieved he would then contact PSISAC. Of course, if his mobile communications were still intact there would be no problem, but his mind-plagued passenger had put paid to that. And so Bragg was now obliged to seek a public tele- or video-phone.

Lynn Craig slept on in the back of the Komet, and she would probably stay down for a couple of hours yet. Not that Bragg was going to take any chances on that; if she woke up, he was fully prepared at a moment's notice to dart her again. But in all likelihood she would sleep the night right through, for certainly she and her boyfriend had had a rough time of it these last couple of days. Moreover, she would be exhausted from her attack (an initial attack, from what Bragg had seen of it), which he knew from personal experience to be extremely debilitating. Well, at that she was lucky; once at PSISAC her father would take steps to ensure that she never had to go through that again.

Since leaving Schloss Zonigen's steep access road, Bragg had neither stopped of his own accord nor been stopped by the police. There had been plenty of police activity on all the roads, even at this hour of night, but every official vehicle he had seen was either on its way to or arriving at some new incident or accident. Plainly things were really hotting up now—and quite literally! Fires burned on the night horizon at every point of the compass; the few civilian cars he saw on the roads were full of frightened, white-faced people, mainly families; and if his own car still had its radio he would have known from non-stop news broadcasts that the increasing incidence of mind-plague had suffered a dramatic acceleration. Even without the news, still there had been plenty of physical evidence for that.

Twice gibberers had tried to flag him down, and twice he had plowed straight through them. The first of these incidents had involved a woman who ran at his car head-on, screaming, so that he couldn't avoid her if he wanted to; the other had consisted of a gang of men and women with blazing torches, strung out two-deep right across the motorway, all of them gibbering. As Bragg had smashed through the double line someone had opened up with a machine-gun, sending a stream of bullets glancing off the roof of the car and shattering one of the rear windows. If the girl had been sitting there instead of lying down, then she would have been in mortal danger.

But then, some few miles beyond Mulhouse toward Troyes, Bragg had seen in the distance the square bulk of a large motel rising against the night, all its lights ablaze, and had decided this was as far as he dare go without assistance. Pulling in, he saw that the motel had been converted into an emergency refuge or harbor area, where neon letters were clumsily strung above the entrance, proclaiming the place an OPITAL.

Ambulances stood in a pool of light in the car park and police vehicles were there in some strength, their sirens blaring and their beacons flashing biliously as they came and went. Not wishing to add to the congestion—wishing, indeed, that both he and his Komet were totally invisible—Bragg climbed the low curb and switched off his lights. But if his actions were noticed no one seemed much interested; and so he drove in the darkness bumpily round to the back of the place over the uneven surface of a field, and there parked the car in a small grove of trees standing some distance apart from the main building. Then he checked that Lynn was still asleep, got out of the car and cautiously made his way to the front entrance of the motel.

Uniformed gendarmes and ambulance men were all over the place and the reception area looked like an abattoir, with makeshift operating tables everywhere and two or three bloodied doctors working at a pace which would shame a field hospital in a war zone—or master butchers on a Saturday morning! But beyond a cafeteria which was now a morgue, where tablecloth-draped figures lay in grotesque rows atop the dining tables, Bragg found the tele- and video-phone booths mainly unoccupied.

Still unchallenged in the melee, he entered a video-booth and came up against a problem: the wiring had been re-routed into an adjoining room which was now a police communication center. All of the booths were the same with two exceptions, and both of these were in use. The doors to the simple telephone booths had been locked, but in any case their cables too were re-routed.

Bragg had no time to spare. Of the two occupied booths, one was being used by a florid fat woman in a flowery nightgown and slippers, the other by a tearful, hysterical couple. Bragg squeezed in behind the fat woman, who immediately turned and offered him a look of outrage at his invasion. On the screen a pimply-faced girl was gabbling away in French, asking what was going on.

"This booth is occupied!" the woman snapped. "Can't you see that? How dare you burst in here and—"

"Will you be long?" Bragg cut her off.

Her eyes popped wide open. "I shall be as long as I shall be!" she declared.

Bragg quickly glanced out through the booth's windows and checked that no one was looking. Then he smiled at the fat woman and fired a dart into her massive right breast. Unable to move or react in the confines of the booth, she simply stared at him aghast, her mouth working soundlessly as he grabbed her breast, tugged the dart from her flesh and put it in his pocket. Then, thrusting the pistol back into its shoulder holster under his left arm, he quickly buttoned his jacket and backed out of the booth, letting the door swing shut in the woman's astonished face. A moment later and she screamed once, and then the door of the booth flew open as she came toppling forward, flopping into Bragg's arms. Grunting, he lowered her to the floor and straightened up.

A hand fell on his shoulder. "What's going on here?"

It was a gendarme. Bragg's French was barely adequate, but he had to make an attempt. "She fainted," he shrugged. "Too fat, I think."

"Is she with you?"

"No," he shook his head. "I saw her collapse. She fell out of the booth. I caught her before she hit the floor."

"Rather you than me!" said the gendarme, frowning at the woman's prone bulk. "But thank you anyway. You speak to whoever that is on the screen in there, and I'll get a doctor to have a look at her."

Bragg thought he had better carry on with his innocent act, at least for a moment longer. "Anyway, what's going on here? Where have all these dead and injured people come from?"

"From Remiremont," answered the other, "most of them. It's a town close by. Some crazy gibbering bastard ran through the main street tossing sticks of dynamite in through the windows! The world is mad! But please excuse me—we are very busy here." Bragg watched him hurry off, turned and entered the booth.

The frightened, pimply girl was still on the screen but Bragg quickly disconnected her. Then he called PSISAC . . .

There were now two main categories of mind-plaguers: live ones and dead ones. And like the redskin of a Wild West more than one hundred years in the past, the only good gibberer was of the latter variety. Specimens of the first were to be caused to metamorphose into those of the second by whatever means available and as soon as possible, and with similar dispatch these were then to be consumed in cleansing fire. It was not cruelty but the economics and statistics of survival, however falsely based or construed. Fear of mental contagion was the reason for the first measure (men could no longer take the chance that there was no such thing, and must therefore destroy any and every carrier), and physical contagion, namely corruption, was the reason for the second: if the mounting number of dead were not burned, the world would very soon begin to stink.

Therefore, any corpse discovered in peculiar circumstances must now be assumed that of a gibberer and join the others on the funeral pyres. The time for niceties like identification, mourning and decent burial was over . . .

In Raron, the once small and very exclusive Klingerman Privat Krankenhaus—until recently a luxury hospital for members of the Swiss, German and French elite—was now a common morgue. Worse, it was a "collection point," a halfway house to the human bonfires. But although the incidence of mind-plague was now one in five leaning toward four, still this had not signaled chaos in the thinly populated area; as yet the people of the Rhône Valley had not been overcome by the general horror of the outside world. To complete their isolation, just after midnight a rail accident had blocked the Neu Lötschberg Tunnel to the north; similarly, the ten miles long south-leading Neu Simplon was now out of commission, blocked by a multiple pileup. A few other routes remained, but these too were gradually closing. The 12:30 train from Montreux had not arrived; traffic was now very thin on the mountain roads and in the passes; the local people kept mainly to themselves and their own villages and counted their inaccessibility a blessing.

Raron was the collection point for the Raron-Visp "catchment area," and the Klingerman Krankenhaus was the depot. As sufferers from mind-plague died or surrendered, were informed upon or otherwise discovered and ultimately "dealt with" (they were, frankly, put down like incurably sick animals, usually by use of painless but lethal drugs, but if violent by whatever means were to hand) their bodies were taken to the Krankenhaus and tagged ready for collection. Every four hours two large lorries would come for them and take them down the valley to a place

near Leuk where a pit was their communal grave.
There, soaked in kerosene, they were cremated.
No words were said over them, they simply
burned.

It was now a quarter after 1:00 A.M. and the
night was bitter cold. In the little hospital, Frau
(*Witwe:*—widow) Inger Gussel grimaced as she
swilled out the large glass-roofed conservatory
which recently had been a reading- and rest-
room. The ultraviolet projectors were no longer
in use and the flowers had long since wilted, but
these things were of no concern. There was no
longer room for flowers and corpses are better
cold. Frau Gussel had been doing this job for four
days now—receiving the bodies of mind-plaguers
as they were brought in, tagging them and log-
ging their particulars where known, finally releasing them to the disposal trucks—and while she
had worked at the hospital for many years and
was well acquainted with death in all its forms,
still she was sickened by what was now a routine
of unrelenting horror. For she as much as anyone
anywhere in the world was aware of the terrible
acceleration of the thing. Indeed, over the last
few days the figures had seemed to lurch drunkenly from peak to peak, climbing ever higher, and
Frau Gussel could see no end to it. The one-o'-clock
lorries had been filled to their tailgates with over
one hundred and eighty bodies; when the 5:00
A.M. collection came around there would probably
be more corpses than space for them.

Here it was the middle of the night, and already
the first of the next batch (*oh, God! She had begun to think of them as batches, like loaves!*) had
been brought in. A young man, his body and
clothes had been wet with melting frost and river
water, his life sucked out by the Rhône's bitter

swirl. Young Rudi Ullman had found him and brought him here, and Rudi had told a sad tale of it.

He had been visiting and comforting his fiancé in Brig (her mother had been taken yesterday) and had stayed late. Driving back toward Raron, Rudi had spotted a huge black dog in the middle of the road. Bedraggled, shivering and obviously exhausted, the creature had simply barred his way, refusing to move. Rudi loved animals and this one was plainly in trouble. He had got out of his car and gone to the dog, which immediately staggered to the edge of the road where it bordered the river. Down there at the bottom of a gentle slope, fixed in the powerful yellow beam of Rudi's torch, he had seen a body half-in, half-out of the water.

The black dog, a Doberman bitch, had then flopped and slithered down the grassy slope to the prone figure at the river's rim, and Rudi had scrambled down after her. Rudi was no doctor but it seemed to him the man must be dead, drowned. Obviously his body had been here for some hours. His head and upper clothing where the dog had dragged him from the river were rimed in frost; his lower body and legs floated and moved in the Rhône's icy eddies; he lay facedown and was completely motionless.

Rudi was a strong young man. Under the dog's watchful gaze he had dragged the half-frozen body up the slope to his car. The dog had tried to follow but was unable; in the end she had given up and simply sat there, her tail giving little thumps of gratitude. Rudi put the body in the back of his car and went back for the dog—but he found the poor, faithful creature already on the point of expiring. Stretched out beside the rushing river, her eyes had fluttered closed, her indomitable will had ebbed along with her strength—and Rudi Ullman had seen no hope for her. There he had left her, brave creature, and there she must remain, frozen to the riverbank.

Well, and if there was a heaven, doubtless dog and master were even now running together as in happier days; and who could say (thought Frau Gussel) that they were not the lucky ones . . . ?

2:30 A.M. and Bragg expected the jet-copter's arrival at any moment. The sooner the better, for things were definitely deteriorating.

The girl had not yet stirred, but as a precaution Bragg had taken time to bind her hand and foot, and he had made ready a gag to still her cries if or when she should recover at some crucial moment. Now it simply remained to wait out these last few minutes, which he guessed would be the longest minutes of his life . . .

When Bragg had got through to PSISAC, Craig had not been available. No time had been lost, however, for Dorothy Ellis had taken the call and was completely conversant with the situation. She had noted Bragg's coordinates and instructions, and in a matter of minutes Craig's commandeered jet-copter and its pilot were airborne. The aircraft was of the latest design and satellite beam–powered, whose range was only limited by the pilot's stamina. To make sure that the latter—a recent recruit at best—would not renege on his new master, one of Craig's more reliable, long-term disciples accompanied him. Craig had earlier allocated this task; the man he had chosen for the job was one Henry Stafford, a fortyish, bespectacled, thin-faced and single-minded micro-electrician from Components Division. He had always been a staunch believer, and never more than now. In his opinion, any man who could not see Craig's prophecies coming to fruition all about him was either blind or a gibberer. Craig could be absolutely certain that Stafford would follow his instructions to the letter.

Bragg, of course, knew nothing of these instructions; nor did Dorothy Ellis. Even if she had known of them, it is doubtful she would have dared mention them to Bragg. For she, too, was a true believer . . .

By now Bragg had taken the girl from the car and carried her to an open field some hundred and fifty yards away from the motel along the edge of the six-laner in the direction of Paris. This was where he had arranged for the jet-copter to land in response to an SOS he would flash from his pocket torch. The pilot could hardly miss the place: not only would he have the coordinates but also the lights of the motel itself, with all the toing and froing of police vehicles and ambulances to guide him in; on top of which Bragg had arranged for an unmistakable welcome of his own.

Nevertheless, the waiting man's nerves were stretched taut by the time he saw the jet-copter's beacons flashing in the sky to the northwest, and not without good reasons. There had already been one false alarm, when he had seen other lights in the sky. That aircraft, whatever it had been, was no more. Before Bragg had been able to react to its presence, the lights had passed dangerously low overhead, showing the shape of a mighty airliner, and moments later the horizon to the southeast had been lit with a terrific flash. Then there had come a dull, booming explosion like a deep roll of thunder. Bragg could only assume that the unknown airliner was just another victim of The Gibbering.

In addition to this there had been shouts, screams and the rattle of automatic fire from the motel-cum-hospital itself, culminating in several small explosions before a police car had gone tearing off down the motorway in the wrong direction—that is to say, against the flow of traffic—hotly pursued by three others. The mind-plague was no respecter of rank, position or power; policemen were no more exempt from it than anyone else. All of which had only served further to fray Bragg's already ragged nerves.

Now, though, there could be no mistaking the *chop-chop-chop* of the jet-copter as it circled high over the motel, waiting for Bragg's signal. Crouching low, he left the girl lying where he could easily find her again and ran back to the Komet parked in the trees behind the motel. It was the work of only a few seconds to empty a jerrycan of petrol in and around the car, laying a thin trail some forty or fifty feet long before throwing down a flaring match and haring back the way he had come.

Behind him the Komet roared up in gouting fire, throwing Bragg's shadow ahead of him where he raced breathlessly across the night-dark field. In another moment he was standing over the girl, his torch flashing its urgent SOS signal at the circling jet-copter. The pilot was good; he brought his machine down without delay and landed it not fifty feet away. As the door in the aircraft's body slid open, Bragg picked up the girl and carried her beneath the vicious sweep of the vanes, until she could be taken from him by Henry Stafford and dragged inside.

By now police cars were bumping about in the

field behind the motel, attracted by the spectacle
of Bragg's blazing car. Then their gendarme oc-
cupants spotted the jet-copter and their spot-
lights were blinding where they turned uniformly
in Bragg's direction. As the burning car exploded
in a bright blast of heat and flame, so the police
cars came lurching over the rough field.

"Let's go!" Bragg yelled over the rush of air and
the rising whine of the rotors. He made to climb
aboard.

"Sorry, old son," Stafford yelled back at him,
pointing a pistol at Bragg's head.

"*What?*" Bragg's eyes bulged where they gazed
up into Stafford's emotionless face. Frantically he
threw himself forward, his arms reaching inside
the jet-copter's fuselage. Even now the aircraft
was beginning to lift off.

Stafford shook his head. "Can't take you,
chum," he shouted. "Craig's orders." He pulled
the trigger—and the mechanism of his pistol
jammed. Cursing, Stafford threw the gun down,
grabbed the handle of the sliding door and
slammed it again and again into Bragg's outstretched arms. Bragg yelled his terror, his outrage, as his feet left the ground and his fingers
scrabbled to find purchase on the rubber-clad
deck of the jet-copter; yelled again, his agony this
time, as Stafford mercilessly stamped on his
hands.

Down below the police cars were skidding to a
halt on the blast-flattened grass of the field; gendarmes were piling out of them, shouting their
bewilderment and pointing skyward. Bragg lost
his grip. His body felt as if it weighed a ton as the
jet-copter began to climb rapidly. His broken fingers were less than useless to him where they slid
along the floor, flopping over the ridges in its

rubber covering. He screamed ... and forced those three or four fingertips which still had feeling to hook themselves onto the sliding door's metal runner.

The jet-copter was more than a hundred feet up now and climbing straight into the night sky. Stafford looked out and down, saw Bragg's bloodless face and bulging eyes, his wide-open, straining jaws. Beneath his dangling figure the headlight beams of police vehicles made stripes of light across the fields. Tiny white faces looked up in shock and amazement.

Stafford shook his head and gritted his teeth. He didn't particularly like this, but ... he shrugged, straightened up. "Orders, chum," he said.

No! Bragg's eyes and mouth silently formed his denial.

Stafford slammed the door.

Two hundred feet later, Bragg's body crashed down like a sack of wet cement across the bonnet of a car, molding it to its engine ...

Some inner sense of urgency brought J. C. Craig awake with a start where he half-reclined in the throne's embrace. His first instinct was to struggle upright, but the throne held him fast in its manacles. He straightened his fingers down the sides of the throne's arms and pressed the release buttons. The skullcap tilted back with a whir of its servomotor; likewise the U-shaped neck clamp, swinging aside, releasing Craig's head. The wrist and ankle clamps sprang open and he was free.

He quickly stood up—perhaps too quickly. He staggered a little and leaned on the throne's arms for support. It had been an unusually long session and it had weakened him. Normally he would still be sleeping and building his strength, but something had awakened him. Craig thought of what had gone before—and froze as his memory found its focus.

Then, feeling the first stirrings of panic deep in his guts, he stepped down from the dais and turned to the computer keyboard.

He typed up: TIME?

Psychomech: 3:50 A.M.

Craig felt his panic give a lurch to match that of his heart, galvanizing him to activity. 3:50 A.M.—he had been on the machine for almost four hours!

He left Psychomech almost at a run, passed through the garage area to the elevator. It was too quiet; something must be wrong; something must have happened while he underwent treatment. He leaped from the elevator as soon as its doors opened, rushed to his study. At the windows he stared out expectantly, almost fearfully, over PSISAC. Then he began to breathe more deeply and fought down the thudding of his heart. From what he could see from here, all seemed in order.

Craig's intercom bleeped, causing him to start. He turned, crossed to his desk.

"Craig here."

"Mr. Craig?" it was Dorothy Ellis, her voice sighing its relief. "Sir, I've been trying to get hold of you for more than three hours!"

"I've been . . . busy," he answered. "Is all well?"

"Yes, sir. At least, I think so . . ."

Craig did not like the sound of that. "Where are you speaking from?"

"Pay and Admin, sir. Switchboard and computer."

"What's wrong with video?"

"Nothing, sir. Intercom was quicker, that's all. As I've said, I've been desperate to get hold of you. Sir, I sent the jet-copter for Bragg and your daughter. They're due back any time now."

"What?" Craig drew air sharply. "Bragg got her?"

"Yes, sir—the jet-copter left just before 1:00 A.M."

That must mean that Richard Stone/Garrison was dead! "Did Stafford go with the pilot?"

"Yes, sir."

Now it was Craig's turn to breathe a sigh of relief. *Oh, God be praised!* "Go to video now," he said.

In a matter of moments her face floated up on the screen. She looked washed out, weary to death. And she was wearing her headset.

"An attack?" Craig was solicitous.

"I . . . I think it's over now," Ellis answered. She took off the headset, waited for a moment, finally smiled a twitchy, nervous smile. "Yes, it's over."

"Good," said Craig. "Now, about my daughter—tell me all you know." When she was finished he said: "Miss Ellis, through all of this so far you have been my mainstay. I would have been lost without you."

"Thank you, sir."

"No, I thank *you*—and you shall be rewarded. Now—what of PSISAC?"

"There has been some activity," she answered. "Nothing much. And nothing official—that is to say, we haven't been bothered anymore by government or the law—but . . ."

"Yes," he prompted her, "but—?"

"The Gibbering, sir—it's going over the top!"

"What?" Craig frowned. "Explain."

"Master computer shows mind-plague incidence as high as one in three, heading toward two."

"What?" Craig's jaw dropped. This was all of three days sooner than previously computed. "Are you sure?"

"Oh yes, sir. Most of our people have suffered attacks—or would have, without their headsets."

Craig thought of his own attack and something of his panic returned, forming a tight knot in the pit of his stomach. "Are the men all right?" he asked.

She nodded. "There's been little for them to do. A gang of gibberers—ex-employees, we think—tried to break in through the west gate. They were dealt with. But outside: it's chaos! Fires everywhere. People in the streets, fighting, panic-stricken. Shouting, screams. Explosions and gunshots. Nothing on TV; very little on radio; the stations have been going off the air one by one. Australia and New Zealand are at war. Some nuclear strikes. Nothing like that here, though. I got that about Down Under from an American broadcast, but that was almost half an hour ago. Since then . . . nothing."

"Communications are very nearly dead, then?"

"Yes."

Craig nodded. "Miss Ellis, you stay at your post. Keep watching and listening. I'm going to speak to the men now, then I'll go down and wait for the jet-copter."

"Right, sir."

He broke the connection.

Responses from the three security control centers and the main gate were all favorable; but even as he spoke to his disciples, still something nagged at Craig. Then he remembered his earlier conversation with Phillip Stone . . .

Satisfied that all was well—at least within PSISAC—Craig went downstairs and out into the complex, mounted his runabout and headed for the sports field. While he awaited the return of the jet-copter, he would speak one last time with Stone. Then—

Then it would be time to put the man out of his misery . . .

Phillip Stone had started to gibber at about 1:30 A.M. It was his initial attack, and it had lasted for more than an hour. In the end, Stone himself had called a halt to it.

The thing had started as he worked at his ropes. He had just begun to feel that he was getting somewhere—had sensed a slackening of his bonds behind his back, where his wrists were tied—and had started to concentrate all his efforts in that area, when suddenly he had heard a distinct *click!*

It was a sound Stone could not mistake: the click of a hammer falling forward onto the empty chamber of a revolver. Oh, he knew that sound well! He had heard it in Russia, and in China too. That had been many years ago, but it wasn't a thing he was likely to forget in a hurry.

It was a form of torture where they load a gun with one round of ammunition and position the live chamber at twelve o'clock. Then the gun is placed beside the victim's head and he is questioned. When he fails to answer or offers the wrong answer, the trigger is slowly pulled. The magazine revolves one space right, the hammer falls on an empty chamber. The process is repeated five times. If the question is not answered correctly on the sixth asking—then the hammer falls on the sixth and last chamber, which the victim knows is *not* empty.

That was just the sort of *click!* it had been . . . and it had caused Craig to still his harsh breathing in a moment and his eyes searched the cold, almost sentient darkness of the sports storeroom. There was no one there—could not be anyone in there with him, and he knew it—and yet he had heard the click. The click . . . and the chuckle!

A low, throaty giggle in the darkness, evil and insinuating. A mad titter of delight.

And slowly, out of nowhere, a picture had formed in Stone's mind—a picture *of* his mind!—his brain, surrounded by a ring of steel. Six revolvers, all of them loaded with one round apiece, and all pointing at the wrinkled convolutions of his own throbbing brain.

Then, for an hour, Phillip Stone had suffered the incredible torture of The Gibbering, and for the first time he had fully understood the mind-plague's horror; for there was no value in attempting to convince himself that this was not, could not be, happening. It *was* happening, and he was the victim. A minute or two would go by while he struggled desperately with the ropes that bound him, and then—*click!* In rotation, clockwise, one by one the revolvers in his head were playing their deadly game with him. And he knew that he would hear thirty such clicks—but that he would *not* hear the thirty-first.

And each time the click was louder, and always the picture in his head was that much clearer: the six revolvers closing in on his brain, touching it, prodding it. And the mad laughter of a constant torment, the crazed tittering like a tide of mad-

ness in his mind. And—*click!* Louder still—until
the sound of the hammers falling had started to
resound like thunderclaps, until Stone had gritted his teeth and screamed his rage and his agony at the unseen chucklers and the fatal
thundering of the hammers in his head.

By the time he had counted twenty-five clicks
he was quite mad, but still the torture had gone
on. Then, before the thirty-first click could come,
he had crashed with his head again and again
into the metal leg of a shelf unit until consciousness had fled him, and only then had he known
peace . . .

Now that peace was being disturbed, and Stone
swam up from darkness like some aquatic beetle
in a night-dark pool. Coming awake he remembered The Gibbering and was sick, throwing up
fluid vile as acid on the storeroom floor. And once
more he kept his face in the shade, for again the
strip lighting was livid and scorching to his light-
starved eyeballs, burning on his retinas like the
bars of an electric fire.

"Phillip," said Craig's pitiless voice. "I've come
to hear your confession before I grant you a merciful release."

Stone had lost his wife, his son, his world. Now
he was losing his mind, and this crazy bastard
wanted him to "confess" that he was in league
with the devil, part of a conspiracy to bring back
the antichrist. Stone's head felt soggy as wet
blotting paper; his skull was probably fractured
on one side. But what the hell?—he was going to
die anyway—and this little shit-bag wanted to
play father confessor to see him on his way!

"Do you hear me, Phillip?"

"Fuck off," Stone coughed the words out with

blood and sickness and froth. "Go and fuck a rat."

"You are Godless," said Craig.

"Do your worst, you scummy little shit," Stone growled, his mouth feeling full of gravel. "I'm a gibberer anyway, so get it over with—do your fucking duty!"

Craig went down on one knee, grabbed Stone's jacket and dragged him out into the light. Then he smiled a thin smile and nodded. "You see? Satan has not prevailed. The Lord's will be done."

Stone squinted up at him. "You know, Jimmy, old pal, I only ever saw one bastard sick as you before—and he was the one who did this to you!"

"What?" Craig's eyebrows went up. "You continue with your stupid riddles? Don't you know you can't win?"

"Jimmy, a while ago I heard voices in my head. They laughed and tittered while I screamed. They threatened and tortured me. Now they've gone—but I know they'll come again. One way or the other I'm going to die, and pretty quickly, I guess. Why should I lie to you or try to confuse you with riddles now?"

"Your master, Satan, will fight to the bitter end."

"My master? And what of *your* master, Jimmy. Don't you hear voices in your head, too? Doesn't someone come to you in your sleep? And is this the one you call your master?"

Craig's face seemed to go very thin. His eyebrows drew together and his eyes became dark, tiny highlights in the flesh of his pale face. "Only the Lord my God comes to me in dreams, Phillip," he husked. "What are you trying to suggest?"

Stone rolled his head to and fro on the floor. The left side of his face was one enormous bruise split by a raw red gash. He laughed mirthlessly, coughed up phlegm and spat it out. "The lord your god? Jimmy, the one who comes to you in your dreams was an obese, crazy, slug-gray Negro bastard with hypnotic and telepathic powers! Hey!—and did he tell you to build an 'oracle,' Jimmy? An even bigger, better Psychomech than the one you prettied up for Garrison?"

Craig flopped down on the floor, sat with his knees apart, his pistol in both hands, pointing it at Stone's battered face. His own face was like a blob of white putty, with two pieces of coal stuck in it for eyes. "What?" he croaked.

"And does he come to you still, Jimmy—even though he's been dead for twenty years? Hey—didn't you ever hear of post-hypnotic suggestion?"

"What?" Craig's hands trembled feverishly and the gun shook with them. Sweat oozed from every pore of his body.

"And does he tell you you'll be a power in the world, second only to him? And you think he's a god—*the* God? Jimmy, he was a flabby hermaphrodite freak! He was a mental mutation!"

"What?" Craig straightened his arms, pointed the muzzle of the gun straight into Stone's left eye.

"Go on, you poor dumb shit—pull it!" Stone croaked. "Pull the fucking trigger!"

Through the open door there came the unmistakable *chop-chop-chop* of a jet-copter coming in to land. Stone stared up at Craig and grinned hideously. "Did you get my tapes, Jimmy? Did you listen to them? No, I can see you didn't. You can't hear anything but that crazy dead man's voice in your head, can you? Well then, do me a favor—

make me one promise—before you kill me. Promise me you'll get those tapes and listen to them."

"Why should I do that?"

"So that I'll know that if you're not mad now, you *will* be when you realize what you've done!"

"What I've done . . ." Craig repeated him, his voice flat and dead.

The jet-copter was nearly down; a blast of pressured air banged the storeroom's door to and fro.

"Yes, what you've done," Stone answered. "I have it all figured out—most of it, anyway. You see, Psychomech's not just a machine, Jimmy—it's a monster!"

Now the whine of the aircraft's engine was changing its pitch, shrilling lower as it landed. Craig put his gun away. A semblance of normalcy had come back into his face. He stood up. "That's my daughter," he said. "God has given her back to me. Can you deny me that, too, Phillip? Anyway, I wouldn't want her to know I killed you."

"Killed me?" Stone's grin was vacuous, awful to see. "Man, I think you've killed the world! What was it you did ten years ago that started the mind-plague going, Jimmy? *What did you ask Psychomech to do for you?*

Craig's eyes bulged. He clapped his hands to his ears to shut out Stone's words, backed away, turned and staggered to the door. He went out, slamming the door shut behind him . . .

The jet-copter was down on the playing field where it had landed before. Craig arrived to find two of his men, Hill and Bellamy, already there. As they lifted Lynn down he ran to her, hugged and kissed her. She was warm—she lived—his daughter was alive and well!

She opened her eyes and grinned at him—

grinned, not smiled—and patted his drawn cheek. "Daddy," she said, froth dribbling from the corner of her mouth. "Daddy, I have hair growing on my brain! Ropes and ropes and ropes of it . . ."

Craig jerked back from her, staggered and would have fallen if Bellamy had not reached out a steadying hand. He stood swaying and staring at his daughter in utmost horror, his mouth working like the mouth of a fish, unable to form words. And all the while she looked at him where she lay like a doll in the arms of his men, looked at him and grinned and dribbled.

He found his voice, said, "Bring her . . . bring her to Psychomech." And to Stafford where he stood in the open door of the aircraft: "Wait here. I have another job for you. Keep the motor running. I'll be as quick as possible."

In the garage area under the Dome, Craig lifted his daughter from the arms of the two men and sent them away. Then he carried her into the room of the machine. Ten minutes later he came out alone, made his way dazedly back to where the jet-copter waited.

At the sports field, Stafford came forward to meet him. "Sir?"

"Take another man with you and go to Stone's house," Craig whispered. "Do you know where it is?"

"Yes, sir—I've been there once or twice."

"You'll find tapes there, cassettes. Bring them to me. They may be . . . important."

"Right away, sir."

"And Stafford—take machine-pistols and be careful. The Gibbering is going through the ceiling."

"Right, sir."

A short while later the jet-copter took off again.

Craig stood and watched it go until its beacons
were green and red fireflies flickering in the flame-
tinged sky . . .

At 3:30 A.M. Hans the Caretaker (the staff of the
Klingerman Krankenhaus had never known him
by any other name, for all that he had worked
part-time at the hospital for over forty years)
woke Klingerman up and told him about Frau
Gussel's condition. Actually Klingerman had not
been asleep but merely lying in his bed and turning things over in his mind. He was an old man
now and his wife long dead, but he had children
and grandchildren in all parts of the world and
he worried for them. These were strange, terrible
times.

Hans had a tiny cottage in Raron; he had himself been shocked from sleep by riotous singing,
crazed laughter, shrieks of horror and death
screams. In the village streets, mind-plaguers
were raping and murdering. Looking out of his
window, Hans had seen a large party of madmen
smashing windows and breaking down doors,
shooting people and dragging women and girls
out into the street to rape and murder them. And
sometimes they murdered them before violating
them . . .

Eventually two uniformed policemen had come
on the scene in a car. They had automatic weapons and there had been a lot of shooting. Hans
had ducked down out of sight until it was all over,
and when finally things seemed to have quiet-
ened down he had dared to take another look. He
had been in time to see one of the policemen kill
the other, then put his weapon to his own head
and shoot himself. For Hans, that had been the
last straw. Reckoning he would be safer in the

Krankenhaus on the slopes where they over-looked the village, he had hurriedly dressed him-self and crept out of town, sticking close to the shadows and hurrying as best he could.

And in the hospital's conservatory, now its morgue—there he had found Frau Gussel danc-ing with a little boy corpse! She had held the small, naked body tightly to her bosom, its little dead feet stiff and dangling above the floor, whirl-ing it round and round amongst the other bodies where they lay; and all the while she had hummed an old Strauss waltz to herself and to her partner. She should have gone home after the 1:00 A.M. collection, but . . .

When Dr. Klingerman went to see her she laughed at first and talked a great deal of many things—nonsense talk, scenes from some real or imagined girlhood—but when she saw his needle she had grown calm, had known it was for the best. One really must not dance with little dead boys. And now she lay with the rest of them, and Hans had tied a tag to her great right toe.

Klingerman sat beside her, holding her dead hand. He had held it while she died and contin-ued to do so, paying his last respects. Also, he had cried a little for her, cried for the whole world . . .

From where he sat, he was able to look down on Raron through the glass wall. There were fires down there now; half the town seemed to be in flames. Klingerman sensed some kind of grim cli-max, was keenly aware of a looming *fertig*, a *Schluss*.

"Hans," he said, "I do not think there will be a five o'clock collection. There are only a dozen bodies here, and they were all brought in before two o'clock. I think it is much worse now, and people are doing whatever they can for themselves—whatever they *have* to do."

"Herr Doktor," said Hans the Caretaker from across the room, where he had been only half-listening. "This one's eyes are open."

"Then close them, Hans," Klingerman tiredly told him.

"They will not stay closed, Herr Doktor. And they are very strange eyes. Also, he is not stiff, this one."

"Oh?" Klingerman got up, left Frau Gussel and went to where Hans stood beside a trolley. Upon the narrow, wheeled table, a young man's naked body lay cold as clay. But Hans was right: his eyes were open, and when Klingerman pressed their lids down over them they slowly opened again. The doctor looked at those strange yellow eyes and for a moment it seemed that frozen fingers stroked his spine. He quickly took a frigid arm, bent it at the elbow, gasped his concern.

"Hans, I believe he is alive! Quick now, go to the operating theater and bring me a defibrilator."

Hans hurried off and Klingerman wheeled the trolley to an electrical supply socket. He put his ear to the cold chest and listened; he sought a pulse high in the column of the pallid neck. And . . . yes, there was life here still, a heartbeat. Weak and fluttering—very intermittent—but definitely a heartbeat!

Klingerman took the tag from the man's right toe and read it. A simple epitaph, it said: "Found in the river . . ." But nothing to say he was a gibberer.

Hans came back wheeling a machine before him. He plugged it in, handed the pads to the doctor, who took them by their rubber handles.

Hans switched on the power. They were lucky to have a supply, but it came direct from a hydro-electric source higher up the valley.

Klingerman leaned forward, applied the pads to the young man's chest, squeezed the grips. The jolting current smashed into the body on the trolley like blows from a great hammer. Klingerman felt the shocks of it in his arms: once, twice, three times . . .

The lights in the conservatory dimmed, went out.

In the sudden darkness, the body on the trolley began to glow blue.

Hans and the doctor backed away, clinging to each other as the naked, blue-glowing figure floated free of the narrow table and turned stiffly vertical through an angle of ninety degrees. The entire conservatory was limned in the figure's blue light, its weird St. Elmo's fire, which now began to pulse like some sinister strobe. The eyes in the gaunt blue-glowing face were very much alive now, and they were golden. Golden beams of light scanned the gaping faces of Hans and the doctor . . . and then the eyes closed.

Faster pulsed the blue light, and faster still.

The figure standing in midair vanished, disappeared.

It was there . . . and it was gone!

The two terrified men felt themselves *sucked* toward where the figure had been. The windows came crashing in; chairs and tables were overturned, bodies strewn everywhere; a great wind howled. But in another moment all was still again and the lights flickered back into life.

Huddled together on the floor, the two old men looked at each other. Hans spoke first, tremulously, in a whisper: "Herr Doktor, are we also mad?"

Klingerman gulped, forced spittle down his dry throat. "Possibly," he whispered back. "Yes, Hans, it is just possible that we are. But I hope not." And then: "Hans, do you take a drink?"

The other nodded. "Oh, yes, when I can afford it."

They continued to stare at each other. Though shards of glass and splinters of wood from the windows lay all around, they had suffered not a single scratch between them. "Tonight we can both afford it," said Klingerman eventually, carefully lifting a long splinter from Hans the Caretaker's gray hair. "I have some very good stuff in my study. Come, let's you and I go and drink some of it."

He stood up, dusted himself down, helped Hans to his feet. "Yes," he nodded, "that seems to me a good idea. In fact, let's go and drink all of it!"

Over the bank of the River Rhône, appearing out of nowhere, the *other* Richard stood naked in the air and gazed down with golden eyes on the sprawling, frost-rimed shape of Suzy the Doberman pinscher. She looked dead, would seem so to any other eyes, but the *other* Richard knew differently. For in Suzy, too, there was something of Garrison, and it was something which clung to life with an incredible tenacity. For hours she had lain there, but still that spark burned in her, however falteringly. She lacked only warmth, strength, the physical ability to carry on; and these were things of which, for the moment at least, the *other* Richard had more than sufficient . . .

The beams of his golden eyes played upon her still form and the frost steamed away. Blackly glistening, she lay there. Still the golden beams poured down, solid bars of brilliant yellow fire now, and slowly the mass of Suzy's body turned into a drifting golden mist. Then the *other* Richard opened his mouth and breathed her in, a cloud of golden vapor, inhaling her like smoke into himself. For a moment longer she stood there on the night air above the empty riverbank—

Then dematerialized . . .

Richard Stone/Garrison had communed with the spirit (the soul, the essence, the memory) of his mother and she had told him to go to Wyatt's house. Now he went there: the merest nudge through the ether of the Psychosphere.

He materialized above a rectangle of empty earth where once Wyatt's house had stood—in gardens running wild on an untended, untenanted estate—and steeped himself in the essence of the place, discovering many of its secrets. He learned of a Machine: a device conceived in the mind of a madman, built to cure madmen, and corruptly employed to drive men mad. And he knew that this was the Machine which had "created" the Richard Garrison supermind.

Now he must go to the place he had called home, to the man he had mistakenly—but lovingly—called father.

He dematerialized and went there . . .

At the Stone estate in Sussex, Craig's commandeered jet-copter had landed inside the wall and barbed wire fortifications, on the large lawn in front of Phillip Stone's house. Ready at its controls, the pilot now waited. His name was Gavin Campbell and he had been George Blewett's private air-chauffeur for three years—three years too

many! But Blewett was dead now, and as the night
had progressed Campbell had watched the world
go mad—and he had made his decision. J.C. Craig
seemed to have found himself an answer, and if
it kept you alive and well in a world which was
sick and dying, that was good enough for Gavin
Campbell.

While he sat waiting, Hill and Stafford had entered the house and one by one the lights had
been switched on. Campbell was not sure what
they were doing in there, but that was not his
business; he was a pilot and they were what they
were: J. C. Craig's soldiers, or his "disciples" as
he seemed to prefer it.

Campbell sat in his carboglass cockpit and
smoked a cigarette, the rotors gently fanning
overhead as the engine ticked over, masking
shadows which flitted over him like ripples of
darkness. He was nervous, not unnaturally, and
his face was pale in the multihued glow from the
instrument panel. On every black horizon, fires
cast their ruddy glow on the underside of a heavy
screen of cloud and smoke. From here it looked
like England was burning. Toward London the sky
was literally lurid, like a scene shot in some remote hinterland of hell.

Campbell shuddered. He was not physically
cold, but he turned up the collar of his flying
jacket anyway . . .

Inside the house, Hill and Stafford had already
checked out all the upstairs rooms and had now
come downstairs again. There was a lot of valuable stuff here but they were not interested; the
world would be packed full of valuable stuff, later.
Mainly they wanted to be sure there was no one
here who might come on them by surprise. As
they explored the place, so they had switched on

the lights. These still worked, however flickeringly, showing that at least one local power station was still operational. Or perhaps this was simply the last drop at the bottom of the bucket.

In Stone's study they found the tapes they were looking for scattered across the floor where Stone had hurled them. The broken recorder was also there. Stafford picked it up and set it on the desk, pressed the "eject" button and snatched the rapidly coughed-up cassette from the air like a piece of toast from a toaster. He glanced at the cassette, shrugged, pocketed it with the rest of the tapes. He turned to Hill:

"These must be what J.C. was talking about. There may be other tapes somewhere about, but these are the most obvious."

"Good," Hill nodded, licking his lips. "So let's get out of here. This place gives me the creeps! It doesn't seem right that a house as big as this should be so . . . empty." He put a hand to his head, touched his headset, gained a little comfort and confidence from it.

"You'd better get used to that," Stafford said curtly. "From now on there's going to be a hell of a lot of emptiness. A world full of it, if you get my meaning. But I know how you feel. Okay, let's go."

As they left Stone's study and went out into the hall, the lights dipped and almost failed entirely. Hill froze, drew air in a startled gasp. He pointed the snout of his stubby, ugly machine-pistol upstairs. *"Look!"*

In the upper rooms of the house, the lights were going out one by one. On the spacious railed landing, a blue luminosity replaced the electrical light with its own eerie glow. "What the hell—?" said Stafford. "We checked up there!"

He made for the stairs. As his foot hit the bottom tread the rest of the lights went out—but the blue glow remained. Hill said:

"Do you . . . do you think we should go up there?"

"We have to," Stafford grunted over his shoulder. "If someone's up there, he could pick us off from a window before we got back to the chopper. Come on."

They climbed the stairs to the landing, Hill bringing up the rear. The blue glow came from beneath the door of a bedroom they had already explored, but now the door was closed. It was Richard Stone's old room, a fact whose significance they could hardly be expected to know. The blue light pulsed out from the crack beneath the door, seeming to form a shallow pool which lapped all along the landing.

"It could be a TV or something," Hill whispered to Stafford where they paused outside the door.

"Did you see a TV in there when we checked the rooms?" Stafford asked him. "Damned if *I* did!" He cocked his weapon. "Are you ready?"

Hill swallowed hard, jerked back the firing mechanism on his machine-pistol, nodded his head once.

Stafford lifted a booted foot and kicked the door open. The lock smashed and splinters of wood flew. The two men were at once bathed in a solid, rectangular shaft of blue light from the open door. Their faces were made ghastly with blue highlights as they gazed into the room, and—

As their eyes popped and their jaws fell open, both men squeezed the triggers of their weapons.

They fired long bursts—which spun them over and over like leaves in a gale. Naked, weightless, they tumbled against a backdrop of stars in an endless void which reached out to eternity all

around them. There was no air to breathe, no
warmth, no life. They kicked for long moments
and screamed soundlessly until their lungs were
empty, then froze.

Richard had sent them to that place where he
had once sent the cabin in the Harz, but without
the protection he had given to the cabin.

Outside the caved-in door of his room, their
coveralls were piled haphazardly where they had
fallen to the carpeted landing. Their headsets
were there, too, and also the cassettes Stafford
had thought to take back to J.C. Craig . . .

One Hour

I T WAS ABOUT 5:00 A.M. AND THE JET-COPTER SHOULD
be back at PSISAC by now; but J. C. Craig found
himself half-hoping that Stafford and Hill would
not make it back, that some accident would overtake them en route. It was the tapes he feared,
Phillip Stone's tapes, which he knew he must listen to once they were in his hands. Yes, for Satan
had found Craig's one weakness—his basic inse-
curity, the uncertainty he felt within himself, his
lack of faith—and had used it to tempt him. And
indeed he had been tempted.

Was there something he should know about his
own past? Why were there blank areas in his
mind, as if selected sections of his memory had
been altered or blotted out? And how did Stone
know so much about Psychomech? What the man
had said at the end there had had more than
a ring of truth to it; his personal conviction—
however misplaced, warped through his satanic in-

volvement—seemed undeniable. For on the very point of death, a man is *not* likely to lie; what is there to be gained from it? One might as well be hung for a lion as a lamb.

As to what Craig had "asked Psychomech to do for him" ten years ago: he refused even to think about that. It could not possibly have any relevance. There could be no connection . . .

After the jet-copter left for Stone's house, Craig had gone back down to the room of the machine. Lynn had been just as he had last seen her: locked into the throne, reclining there, fighting the mindplague with all the strength which Psychomech fed into her. Now she fought, battled it out in feverish dreams; but she would return from those mad dreams safe and sane, and a headset would keep her that way until all of this was over. Which would not be long now.

How long? Back in his study again and wondering if there was any new information on that subject, Craig got Dorothy Ellis on his viewscreen and asked her.

"The figures are level-pegging, sir," she told him. "Fifty-fifty and still rising. Half the people in the world have gone mad, and the other half is well on its way to joining them. Master computer says the plague will be at its peak—total saturation—in just one more hour."

Craig slowly nodded, tried not to look surprised despite the fact that things seemed to have speeded up out of all proportion to expectations. "And communications from outside? Tele- and video-phone? TV, radio?"

She shook her head. "Something on BBC fifteen minutes ago but I could make nothing of it. It was . . . gibberish? Nothing since then. The stations are clear right across the wavebands. Oh, there's continuous music from two or three stations, but nothing else."

Craig frowned. Something failed to connect here. "What about incoming computer information?"

She looked surprised. "But we've had nothing for more than two hours, sir! I thought you knew that?"

Craig stared at her tired, lined face for long moments, then said: "Miss Ellis, don't we have something of an ambiguity here?"

Before she could ask what he meant, Craig's intercom bleeped.

"Wait," he told her. And: "Craig here. What is it?"

It was Bellamy on the other end. "Chopper's back, sir! We've spotted its beacons. It'll be down inside a couple of minutes."

"Good! Keep me posted."

"Sir?"

"Yes?"

"Something out of the ordinary here, sir," Bellamy sounded puzzled. "Sir . . . I'll get back to you."

Craig turned back to the face of Dorothy Ellis on his screen. "Miss Ellis, if we've had no communications with computers at other information outlets—indeed, no communications of any sort for more than two hours—where is *our* computer getting its figures? I mean, is it projecting the curve and computing on that basis, or what?"

"Wait, sir," she said. "Let me find out."

Bleep!-Bleep!-Bleep! from the intercom.

"Yes," Craig snapped.

"Sir!" (Bellamy's voice again, but out of breath now, gasping.) "Sir, the chopper's circling over PSISAC right now—but its rotors aren't turning!

Its fans are standing still, sir! *Its bloody engine isn't working!*"

"You mean it's crashing?" Craig's eyes widened. He glanced apprehensively at the ceiling, gritted his teeth and shrank down into himself.

"No, sir—it's flying quiet and sweet as a bird up there—there just doesn't seem to be anything holding it up, that's all!"

The man must be gibbering, Craig thought. "I'll be right down," he snapped. He got up and headed for the elevator—but the voice of Dorothy Ellis stopped him in his tracks:

"Psychomech, sir," she said.

He whirled, strode back to his desk. "What? What do you mean, Psychomech? What are you talking about?"

"The source of our information on mind-plague figures, sir," she told him. "Master computer is getting it direct from Psychomech."

Craig felt the short hairs stiffen at the back of his neck. "I have to go now," he said, "but I'll get back to you. Meanwhile . . . check that out again, will you?"

He cut her off and hurried downstairs . . .

There was no longer any *other* Richard. Richard was whole now. He understood and was no longer apart. He knew that he was a power in the Psychosphere, and how he came to be that way: through his father's weird legacy. The only distinction there had ever been between *him* and the *other* was that his subconscious self had known these things instinctively, while his conscious self had had to discover them gradually. For the Psychosphere guarded its secrets jealously, and the toll it would exact from unwary explorers might be devastating!

If Richard had demanded to know all right from the start—if from the beginning he had been made fully aware of his real potential—then his very being might not have been able to bear the knowledge. How will a man react when he discovers he is superhuman? Power corrupts—and what of ultimate power?

The one thing he did not yet understand was conservation: the most efficient use and balanced application of his paranormal powers. A tiny battery will drive a toy motor for many hours; used to power an electric fire it will drain instantly, without raising the temperature the smallest fraction of a degree. Richard could have transported Suzy, but he had absorbed her; he could have merely levitated from Switzerland to England, but he had teleported; he might simply have blasted Stafford and Hill out of existence, but he had hurled them across several light-years. And he could have caused Campbell to fly him to PSISAC, but instead he had let Campbell go and himself had flown—carrying the jet-copter with him! And so once again his psychic battery was very nearly drained, and with it his merely mundane strength. It was as much as he could do to keep the jet-copter from plummeting to earth as he felt the power flowing out of him . . .

The sight which greeted J. C. Craig as he halted his runabout at the edge of the sports field and dismounted was one to stun the mind. Most of his men were already there, standing in groups of twos and threes, their disbelieving eyes turned up to the sky, staring in dumb amazement. They did not understand—but Craig understood at once, or believed that he did.

"Power of the devil!" he hissed to himself as

the jet-copter came floating silently down out of a grim, bloodied sky.

Its navigation lights were blinking and it sat upright in the air, as indeed it should; but Bellamy had been perfectly correct: its rotors were not working and there was no sound from its engine. And in the carboglass cockpit—something sat there which glowed a pulsating blue, lit (in Craig's eyes) with the light of demons and death and the bottomless pit. Lower sank the aircraft, floating down light as a feather, until Craig could clearly see the blue-glowing face of the man in the cockpit—the face of Richard Stone, the antichrist himself!

Bellamy was the first of the men to recover his senses. He too had recognized Richard Stone, and now he approached Craig. "Sir, with what we have here we can blow the bastard right back to hell!" he said, patting the heavy weapon which he cradled in his arms. "He might have the devil in his soul, but on the outside he's just flesh and blood like anyone else."

Craig glanced at Bellamy's gun. The thing was a recoilless cannon; it fired 18mm explosive shells. The rest of the men were carrying side arms and machine-pistols. Craig snorted his scorn. Weapons such as these, against Satan? Toys!

"No," he shook his head. "Useless!"

"What?" Bellamy looked again at his cannon. "Did you say useless?"

"Against him, yes. You don't understand what we have here, do you? You see that light—that blue fire inside the cockpit, surrounding him?—Satan's protection! Open your eyes, man: the aircraft floats on thin air! His power is . . . awesome!"

The jet-copter was almost down now, mere feet

above the grass of the playing field. Suddenly the blue glow began to pulse less powerfully; it flickered, died away entirely. The aircraft fell, bounced on its pontoons, tilted awkwardly to one side and stood balanced like that, with two of its vanes dug into the earth. The figure in the cockpit was now slumped over the control panel, unmoving.

"Hold your fire!" Craig yelled as his men moved forward, their guns at the ready. "He's full of tricks, this one. Keep well back." As they grudgingly retreated and formed themselves into a circle about the grounded machine, Craig turned to Bellamy. "Go and take a look—but be careful!"

Bellamy loped forward keeping low to the ground, peered for long moments into the cockpit, returned. "He seems to be out cold. He's breathing, but slowly. Looks like he's asleep to me. Also, he has one of our headsets. He's wearing it round his neck."

Craig grabbed his shoulder. "He's what? One of our . . . headsets?" The worried look lifted from his face and he slammed a fist into the palm of his hand. "Bellamy, you've just delivered the antichrist right into my hands! Stay here, take charge. Keep the men well back from that machine, and make sure no one fires on it! Oh, and have them break out the dogs."

He ran to his runabout, mounted it and returned to the Dome. He went to the room of the machine and looked at Lynn; she was sleeping now, no longer nightmaring. He knew he should let her rest but wanted her out of it. He freed her, half-carried her to the elevator; he supported her all the way to her bedroom. Too dazed to question what was happening, still half-asleep, she let him lie her down upon her bed. He kissed her, touched her brow, told her to sleep.

Lynn closed her eyes and they stayed closed. Craig waited for a moment and then, aware that time was of the essence, hurried to his study. He got Psychomech on the remotes, typed in:

> HILL
> HEADSET 8
> LOCATION?

Psychomech:

> HEADSET 8
> SOUTH
> COORDINATES: 817,319

So, Hill was still at Phillip Stone's place. Doubtless he was dead. That left Stafford and Campbell. Craig typed up:

> STAFFORD
> HEADSET 3
> LOCATION?

Psychomech:

> PSISAC

Craig slapped his thigh, laughed out loud. The bastard had taken Stafford's headset! Well, whatever his reason had been, it would be his undoing. He typed up:

> HEADSET 3
> IMPLEMENT OVERLOAD

Psychomech:

SPECIFY LOAD

Craig grinned his delight, his lips drawing back from his teeth in a totally insane grimace. Deliberately, with enormous satisfaction—well knowing what the answer would be but deciding to play the game out to its full—he typed up:

WHAT LOAD WOULD CAUSE
DISINTEGRATION OF THE CORES?

Psychomech:

0.0525 M/WAVE

Craig:

WAIT

He got vision on the sports field area, linked his intercom to all outdoor loudspeakers, and said: "Men, this is Craig. Keep well back from that aircraft. I am about to destroy it. Take cover, get behind buildings, anything. Keep close to the ground. Bellamy, let me know when they're safely out of the way."

A minute or two passed, then Bellamy's voice came up on the intercom: "Sir, I have a CCTV camera with me. Do you want a link?"

Craig could already see the jet-copter on one of his screens, but distantly and from a poor angle. "Yes," he said.

Another screen snapped into life, swam into sharp focus. Bellamy zoomed in on the aircraft, gave Craig a view of the cockpit, of Richard Stone's upper half where it lolled over the control panel.

Sure enough, a headset circled his neck like some false priest's dog collar.

On Psychomech's remote keyboard, Craig typed up:

PREPARE TO IMPLEMENT
OVERLOAD OF 5.25 M/WAVE

Enough to melt the chopper, Stone and all to so much fused slag!

Psychomech passed on the load requirement to a PSISAC satellite, said:

OVERLOAD READIED

Craig's fingers hovered over the keyboard. He licked his lips in anticipation, tasted victory. He trembled with pleasure, glowed with triumph . . .

"Dad?" said Lynn from the open doorway. "Dad, what are you doing?" She was still half-asleep, leaning against the doorframe. She pushed herself upright, came stumbling into the study, looked at the screens and blinked. Then her eyes widened, grew alert. "Dad—that's Richard on those screens!"

"You should be in bed," Craig stammered. "You should be resting." His fingers trembled on the plastic keys. He glanced at the screens, tried to smile at Lynn at the same time but only succeeded in grimacing.

She stared at him in horror. "Dad? Dad what . . . are you . . . doing?" Staggering toward him, she was choking the words out—choking out her accusation. "Dad—that's Richard!"

"Lynn, he's the antichrist!" he blurted. "Him, Richard Stone! He's Satan himself, girl—and I have him just where I want him!"

"No!" she cried, her slender fingers reaching toward the remotes.

Before she could touch them, Craig typed up:

IMPLEMENT

Craig shielded his eyes where they were locked in fascination on the screens. Lynn followed his gaze. She saw—heard—what happened, and fainted away on the floor at her father's feet.

Craig's study turned white in the sudden blinding glare from the screens, and he blinked his eyes to relieve the pain of watching through spread fingers. Then—

—Nightmare!

But before that, Richard had also nightmared:

Alone he wandered through a dead and sterile world, and knew that of all mankind he was the last. No balefires now on the far horizons, for there was no one to light them. The mad monster machine god had eaten them all—all except Stone.

He came down from barren, windswept mountains across foothills of yellow, withered grass to stand at the edge of a vast white desert of bones. Ah! And how the vampire must have feasted here— that beast of plastic and steel and weird energies— that iron octopus which battened on sanity, leaving only madness and mayhem in its wake.

The desert was an ossuary, the last charnel house, the massed grave of mankind. Standing at its edge and gazing bleak-eyed across leagues of bones, Stone wrapped his rags around him and shivered in his loneliness. Miles of crumbling mummies littered the desert's floor to its harrowing horizons. Here were dunes of dusty skulls, defunct storehouses of all Man's knowledge, where now the desert winds keened through sightless sockets and played upon rib cage harps. Here was the Mortuary of Mankind, and nowhere a bell to toll the final knell.

For long and long Stone stood there, and though he was young he felt old as time. Here would be as good a place as any to lie down and give up the ghost, and join the Great Majority; and yet he could not do so. No, for what had been for him an eternity of mindless horror and panic-flight had now become a query and a quest. He sought answers, desired to know why and to what end.

Except . . . who was there to answer such questions now?

He set out across the desert, picking his way carefully between the piled relics of his race, unwilling to stir up their ill-slumbering ghosts. Behind him, slowly the foothills merged with the horizon; behind them the mountains grew misty with distance; until Stone became as a lone spark of life in these endless leagues of desolation and death. The earth beneath his bleeding feet grew brittle with desiccation, where great cracks spread out like cobwebs carved in dusty concrete; but her the skeletal debris was spread more thinly and he was able to go forward at a greater pace.

Here too, for the first time, Stone became aware of the silence which had gradually grown in his ears like some malignant polyp, shutting out all sound. Even his footfalls were muted, as if he trod in deep snow; the very desert seemed to hold its breath . . .

Utter silence fell like a shroud upon the place.
Then—
Across a mile of gleaming white shards that shimmered under a bitter sun, Stone became aware of motion. Flying heels kicked up the dust of the

dead and marble limbs moved in the rhythm of running. A voice, it seemed, called to Stone across this wasteland of wasted lives. Old chords were struck: he knew the motion of that flying figure, recognized the ring of that voice.

He, too, began to run. Hope struck sparks within his breast, fanned them into flames which, in another moment, leaped high and consumed him. It was—it could only be—Lynn!

The last man in the world ran toward the last woman across a plain of bones.

They flew toward each other, arms reaching, the distance between narrowing down. The cracks in the desert's floor were wider now, as if some mighty quake had split the earth; but in their haste the two leaped the fissures as they drew together. Only a hundred yards to go . . . fifty . . . twenty.

Stone dug in his bleeding heels and skidded to a panting halt. Lynn, too . . .

They stared at each other across a distance of a dozen short paces . . .

The desert laughed . . .

And so did Lynn! She laughed around coarse tufts of hair sprouting like grass from her mouth! She laughed and tittered and screamed and choked on it—and she gibbered! Great ropes of hair grew out of her ears, her nostrils, the corners of her bleeding eyes!

The fissured earth at her feet cracked open with a dull rumble and she was pitched down, shrieking, into oblivion—but before the desert could close on her again, Stone looked down into the midnight vaults beneath, into the lair of the mad god, and saw the cold gleam of metal and the pulsing lobes of a monstrous mechanical brain!

A trap!—but then, he had known it was a trap. He made no move to flee but waited—waited as

*the earth split wide again beneath his very feet and
lashing cable and conduit tentacles erupted upward through dust and bones—waited as they
snatched him up and dragged him down into darkness. Above his head the riven rock closed like the
jaws of a vise, and here in putrid bowels of earth
he felt his ears pierced by brain-probes and his
eyes displaced by greedy probosces. In his brain,
the monster god gloated, said:* NOW I HAVE YOU!

*But Stone only smiled as the horror tasted his
brain—and smiled again as it snatched back its
seared mouths and screamed the first of many
screams.*

*Then, guided by its screaming, he reached for it
in the darkness, searched it out until he found it
cowering and quivering there.* NO, *he finally answered it then.* NO—NOW *I* HAVE YOU!

Like Craig up in his study in the Dome, his men
closed their eyes against the searing glare as the
jet-copter's carboglass cockpit became the center of an inferno of heat and light. A moment
later, while yet the shock wave of the first blast
raced outward, and the fuselage of the aircraft
followed suit, its aluminite body burning like a
petrol-soaked rag in the incredible heat. Two
more explosions followed in short order, and as
the glare died away and blazing debris rained
down on the playing field, Craig's men shielded
their eyes to look upon the spot where seconds
ago a flying machine had stood.

The earth was scorched and blackened as by a
great bonfire; while above, a curling puffball of
black smoke shot with flames *whooshed* upward
like some demoniac smoke-ring. But between the
mushroom cloud and the earth, pulsing in the
tortured air like a great alien heart, a naked,

nightmare figure defied gravity and surveyed the scene with eyes of molten gold. Its flesh was of a translucent blue, through which the bones showed its perfect skeletal form. It was human—it was *in*human—it was superhuman.

And now it drifted down to earth and stood amidst the licking flames and smoldering debris of the exploded aircraft.

Someone, in his shock, had accidentally released his dog. Trailing its lead the beast barked as it raced toward the blue-glowing figure. The rest of Craig's men, seeing this and believing it to be a signal, also sent their dogs to the attack. Nine snarling alsatians, excited to fever-pitch, zeroed in on the man-thing where he stood in smoke and smolder. Richard saw them coming, opened his mouth and breathed out a cloud of golden dust—which materialized into a red-eyed hound big as a pony!

Before the pack could swerve aside or even change its course, Suzy engaged it in battle. Except it was not a battle but a slaughter. She ravened like a wolf among kittens. She snapped her jaws: again, and again, and yet again. And four times blood flew and howls of agony were cut short, and four canine bodies crumpled to earth, twitching their lives out at her feet. Without pause she pounced, and the back of the fifth as broken. She bit off the head of a sixth; shook the seventh to death like a rat; turned on the last two and snarled her rage. They held back, turned, leaped away in a blind panic, yelping their terror. And Suzy, her fangs gleaming like ivory scythes, loping after them.

And while she tracked down those last two members of the pack through PSISAC's great maze of alleys and buildings, so her master reached out his megamind and searched . . . and found what he was looking for. Phillip Stone was here, and he was alive. Likewise Lynn: alive and well. But there was a third mind here whose power was almost as awesome as Richard's own.

Craig's "Soldiers of Christ" had learned all about killing this day; they knew how powerful their weapons were and how frail flesh and blood. Now, bolstered by Richard's seeming inactivity, they crept forward upon him and aimed their weapons—all except Bellamy, who remembered what Craig had told him. Richard apparently ignored them. Inches above the cratered, smoking earth, his upright, glowing body had commenced a slow turning upon its own axis . . . and he had commenced a silent conversation with Psychomech . . .

Up in the Dome, Craig was panicked almost to immobility. Here he stood in what should be the very moment of his triumph, rooted to the spot by terror. He could see on his screens all that was happening; knew that a monstrous beast—dog—demon—creature was loose somewhere in the complex; knew also that Satan's power was greater than even he had suspected, and that all he had planned and fought for now stood in jeopardy.

His daughter lay on the floor at his feet, fainted away; his men were up against forces they could not begin to understand; and now, for reasons beyond Craig's own comprehension, even his Psychomech remote controls appeared to be going crazy. Craig sensed Doom rushing upon him, and in a suddenly alien and unpredictable world all that was still sane in him responded in a completely human and predictable manner: he thought only of Lynn's safety.

Controlling his terror, he called Bellamy to the Dome, then tried to make some sort of sense out of what was happening with Psychomech.

Independent of the keyboard, words and figures were flashing up onto the machine's remote screen, coming and going so rapidly that Craig was barely able to follow the story they told. On his main communications viewscreen, Dorothy Ellis was now reduced to a black mouth in a chalky face—an incredibly mobile mouth that demanded to know what was happening, that screamed about the master computer and the fact that it had gone berserk—an utterly hysterical mouth obeying the commands of an exhausted mind in a completely fatigued body.

Craig did not know which way to turn.

He collapsed into his chair, clapped his hands to his ears, gritted his teeth and tried to shut the world out. But the pictures were still there on the screens and Dorothy Ellis continued to mouth her frenzied protests and demands, and Psychomech ran on and on through its impossibly rapid dialogue with some equally impossible inquisitor, and—

Craig's hair stood on end. Yes, that's what it was: Psychomech was talking to someone—*but at such a speed and in such detail that no merely human mind could possibly absorb or even begin to understand all it was being told!*

Craig switched off all communications except Bellamy's audio link and sat, mouth agape and eyes bugging, watching Psychomech's screen. The machine talked to someone, yes—but to whom—and telling him what?

Craig must stop this . . . must stop it now! He

reached out hands he could barely control, cleared the screen and typed up:

CRAIG: WHAT IS HAPPENING?

Psychomech: WAIT, and again the facts and figures flashed and flickered on the screen, coming and going faster than the eye could follow.

Craig would not be put off. He cleared the screen again, typed up:

WHAT IS YOUR CURRENT FUNCTION?

Psychomech: WAIT—WAIT—WAIT, followed by a yet more rapid flow of detailed data. There were snatches from the Holy Bible in the screened jumble, echoes of conversation Craig himself had held with the machine, headset recognition patterns and ten-figure coordinates, and other figures that marched in columns up and down the screen in endless procession. It hurt the eyes to watch and the mind to follow. Briefly displayed, Craig saw the exponential curve of mind-plague incidence—saw it bending and turning back on itself—before Psychomech's madly frenetic "chatter" continued unabated. And in one corner of the screen, rapidly approaching the four and a half billion mark, a constantly changing set of numbers showed the score of those eliminated from Psychomech's search, and those still to be examined.

Craig began to understand.

Clammy in his terror, he made one last attempt to cut in on what was happening. He cleared the screen, and—

WAIT! Psychomech silently shouted at him.

"Craig, this is Bellamy!" his intercom blurted.

"I'm at the Dome but I can't get in. The doors are locked." The man's voice was high-pitched, hysterical as a girl's.

"I'm coming!" Craig barked, amazed that he could still give his own voice a measure of authority. He picked up Lynn and staggered with her to the elevator, carried her downstairs and through the boardroom, drew back the catch on the outer door.

Bellamy almost fell inside.

"Take her," Craig hoarsely told him. "Look after her. Get out of here, as far as you can go. It's all gone, all of it . . ."

Bellamy looked at him and knew he was mad. He did not argue but took the girl from her father's arms, carried her into PSISAC's shadows and made for the main gate. Craig watched him creeping stealthily away, turned and went back inside . . .

As Craig's men edged closer to the glowing, pulsating, slowly rotating man-thing, so it it began to rise up again from the scorched earth until it stood a good seven or eight feet above the ground. But by that time Craig's marksman, an old Bisley shot called Goodwin, had joined the party from his post on the wall at the main gate. Now, taking what cover they could, still forming a rough circle about Richard where his radiance burned over the playing fields, touching all and everything with its strange foxfire, Goodwin and the rest prepared for a concerted attack upon him.

The marksman started it with a burst of tracer fire from a long-barreled machine-gun, aiming slightly to one side of Richard and then traversing across the target. The tracers alternated with explosive shells, the first for locating and burning and the second for disintegrating. The weapon was like a great hosepipe, and when its stream of blistering fire and hot, explosive steel hit Richard, then his blue-glowing figure at once stopped turning. Limned in the searing incendiary glare he became even more of a target, impossible to miss. Now the rest of Craig's men came out into the open, blazing away with all they possessed. One or two of them hurled grenades; the rest used machine-pistols; in seconds their aerial target was lost in smoke and fire as the complex was shaken by blast and the jarring concussions of massed automatic fire.

"Pour it on him!" yelled Goodwin, firing a continuous stream of sodium and steel at the now totally obscured target. They were the last words he ever spoke.

Flickering like slow, golden lightning from the heart of the aerial bomb-burst, a tendril of weird energy tracked the stream of tracers back to Goodwin and touched, then enveloped him. His flesh became liquid as water in a single instant, so that it fell from his crouching skeleton, which immediately toppled forward in a clattering of naked bone. His weapon smoked, turned white hot, atomized in a blast which knocked men off their feet fifteen yards away.

Several among the others now found that their grenades were armed, exploding before they could get rid of them. Weapons melted in hands which became fused blobs of flesh. The automatic fire ceased; screams of terror and agony filled the air; men exploded, dissolved away, were smeared to the ground like crushed beetles.

The "attack" had lasted perhaps fifteen seconds, the retribution five . . .

* * *

In Craig's study the mass of information flickering across Psychomech's remote screen came to an abrupt end. The last column of figures marched off the edge of the screen into eternity; except for the run of mind-plague calculations in one corner, the screen was empty. Then—

PSYCHOMECH TO CRAIG

Trembling, Craig typed up:

CRAIG HERE

Psychomech:

I HAVE FOUND GOD

Craig's skin itched where it crawled on his back, his limbs, his scalp. He wanted to believe that the machine was right, but he suspected that it was wrong—horribly wrong. With hands he could barely control, he typed up:

HOW DO YOU KNOW THAT THE ONE YOU HAVE FOUND IS GOD?

Psychomech flashed up more impossible-to-follow information onto the screen, spoke of miracles, of a man walking on air, of life after death, of invulnerability, of a man with a megamind, a mind of godlike strength and near-omniscience. The machine duplicated and reiterated Craig's own definition of the god he had tasked it to discover, delineated each identifying property and aspect of the godlike creature it *had* discovered, and concluded: HE IS GOD

"No," Craig shook his head in frantic denial,

almost as if he believed Psychomech could see and hear him. And perhaps the machine could. "No, you are wrong." But this was judgment before the fact; he still did not know for sure Psychomech's meaning. It could be that indeed the machine had found God. He typed up:

WHERE IS THIS GOD?

Psychomech at once answered:

BEHIND YOU

A blue, pulsating glow bathed the study in eerie light. Craig whirled—

Beyond the curving windows, standing on the air, gazing in with eyes of gold, Richard Stone's translucent, zombie-figure was a hideous human neon!

Craig fled.

He bounded, choking, for the elevator. Heart pounding, he clawed at its walls for support as he descended to the Dome's garage. He wrenched a fire axe from the wall and drunk with adrenaline lurched mindlessly to the room of the machine. He entered and staggered down the tunnel of Psychomech's throat to the throne. There, at the foot of the dais steps, he tossed down his axe, drew out the keyboard on its swivel arm and tried one last shot:

ERROR: RICHARD STONE IS NOT GOD. HE
IS THE ANTICHRIST

Psychomech:

A MEASURE OF THE ANTICHRIST IS HIS
CAPACITY FOR EVIL. I AM CAPABLE OF
GREAT EVIL. I HAVE BROUGHT GREAT

EVIL INTO THE WORLD. I AM THE
ANTICHRIST. THEREFORE RICHARD STONE
IS GOD.

Craig (desperately):

INCORRECT! YOU ARE A MACHINE. YOU
WERE NOT BORN OF EVIL BUT METAL,
PLASTIC, ELECTRICAL CIRCUITS AND MAN-
MADE ENERGIES. I MADE YOU!

Psychomech (after a pause):

THEN YOU ARE THE ANTICHRIST

All about Craig, the machine began to throb
and vibrate. Its lights flashed with stroboscopic
intensity; the very concrete beneath Craig's feet
trembled with pent power. Foaming at the mouth,
Psychomech's maker typed up:

WHAT ARE YOU DOING?

Psychomech:

THE EVIL MUST END. RICHARD STONE/
GARRISON DEMANDS IT. THE
PSYCHOSPHERE IS FILLED WITH EVIL. NOW
I DRAW IT BACK. THE BALANCE IS
RESTORED. I FEED UPON EVIL. I DESTROY
IT. I DESTROY MYSELF. I FREE THE MINDS
OF MEN . . .

In the corner of the screen the mind-plague figures ran faster and faster *in reverse*. By the thousands the number decreased, by tens of thousands,
then millions, faster and faster.

"It was you!" Craig screamed uselessly, accusingly. He began to laugh, roaring with mad, hysterical glee. Ungovernably he laughed and screamed and cried. "You caused The Gibbering! No, *I* caused The Gibbering! Phillip Stone was right! You are right! *I am the antichrist!*

He typed up:

I AM THE ANTICHRIST

And Psychomech said:

GET THEE BEHIND ME, SATAN!

Craig laughed uproariously and slapped his thighs, tears streaming down his cheeks in a flood. The antichrist, yes. And now the Machine would rob him of his greatest triumph: the total destruction of mankind. But Craig—no longer the instrument of God's will on Earth but spawn of hell itself—would not allow it.

His laughter became a bellow of rage, the warped howling of a demon denied. He snatched up the fire axe . . .

Bellamy had Lynn over his shoulder in the fireman's lift position, leaving his right hand free to use his machine-pistol if that should be necessary. He had kept to the shadows all through PSISAC's alleys and ways, and was now close to the main gate.

Bellamy did not know what Craig had meant by his statement: "It's all gone, all of it," but obviously the man had seen some hope for his daughter, and therefore for Bellamy, too. His instructions that the two should now "get out of it, as far as you can go," simply meant that the complex itself was no longer safe. Bellamy could hardly argue that point, not with that spewed-up dog-creature running loose, and with its blue-glowing, inhuman master wreaking havoc among Craig's remaining soldiers. Just exactly what was happening back there he could not say, but he had heard the explosions and the automatic fire—and the screams. So Craig was obviously right: this was no longer any sort of place for the likes of Geoff Bellamy.

As for the future:

The more Bellamy thought about it, the more he relished his future. He was not exceptionally bright and had never really understood the connection between Craig's machine and the headsets; he simply accepted that the headsets worked, and that while he wore one The Gibbering could not touch him. Therefore he had the means to go on: he and the girl possessed the wherewithal to remain sane in a totally aberrant world—a world where all others were now dying or killing themselves off. All they must do was stay safe until it was all over, and then the world would be theirs.

Well, and if he had had to choose a mate, he could hardly have done better. Lynn Craig was a whole lot of beautiful woman-flesh, and from this moment forward it was all his. The girl and her body now, and ultimately the whole wide world. And if there were other survivors—if a handful had remained sane, as Craig had predicted, when all of this was at an end—Bellamy would make himself a king amongst them and God help anyone who opposed him. There might even be other beautiful women, too . . .

Phillip Stone had been deep in the mire of mind-plague again—lost to the torture of the falling hammers where they *clicked* down onto empty chambers—when suddenly the terror had been blanked from his mind. Lying there on the cold floor of the sports storeroom, it had felt as if a soothing balm of sweet water were suddenly poured over his hot and smoldering brain. And in his mind he had heard:

DAD, GO TO THE MAIN GATE. SUZY IS THERE. SUZY THE DOG. SHE WILL PROTECT.

"Son?" Stone whispered. Or was this simply another facet of The Gibbering? No, for this was not the first time he had heard real voices in his head. Long, long ago he had "talked" to Charon Gubwa in precisely this fashion. Moreover, he had known and recognized Richard's mind-talk as surely as he would know his real voice.

"I can't go anywhere, son," he said. "These ropes . . ."

No sooner was the word spoken than he felt moisture on his wrists, his ankles. Small pools of sticky, fibrous liquid dripped from him: all that remained of his tough bindings. He stretched, flexed his cramped, aching muscles, groaned as great pain swamped him. His head felt pulped on one side; his vision was blurred; when he dragged himself to his feet, his legs almost buckled under him.

"I won't make it to the main gate," he said.

DAD, BE WELL, Richard told him.

And he *was* well.

Outside he found a runabout, mounted the tiny three-wheeler and turned it in the direction of the main gate. The place was ominously quiet now, but from the Dome's central bulge came a low throb of power, and an irregularly pulsating greenish glow that came and went and bounced concentric waves of light off the lowering clouds . . .

Bellamy had reached the main gate and must now leave the shadows and go along the open road

and through the fortifications to the world outside. Stumbling a little under the girl's weight, he
came around a corner and into a floodlit area—
and at once gasped and went into a defensive
crouch. He had already ditched his 18mm cannon in favor of a lighter weapon, and now swung
up the muzzle of his squat machine-pistol.

The massive dog was there, standing like a
black statue in the middle of the road, her ears
flat to her head. Large as a small horse, Suzy's
snarl was the savage grin of a saber-tooth; the
gleam in her red saucer-eyes was one of pure
murder. And she spotted Bellamy immediately.
No more than twenty paces stood between them—
a leap or two for the black beast-creature. She
crouched to spring.

Behind Bellamy, Phillip Stone came careening
round the corner of a warehouse. Bellamy spun
around, released a burst of fire from his weapon.
Taking in the scene at a glance, Stone had already applied his brakes and kicked the runabout
out from beneath himself as he leaped free and
rolled under the stream of sudden death from
Bellamy's machine-pistol. Suzy's snarl of rage was
an awesome sound as she began to feed power to
her bunched muscles.

"No, Suzy!" Stone yelled, seeing her tensing
herself. He could scarce believe his eyes where
the dog was concerned, but guessed that this
must be Suzy; and if the massive dog pounced,
then Lynn, too, was almost certain to be hurt.

Bellamy spun again, went to one knee, toppled
Lynn from his shoulder. He took his gun in both
hands and aimed dead center between Suzy's
eyes. Stone sprang to his feet, raced forward.

A blue light pulsed overhead. Golden fire

reached down, touched Bellamy. Stone skidded to a halt mere paces away from the kneeling man.

Bellamy's jaw fell open and he jerked his head from side to side. It was as if some invisible force held him rigid, drawing him to his feet. He fought against it, his eyes bulging. His weapon fell from nerveless fingers and his head cranked backward almost mechanically until he stared up into the sky.

Richard Stone/Garrison stood in midair. The golden fire streamed from the index finger of his right hand, which was pointed at Bellamy.

Bellamy gave one short high-pitched scream as his flesh split open at his skull and folded back as if unzipped from his bones. Hot steaming flesh and viscera fell to the tarmac as his skeleton was drawn intact from his body and hurled into the clouds . . .

Richard teleported himself, Phillip Stone, Lynn and Suzy out of PSISAC. In a moment Stone and the dog stood on the summit of a low hill some miles southwest of Oxford. Lynn lay on the grass at their feet and Richard stood in the air some fifty feet overhead. Between the hill and the city's sprawling shadow, sandwiched between the dark earth and a red-tinged cloud ceiling, PSISAC pulsed hemispheres of green light like some huge and terrible beacon in the night. Far to the east the cloud cover was broken; the coming dawn's light lent the world's curve a milky rim.

Lynn moaned and woke up. Phillip Stone went down on his knees and cradled her. Suzy, just a dog again, licked Lynn's face and whined.

MELTDOWN, Richard told them in their minds. PSISAC IS FINISHED. OXFORD WILL BE DESTROYED COMPLETELY AND HALF THE COUNTRYSIDE AROUND—UNLESS I CAN HELP.

"Meltdown? How?" Phillip Stone wanted to know. "PSISAC isn't nuclear powered."

PSYCHOMECH DRAWS OFF ENERGY FROM THE PSYCHOSPHERE. THE MACHINE RESTORES THE BALANCE. IT IS LIKE A GREAT WHIRLPOOL OR A COSMIC FLYWHEEL: STOP IT DEAD AND ITS ENERGY MUST GO SOMEWHERE. BUT THE MACHINE CAN ONLY ABSORB SO MUCH.

"Then we're in danger even here!"

The blue-glowing figure in the sky soared higher, became still again. I CAN HELP.

By now PSISAC was a dazzling green glare of stroboscopic brilliance too bright to gaze upon, so that Phillip Stone, the newly awakened girl and Suzy must turn their eyes away; but while they cowered there on the hillside and shielded their faces, so Richard reached out his megamind and bridged the gap between himself and the monster machine-brain of his nightmares.

He bled off energy from Psychomech.

An arc of fire like some livid rainbow of painful unknown colors and otherworldly energies curved up from PSISAC's heart and down into Richard Stone/Garrison . . . and was at once sent arcing away over the eastern rim of the world into the dawning sun. For full fifteen minutes the display continued, with Richard's blue-glowing body acting as a way-station for energy to power a planet. And then the rainbow arcs—from PSISAC to Richard, Richard to solar orb—grew dim, faded and flickered out.

Now PSISAC was a dome of green fire lighting up the night—a great dome laced with red and white lightnings that chased each other in crazy patterns and intricate traceries over its ever-changing, throbbing surface.

Lynn was fully awake. She sat up, brushed away

Phillip Stone's encircling arms, cried: "My father! Richard, *what about my Dad?*"

LYNN, LYNN, LYNN, he sighed in her mind. TOO LATE. IT HAS LONG BEEN TOO LATE FOR JIMMY CRAIG.

And as her tears came he teleported girl, man and dog to the house in Sussex. Then he stood alone on the wings of a wind which came up from nowhere and blew away the lurid clouds; stood there in dawn's first feeble light and watched PSISAC and Psychomech in their death throes . . .

In the heart of the Machine, James Christopher Craig swung his axe again and again. The damage he caused was at first superficial, for he had built the Machine to last. But gradually his efforts began to make an impression. The edge of his axe bit through cables and pipes; lubricating fluids spurted and showers of sparks danced and flashed; bright metal became dull and dented and plastic casings shattered under his onslaught. Out went the chaotic computer screen in a single mad swipe, and keys from the keyboard flew in disarray.

Craig stumbled up the dais steps, aimed a blow at the throne's delicate skullcap and upper mechanisms—and missed. He tripped and the axe flew from his fingers. He fell, still turning with the momentum of his swing, and flopped down into the throne—which at once grabbed him.

The hinged helmet crashed forward, trapping his skull; the jointed arm swung into position, its U-shaped clamp closing on his neck; the wrist- and ankle-clamps snapped shut, pinning him inextricably to the throne like an insect on a velvet display board. Craig heaved his trapped body and screamed and struggled, but the Machine paid no heed. He reached down his fingers to claw at the release buttons, but Psychomech ignored him.

One of the cables he had cut through controlled the function of the anesthetics and brainsalves; their needles slid home but delivered nothing but pain. Other servo-motors and mechanisms had been damaged. The "teeth" of the wrist and ankle-clamps gripped; their needles slid in and out, in and out. The microscanners were blind now; their cerebral and intravenous probes and minute feeder-nozzles drilled through muscle and bone, stabbing and jetting indiscriminately.

Even before the brain probes, Craig's fear-centers had already been stimulated as never before; but running amok now, Psychomech fed him all the world's horror, all the misery and torment of The Gibbering, all the nightmares of a billion minds.

Craig's eyes flew out and flopped on his cheeks, melting. His brain burst, exploding out through scarlet eye sockets and ruptured ears. He baked as the Machine grew hot, white-hot. Like some strange mad Christ crucified on a mechanical cross, Craig died.

The Dome's foundations melted and the building sank down into a lake of metal, plastic and concrete lava. All of PSISAC's buildings leaned in toward the sinking center, toppling. A wave of white heat spread outward, cooling rapidly. Buildings outside the complex burst into flames. Walls a mile away were briefly scorched. Two miles away, it was as if a breath of hot air had been breathed by some vast and unseen beast.

But the beast was dead. It had been Psychomech's dying breath.

The Balance was restored . . .

Epilogue

IT WAS CHRISTMAS AND THE SNOW HAD COME.

Richard walked with Suzy on the Sussex Downs, their feet leaving tracks in the snow. Warmly wrapped, the young man breathed clean air and looked out of aeon-wise eyes on a land made fresh and pure and white. It might well be a scene from one of his dreams, except that the mad monster-god no longer pursued him . . .

When it had all been over, Richard had told Lynn and his father (he accepted Phillip Stone as his father now, and was in turn accepted) that his Garrison facet was gone forever, that he had drained himself utterly of paranormal powers. It was better that they should believe this—better for the world that it should never know—that the thing lie dormant in him and perhaps, eventually, leave him entirely.

But now, hearing some distant call, he had

come out with Suzy to walk in the snow and climb the sweeping uplands. Lynn and his father had stayed home, listening to the news on the radio and making their plans as the world licked its wounds and looked to a great new beginning.

And here, where a field of snow climbed like a white wave to a blinding horizon, now man and dog heard the call again. Carried on the currents of the Psychosphere, it came from far, far away, from somewhere beyond the rim of the world, beyond the span of galaxies. And it was not meant for Richard but for Suzy.

"Do you hear him, girl?" Richard asked, and in answer the great black bitch whined, barked and licked his dangling hand.

"Maybe he misses you now," Richard told her. "I'll miss you too, but you're more his than mine. How far, Suzy, how far? And do you think you can find him?" He fondled her ears, pointed toward the crest of the hill.

"Go, then, and I'll help you on your way."

She barked again, wagged her tail furiously, stood up on her hind legs and licked his face— then sprang away and began to race up the hill, her tracks appearing in the snow as if typed there. A black dot against the endless white expanse, at first she seemed to grow smaller as she neared the crest.

Richard's eyes burned golden.

The spaces between the typed periods of Suzy's tracks grew wider; her leaps were enormous, her form huge and expanding. A sweeping black cloud whose shape was that of a dog reached the top of the hill—and kept going.

Suzy went back to the one she had always loved.

Richard watched her go, then turned back and headed down the hill. He too went home to the ones he loved. And as he walked, so the golden fire in his eyes slowly went out . . .

THE
BEGINNING